And Don't Forget the Roses

– P. J. PATERSON –

Printed and bound in England by www.printondemand-worldwide.com

http://www.fast-print.net/bookshop

And Don't Forget the Roses

Copyright © P. J. Paterson 2017

ISBN: 978-178456-499-5

All characters are fictional.
Any similarity to any actual person is purely coincidental.

A catalogue record for this book is available from the British Library

First published 2017 by
FASTPRINT PUBLISHING
Peterborough, England.

And Don't Forget the Roses

P. J. Paterson

Contents

Contents

Note from the author:

And Don't Forget the Roses was written, produced and edited in the UK where spellings and word usage can vary from U.S. English. The use of quotes in dialogue and other punctuation can also differ.

Acknowledgements

To Emily, and all the children of the
world who have succumbed to illness.

To Kimberley, editor and fellow biker – thank you.

To the Bard, for his undeniable and
exceptional contribution to English literature
and language worldwide.

Prologue

Sam had kept his final promise to his late wife Annie, but sitting on the steps outside the National Gallery in Trafalgar Square, London, he could hear a woman shouting and screaming behind him; their meeting would alter the direction of their lives forever.

Soon after Penny met Sam that very first time, she felt as if she knew him because of her inner sense of being able to trust him. *But how can I trust you if we've never met before?* she asked herself.

Was their meeting by accident? Or had fate, or a force beyond their control, drawn them together?

They both bore scars from their past. Sam's due to betrayal of love and trust – caustic memories that ate away at his soul. Penny's was guilt from early childhood, lonely and friendless – a guilt that sapped her belief in herself.

When their friendship takes on a momentum of its own, Sam becomes drawn into her life as an actress, and the lives of her two eccentric aunties. But behind the scenes, simmering revenge and betrayal is being acted out . . . a plot that could not only destroy Penny's career and sanity, but the good reputations of her two aunties . . . and Sam.

Chapter 1

Time to Pass

Sam once again climbed the stairs to his bedroom. No big deal. It was something he had done in this house for the past five years, ever since he and his wife Annie had moved there. But for Sam this walk was getting more and more stressful. He had no choice. He had to do it and he wanted to do it. He entered the bedroom as slowly and as quietly as he could, and walked over to his sleeping wife. As he stood over the bed, he could see a shaft of light from the late afternoon winter sun cutting though a gap in the curtains, and it shone on the pillow above Annie's thinning, silver hair, so different from two years' earlier when it had been long and auburn.

Sam knelt down next to the bed and put her hand in his, gently holding it, trying to resist the urge to stroke her pale and cold skin. He knew that even with the medication she was being given to sedate her, the pressure on her frail body could disturb her . . . even the loving touch from her husband of thirty years.

Throughout that night, like many nights before, he tended to her needs as much as he could, but he was so grateful for the visits from her doctor and the Macmillan nurse.

Morning dawned, but not for Annie. She passed away shortly before the sun rose, Sam by her side till the end, still holding her now lifeless hand. Sam lent over and kissed her lips one final time, wiped the tears from his eyes, and walked out of the bedroom into the comforting arms of their two daughters.

The details of the funeral were already in place. It wasn't like a coronary or a fatal accident. If anything, cancer gives both of you time to consider the unthinkable.

Neither Sam nor Annie were regular churchgoers, although, like many of their friends, they went to midnight mass on Christmas Eve, but that was about it. So the funeral was to be held at the crematorium, and her ashes placed in the garden of rest.

But first Sam and Annie would make one last trip together.

Chapter 2

Away Day

Sitting on the steps outside the National Gallery in Trafalgar Square, Sam felt strangely calm. He had kept his promise to Annie – made such a long time ago – and with his backpack beside him, he looked up at the blueness of the sky. It was a dry, bright spring morning, and the warmth of the sun eventually broke through the calm and revealed the reality of how he was really feeling – he was lonely.

Reaching into his jacket pocket, Sam pulled out his phone. He needed to ring Maggie, his beloved eldest daughter, as he said he would as soon as he came out of the gallery. Just then, above all the noise of the traffic and tourists around him, a woman's loud voice broke through, shouting insults and swearing. Sam instinctively turned around to where the racket was coming from, and at a glance saw her shouting into her phone and heading down the steps in his direction. Suddenly, like a footballer taking a penalty, she scooped the toe of her foot under the backpack and lofted it high into the air, it landing several steps further down from where he sat. He rushed forward to retrieve it, followed by the young woman, who knelt down to help him pick it up.

"I'm ever so sorry. I don't know what to say," she said looking at him.

"By the sound of the conversation you were having, you've said plenty already," Sam barked.

"I didn't do it on purpose," she continued. "It was an accident, and I am very sorry." She scowled at him. "But as for being abusive on the phone, I make no apologies for that."

Sam could see she regretted her actions, but wouldn't be chastised.

"I feel sorry for the person on the other end of the phone," Sam replied.

"Don't be. The shit deserved every word," she snapped. Then the young woman looked concerned. "Have I broken anything?" she asked, more softly.

"No, you haven't," Sam replied, looking into her lovely hazel eyes, and for a moment he almost forgot why he was there and gave a gentle smile.

"How do you know?" she asked. "You haven't looked inside. I'm sure I heard a clunk when it landed."

Sam knew he was in a predicament. Should he insist that there was no need to check? Or tell her the real reason why he knew the contents weren't damaged? He could tell by her persona she wasn't the type of woman to be fobbed off.

"OK, I'll check, if that's what you want," Sam sighed. "Sit down and I'll explain why I'm sure the package inside the bag isn't damaged."

He paused and studied her brown, wavy hair – it had just a hint of natural auburn that was glinting in the sun as it cascaded onto her shoulders. He noticed her prominent cheekbones, which gave her the air of a cultured, self-assured person, and the perfectly manicured eyebrows and understated make-up that enhanced her natural complexion. Sam detected a hint of quality perfume too, and noticed the single diamond studs in her earlobes. This was a lady who was naturally beautiful. Visually she didn't need to be loud to be noticed, but the abuse that came out of her mouth . . . well, that was a different matter!

Suddenly she stood up and rubbed her arms. She looked down at Sam.

"I'm sorry about that, I felt all goose-bumpy and creepy, as if someone had just walked over my grave," she murmured.

"Perhaps it would be easier for me if I knew your name?" he asked.

Now it was she who paused to look at him. Early fifties, she guessed, by the greying hair. He was of slim build, but not skinny, and he was clean-shaven and tidy. His brown eyes looked tired and red as if he'd been crying, or maybe it was lack of sleep.

"It's Penny . . . Penny McCain," she replied.

"Well, Miss McCain–"

Sam was about to give his name when she interrupted, saying, "Please don't call me Miss McCain. I've got two elderly aunties, and being called miss makes me feel old. Penny's fine." She gave him a smile, then an inquisitive look. "Do we . . . ?" But she stopped without finishing her sentence.

Sam looked at her. "Do we what, Penny?"

"No matter, it's not important," she replied. "Sorry I interrupted. Your name is?"

"It's Sam, but a lot of people just call me Farmer."

"Why? Are you a farmer?"

"Good god, no!" Sam smiled. "Farmer's my surname, but don't call me Mr Farmer, it makes me feel old!" he said as he grinned at her.

"OK. OK. Duly noted."

"Good, good."

"So, what's in the bag, Sam?"

"Well, it's not a bomb, so you don't have to worry." Lifting his backpack onto his lap, he looked at Penny seriously now, and speaking in a quiet tone began to explain: "My late wife Annique, Annie as we called her, used to come here as often as she could. She was French, you see, from Marseille .She studied art and design at the *L'ecole des Beaux*, Paris, before continuing her studies at the Academy here in London. When she finished her degree she moved to Exeter to teach art at the university. Sam gave Penny a pensive smile. "I first met her in Weymouth where she was partying with friends at the weekend, and well . . . the rest is history really. We married two years' later and set up home in Exeter. Annie loved art galleries – the Tate, the Louvre – but especially the National Gallery here behind us." Sam paused, gathering his thoughts. "I hope I'm not boring you . . ."

"No, no, please go on," Penny insisted. She'd sat back on the step beside him now, and was surprised at feeling interested in what this stranger had to say.

People were walking past them on both sides, but Sam seemed oblivious to all that was going on around him. He wanted to tell Penny why he was there and nothing else seemed to matter.

"Annie would come up to London as often as she could to see new art collections or exhibitions," he continued. "'All the usual suspects', as she called them: Monet, Van Gogh, Baptiste and so on." He had his hands resting on the bag and was gently tapping it. "As you can see, there's a Van Gogh exhibition on now, which she planned to visit, but her true love was Monet and his exhibition isn't on until next year."

Now Sam looked at Penny with a more sombre expression, and his voice was trembling slightly.

"Two years ago she was diagnosed with a brain tumour, but by the time the doctors found out, it was too large to operate. They tried chemotherapy but it only prolonged her agony. Within months she went blind . . . she was so upset that she could no longer see her beloved art. But she's gone now, at rest from all the pain and drugs. I miss her." Sam swallowed to clear the lump that had formed in his throat. "She was my rock." He raised a small smile to help resist the temptation to weep. He drew a large breath. "It was Annie's last wish to come back to the National one more time–"

Penny quickly butted in, saying, "Oh my god, are you telling me she's in that bag?" The shock of that possibility was ringing in her voice.

"Yes, well, her ashes are . . ." Sam said.

"Oh shit, and I almost messed it all up!" Penny exclaimed.

"No harm done," Sam told her. "Her ashes are in a strong container. Not even an elephant could damage it – even a pretty elephant like you." Sam managed another little smile to reassure her. "Anyway, I've kept my promise to her. I'll take her back to Devon, and then sort my life out. I know that sounds a bit callous but that's what she wanted me to do. That's what I would expect her to do if I had died."

"How long ago did she pass away?" Penny enquired, in a soft, gentle tone.

"A few months ago," he told her. "I'm here till Monday, and plan to lay her ashes to rest next week. We have two daughters. Maggie, who's like me. And Estelle, who's more like Annie with her long red hair and stunning green eyes. They are in their twenties now, all grown up and moved away." Sam stopped and looked at his bag again. "So, there you go, now you know everything." He gazed at her and saw she had tears in her eyes. She quickly wiped them away. "You silly thing, there's no need for that," he said kindly.

"It's so sad, so lovely," she said, sniffing at the same time. "How long were you married?"

"It would have been thirty years this August. It was a good marriage. It almost went into meltdown once, many years ago, but she stood by me and we got through it."

"Was someone else involved?" Penny enquired.

"No, it was a family matter. Why do you ask?" he said.

"No reason, just being nosey . . . sorry." She knew her inquisitive mind had got the better of her again.

And Don't Forget the Roses

"Right, Penny, your turn. What was that heated call about?"

She looked at him, her eyes suddenly large and angry.

"I was on the phone to my fiancé, Toby. I live here but he works mostly in the northeast, so we don't see each other that often at the moment." Then she abruptly stopped talking about him. "Tell you what, Sam," she declared. "My arse is getting cold sitting here. Let's go and get a coffee across the road. All this traffic noise and emotion is doing my voice in."

He gazed at her, not sure whether to frown or smile in reply to her suggestion. It was most curious that only minutes before he had been sitting here on his own feeling calm, but lonely, and now he had a complete stranger – an attractive stranger, but a stranger nevertheless – wanting to go for a coffee with him.

"Yes," Sam replied politely, "I would like that." He stood up. "Arrgh! My old bones are a bit stiff!" he laughed, picking up his backpack as they headed off for a coffee. Penny led the way, and Sam followed.

She was elegantly dressed in a light Highland tweed skirt, which came just below her knee, and brown patent leather boots. She wore a dark cream roll neck sweater under a leather three-quarter-length coat – almost the same shade of tan as her boots. He guessed her age at early thirties, as she had that look of maturity about her. From the tone in her voice, Sam thought he detected a slight accent from the borders, but he wasn't sure.

Penny walked into the coffee bar and down to the far end.

"Down here, Sam," she said. "Plenty of room for your bag and its quiet . . . well, it's as quiet as it can be in London!" She looked at him as she removed her coat.

Sam sat down opposite her, which gave them both the opportunity to study each other over their drinks. Sam ordered their coffees, along with two large Belgian buns.

"You were telling me about Toby," Sam reminded her.

"Yes, that shit. OK. We'd arranged to buy my engagement ring today. He came down last night from Newcastle and stayed at his mate's flat as I was working late. So we arranged to meet outside the gallery at eleven . . . that's better," she said, sipping at her coffee. "I got a call from him saying his mate had got them two tickets to watch the rugby at Twickenham, and he'd get one next time he's down." Penny stopped talking, looked at Sam and smiled. "That's when I crashed into Annie, sorry, again." Then Penny's smile disappeared.

"So, no ring today," Sam said. "I feel sad for you. It's a special occasion in a woman's life."

"You don't have to tell me. Don't worry, he'll be sorry. I had hoped we would get a picnic, take it to the park and enjoy the good weather and our time together," she said, looking disappointed. "Oh well, the best laid plans, as they say . . . So, what's next for you today?" she asked.

He looked at her with a studious expression and thought for a few moments.

"Well, I thought I might take my new-found friend to the park for a picnic."

Penny frowned at Sam, taking in what he had just suggested. She felt unsure, but at the same time something niggled away at her: *why did she get the feeling they knew each other?*

"Yes, why the hell not! I have hours to spare, thanks to Toby, and I'll be able to tease him about that. I'll tell him I met this lovely man who treated me to a picnic," Penny giggled.

"At fifty-two, I think I'm past the competition stage! But if he gets jealous, just tell him he shouldn't have stood you up."

Penny laughed at this comment.

"What about the saying, Sam – 'Many a good tune . . .'?"

"That depends on the tune, and what the instrument is," Sam replied with a grin.

She looked across the table, unable to resist staring at him, with her chin resting on her hands. He noticed what she was doing but said nothing.

"Sorry, Sam, I'm staring at you," she suddenly said.

With a polite smile, he replied, "Come on then, let's get that picnic."

He picked up her coat from the chair and helped her put it on. He thought he would feel awkward going to a park with another woman, with Annie's ashes in his bag, but he didn't. Instead he laughed to himself. *Ha-ha*, he thought, *she always enjoyed a good picnic, did Annie.*

Chapter 3

Picnic in the Park

Which park is nearest?" Sam asked as they left the coffee shop.

Penny stood on the pavement, looking around, trying to find her bearings.

"Green Park is nearest. Not much of a walk," she said, thinking it would be wiser to walk somewhere rather than get into a taxi with a complete stranger – even if she did feel at ease with him. She felt a strange sense of excitement about going for a picnic with Sam, and led the way to a small delicatessen she knew.

They loaded up with French bread, *foie gras*, potato salad and a healthy wedge of Camembert, all to be washed down with a bottle of Chardonnay. They also grabbed the obligatory plastic knives and cups, and then set off to the park.

Sam had no idea which direction to take.

"'*Lead on, Macduff*'," he said, and nodded his head in a forward motion.

Penny chuckled to herself, aware he had just misquoted the words, knowing he should have said, '*Lay on, Macduff,*' – but decided to ignore his misquote of the Bard out of politeness.

"'*And damn'd be him that first cries, "Hold, enough"*,'" Penny retorted.

"You know your Shakespeare!" Sam laughed.

"Oh yes, just a bit . . ." she replied, laughing too. "So, how do you know about Macduff?" she asked as she picked her way through the traffic and crowds with ease.

Sam, on the other hand, was trying to keep up alongside her, but had to drop back several times, not only because he hadn't a clue how to get to Green Park, but because he was used to walking behind Annie when they were in London – he found it safer to keep an eye on her that way. Besides, Annie always had a good sense of direction. Old habits die hard!

After what seemed quite a walk they arrived, and at last he was able walk beside her and answer her question.

"*Macbeth*," Sam belatedly replied. "Got dragged to the theatre in Plymouth by Annie, and left feeling slightly shell-shocked by the power of the tale."

"You got off lightly, Sam, believe me. I know two elderly ladies for whom Shakespeare is '. . . *their night, their day'*."

Sam now felt he might be out of his depth with regards to Shakespeare. Somehow he thought that this young woman knew quite a bit more about the Bard than he did.

Penny found a nice spot under the shade of a leafy ash tree and removed her coat ready to sit on it.

"Oh, don't do that," he said. "You'll get grass stains on the leather. It'll be a bitch of a job to remove." He gently put his bag down where he could keep an eye on it and took off his jacket. "Here, sit on mine."

"Thank you, kind sir, that's very considerate." Penny smiled as she sat down and kicked off her boots. "My poor feet!" she said, rubbing her toes. She then looked at him. "Come on, get the wine out," she ordered, "and I'll sort the food. Chop-chop!"

"Nag, nag, nag!" he said, pouring the wine into plastic cups. "Here you go – enjoy!"

Sam put his cup up to hers. "Here's to a friend new and friends past."

She gave him a sad smile. "Yes . . . to friendships new and old," she said, and then knelt forward and gave him a gentle kiss on the cheek, and as she drew back, stroked the skin she had just kissed.

He looked surprised that she had done such a thing, but then smiled too. "Thank you," he said

"Tuck into your food, Sam!"

For a few minutes they quietly ate, breaking the bread and slicing into the Camembert.

"Do you know it's been years since I've been on a picnic," Penny then said. "At work I only grab snacks and whatnot, and in some unusual places, but you can't beat a picnic. Thank you for asking me." She suddenly realised how hungry she was.

"So what sort of job do you do that requires you to have lunch on the hoof?" he asked, watching her as she sipped her wine.

"I'm an actor. I do theatre and TV, and the occasional film work in some out-of-the-way locations, but my first love is the theatre."

"Let me guess . . . Shakespeare?"

In answer she leant over with her plastic cup of wine and offered it up to his.

"Here's to Shakespeare! A man who will outlive us all!" she proclaimed. "God, I sound like my Auntie May," she laughed. "That's what she would say!"

Penny was now beginning to relax her guard with this man she had only met, purely by chance, just a couple of hours before. It may have been the wine, or the fact that she was enjoying his company, but she found herself telling him with enthusiasm about Shakespeare – his plays, the sonnets – everything that she loved about them.

"So, where did it all begin for you, this love of acting?" he asked, passing her another slice of Camembert.

"Mmm, thank you, Sam." She paused a while, consuming her cheese. "My aunts sent me on course for treading the boards, as they say. . ." she replied, and then pensively looked down at her tweed skirt, picked at the hem, and pondered just how far back she wanted to go without reliving the pain of her early years, "when I moved to London from Edinburgh."

"Ah!" Sam exclaimed. "I thought I detected a slight Scots accent."

"I moved in with two aunties when I was quite young. They introduced me to the Bard, as well as Noel Coward, Samuel Peeps, George Orwell, Shaw and not forgetting the Bronte sisters – the list goes on and on and on," she said with a wry smile, stopping to sip her wine.

"Tell me about your aunties," Sam replied, offering her a top up.

"No thanks, sweetie, any more and I'll need a pee, and I'm sure crouching behind a tree in a Royal Park is still a hanging offence!" she said, laughing.

Sam was now completely consumed by every word this woman spoke – soft, rounded, ever so slightly deep in tone and concise. Everything she uttered was with purpose, even if she resorted to using language not befitting a lady!

"My aunties," she said, drawing a large breath. "Auntie June and Auntie May are considered to be two of the greatest living Shakespearian actresses of their generation. They're two lovely ladies with minds as sharp as razors and full of mischief. You'd like them."

"Does that mean I may get the opportunity to meet them one day?" he asked.

Penny made no attempt to reply, but looked at Sam with a thoughtful smile. She then started rubbing her feet again.

"God, they're sore. I wear some bloody heavy costumes and ridiculous shoes at times. Last week I played a tart and I had to run away from this man who was going to strangle me – which he did! Anyway, I had to wear these stupid stilettos. My poor feet were sore and swollen for days. If I don't get bunions, I'll be lucky!"

Sam looked at her shapely feet and her smooth legs, leant over to Penny's coat, rolled it up into a pillow shape, and then said, "Here, put your coat under your head and lay back."

She looked at him with a curious expression on her face, but said nothing, aware again of that inner sense she could trust him.

"Go on, trust me," he said.

As Penny lay on her back with her head on her coat, Sam moved to her feet and started to massage them. She felt his strong hands on them, and although her feet were sore, what he was doing felt soothing.

"Bloody hell, Sam, that feels lovely, thank you."

"Even at my age, I still have my uses," he replied with a look of concentration on his face.

"Uses! If you weren't going home Monday, I'd employ you as my personal foot masseur!" She paused for a moment, then laughed. "Ha, if I told my friends that I met a guy for the first time today, and then let him massage my feet in the park a few hours later, they wouldn't believe me. I wouldn't believe me!" she proclaimed with another laugh. "How about you, Sam? I bet you never imagined this happening?"

He worked the bones of her feet with his thumbs, firmly, but not so as to irritate or hurt her. Occasionally he looked over to her, and watched her lying there, resting and enjoying the pleasure he was giving her.

"I haven't given it any thought," he said. "One minute I'm sitting on the steps in Trafalgar Square, feeling lonely, and then a few hours later I'm here massaging the feet of a beautiful woman. Someone up there must love me, as they say."

"It could be Annie, Sam," Penny said, lifting herself up on her elbows and smiling.

He looked at her with a sad expression on his face.

"That would be typical of her. She always looked out for me. We looked out for each other. Only her ashes are in that bag; her spirit is up there somewhere." He gazed up into the afternoon sky.

Penny moved her feet away from Sam's hands. She now felt a little awkward after what she had just said about Annie. So much had happened in the few hours since they'd met. They got on so well, though, like they had known each other for years.

She rubbed her feet.

"Wow! They feel lovely. Thank you again." She moved her hand over to Sam's and gave it a light squeeze.

"You ought to get Toby to massage your feet with warm, sensual oils. It's so good if you've been on them all day," he said, noticing the dimples on her cheeks when she tensed her jaw muscles.

"No chance," she told him sternly. "Knowing Toby, he'd be rubbing my feet for about thirty seconds before trying to move his hands up my thighs. That the last thing I need after being on my feet all day!"

Can't blame him for that, Sam thought, glancing at her shapely legs.

"Are you working tonight?" he enquired.

"Yes . . . Oh shit! What's the time?" she said, grabbing her phone. "4.20! I've got a reading tonight in Staines at 7.00pm!"

"Reading? What's a reading?" Sam was intrigued, but at the same time he felt deflated that the wonderful time he was having with her sounded like it was coming to an abrupt end.

"Reading passages from Shakespeare's plays and sonnets," she quickly informed him, standing up and brushing herself down.

"Tell you what . . . you said you're not going home till Monday . . . meet me here tomorrow at midday sharp. Got to dash, Sam. You'll be here, won't you? I don't want to be looking like a tart hanging around in the park." She pushed her rejuvenated feet into her boots.

"Don't worry, I'll be here," Sam replied, surprised and quietly elated she wanted to see him again. "You go. I'll clear up. See you tomorrow." She started struggling with her coat. "Here, let me help. You're all fingers and thumbs," he said, holding it open for her.

Gathering her thoughts, she looked around for the correct path to take her out of the park.

"I really have enjoyed today, thank you," she said, reaching for his hand and giving it another tender squeeze. "Must go."

Sam watched her disappear out of the park.

"Well, Sam, what would Annie make of this?" he said, chuckling to himself as he packed up the remains of the picnic.

Chapter 4

Maggie Won't Believe Me

Sam opened the door to his hotel room, placed the backpack by the window and slumped down on the bed. He gazed up at the ceiling and thought *you couldn't make today up if you tried*. He closed his eyes and fell into a deep sleep.

He stirred at the sound of ringing, and was still half asleep he reached for his phone, but soon realised that it was the hotel phone. He picked it up in a sleepy daze.

"Good evening, sir, I have a call for you," the female voice said, sounding jolly and polite.

"Thank you, put it through," he replied, having no idea who it was.

"Hi, Dad. I've been worried sick! I've been trying to contact you all day. Why didn't you answer your phone? You said you'd phone me when you left the gallery."

Sam suddenly remembered that he was about to ring Maggie when Penny hoofed his backpack down the steps outside the gallery.

"Sorry, Mags, I put it on silent when I was in there and forgot to switch it back on."

"Dad, you plonker, you're always doing that!"

"True," he admitted.

So what did you do once you left the gallery that made you forget to phone me?" she asked, curiously.

Chapter 4

Sam grinned to himself and then told her how he'd spent his afternoon. He had the feeling she wouldn't believe him – and he was right. Even by the time they ended their conversation, she still didn't.

"10.30 already," he said, checking his watch.

A quick pint from the bar, he decided. He wondered what Penny had planned for them tomorrow. It couldn't be any more eventful than today, or could it?

Chapter 5

Starting a New Day

It had gone midnight when Penny returned home after her evening reading Shakespeare. Opening the door, she could hear a strange noise coming from the lounge. It was Toby, passed out on her settee, snoring loudly, smelling of tobacco and stinking of beer. Being over six feet tall, he looked uncomfortable hanging over each end of her two-seater.

"Toby, you shit," she said quietly. "What do you look like?"

She switched off the light and went up to bed. Getting undressed, she recalled her day. *Poor Sam. I hope he'll like what I've got planned*, she thought, smiling to herself.

She knew she could have just said goodbye to him in the park, so why didn't she? That would have been the easy option. Her life was hectic enough, without being a Good Samaritan. Then she thought of Toby. It was a good job she loved him! She decided to let him stew for a bit, but he wasn't going to be let off the hook that easily after what he'd done: standing her up. *The shit*! she thought again, with a wry smile, as she rolled over and fell asleep.

"What the . . .? Toby, get your grubby hands off my tits!" Penny yelled, realising he had clambered in beside her. She looked at the clock with sleepy eyes. "God, it's 3.30 in the morning! You're out of your sodding mind if you think you're sleeping in this bed tonight. You stink of beer and I haven't forgiven you for standing me up. Piss off and go and sleep in the spare bed."

"If I don't get some sleep, I'll look like a bloody hag in the morning," she muttered to herself.

Sam awoke early at 6.00am; a force of habit for him. He'd been getting up at that time for over two years, tending to Annie's needs, sometimes never getting to bed at all. Although it was all over now, he still got up at that time. He couldn't see the point of staying in bed any longer, now that he was on his own.

Six hours to kill, Sam thought. *Shower, shave, breakfast and a stroll around the block, I reckon*. He still wondered what Penny had planned for them.

After his walk, he freshened up and then changed into smarter clothes than the ones he'd worn the day before. This time he chose a pair of light tan trousers creased down the front, with a dark brown leather belt and short-sleeved white linen shirt – which he wore tucked in. Even at fifty-two he still had a good physique. He finished off with light brown shoes and a smart cotton jacket. Looking in the bathroom mirror, he studied himself. His dark brown eyes still looked slightly bloodshot, as they had been the day before. He combed his hair, now mostly grey.

He picked up his phone and set off to meet Penny and the mystery date.

"Circle Line south, third stop, and then a five-minute walk . . . I should make it with half an hour to spare," he said with mixed emotions of amusement and confusion. It was very strange that this was happening to him, and he didn't know why, but he wasn't complaining; he was on his way to meet a person whom he found interesting, apart from being beautiful.

Penny reached over to her bedside table and fumbled for her phone; the ring tone was now getting on her nerves. She grabbed at it, endeavouring to press the green receive button.

"Yes?" she said, in a half-hearted way.

"Hello, dear, it's May. I hope I haven't phoned you too early."

"What time is it?" Penny asked, lethargic from being woken up.

"9.50, dear. I just wanted to confirm you're still coming for lunch."

"Oh no, I've overslept," Penny said to herself, very quietly. "Yes, yes, I'll be there. Sorry, May, I've overslept. It's a good job you phoned, otherwise I'd still be out for the count."

Still speaking in a hushed voice, so that Toby couldn't hear what she saying, she added, "If it's OK with you, Toby won't be coming, but I'll be bringing a friend along. He's not long lost his wife, and I couldn't think of a better way to cheer him up other than meet you two." Penny knew her aunties wouldn't hesitate to say yes.

"Of course he'll be welcome! What's his name, dear?" May enquired.

"Sam. You'll like him. He's got sad eyes, though."

"Well, what do expect? The poor man's just lost his wife. You would hardly expect them to sparkle, now would you?"

"I'm sure after an afternoon with you two, they will!" Penny laughed quietly down the phone. "Look, I'd better get up and shower. We'll be with you about 12.30."

"There's no rush, dear, we won't finish off the roast until you arrive."

Penny climbed out of bed and quietly looked in on Toby in the spare bedroom. He was still fast asleep on top of the bed, naked.

"Oh my god. What a sight to see . . . and before breakfast too," she murmured. She closed the door and went to get herself ready to meet Sam.

On her way out, Penny quickly jotted down a note to tell Toby not to bother about lunch at her aunties, and that she'd see him later. She put the note by the coffee pot, knowing he was going to need some. She checked herself in the hallway mirror, pursing her lips to even out her bright red lipstick, and then walked to the park. She had a good half an hour to spare.

Chapter 6

The Shakespeare Sisters

Sam scanned the park looking for Penny; he felt apprehensive. He kept asking himself why such a fine young woman would bother befriending him. It was a meeting that had happened by accident and turned into a fabulous afternoon with her, but he was puzzled. Why had she wanted to meet him again? She didn't strike him as a person who had time to spend forming new friendships with people outside her life as an actor. He didn't think it gave her that luxury.

Time was cracking on. He'd been in the park for over twenty minutes, having arrived early, but it was almost midday now and he was starting to become aware of people looking at this 'poor man standing on his own'. He smiled at a young woman pushing a pram, with a toddler in hand, and a couple of dog-walkers. He didn't want to sit on a bench as it made him feel even more awkward than standing around in his shirtsleeves, his jacked folded over his arm. He checked the time on his watch – even though he'd done it countless times already since he arrived in the park – and again he looked around to make sure that he was at the exact spot where they'd been yesterday. The midday sun now beginning to beat down on him as he patiently waited for her.

Well, Sam, he thought, *give her till half past then start to worry*; but just as he got that thought out of his head, he saw a wonderful young lady heading towards him in a full, red and white polka dot dress with thin shoulder straps which showed off her elegant neck; her shoulder length hair hung down over her shoulders.

Penny waved as she strolled towards him.

"I'm so sorry, I bet you thought I'd stood you up," she said as he gave her a welcoming peck on her cheek. "It was my bloody shoes – a lovely red pair – but I couldn't walk in them. I got two hundred yards and had to go back and change them!"

Sam gazed at the beautiful woman in from of him.

"Anyway," Penny continued, "when I got back home, I couldn't get the other shoes I wanted to wear as they are in the spare bedroom where Toby was, and I didn't want to wake the bugger up, so slipped these white ones on and found this matching handbag. I love this style, don't you?" she asked, her hazel eyes beaming at him.

Her beauty had him breathless, and he felt a strong sense of pleasure as he gazed across at her.

"If I were a scholar, I would say something profound or recite a sonnet for you," he replied with a smile. "You look absolutely stunning. I love that dress; the whole outfit. I'd like to say you make me feel twenty years younger, but my daughters would accuse me of being on drugs if they heard me say that!" he joked, watching her do a twirl for him.

She took a step back, looked Sam up and down and then stepped forward again.

She frowned.

"May I?" she asked.

He looked at her curiously.

"Be my guest," he replied, not knowing what she intended to do.

She lifted his arms out as if he were a scarecrow, loosened his belt and then put her arms around his waist and proceeded to pull out his shirt. Working her way to the front, she pulled on the shirt hem to remove any creases and then retightened his belt.

"Mmm, flat tummy," she smiled.

Brushing him down with her hands, she smiled and stood back to admire her work and remarked, "That's better. You can put your arms down now." She giggled then and looped her arm in his and gave it a squeeze. "Well, Sam, you old man," she continued, "they say you feel as young as the woman you're with, and I'm twenty years younger than you, so I've just knocked them off you!"

"That was a surprise, but why do I think you've got another one up your sleeve?" he asked.

"You'll like this one, Sam."

"I liked the last one!" he said, and they both laughed.

She led them in the direction she wanted them to go, and as they walked Sam asked her about her evening.

"Have you ever been to a Shakespeare reading?" she enquired.

"No, I only know as much as you told me yesterday."

"Well there are three of us – me, Ahmed and Patch; we call him Patch because his surname is Patchette. He knows his Shakespeare, but can be a bit of a knob at times."

Sam frowned at her frequent use of expletives, and wondered if she would ever call him a shit or knob one day. *I'd be pissed if she did*, he thought.

She continued to enlighten him on her readings, saying, "We hold the readings all over the place – in pubs and churches, anywhere really. We even did one a rugby club once. That was fun. A few in the audience tried – and failed – to heckle us. You're on to a loser when it comes to the Bard. With verses from various plays and sonnets, we had the rest of the audience laughing at the pricks who thought they were clever."

They had left the park now, and Penny was taking them down

back streets and avenues. Sam still didn't have a clue where he was going.

"Ahmed and I read a selection of passages from plays and sonnets selected by the audience, and then Patch interprets. I enjoy doing them," she continued. "The money's no good but it's a way of getting Shakespeare out there. That's what he would have wanted. Besides, my other work pays the mortgage. We did a golf club once – God, they were as thick as shit! All they wanted to do was get me pissed and get inside my knickers."

Sam was again surprised by Penny's bluntness and choice of words, but like the saying goes, he thought *you can't tell a book by its cover* and found himself mesmerised by her fluent, almost artistic, delivery.

"Brash, aren't I?" she admitted, noticing his frown at her bad language. "I'll try not to be, sorry," she said with a flutter of her lashes.

"I bet when you visit your aunties you're all peaches and cream," he replied.

"Not always. They irritate me sometimes, but I try my best to be respectful to them. Most of what I know is due to them."

They turned into a small cobbled mews – dwellings that were formally stable and coach houses – an enclave of peace within the bustling city. Some had been painted in pleasing pastel colours, but others still showed their London-brick walls, and all had an abundance of flowers and plants cascading from window boxes that added to the beauty of the tranquil setting.

"Wow!" was all Sam could say.

Outside one they noticed a pair of legs sticking out from under an old 1950s car.

"Hi, Harry," Penny called as they stopped, and the rest of the body appeared from under the vehicle and stood up.

"Hello, angel. God, you wouldn't look amiss in my old banger in that dress!" he declared, making her smile as she gave a little curtsey for him.

"Harry, this is Sam, a mate of mine from Devon," Penny smiled, her arm still linked in Sam's.

"Good to meet you, old boy. Won't shake your hand. I'm all grubby!" Harry laughed, and then turned to Penny and asked, "Where's that young man of yours? I hear congratulations are in order!"

Penny scowled, and replied, "He's at home with a hangover, Harry, and the bugger hasn't even bought me my ring yet."

"Oh! He hasn't, has he?" Harry replied and not holding back with his opinion, said, "Tell you what, Sam, that young man of hers doesn't deserve her. I've known this lass since she first came here as a child. I know she can be a bit loud at times, but under that visage is a loving woman busting to get out!"

Sam looked at her, and noticed that she blushed.

"He always does that to me, the bugger!" she laughed, leaning over to kiss him. "We must go, Harry, they'll be waiting for us," she said, taking a few more paces towards the house next door with its white timber sash windows. They stepped into the oak panelled hallway. "Come on, Sam," Penny said. "Come and meet my aunties."

Waiting in the lounge was an elderly lady in her seventies, wearing a flowery dress and apron. Penny stood to one side and introduced Sam to her Auntie June.

"It's nice to meet you, and no you don't," Sam said. Auntie June looked puzzled at his remark, and Sam grinned as he added, "No, your bum doesn't look big in that . . ."

June gave out a hoot of laughter, and cried, "You cheeky bugger! May! May!" she shouted, "Penny's here with her new friend!"

She led the way into the dining room where Sam could see the back of a lady in the kitchen, just closing the oven door. She turned around, and he saw this goddess of a woman with big breasts and wearing a bikini: it was Auntie May wearing *her* comical apron!

Sam felt a sharp pain in his ribs and a voice in his ear: "Don't even think about it!" Penny hissed.

Penny saw him suck his bottom lip as if to say *My lips are sealed*, and then he winked at her with a cheeky smile. They walked into the kitchen, and Penny gave her auntie a hug.

"Be a dear, Penny, and fill up the kettle while I introduce myself to this handsome man of yours. Sam is it? she asked, as she showed him the side of her face for a polite kiss.

"May," Penny moaned, "this bloody tap! Why don't you get it fixed? Your water bills must cost you a fortune with it dripping all the time." She looked at Sam. "Can you turn the bloody thing off? They both have arthritis in their hands. It's ridiculous that they don't get a plumber in."

"Plumbers! It's like they have a licence to print money, especially in London, dear, you know that," May complained.

Sam walked over to the kitchen sink, realising his opportunity to help, and then turned and said, "I'm just popping out for a moment." He returned within minutes with a handful of Harry's tools. "Could you go to the bathroom, Penny, and open all the cold water taps and flush the loo for me," he asked.

"Why? What are you doing?" she asked, looking curious.

"Trust me, I know what I'm doing," he said, reassuring her with a nod of his head.

June and May stood arm in arm, paused as if frozen in time; they were wondering what he was preparing to do. Penny went upstairs to the bathroom and did as Sam instructed, and then the three women watched with fascination as he dismantled the tap and showed them cause of their problems.

"This black bit of rubber, here, it's the washer," he explained.

"I'll take your word on that. I haven't got a clue what you're talking about," Penny replied.

"Don't look so worried, I've done this loads of times," he told her, putting the tap back to together – with the aid of a drop of washing up liquid.

"You're going to do the dishes as well, are you?" she asked with a curious smile.

"No! I haven't got any grease to tighten the threads, so this stuff will do for the time being." He turned to the aunties – who were peering at the tap. "There you go, ladies, all done," he said, picking up Harry's tools. "Be a love and go back upstairs while I turn the water back on. Give it a few seconds before you turn the taps off, it'll let the air out."

He left to return the tools to Harry, and when he walked back into the kitchen he laughed when he saw all three women standing at the sink taking it in turns to use the tap as if it was a new invention!

"Well, bugger me, it's like new!" June exclaimed. "Thank you, dear. A useful man – what a rarity!" she exclaimed. "Quick May, go and ask Harry if he has any chains, coz he's not leaving here!"

May returned to cooking the lunch, and she began to recite a passage from *Macbeth* while she stirred the gravy, soon joined by her sister and Penny:

"'O well done! I commend your pains;

And every one shall share I' the gains;

and now about the cauldron sing,

Live elves and fairies in a ring,

Enchanting all that you put in. . . '"

When they'd finished, Penny stood in front of Sam with her hands on her hips, smiling in amusement.

"Well, that's a novel way to impress new friends, you smoothie, you!" She kissed his cheek. "Thank you. That was kind of you!" she added.

Sam shrugged his shoulders in reply, slightly embarrassed at the accolade bestowed upon him.

"Go on, dears, go through and get seated," May said, pointing to the large mahogany dining table set for lunch. Sam's eyes were drawn to the framed theatre programs hung on practically every inch of available wall space. There were photographs of the sisters in various costumes with the play titles and dates; the great and good of the theatre world in years gone by.

"You're sitting over there opposite me, Sam, so I can kick you if you misbehave," Penny joked.

"I hope you're not a fussy eater, dear," June said. "That Toby of hers doesn't like this, and doesn't that! One day I'll give him beans on toast, but I reckon even then he'd make a fuss."

"Come on, Auntie June, give Toby a break. He's a darling really," Penny said, springing to his defence.

"I'll say no more, dear. I'm sure Sam doesn't want to know about your poor taste in men."

"Auntie June!" Penny uttered. "God, you drive me mad at times."

"She's only teasing you. The more you bite, the more fun she has!" Sam told her, enjoying the banter going on between them.

"I can't remember when I last had a delicious meal like that, and in such good company too!" Sam declared, thanking them. He silently recalled how the complications of Annie's cancer had meant that her food had to be easy to swallow, and how he'd felt that it was cruel to treat himself to a roast dinner, or a succulent Ribeye steak, when his lovely wife had had to endure mush akin to baby food.

May looked across the table at him, frowning and shaking her head. "This is no good, it won't do at all," she said.

"What's the problem, May?" Penny asked, suddenly concerned.

"Harry next door . . . his bloody cat is called Sam. Every time I look at our new friend here, I think of that matted ball of fur."

Sam laughed. "Well just call me Farmer; lots of people do. Annie used to call me Sam when I was in her good books, but Farmer when I wasn't!"

Suddenly the mood changed, and Sam could see the sadness on the two elderly ladies' faces when he mentioned his late wife.

June looked across the table to him.

"Here we are laughing and joking," she said, "and we haven't said how sorry we are about your dear wife."

Looking thoughtful, he smiled at his hosts.

"I won't even try to say something profound about my loss, but I know Annie would be happy that I have had the good fortune to meet three wonderful ladies who have brought a smile to my face." Then looking directly at Penny he said, "Maybe Annie had a hand in the fortuitous way we met, and how I find myself here today . . ."

She was taken aback by his words, fully aware of what he meant. Suddenly the hairs on the back of her neck stood up, and she became very self-conscious. *Why?* she thought. *Why am I self-conscious?* As an actor she was used to attention. She thrived on it. It was her oxygen. Her aunties had taught her the craft of acting – to feel passion, remorse, hate, sorrow, all the emotions, an accumulation of emotions, she could call upon – but she felt perplexed that those few words Sam had just spoken had got under her skin. Looking at him thoughtfully, she stood up and declared, "Right, Sam Farmer, you and me are doing the washing up."

"OK, bossette, that's fine by me," he replied, smiling.

A cackle of laughter erupted from the aunties, who were clearly amused at Sam calling their niece 'bossette'.

He glanced at her pillar-box red manicured fingernails and thought *I'll wash*.

"I would have washed!" she protested.

"Yes, I'm sure you would," he replied, giving her a wry smile. "But I've seen your nails. I bet doing the dishes in your house is putting them in a dishwasher."

"Well, we girls are the fairer sex," she giggled. "You men have to take care of us." She wriggled her hips to accentuate her femininity.

Sam looked towards the kitchen door to see if they were alone.

"Rubbish," he whispered. "I get the feeling you're more capable of looking after yourself than you make out!" he said, flicking soap suds at her.

Penny was enjoying the banter immensely, this *now* time she was having with Sam. It was relaxed, uncomplicated fun.

"You can't do the dishes like that, not after all the effort I put in getting you looking nice. Here put this on," she insisted.

"Oh, I'm so thankful, Miss," he quipped, putting on May's apron.

Penny found herself pondering her new friend. He'd been polite and a real gentleman with her over the weekend, right from when they'd first met on the steps. He'd shown his vulnerability and the raw emotions over the loss of Annie, but she could see glimpses of the fun side of his personality beginning to shine though. Engrossed in washing the pot and pans, he didn't notice her gazing at him . . . or so she thought. She began to wonder how they could keep in touch without giving him the wrong impression. He was a nice guy, and it would be good to have a pal from outside the acting world; *more importantly a man who could repair taps*, she chuckled to herself.

"Penny for your thoughts," he said, and then laughed. "I bet that's been said a few times!"

"Just a few, and it doesn't get any funnier. In fact the last person who said that was crossed off my Christmas card list," she replied, teasing him.

"Ouch! Point taken," he replied with a sheepish glance.

"So what do you think of my aunties?" she asked.

"They're lovely. I like their sense of humour, but I bet they can be buggers at times though!"

"Oh yes. They plot and plan – just like a couple of Shakespeare's characters!"

"I can see they think the world of you. You're probably more like a daughter to them than a niece," he observed.

Penny gazed out of the window, drying the plates. She thought about what Sam had just said.

"They are sweet, but hard task masters. It wasn't easy living here. That's probably why I'm a bit loud sometimes and can be a selfish bitch," she admitted, pulling a face.

"As long as you don't practice being a bitch with me, coz it won't work," Sam warned, giving her a stern look.

"Oh, I don't have to practice, I've got it off to perfection–"

Penny was suddenly distracted by the sound of a familiar voice.

"Hello, pet!" said Toby, as he poked his head around the kitchen door. "I thought I'd come over and surprise you!"

She turned to look at him, startled like an animal caught in the headlamps. *Oh yes, it's a surprise alright*, she thought, and then, *shit. . .*

"Hi, sweetheart," she said in a joyful tone as Toby gave her a kiss on her lips, his eyes glancing at Sam.

"So, what are you doing here?" she asked, trying to look pleased to see him, but still feeling aggrieved about his behaviour the day before.

"I thought I'd come and collect you, pet. We can walk home together seeing as it's a lovely afternoon," he replied, looking directly at Sam. "Who are you then?" he enquired abruptly in his broad Geordie accent.

Sam looked back at him with a cheerful smile, and dried his hands on the tea towel to shake his hand.

"I'm Sam, nice to meet you," he replied, taking a firm grip of his hand.

"He's one of my aunties' old friends, babe. He pops in now and again to do odd jobs – don't you, Sam . . ." she said, seeing him nod in agreement.

"Really?" Toby asked, looking at him curiously. "I like your apron, it suits you."

"I thought so too," Sam joked as Penny quickly left the kitchen to go and speak to her aunties. "I think it brings out the feminine side in me, don't you think?"

He sensed Toby was trying to be clever, but he wasn't fazed. He knew he could give as good as he got, and some! Penny quickly returned, slightly anxious and feeling embarrassed for Sam; it had been her idea for him to use the apron with the picture of a bikini-clad girl.

"Go into the lounge, sweetheart, while we finish off here," she said. "Then we can go."

"Wye-aye, pet," Toby replied, shooting a piercing glance at Sam as he disappeared out of the kitchen.

"I'm so sorry he saw you with that on," she said.

"Don't be. It was a bit of a laugh, no harm done."

"The bugger. I didn't want to go yet. I was enjoying it here," she said with a deep frown on her face.

"Well, stay then."

"Good God, no. My aunties hate him, but they tolerate him for my sake," Penny replied, not bothering to hide their opinion of him. "I quickly asked them to tell Toby you're an old friend of theirs, otherwise I'll have to explain how we met, and that's not for him to know, if that's OK by you?" she asked.

"I'm fine with that. We'll keep it our little secret," he agreed with a wink.

She smiled, wondering why she genuinely felt angry with Toby for turning up; he was her fiancé, after all.

"I'll stay for a coffee and then make my way back to the hotel," he said, looking into her eyes. He took her hands in his. "Thank you for a wonderful day – and an eventful weekend, for that matter. I hope we can keep in touch. I'll leave my phone number with your aunties . . . but if you don't want to, that's fine."

She shrugged her shoulders, and said, "Well, if I have time, I'll think about it." She gave him a cheeky smile, and then a quick peck on his cheek. "Something tells me we haven't seen the last of each other, Sam Farmer." She studied his face with a curious look. *Where the hell do I know you from*? she thought as she moved her hands around his waist to untie his apron. "Joking apart, I would like to know how you are getting on, but I'm not easy to contact when I'm working, I'm all over the place. I've got film and TV work coming up, so will be very busy for the next few weeks."

"Well, why don't we just text each other first to see if it's OK to phone?" Sam suggested.

"Sure, and thanks for sorting the tap out by the way. Most men I know would be worried about breaking a fingernail!" she chuckled, running her fingers through her hair and then smoothing them over each eyebrow. "God, I bet I look a mess!"

"Well, if that's what you call a mess, you can look a mess

anytime you like," he laughed. "You look fine. So, are we all done here?" he asked, as he gave the kitchen a quick look over.

"I reckon so. Let's go and rescue the old ladies from Toby," she said, leading the way back to the lounge.

Oh, Sam, if only you were twenty years younger, he thought to himself as he watched her walk away from him.

Toby sat sprawled on one of two country-style settees that were positioned opposite each other. He was resting a can of lager on the arm. (On his last visit he'd spilled the contents of his can over the blue and black tweed fabric, and it had taken the sisters ages to clean it up.) Along one wall was a floor-to-ceiling mahogany and glass display cabinet filled with memorabilia and awards that the two sisters had acquired during their years in the theatre. They both sat together on the other settee, trying to make polite conversation. They found it hard work talking to Toby and felt they had nothing in common. Yes, he was an actor, but a minnow compared to them, and he had never embraced Shakespeare as they and Penny had done. They tolerated him for the sake of their niece, telling each other she was a grown woman and that it was up to her who she loved, and they must try to accept that as far as possible. But they were more than capable of hatching their plots given half a chance; just like *Macbeth*'s witches, as Toby sometimes called them.

Penny walked into the room, still chatting away to Sam.

"Well, sit down both of you and I'll make the coffees," May told them.

"Not for me thanks, Auntie May. Toby and I will be off. It's a fair walk home and I've got a busy day tomorrow. I don't want to be late back," Penny replied with a forlorn smile. "Come on, babe, off your backside," she ordered, looking at Toby. "God, you look rough. Didn't you get much sleep last night, hun?" She looked across at Sam. He was well aware that Toby had slept in the spare bedroom the night before.

And Don't Forget the Roses

The two sisters got to their feet to see the couple to the door. Sam walked over to Toby, looked him in the eye, and shook his hand again. He gripped his hand firmly, as if to say *Match this*!" Toby's handshake was not up to his. He had soft skin and a distinct lack of firmness in his wrist. Toby couldn't even look him in the eye – which in Sam's book said a lot about a man.

Penny was still yapping away to her aunties, but then gave each of them a hug. From the corner of her eye she could see Sam smiling at her and waiting to say goodbye.

"You see, Sam, I've managed to put a smile on your face," she said, holding his arms as she gave him a kiss on the cheek. She whispered in his ear, "Take care." Stepping back, but still looking straight at him, she spoke in a soft measured tone, adding, "I hope this weekend has provided you with a light at the end of your tunnel." She could see he was moved by her caring words, and felt the urge to give her a hug, but he knew it would annoy Toby. That didn't bother him, but he didn't want to cause friction between Penny and her future husband.

"Well, I'm touched by such tender words. I only hope that what I do in the future does justice to them." They stood there smiling at each other, not saying anything more.

"Come on, pet, let's go," Toby said, taking her hand.

The aunties stood at the front door and watched them walk out of the mews.

"Sam, you're staying for a coffee aren't you, dear?" asked May.

"Yes, I'm parched," he replied.

"Good. You can tell us all about yourself and how you came to meet Penny."

Sitting on the settee opposite them, he put his cup on the coffee table.

"Tell us, Sam, do you have any children?" May asked, interested in finding out as much about this man as they could.

"Yes, I do. Two beautiful daughters. Maggie and Estelle. Maggie's a vet – Mayhem Maggie I call her – and she's vivacious and full of life. Estelle is an art restorer; old head on young shoulders like her mother. They've 'flown the coop' as they say, but we keep in touch all the time."

Sam knew they hadn't finished with their questions; Penny probably wouldn't tell them anything, so they had to find out for themselves.

"So, what business are you in, dear?" June enquired, looking uncomfortable in her seat. "Oh this bloody hip," she declared with a wince as she rose to her feet. Sam stood up, offering to help her, but she politely waved at him to sit down. "So, dear, you were saying . . ." June then said, wanting to continue the interrogation.

"I live near Exeter, in Devon, and own a property letting agency."

"So, that's how you know about tap washers?"

"Not quite, June," Sam replied. "When I left school, I worked for a builder and learnt many skills." He paused, the two ladies hanging on his every word. "Being brought up in Southampton I loved the sea, so later on I joined the merchant navy and enjoyed every minute of it – well, almost. I learnt some harsh lessons along the way about life and myself, which have held me in good stead over the years."

"More coffee, dear?" asked May, rising to her feet, knowing the longer he stayed the more they would find out about him.

Sam nodded and smiled, continuing, "When I decided to make my life ashore again, I went 'back to my tools', as the saying goes." He noticed June listening to him, but that she was slightly distracted at the same time – no doubt thinking of jobs he could do for them!

"Surely a man like you must have a chest full of stories, Sam!" June responded, probing him.

And Don't Forget the Roses

"Oh yes, but you don't want too much excitement for one day! After all, you've had Toby here."

The sisters let out another cackle of laughter.

"You like him as well, do you, dear?" May asked, with a twinkle in her eye, realising he would know it was a tongue-in-cheek question.

Sam didn't reply, but instead said, "To answer your question about how I met Penny – she tripped over my bag outside the National Art Gallery. Luckily she didn't hurt herself, but we got chatting and then I took her for a coffee. She's a nice, intelligent young lady, and I enjoyed her company."

June walked over to the cabinet and picked up a framed photograph from one of the shelves. She handed it to Sam.

"This was taken nearly forty years ago, dear."

He looked at it. It was of three women with their arms around each other, but the woman in the middle was . . . Penny?

"No, it can't be!" he said as he studied the face with disbelief. He looked up at June.

"It's Penny's mother, April – May's twin sister," June said briefly, turning to look at her. "I was the first by six years, and then April and May came along. Father was always a bit eccentric and rather bohemian. I suppose if we'd had another sister, she would most probably have been named Augustine!"

He gazed at the picture again; he saw Penny's eyes staring out at him.

He shook his head and said, "It's uncanny . . . they look so alike. My youngest daughter Estelle looks a lot like her mother, but Penny and her mother could be the same person."

May watched him as he studied the picture.

"April was so beautiful, just like Penny, and I think she was the most talented of the three of us," said June, sounding gracious, and tears began to form in her eyes.

He listened as they told him about Penny and her mother. He knew they didn't have to tell him anything – a few hours before he had been a complete stranger – but now it seemed they had accepted him like a friend, someone they liked and trusted, just like their niece had done.

"I take it that Penny's mother died?" Sam asked quietly.

"Yes, Sam," replied June. "Penny's mother died when she was eight and she came to live with us. As you can see, she has her mother's looks, but more importantly, she has her mother's talent." June then rested herself on the arm of Sam's settee and smiled at him. He could see the emotion in her face as she continued, "Penny struggles with memories of her mother and early childhood. Vague as they are, they seem to hold her back."

May reached out her arm to Sam, gesturing that she would like to hold the photograph. She ran her fingertips around the silver gilded frame, and then faintly said, "The Shakespeare Sisters. Oh what happy times they were." She then lovingly kissed it, the window to her sister, remembering the good times and the regrets that never went away. "One day, Sam," said May, her voice now sounding resolute, "Penny will get a part which will blow away her ghosts and leave her audience breathless." She stopped, and let out a forlorn sigh. "I just hope I live to see it."

"Oh don't be so bloody melodramatic, dear," June spouted.

"I'm sure you will, both of you," Sam said, giving May a kindly wink.

"She'd better get her skates on. None of us are getting any younger, not even you, Sam."

Sam thought about what May had just said. It almost had an air of permanency about it, as if they'd decided that they'd be seeing much more of him in the future.

"When do you plan to go back to Devon, dear?" June asked.

"Tomorrow. I arrived on Friday night, and I had a personal matter to attend to yesterday – just before I met Penny. Today I'm here, and tomorrow I'm off to the tailors," he said, seeing June's eyes open wider with interest.

"Really, dear, do tell, do tell!"

Sam then looked at the sisters with a pensive smile, and replied, "During Annie's illness I lost a lot of weight, so now many of my clothes hang off me, particularly my suits, so I'm treating myself to two new ones from Saville Row. Extravagant I know, but I always promised myself that one day I'd have my suits made there."

"Good for you, dear," June declared, putting her hand on the back of his head and gently stroking it.

"I have to start rebuilding my life sometime, so I may as well start with my wardrobe." He stood up then to stretch and liven up his body. "Now, I've taken advantage of your hospitality long enough. It's time I went. I hope you don't mind, but I've left my phone number and email address on the notepad by your phone . . . for all of you." He hesitated then, trying to pick the right to words to say next. "Look, I hope you don't think it forward of me, but I see your kitchen window is kept open using a block of wood. You must allow me to repair it next time I'm up – in a few weeks' time – and before you suggest it, I don't want any money for doing it. I'll do it as a friend," he said. His tone of voice told them not to bother to argue.

"That window's been like that years, Sam, I wouldn't bother yourself–" May replied.

"Hold on, dear," June interrupted. "Do you read, Sam?" she asked, as she walked over to a bookcase in the alcove. She selected a book from the shelf.

"Yes, all the time. And when Annie was ill I used to spend hours reading to her."

She put the book in his hand as he spoke, saying, "*The Tempest.*"

"Well, thank you! I know of it, of course, but I've never read it." He kissed her cheek for her kindness.

"I wouldn't thank me so readily, dear, it's written in the original text." She smiled gently, holding and squeezing his arm. "Phone us if you get stuck, or call Penny. It was no different for her, dear, when she first read them."

He laughed, shaking his head in disbelief. "My daughters will never believe me when I tell them how three lovely ladies have befriended me!"

"Oh, I almost forgot," May said, waving a piece of paper in her hand. "Penny told me to give you this. It's her phone number, the same one we use. She uses two phones: one private; one for work. I've put our number and address down as well, so keep in touch."

The sisters stood and waved at him as he left the mews.

May wanted to phone her niece to see if she got home safely, but really she just wanted to say how nice she thought Sam was, and said so.

June stopped her. "Don't be so silly, May. Penny will no doubt phone us later – you can tell her then."

Toby took hold of Penny's hand and started to walk at a brisk pace.

"What's the hurry, hun? There's no rush . . . we've got plenty of time," Penny said.

"I thought we'd get the bus back actually, pet," he suggested. "We haven't seen much of each other this weekend, and I'd rather be home with you than spend the next hour walking the streets."

She turned to him with a look of indignation on her face, and her eyes raged at him. She stopped dead in her tracks and pulled her hand out of his grip. She knew exactly what he meant by time at home: *sex.*

"That's OK. You catch the bus and I'll see you later," she said, walking away, leaving him standing alone on the pavement.

"Hold on, pet. OK, OK, we'll walk," he said, taking hold of her arm again and forcing a kiss on her cheek.

"So what's with that old guy you were with in the kitchen? Some fancy man of the witches, I suppose?"

Again she stopped and again she became indignant at his remarks.

"You bastard, Toby, you have no right to keep calling my aunties that. It's disrespectful and they don't deserve it. You'll never match up to their achievements," she said, putting her hands in her dress pockets out of his reach.

"God, you're tetchy," he moaned.

She scowled at him, feeling despondent at what she perceived as his immature attitude.

"For Christ's sake, you're acting like an arsehole. Why is that?" she asked, now taking the opportunity to get some thoughts out into the open. "It's as if since I said I'd marry you, you've stopped being the Toby I fell in love with. Are you having second thoughts? Because if you carry on like this, I think I may start to."

Toby was visibly taken aback by her bluntness, but then countered it by giving her a cheeky grin, putting his arms around her waist, and kissing her lips.

She found it difficult to respond in-kind as he embraced her and pulled away. She gave him a weak smile.

"You asked me about Sam. Well, I hardly know him, and *you* certainly don't. You may act the hard man on TV, Toby, but somehow I sense if you piss *him* off he won't be acting." There was a chill in her voice as she spoke; she wasn't to know how true those words would become. "Come on. Let's get home," she said with a frown.

Toby didn't reply to Penny's question about having second thoughts, and he knew he'd got off the hook lightly this time.

"Hi, Auntie June, it's me," Penny said.

"Hello, dear. I thought you might call before you went to bed," June replied.

"I've sent Toby back to his mate's flat for the night. I have to be up at four. I've got some early morning scenes to do at Shepperton Studios," she told her. "So what did you think of him then – Sam, I mean – sweet, isn't he?" She was curious to know her aunties' opinion of her new friend.

"He's charming, dear. We had a lovely time chatting away."

"It sounds like I've lost him to you two already," Penny said with a giggle. "Did he tell you how we met?" she asked, wanting to know how much he had told them.

"Yes, dear," she replied. "You kicked his bag or something and then went for a coffee. How very romantic, dear."

"Auntie June, you bugger," she retorted. "To tell you the truth I should have walked away after I said sorry, but there was something about him, and he had those sad eyes. Of course, I didn't know at the time why that was . . ." Penny paused. "June?" she asked, in an inquisitive tone of voice.

"Yes, dear?" June replied.

Penny spoke in a soft voice, sounding cautious: "Have you ever met someone who you think you've met before, but you know you haven't?"

"Can't say I have, dear, why?"

"I'm not really sure. I know it sounds silly, but I keep getting the notion that I know him. How spooky is that?" she said, now sounding confused.

"Maybe he's a lover from a previous life, dear, come back to look you up," June said, laughing down the phone.

"He's a bit late, though, isn't he? I'm spoken for! You two can have him."

They continued to talk about her aunties' new unpaid handyman, his planned visit to the tailors, and the book she had lent him. Penny felt slightly concerned for Sam. Like she'd said, Shakespeare was '*their night, their day*' – how would he cope with their adoration of him? Penny finished the conversation then, to get to bed. She knew only too well how June liked to chat.

June relayed to May what they had talked about and that it seemed Toby didn't like Penny getting on so well with Sam.

"Somehow I don't think Sam will have sleepless nights at the thought of not having Toby as a mate," said May, and the two sisters cackled once more with laughter.

Penny sat in the middle of her bed, surrounded by scripts and schedules for the following week, looking at her feet, and smiling about the man who she'd let loose on them, still wondering why she had. She didn't regret it for a single moment, but was just curious as to why she felt so at ease with him. Then she thought of Toby and how intolerant she had been with him earlier that day . . . and the lack of regret for being so.

Chapter 7

Tailormade

Arriving at the tailors was just as Sam imagined. A young man, who introduced himself as 'Simeon', and who meticulously took his details in between the small talk, greeted him.

"Oh, you live in Devon, how wonderful! Scones and clotted cream!" Simeon purred, with a dreamy look on his face.

"Ah, but do you put the jam on top of the cream, or the cream on top of the jam?" Sam asked.

Simeon answered with a puzzled expression, and then said, "We'll need to take your measurements now." He led him into Mr Bloomfield's fitting room.

An elderly gentleman in his late seventies greeted Sam. He was standing next to his desk and shook his hand. The rather rotund, but very smartly dressed gentleman soon got down to business.

"I'm Solomon. Good to meet you. Now stand over here, please, and we'll get started."

He had an eastern European accent, possibly Polish, but his command of the English language made Sam aware he'd been a British resident for quite some time.

Solomon took all the various measurements: inside leg, outside leg, arm, chest and neck.

"You have a good posture, Mr Farmer," he observed. "My suits will fit well on you."

Sam enjoyed discussing the details regarding choice of colours and various cuts, and looking at samples of fabric. It had certainly been a long time since he had treated himself to a bespoke suit. He finally left the tailors – with his bank balance rather reduced – and headed back to the hotel to collect his bags. He then went on to the station for his train back to Devon . . . and to close a chapter in his life.

Auntie May was outside in the morning sunshine chatting to Harry as he worked on his old car, as usual.

"Harry, dear, what do you think of Penny's new gentleman friend?" she asked.

"He's the only man she's brought back who knows what hands are for, other than lifting pints!" Harry called out from under the car, with a laugh, in his usual candid way. "I think he'd be good for her. A proper man – not one of those airy-fairy actors she usually hangs around with. Good luck to them."

"Oh no, dear," replied May, countering his assumption. "The poor man has just lost his wife. I think a relationship is the last thing on his mind at the moment," she said, used to talking to the lower half of Harry's body as it protruded from under the car.

Harry pushed himself out, stood up and turned to May.

"Ah, lost his wife, eh . . ." he said, just as his wife Betty appeared with a mug of tea.

"What's he saying now, May? Still planning to do me in?" She laughed in an *I've heard it all before* way. "He can't even keep this heap of rust on the road, let alone look after himself. You'd think after fifty-one years of married bliss the old fool would know that," she said, as she put her hand on top of Harry's balding head, polishing it with her fingers.

May chuckled too; she'd heard this same patter for over forty years but it still made her laugh.

Chapter 8

New Direction

'Now the stage is set, let the acts of love and betrayal begin...'
–Shakespeare

Sam walked into his lounge where he and Annie used to spend so much time, but now it was quiet and soulless. He looked around at all the familiar furniture and the many pictures of them both with their two girls in happier times, and he realised that the house just didn't feel like home anymore. He'd continued to sleep in the spare bedroom as he had done for the many months before Annie's death, as he just couldn't bring himself to sleep in their bed again. And that night, lying there gazing into the dark, he decided it was time to move on.

Just before midday, the next day, he left the house with Annie's ashes. They were to be placed in the garden of remembrance. A rose by the name of *Our Annie* would also be planted in memory of her, with a small brass plaque. As he lingered at the gates to the garden, he started to tentatively consider what life next held in store for him. *What will the future bring?* he thought as he started to wander home.

He was completely unaware that his future had already begun.

oOo

Standing in the open plan lounge of his new home on the edge of Dartmoor, Sam gazed around the room, planning where his furniture would eventually go. He could hear his two daughters upstairs laughing and giggling.

"Dad! Have you seen the state of this bathroom? I wouldn't wash a dog in it!" Maggie remarked, coming back down the stairs with Estelle close on her heels.

"So what do you think?" Sam asked, looking excitingly at his daughters, and laughing at Maggie's observation of the bathroom. He really hoped they loved the cottage as much as he did – his new beginning.

"This place reminds me of you, Dad," Estelle joked. "Old and in need of TLC."

"Come on, you two," he said, standing in the doorway, beckoning them out of the cottage. "I promised you a drink in the pub, and I'm thirsty."

He took one daughter on each arm and led them down the country lane to his new watering hole, The Bal Maiden Arms.

"So, Dad, what are you going to do now you've got more time on your hands?" Estelle asked as they sat down in the beer garden enjoying the midday sun.

"I told Uncle Oak I'd go over to Canada to see him," he said thoughtfully.

Maggie reached for his hand, knowing that that decision hadn't been made lightly. Both girls knew his past still haunted him, and to reach out to Oak in friendship was not only brave, but was part of his new beginning.

"Oh yes," he said, his face suddenly lighting up with excitement, "and I'm reading Shakespeare!"

"Wow! Why Shakespeare, Dad? He's a bit heavy for you!" Maggie replied, looking puzzled.

"I know, odd isn't it," Sam said, sipping his beer. "It's a long story, but someone has loaned me *The Tempest* to read." The girls looked utterly bemused at the thought of their father reading

Shakespeare. "I only really took it out of politeness, but once I got into it, I was hooked," he continued. "I don't feel out of my depth at all." Their looks of disbelief were now replaced by curious interest, and it made him smile.

"Well, here's to you, Dad!" Estelle replied, holding up her glass of white wine to him. "I'm impressed. I studied Shakespeare for my A-level English Literature exam, and *I* struggled. But if you ever go to one of his plays, I'll come with you," she said enthusiastically.

Sam thought, for the thousandth time, how much like her mother she was – always into anything arty or classical.

"I may just do that," he replied.

Chapter 9

Dried Bread

Thank God it's Friday, Penny thought as she again dragged herself out of bed at 4.00am and made her way to the kitchen for a slice of toast.

"Bollocks, no butter *or* jam left," she muttered as she waited for her car to pick her up. She glanced out of the window. "Dry toast *again*, and it's pissing down with rain. Shit. I'm going to get soaked," she moaned, scanning her eyes around the room. "Now where are my scripts?" She rifled through her bag and sifted through some newspapers and mail around on the kitchen worktop . . . there they were.

Angie, her close friend and agent, knew Penny's on-set work would be finished by lunchtime, so she'd arranged an audition for her for a forthcoming Noel Coward review. Penny missed the theatre, but as hard as she tried, very little came her way – and when it did it wasn't the meaty roles she hankered for. Several times – even when she knew she had impressed the directors and nailed the character she had been asked to portray – the part still went to a less capable actress.

She checked her private phone for messages.

"Angie. Angie. June. Angie. Toby. Angie. I see . . . no Sam. Maybe he'll phone June. Bugger. I forgot we're going out tonight," Penny said, out loud. She knew Toby wouldn't be happy, but she'd have to text him later. Hearing the toot of her driver's horn outside, she grabbed her coat and work bag.

June was sitting at the dining room table having her breakfast: a cup of minted tea and a slice of lightly buttered toast coated with a tasty portion of Marmite. May wouldn't be down for a while; she took tablets to help her sleep, but then wondered why she couldn't wake up in the morning!

As she sipped her tea, June flicked through her diary. Although they were retired from the stage, they both still played an active part behind the scenes. With their love and wealth of knowledge of Shakespeare and the theatre, they held master classes at the Globe, Shakespeare's spiritual home, as often as they could, as well as making occasional visits to schools and colleges to inspire a new generation of actors – particularly Shakespearian actors. They regularly received invitations to charity dinners and theatre award events, but they found them tedious, and nearly always ended up sitting at a table full of 'overactive egos', as June described them, so they'd become very selective with their attendance at such events.

As May eventually sat down with her cereal and glass of fresh orange juice, June looked over to her. As with every morning when she came down for breakfast, May was still in her nightdress – a habit from her younger days when she would often leave the theatre and go to dinner parties, sometimes until the early hours, and not arise until midday or later – May had definitely been the party animal of the three sisters.

"You do remember that we are going to the Globe tonight with Penny, don't you, dear?" June asked.

May took a deep breath, and then held it for a few seconds before letting it out. She slowly turned her head to face her sister and said, "Yes, dear, you reminded me twice yesterday, and I haven't even finished my breakfast and you're reminding me again."

"Sorry, dear, but we both know how forgetful you are these days, dear, and I didn't want you to forget."

"Sometimes, June, I wonder which one of us has the poor

memory, but I thank you for reminding me all the same." She then smiled at June as she put her hand on top of hers and gave a pat. "Come on, May, get dressed, we have a lot to do."

The sisters were in their bedroom sorting out their eveningwear when May heard the phone ring.

"Bugger, I left the phone downstairs, I'll go," she said, and she rushed out of the room. "Hello?" she answered, sitting down on a dining chair and panting to catch her breath.

"May, is that you?" Penny asked. "Just to let you know I'll be with you around 6.30. We can get the Tube or a taxi, I don't mind either way."

"Tube, dear. We've told you before not to waste your money on taxis – far too expensive. We'll be ready from 6.30, dear. Is Toby here this weekend?" May enquired.

"Bugger! I haven't texted him yet," Penny reminded herself. "Yes, he'll be here tonight, but I'll tell him we're going out, so he'll have to watch telly or go to the pub. Knowing him, it'll be the pub," she replied, checking her other phone for messages while she talked. "Have you heard from Sam at all?" she casually asked.

"No, not yet, dear," replied May, "but I'm sure he will be in touch. He strikes me as the dependable type. Don't forget, he's got a lot on his plate. When he was here, he said he had to make a lot of decisions about how to move on, etc., so I expect he's quite preoccupied."

Penny was just about to speak, when a text massage appeared from Sam.

"Well, bugger me, bang on cue," Penny mumbled, as she read his message.

"What's that, dear? Well what?"

"Sorry, May, I was mumbling. Sam has just texted me. I'll ring him now and tell you how he's getting on when I see you," she said, hastily ending her call.

"Hi, Sam. Sorry, I was on the phone to May," she explained, and all in one breath.

"Hello, babe. Sorry, perhaps I shouldn't have called you that, that was presumptuous of me," Sam said apologetically.

Penny thought it was sweet that he felt the need to apologise; most men she knew wouldn't bother.

"That's OK, Sam. 'Babe' is fine," she answered, with a laugh in her voice.

"But I refuse to call you pet!" he told her.

"Oh please don't! With Toby it's 'pet' this and 'pet' that, all the time. I think he forgets I've got a *name*." (Sam noted a tinge of sadness in her voice when she said that.) "So, bring me up to date on everything!" she declared eagerly.

Sam had discovered that she was endlessly interested in how he was getting on. They had already spoken briefly during the week, but it seemed she had boundless enthusiasm to talk and listen.

"Well, I've bought a cottage on the edge of Dartmoor, but it's in a bit of a state," he told her, "so it'll be a few months before I move in."

Penny was pleased at his news, yet felt sad hearing him talk about how he was rebuilding his life alone without Annie.

"That's great! A new start for you, I guess? So what other plans have you made?" she asked.

He thought about whether he should say anything about his next bit of news, but couldn't take the long reach back into his past to explain the true reason why he wanted to go.

"I met an old friend of mine from Canada at Annie's funeral. So . . . I'm going over to see him. He has a son and a daughter who I haven't seen since they were children." His voice was now quiet and subdued; he felt it inappropriate to be anything other than that.

"Canada. I've always wanted to go there and see Niagara Falls, you lucky man. Bring me back a Mounty!"

"Get Toby to take you there on your honeymoon?" Sam suggested.

"Yeah, in my dreams," she replied with resignation, knowing it was unlikely. "So, when do you plan to come back up?" she asked, and keenly awaited his reply.

"In about two to three months," he said.

"Sam! That's not funny! I've got two elderly ladies here, pining for you!"

"OK," Sam laughed, "possibly in two to three weeks. Is that better? I'm just waiting to hear from the tailor. So what about you? What's new?"

"We're off to the Globe tonight to see one of June's protégés. I'm looking forward to it."

"Sorry, you said June's protégé?" Sam enquired with interest.

"Of course, you don't know, sorry. Although my aunties are retired from the stage, they still keep a hand in teaching and mentoring up-and-coming actors; they love it, it keeps them active," she explained.

"Have you performed there yourself?" he asked.

"Yes, a few times, but only minor roles. It's wonderful, yet daunting. The atmosphere and proximity of the audience is unique. I'll take you there one day," she replied enthusiastically.

"I'll look forward to that very much," he said, thinking how envious Estelle would be.

"Look, I have to go. I have to go and pick up my aunties. Toby's back tonight, so we'll have to chat next week," she said hurriedly.

Chapter 9

"Oh, and I'll tell my aunts that you phoned – they were asking after you," she added.

She reluctantly ended the call to get ready. As she sat at her dressing table she glanced down at her ring finger. *Still no ring,* she thought sadly. *I won't hold my breath.*

Chapter 10

Meeting of the Foe

Penny and her aunties eagerly made their way to the Globe, to be greeted by the sisters' close friend of many years, producer and theatre director, Sir Richard Roddington. It was always an honour for the theatre to have the two ladies attend a production.

"It's a brill night for a show, ain't it, sir, no wind and nice-un-warm," Lesia said.

Lesia was one of the ticket girls, and was standing next to Sir Richard as they waited by the main entrance for the ladies to arrive. Her lack of cultured English was of stark contrast to the words spoken on the stage just feet from her. She was of Afro-Caribbean parentage and slightly overweight for her height and age – and was very excited to be given the role as usher for the special guests. She kept fiddling with her skirt, pulling at the hem, and if it wasn't her skirt, it was her hair.

"Stop preening like a parrot, girl! Despite what people may say, they're not the witches of *Macbeth*!" Sir Richard boomed. *They are Emilia and Desdemona to my Othello*, he thought, as he gazed towards the Thames on the ebb, flowing toward the sea.

From Blackfriars Tube Station, Penny and her aunts made their way along the Embankment to Millennium Bridge, and then made the short walk across to the Globe. For them it wasn't just any theatre they were attending, it was their *crucible*.

"Ladies, good evening," said Sir Richard, putting his hand out to greet them, and then giving them each a polite peck on each cheek. "As always, it's an honour to see you here again. And hello, young lady," he added, as he kissed Penny's hand with a gentlemanly flourish. "So how did your audition go today?" He seemed genuinely interested in her reply.

You're well informed, Penny thought.

"As usual it was a case of 'Don't contact us, we'll contact you'," Penny told him, unable to hide the surprise on her face that he knew about the audition.

"Surely not?"

"We'll see," she replied. "Sometimes I think someone out there doesn't like me. Well, it's their loss, isn't it, May?" she said, taking her aunt's arm as Lesia showed them to their seats.

Penny thought about Toby and the one time she had taken him there, remembering that he had been bored stiff.

As they settled themselves into their seats, a voice come over the theatre's sound system: "Ladies and gentlemen, please welcome Dame June McCain and her sister, Miss May McCain, affectionately known as the Shakespeare Sisters."

The audience in the theatre rose to their feet to applaud them.

May turned to her sister and quipped, "Do a royal wave, dear."

"Oh do shut up, May, you know I don't like this sort of attention anymore."

June looked over to see Penny, also standing up applauding.

"Don't encourage them, dear. Just wait until I get my hands on the young man who announced us." Then she gave a wry smile.

"Don't be so old, June, it's only because they love you," Penny called, trying to make herself heard above the din.

"I know, dear, it is rather nice really, but you have to watch the buggers or they take liberties. They'll have me selling ice cream in the interval next!" she said, and she gave a loud hoot of laughter.

With the expectation of the performance and the noise and chatter of the audience, the whole of the theatre had come alive.

"God! I do love it here," Penny said with child-like excitement. "It's so untethered. You can't help but revel in the passion of it all, can you?" She looked at her aunties with a big smile on her face, and then everyone settled down to watch the performance.

Penny arrived home just before 11.30 after seeing her aunties safely home. As she walked in to the hallway she could see Toby's kit-bag on the floor.

"Toby, hun, are you in?" she called, walking around the house, turning off all the lights he had left on. Then she entered the lounge to see a note: '*Waited till 9.30 so gone to Pete's, will crash out there. See you tomorrow morning. Toby xx.*'

"The little shit," she said. "He knew I'd be late. Any excuse for a piss-up with his mates." She let out a despondent sigh.

"Hi, June, I'm back. Toby isn't here. He was, but he's gone to his mate's flat. I'll see him tomorrow. Thank you for a lovely evening. I'll phone you next week sometime. Love you both, night, night," she said into her aunties' answer machine.

"You sod," she groaned as she went through to the kitchen. "Thanks for not doing the washing up. What a bloody mess."

She stood for a long time in front of her kitchen sink.

Chapter 11

Cod and Chips

Saturday morning. Having a lie-in until 9.00am was sheer luxury for her after having to scrape herself out bed at four for the last week. After a shower she phoned Toby.

"Come on, Toby, answer your sodding phone," she muttered. "Toby! It's Penny. I hate leaving messages on your phone. Call me back. I want to know what our plans are for the day."

She checked her emails. There were the usual messages from Angie her agent, and she wrote all the information in her diary – which was looking pretty full over the next few weeks. She had auditions booked, and then the start of rehearsals for a three-part drama on television. Her time with Toby would be limited.

When 11.00am came and went with still no reply from him, she reached for her phone to call him again, but it rang just as she did so . . . why did that always happen? But it wasn't Toby's number.

"Hi, sweetie, it's Archie." Her friend sounded chirpy.

"Hello, Arch," she replied, already having an idea of what was to come. "For what do I owe the pleasure, you rascal?" she asked.

Archie was a well-known and respected theatre critic, and an old pal of hers and her aunties. She knew that any call from him had something to do with eating, drinking and generally having a good time – with occasional mayhem thrown in for good measure – and mostly in expensive Michelin-rated restaurants and five-star hotels. He wasn't a self-made man, his father was – but he had used his inheritance wisely. As well as stables and stud farm in Sussex, he had many fingers in many pies, and he knew everyone who was anyone – especially those connected with the theatre. Now in his mid-forties, with dyed black hair to disguise the onset of grey, his light-blue eyes and rotund appearance (due mostly to an exorbitant lifestyle) gave him an air of boyishness which he used to his advantage – particularly with other men. Archie was a man you would never miss in a crowd, a staunch advocate of the Queen's English as he'd had this fine language drummed into him from his days at Eton and Oxford.

"Well, sweetie," – his voice was bright and crisp, and he wanted to tell her about a man he'd met – "there's this lovely Yank from the back end of nowhere who's come over to sound people out. He's thinking about writing a new take on the *Shrew*, not an airy-fairy version, but earthy and gritty. He's got me interested, sweetie." (He ended his last sentence with more of a sexual connotation than an informative fact.)

"Most men do, Arch," said Penny, laughing.

"Oh, Penny dear, you must meet him. I'm convinced it would be beneficial to both of you. He's asked me to introduce him to you. Go on, sweetie," he minced, almost pleading, eager and excited at the prospect. "I'm having one of my soirées tonight at Claridge's. Do come, and bring that young boy of yours along."

"Archie, you bugger," she replied. "He hates being reminded that he's younger than me!" But she was becoming increasingly annoyed with Toby for messing her about, and without much thought she murmured, "Yes! Bollocks to him. I'll go, and he can either come with me or go back to his mate's flat again."

"What was that, sweetie?"

"OK, Arch, I'll be there," she said emphatically.

"Fantastic, sweetie. I'll get a car to pick you up at seven thirty. Sooo pleased you will come. You can tell me all about this new man of yours."

Sam? she thought. *How the hell do you know about Sam?* Then suddenly she realised her aunties must have told Arch about him.

"Archie, don't you dare go stirring it, he's a nice guy!" She knew what mischief he was capable of.

"Yes, yes, sweetie, I promise, but when do I get to meet him? May says he's quite a man, but I think she's just trying to tease me," Archie replied, now probing, playing with her.

"Well, you'll have to wait. He's not back for a couple of weeks," – she actually wasn't at all sure if introducing Sam to Archie would be wise for either of them! – "so we'll see," she replied, unaware that Toby was standing in the doorway.

"We'll see what, pet?" he asked, screwing up his eyes at her.

Suddenly turning around she saw him, and felt that she'd been caught out talking about another man. She wondered how much of the conversation he had heard.

"Archie, sweetheart, Toby's just come back. I'll see you tonight."

"Toby, hun," she said, greeting him from the comfort of her settee.

He leant forward to kiss her, but she turned her face away with displeasure.

"God, Toby, you stink of beer and you look rough. Go and have a shower. Have you eaten? I'll cook something."

She didn't like him drinking – especially the amount he consumed when he was with his mates.

"No, pet, I'm not hungry," he said, with an angry stare. "So, what's this about tonight? We are *not* going out with that shirt-lifter," he stated loudly, his body language becoming intimidating.

She looked straight back at him; she had no tolerance for his bullying.

"Well, I am. You've been invited, but if you'd rather go and play with your mates than spend time with me, that's your decision. I told you last week, I'm not your old lady sitting at home, patiently waiting for her man to come back with cod and chips wrapped up in newspaper. The morning is ballsed up now, so let's make the best of the afternoon, shall we?" She was aware that she was barking at him in a concise and measured way. *I'm not going to be cowed by you, Toby*, she thought, and waited for his reply.

Toby then took the *I'm sorry, I've been a naughty boy* approach, sat next to her and put his arms around her waist, pulling her into him.

"OK, pet, whatever you say," he said, giving her a cheeky grin as he went to kiss her.

But she stopped him. "Sod off, Toby. You need a shave and a wash before I let you get near my skin."

"Toby, you're not wearing those jeans! It's Claridge's, not a sodding Kentucky Fried Chicken! You've got smart trousers upstairs! Now hurry up!" Penny screeched as she waited for him.

Toby returned a few minutes later.

"There you go, pet, I look a proper poof, for a poof's party," he said scornfully, wearing a pair of light blue trousers with a short-sleeved pale blue shirt. "God, you wind me up, there's no need for it."

"If you ever get your backside down here from the north and do some proper theatre work, Archie's the last man you'd want to piss off," Penny roared. She now felt that Toby simply didn't understand how things were done at all. She knew if you were a 'dime-a-dozen actor', like her aunties called him, he'd have to be seen with the right people – and Archie was definitely in that category. "He's introducing me to an American writer who wants to explore the possibilities of writing a new interpretation of the *Taming of the Shrew*." Penny looked sternly at him, her piercing hazel eyes searing into his, leaving Toby in no doubt that she was not going to put up with his belligerence. "You may look at your career as a Monday-to-Friday job, but mine is twenty-four-seven, is now, and will be for some considerable time. Is that understood?"

He turned away without saying anything, and then walked towards the front door. He stopped and turned to look at her.

"Your chariot awaits, m'lady."

Now calmer she went up to him, smiled, and kissed him on his lips – a soft tender kiss – and then whispered, "Thank you, my fair prince."

Chapter 12

Claridge's

"Come on, Toby," Penny whispered, gently manoeuvring him off the red carpet after having their photographs taken.

"Penny darling, you've made it, good," a voice called out from somewhere in the crowd.

"Hi, Angie!" Penny replied, walking over to her agent and greeting her with a friendly hug.

"Hello, Toby, you're looking smart," she said, showing Toby the side of her face for him to kiss.

"Hi, pet," Toby politely replied with a false smile.

If there was one person he really didn't like, it was Angie. Not because she was a lesbian – although Toby did have homophobic views – but because Penny and Angie were very loyal friends and he felt threatened by her, as if there were three people in their relationship. If push came to shove, he was never sure whose side Penny would take if it came to it. Angie, on the other hand, couldn't care a toss what Toby thought of her, or her connection with Penny. Now in her forties, she had an aura of motherly calmness about her; but those who knew Angie were well aware that this tall, heavy-framed and robust woman with cropped red hair didn't take fools gladly, and if someone was foolish enough to cross swords with her, she wouldn't hesitate to cut them to pieces with her scalpel-sharp tongue.

"All the usual suspects are here by the looks of it, Angie," Penny said, scanning her eyes around the function suite. "There's

George over there. Come on, you two, I'm going to say hello," Penny informed them, taking Toby's hand.

"Hello, gorgeous," George Dawson said as he greeted her with a kiss. (Penny positioned herself to talk to him and the two other gentlemen standing to his right.)

"You know Adrian Foster and Peter Gifford, don't you?" George asked, as they greeted each other.

George Dawson was a widely-respected theatre producer, so much so that Penny would have dearly loved to appear in one of his productions. She had done many auditions for them, but as yet had not been chosen for any leading roles.

"Have you met my chap, Toby?" Penny asked as she introduced him, having in the back of her mind that although she wasn't successful with the men in front of her, Toby might have better luck.

"Grand to meet you, I'm sure," said Toby; but he came over as not being particularly interested in talking.

"I've heard congratulations are in order, Penny?" George enquired, glancing at Toby, not sure what to make of him.

"*Yes* Toby, when are you going to get this lady her ring?" asked Angie, knowing damn well he kept letting her down.

"Any date set yet?" came the question from Peter Gifford

"No plans at present," Penny replied, with a look that said *it's not going to be anytime soon, either.*

"I hear, Toby, they may be writing your character out of the next series?" George said, looking at him, noting the surprise on his face at the news.

If this was true, it wasn't something he was aware of . . . he hadn't heard of any plans to kill him off?

"Nah," Toby retorted, sounding brash. "They only put that out to stop uz actors asking for more money. You know how it works." Toby scowled at him, thinking *You twat, who told you that?*

"Well, I think it would be lovely if you came back up here, hun, I could see more of you, and . . ." she paused, "I might get the engagement ring you promised me." She smiled, kissing him on his cheek. "Look, we must find Archie."

"He's at the bar, darling," said Adrian, trying to catch the eye of a waiter for a refill.

Archie was found standing at the bar in the cocktail lounge, looking rather dapper in his royal-blue pinstriped suit. He wore a rather garish bright pink shirt under a paisley waistcoat, all topped off with a blue and red silk polka dot cravat.

"Penny, sweetie, so pleased you could come! And you've brought your boy with you, how lovely!"

Penny scowled at him for calling Toby a 'boy', and realised he was teasing her, again.

"Now, sweetie, let me get you a drink and then introduce you to the Yank."

When it came to Penny, Archie would do all he could to promote her career, but he didn't want to promote Toby's. Like her aunties, he knew her acting abilities put his in the shade.

"Toby, sweetie, let me introduce you to two young ladies who have asked to meet you," Archie purred, linking his arm with Toby – who tried to shrug him off – but Archie was having none of it and led him away, leaving Penny at the bar sipping her white wine. He returned with a rather strange-looking man. He was very tall – *very tall* – standing at least six feet seven inches, with a long, drawn face and wide mouth, and a jutting chin finished off with a purple goatee beard.

Who the hell is this? she thought.

"Penny, sweetie," Archie said, looking excited as he took the man's hand, "this is Aaron Akkron, the lovely man who wanted to meet you."

She put her hand out to shake his. It was like an adult holding a baby's hand, and her fine, delicate fingers disappeared completely into his palm. He could have wrapped his thumb and forefinger around her hand and she would still have room to pull it out.

"Hello," she said, politely, smiling at the huge man standing in front of her.

"Now, let's not hog the bar, sweeties," Archie said, pointing over at a pair of large Chesterfield sofas that were facing each other with a glass coffee table between them. Sitting down opposite him, and gazing at Aaron's face, Penny detected softness in his bright blue eyes that made her feel at ease with him.

"Archie informs me you are interested in the Bard?" she asked, not wanting to say any more than necessary; she was more eager to hear what this man had to say.

"Yes, ma'am," Aaron replied, and his American accent resonated around her. "Archie here told me he knew you, and your aunties – the famous McCain sisters – and I've read all there is about them, and you, too, ma'am."

"Me too?" Penny enquired.

"Oh yes, ma'am. Back home where I come from, Shakespeare is pretty big. At my high school, every year we have a Shakespeare month. We put on plays, read his sonnets and dress in period clothes."

She gazed at the man opposite her, all odd-looking and awkward; but he spoke with such conviction and passion that she couldn't fail to be impressed.

"Tell me, Aaron, where is home?"

"Nelson, Kentucky, ma'am."

"It's Penny," she said kindly, and she smiled at him. "Call me Penny."

Archie could see his job was done, so he left them to chat.

"I say, sweetie, I'll find that boy of yours and keep him occupied," he said as he departed, blowing them both a kiss and heading back to host his other guests.

"So, Aaron, you're a writer?" Penny asked. She sipped her wine.

"Yes, ma'am . . . Penny. I rewrote a few plays, played around with the plots." He stared at Penny's face to see if he was boring her, but her eyes where focused on him, making him comfortable and confident. "I rewrote *Midsummer Night's Dream*, and called it, *Midsummer Nights on the Kentucky*."

She giggled and asked, "What did you call Puck? Chuck?" She giggled again.

"No, ma'am, I didn't think of that," he replied, smiling at her. "I've brought a lot of my stuff with me, if you'd like to read it?" He looked at her, anxious to hear her reply.

"How long are you here for, Aaron?"

"Two more weeks, ma'am, Penny. I'm going to Strateford tomorrow."

"That's pronounced Stratford, Aaron," she said with a smile, as she gently corrected his error.

"Sorry . . . Penny. Then on to Oxford. I plan to be back here in six days' time."

"If you want to, Aaron, leave some of your plays and writings with Archie, and I'll pass then on to my aunties to read – they'll give you their honest opinion."

She could see the trepidation on his face at the thought of giving his work to her aunties – not just any ladies, but the *McCain sisters*.

"Don't worry," she continued, trying to reassure him, "they are very open-minded about how writers interpret the Bard's plays.

Just about every modern love story is loosely based on *Romeo and Juliet*." (She knew there were no better persons alive than her aunties to give him constructive advice.) "They don't see it as diluting his works, but keeping it fresh."

But Penny could see he was still unsure, so she said, "Look, Aaron, I took a friend of mine to my aunties for Sunday lunch and they gave him *The Tempest* to read. He felt nervous, too, not only about reading Shakespeare, but also about being advised by them, but there's no need to be. In a thousand years' time, Shakespeare will still be performed in its true form, but there will always be interpretations," she told him, scanning her eyes over the strange but gentle-looking man. "We have a saying: 'Nothing ventured; nothing gained'." She gave him a reassuring smile. "If you want to be taken seriously as a writer, then they are ones who can advise you."

Aaron, on hearing her reassurance, beamed a smile that filled the room.

"Oh my, the McCain sisters reading my plays, I can't believe it! Thank you, ma'am . . . Penny." Aaron was rolling his long hands over and over each other, and wriggling with excitement. "Wow!"

Then his smile became considered, as if he was reading her inner thoughts.

"This new friend of yours," he asked. "Have you known him long?" Aaron's question came over as sincere, but curiously direct.

Penny was puzzled why this man, who she had only just met, had asked about Sam, and she found it hard to give a definitive answer.

"No, I haven't, but it feels like I have known him forever. Does that make sense to you, Aaron?" Penny asked, running her fingers across her brow.

Aaron nodded his head. "What's his name?" he asked, with sensitivity, his blue eyes now concentrating fully on her face.

"Sam," Penny replied, without even thinking, as if he was willing the name out of her.

"I hope I get to meet your guy," he said, still gazing at her.

"Maybe," she replied, in an almost dreamy tone of voice, "but he's not 'my guy', he's just a friend. My guy is over there somewhere." She pointed into the crowd of people just outside the lounge area. Then she suddenly frowned back at him, wondering why he was so interested in Sam; she was unaware of Aaron's ability to decipher her subconscious.

"Come on, Aaron, it's about time we joined the other guests, and we need to find Archie. I think he wants to introduce you to a couple of theatre producers."

She took his arm; it felt a very long way up.

"Hi, hun, trying to find a new model to replace me?" Penny asked, as she walked up to Toby. He was deeply engrossed in conversation with two very pretty girls fresh out of drama school.

"Hi, pet, I saw Herman Monster talking to you. Was that him? The writer?"

Penny scowled at Toby, once again unimpressed with his attitude.

"Yes, Toby, that's him, and if I was you, I wouldn't upset him. His hands are as big as snow shovels. I don't think he would hit you, though, just dig a very deep hole with them and throw you into it," she said, making sure he understood her displeasure.

"Wye-aye, pet. All the same, he's a big lad. Now, do you know were the food is? I'm starvin'."

"Toby, if it's not beer, it's food," she said, looking at him in exasperation.

"Well, pet, sex comes first on my list of priorities," he said, grinning at her. "Lead the way, pet."

No sooner had Toby said that, than Archie appeared.

"Sweetie, glad I found you. Spoke to that giant of a man, the Yank - he's like a boy waiting for Thanksgiving. I'm sure the girls will love him!"

"Hi, Arch. If you are talking about my aunties, there's one problem . . ." she said, looking seriously at him. "How the hell is he going to get through their front door? He's not very wide, but he's *so* tall!" she asked, breaking out into a fit of laughter.

"Yes, he is a big boy," Archie said, sounding like it was feeding time for his passion for young men.

"Now, Archie," Penny said sternly, "you leave Aaron alone, he needs help, but not the sort you've got in mind." She was giving him that look of hers that said *behave*!

"Don't worry your pretty head, sweetie, this is strictly business. Besides, his hands are far too big, if you get my drift?"

"*Archie!*" she screeched, looking around in case anyone else had heard what he'd just said. "You really are a bugger at times! Now, where's the food? This man of mine is starving."

Chapter 13

Moving On

"That's about the lot, Mr Farmer. We've taken our boxes, so if you'd like to sign here we'll be on are way. Enjoy your new home."

Sam watched the removal truck drive away and then walked back inside; furniture and boxes of various shapes and sizes filled all the rooms.

"Right, Sam," he said, talking to himself, "where did you put the beer and your phone?"

His new home was a far cry from the modern design of house he had moved from. The cottage was entirely different: a two-bedroom, semi-detached house built in the 1780s of stone and cob, with a heavy laid *Delabole* slate roof. This former farm labourer's cottage was just what Sam wanted, and it had the advantage of being only five-minute walk from the village pub.

Penny phoned just as he was contemplating a bath, so he sat on his bed for almost an hour while they chatted, bringing each other up to date. He told her about his inglenook fireplace, the oak floors and the exposed ceiling beams, while she told him of the meeting she'd had with Aaron Akkron, and that Toby still hadn't bought her an engagement ring. He once again apologised to her for letting her aunties down – although he had spoken to them himself – and said he had hoped to be in London sooner, but what with work, selling his old house and getting this new home ready, he had been so busy. . . It was now over two months since they'd first met.

"June!" May shouted to her sister, who was hanging the washing out in the courtyard. "June! There you are. Just had a call from Sam. He's coming up Thursday for five days."

June turned to see her sister walking up the path towards her.

"That's nice, dear, but how about you help me first before you put the flags out!"

Sam was an hour from Paddington Station when Penny phoned.

"Hi, sweetheart–" Sam answered.

He was about to continue when she butted in, saying, "I take it you're staying at the same hotel like last time?" Her voice was hurried, and she continued, asking, "Hope you've got some smart cloths with you, coz I'll pick you up at six thirty. Don't bother to eat. Must go. Bye."

"Well, Penny, nice to talk to you too," he laughed to himself.

Christ, he thought, looking at his watch, *she's cutting it fine.* He texted her to confirm the hotel: 'Don't be early, I need time to do my nails lol. Sx'.

Arriving at his hotel with half an hour to spare, but not bothering to fully unpack, he showered and shaved. He put on a pair of black trousers, black shoes, a blue and white striped shirt and a navy-blue tie. He'd also brought his navy-blue blazer with him.

"Well, miss," he mused, looking in the mirror, "this is as good as it gets . . ."

Sam was outside the foyer for less than two minutes when Penny pulled up in a taxi.

"Sam! Sam! Over here, hun!" she called to him through the open door, gesturing for him to get in.

"Hello, babe," he said. He planted a kiss on her cheek as he climbed in next to her, and her musky perfume filled his senses.

"Sorry to rush you, it's been that sort of day. You're looking very smart!" she smiled, giving him the onceover.

"What? Aren't you going to pull me apart? I was looking forward to that!" He could hardly take his eyes off the vision of beauty and sophistication sitting next to him. "And as per the last time I saw you, you look stunning."

She was wearing a body-hugging black jumpsuit with a low-cut neckline that offered just a peep of her cleavage, and a white linen blazer rested over her shoulders. Her beautiful hair shone and was parted to one side and held in place with a pearl leaf-shaped hair slide.

She searched in her handbag.

"Got you, you bugger." She switched her phone to silent mode. "Sorry, Sam, you're wondering where I'm taking you?" she asked. "It's an actor's guild – charity event – not too formal, but I thought you may like it."

Sam noticed a strand of hair had dropped over her right eye, and tenderly brushed it back into place with the tips of his fingers. He scanned her face and he smiled at her, his eyes full of care.

"It sounds interesting! Thank you. I'm looking forward to it," he said, and then felt compelled to ask. "Is your man going to be there?"

Penny replied without hesitation: "Good God, no. Toby finds this sort of thing extremely boring. What pisses me off . . ." she said, now speaking in a more aggressive tone of voice, and looking through the taxi window to see where they were, "is that he got a scholarship to drama school. Where the hell does he think the money came from? He's got no idea." She reached for her bag and pulled out a small bottle of White Musk perfume.

"Jo Malone. I thought it was," Sam confirmed. "I like it."

"Well done, Sam. Is that what you wear?" She let out a happy giggle as she dabbed it behind her ears and between her breasts.

"No, but I recognised it."

"I bought it today. I'm glad you like it," she said, picking up her bright red lipstick and coating her lips. She could see Sam watching her as she pursed them. "Want some?" she said and giggled again.

Sam also laughed and she put her hand on his and gave it a squeeze.

"It is nice to see you again. You're looking a lot brighter," she smiled.

"I'm feeling brighter all the time, especially since I've been in this taxi . . ." (They both laughed at that.) "How are your feet?"

"Killing me, but we haven't got time for you to massage them now, Sam," she said, with a faux sad frown.

Sam was tempted to tell her what he'd brought up with him from Devon, but decided to keep it as a surprise.

"We're here. Come on. By the way . . . you're not camera shy, are you?"

Penny linked her arm around his as they walked into the foyer of the hotel, to be greeted by Sir Richard Roddington, her aunties' old and much-valued friend.

"Penny, darling, glad you could come!"

Penny introduced the two men and they chatted for a short while before having their photographs taken – standard procedure before the evening's event. She then took his arm again and said, "Come on, let's mingle. There's Angie, my agent, I know she's dying to meet you. She's over there talking to some people you may recognise."

Sam was about to reply when an immaculately dressed man approached them. He stared directly at Sam, who looked straight back at him with a polite smile.

"Is this him? Is this Farmer?" he purred, not turning his head to look at Penny, but scanning Sam as if he was inspecting the goods.

"Yeess, Archie. This is he. This is Sam." She squeezed Sam's arm into her body. "Sam, sweetheart, may I introduce you to a very dear friend of mine and theatre critic, Archie Goodmann."

Archie moved nearer to Penny to kiss her, and then turned to Sam, putting his hand out to greet him.

"Oh, how wonderful. A man with a strong grip!" Archie proclaimed. "Not like that boy of yours, sweetie!"

Penny was now feeling slightly uneasy about what he may say next, and she had every right to.

"Tell me, Farmer, are you gay?"

"*Archie*! No, he is not!" Penny exclaimed.

Sam looked straight at Archie, his face deadpan, and replied, "No, I'm not Archie . . . but my boyfriend is," and winked.

Archie let out raucous laugh at Sam's response, and then looked back at Penny – who seemed un-amused at Sam's quip.

"Don't encourage him, Sam! He's a bloody rascal! Aren't you, Archie? And don't call him Farmer . . . it's Sam."

"Oh, it's got to be Farmer, sweetie, that's a strong man's name. The name Sam conjures up soft hands and cuddliness," Archie replied. "You're not a softy, are you? *No*. You're all man. I like you Farmer." Archie then reached over to Penny's hand and gently kissed it. "Tell you what, sweetie, he's your Sam, but to me, he's Farmer."

Sam just shrugged his shoulders in response and smiled. He thought it unwise to say anything further, especially with Penny about to rip his arm out of its socket.

"That's it then, decided. Come on, you two, let's get a drink," he declared, taking his two guests one on each arm.

Penny introduced Sam to all the good and the great who were

present. He knew his girls wouldn't believe him when he told them.

"There's Angie, Sam," she said, taking hold of his hand.

Angie was swopping her empty glass for a full one from a passing waiter.

"Angie, this is Sam," Penny announced, with an air of excitement in her voice.

"Well, Sam, welcome to our world. God, you're handsome! No wonder the old ladies have taken to you!" Angie laughed, putting her arm around Penny's waist. "And of course, this lovely lady has taken to you too," she added.

Penny shot a shy smile at him, and said, "She's sweet, isn't she? But don't let that mumsie look of hers fool you; she'd rip your balls off if she had to," she laughed, giving Angie a kiss on the cheek.

Sam could see Angie exuded an air of authority, which he realised was a necessary trait in her dog-eat-dog world of being an agent.

Penny did not leave Sam's side all evening as they chatted to all the guests, but suddenly she turned to him and said, "Let's get out here. Fancy something to eat? Those canapés wouldn't fill a cat."

"Food. Now that sounds a good idea. Where do you fancy?" he smiled.

"Leave that to me. I know a few places." She led him towards the foyer. "Can you see Angie or Archie?"

"Yes, they're over to our right, by the bar."

As they walked towards them, Penny waved. "Hey, you two, let's go eat."

Archie down his brandy in double-quick time. "Excellent idea," he declared.

And Don't Forget the Roses

The four of them made their way outside.

"OK, hun. Chinese, Indian or Italian? Choice is yours."

Without hesitation, he replied: "Italian. Love Italian."

"Meatballs," Archie stated, emphatically.

"Good idea, Arch," Penny agreed, taking Sam's arm as the four of them head down the road. "Romeo's, it is."

Chapter 14

The Past

"Sam, do you want a coffee, dear?" May was preparing lunch.

"Not just yet, May, thank you. I want to try and finish this window before lunch."

"Have you heard from Penny today?"

"No," he answered, shaking his head. "I generally don't contact her before five, and even then, I text her first."

May looked at him, her smile kindly and warm.

"No doubt she'll phone later, dear. Knowing her, she's probably got something planned for you again tonight." She huffed and puffed a little as she tried to grate a carrot. "Sam, be a dear, grate this for me will you. With the way my hands are these days, you'll be lucky not to get grated fingernails in your salad."

"What *would* madam say?" Sam asked, laughing. "If she turned up and saw your fingers covered in plasters, she'd blame me."

"I'm sure she wouldn't, she knows what we're like. Besides, she can't cut an onion without drawing blood!"

"I see . . . she can act, but she can't cook."

"Oh no, Sam, she's a brilliant cook, she just can't cut onions without chopping her fingers off!"

Sam laughed at May's observation.

"Window done, May, what's next?"

"It sounds like June is calling for you upstairs, dear. Go on, I'm almost done anyway."

"Just the man!" June said, sitting down on an old chair, her breathing rushed due to over exerting herself.

He could see she was looking flushed, and noticed that the heavy boxes near her had been moved.

"June, what are you doing? You've worn yourself out," he said, looking at her with concern.

"I'll be OK in a minute or so, dear," she replied.

"No, you won't. Come downstairs and have a rest." (He wasn't actually sure if he should be so assertive with her. After all, it was her house. But he thought it wise to take control rather than have her drop dead in front of him.)

"Let me sit here, I'll be alright," she panted, as she put her hand out to him. "Right, dear," she continued, and then stopped to mutter obscenities to herself due to her sore hip. Her face was distorted with discomfort.

She muttered a bit more, and then turned to Sam and said, "May and I have spoken to Penny and we think it's wrong that you come up here to see us and spend a fortune on hotels bills. So, if you agree, we would be more than happy for you to stay here."

Sam looked at her, feeling flattered by their kindness considering they barely knew him.

"That's all well and good, June, but what if I want to bring a woman back?"

June looked shocked at his reply, having not considered the possibility prior to asking him. Then she saw a broad grin spread across his face.

"You bugger, Sam!" she screeched. "You had me going then! Wait till I tell Penny!"

"Oh Christ, now I'm in trouble!" he exclaimed, feigning a worried look.

"Well, dear, what do you think?" June asked, when she'd finished chuckling. She fixed him with a look.

He looked around the room. There was a large bookcase standing against one of the walls, every shelf filled with rare and valuable books. The floor area was almost entirely taken up with boxes of various shapes and sizes. Even the single bed was barely visible under more boxes and bundles of clothes. The window looked out over the courtyard and the small, grassed area at the rear of the house. He looked at her, still sitting in the chair, still looking at him.

"I don't know what to say? Yes, if you are sure, but where are we going to put all these boxes?"

June looked at Sam and let out another chuckle.

"Take a look in the boxes, dear," she instructed.

He opened one, then another, and another.

"They're all full of old costumes and scripts," he whispered, looking across at her a little non-plus. "So, what do you want to do with them all?"

June then stood up, using the arms of the chair to manoeuvre herself to her feet. She tentatively walked to one of the boxes, cussing her hip again as she moved.

"These are mostly Penny's, dear," she replied, removing some of the contents. "When she was a child she used to dress up and act out scenes. Sometimes the three of us would re-enact *Macbeth*, amongst others. Oh, they were happy days, Sam, but as you well know, dear, nothing stays the same does it, time moves on. . ." She looked wistful as she reminisced.

"You still haven't told me what you want done with these boxes?" he asked softly, as she held up a silk blouse and sighed.

"I'm sorry, dear, I got distracted."

And Don't Forget the Roses

She was about to decide about the boxes, when May appeared.

"Lunch, dears, when you're ready," she announced from the doorway.

June turned to acknowledge her, saying, "OK, dear, we're coming now."

"June? The boxes . . . what do you want me to do with them?" Sam asked again. He took her arm gently.

"The boxes, dear? Oh, nothing. They're being collected on Monday by a youth drama school," she replied. "Come on, Sam, our salad's getting cold."

After lunch June pointed in the direction of the lounge.

"Go and sit down, Sam, and I'll bring you a cup of tea."

He entered the room to see May was already in there, sipping her coffee. When June pottered in with the tea, she didn't sit down but instead stood awhile talking to them.

"God, this hip of mine is a pain in the arse," she hissed.

Sam felt for her, always being in pain. She'd already told him she couldn't afford to have the hip operation done privately so had to wait her turn in the NHS queue, but like she said – how long is a piece of string? He sat in one of the settees and looked over to her; there was something he very much wanted to ask her, so after offering consoling words about her hip he asked quietly, "I know it's none of my business, but what happened to Penny's mother? When Penny speaks of her childhood, it's as if it only began from the time she came here."

"I suppose it–"

"Please, June," said May, interrupting her. "May I tell him, please?" Her voice was quiet and sincere, and she looked at her sister with a forlorn expression on her face.

"Of course, dear, of course."

With winces of discomfort June sat down next to May, and

held her hand as she began to speak. Sam had no idea that once he was aware of the facts about Penny's past, his feelings towards their niece would change and he would understand why sometimes she was belligerent and outspoken.

"You see Penny, you see April," May began. "Intelligent, beautiful, charismatic, and above all, a wonderful actress."

She took a deep breath, and Sam watched and listened intently as she told her story in a concise and measured way.

"April was by far the most talented of the three of us, as I think I may have mentioned before. I don't know if Penny has told you how we educated her with regards to Shakespeare? It was the same way our father taught us. For example, Sam, we were told to read *Romeo and Juliet*, and then given a line of script to find in the book. We had to then write about that particular line. It took June and I ages, didn't it, dear?" May turned her head to look and smiled at her sister. "But everything seemed easy for April, her brain was like a sponge and she learned so quickly. By the time she was twelve she could already speak French and Italian fluently – and so could Penny at the same age. But we were never jealous of April, were we, June? We were in awe of her. She was our lovely sister.

"When April and I started our careers as actresses, it was April who stood out. Her reviews were outstanding, her acting abilities limitless." She indicated the photograph that had been taken of the three of them, the photograph that she had shown Sam a few months before. "A few years after that photograph was taken, April met a budding young actor. His name doesn't matter now, but like Penny and Toby, April's relationship with this man was also doomed. He entranced her; she couldn't see that he was using her to promote his own faltering career. We talked to her, hour after hour, but she didn't listen, she didn't want to, she was in love, and he loved her . . . so she thought." May turned to her sister. "Be a dear and get me a glass of water?"

"No, I'll get it," Sam said, returning with glasses of water for each of them.

"April found herself pregnant, Sam," she said, her voice sounding desperate, as if it was happening in the present not the past. But in her mind, it was, as she was reliving every painful memory. "April was overjoyed with the news. She couldn't wait to tell her man and live happily ever after. But that's a fairy tale ending . . . real life isn't as clear-cut as that is it, Sam?

"Soon after April gave him the good news, the bugger did a runner. Got on a plane and disappeared to America." May reached for her hanky and dabbed the corners of her eyes, her memories now prompting the tears that flowed out of her. "April was distraught with disbelief and the sense of betrayal; she was a broken woman, Sam, broken, and she vowed to never act again. She said to act about everlasting love would be a lie, and she could never act a lie."

Sam stayed silent; he was thinking about Penny and her mother, and the similarities with his past. He could hardly believe what he was hearing.

"A few months into her pregnancy, April moved to Edinburgh to live with our mother, who returned there when our father died. April gave birth to twin girls: Megan and Penny. She never kept in touch with us once she left London – we think she wanted to forget every aspect of her life before the girls came along – but we were kept up to date, of course, by Mother."

June was looking at Sam, studying him. He hadn't said a word and his eyes were intensely focused on her sister. She wondered what was going through his mind.

"When the girls where four, our mother died," May continued, "and April stayed in the house with her daughters. But all news from then on was lost. We wrote to her, sent birthday and Christmas cards, but we never received a reply." May paused, and long moments passed as she composed herself.

"When Megan was five she developed leukaemia. The doctors did their best, but she died when she was eight."

Suddenly Sam breathed in and held it for a few seconds. May stared at the picture of the three sisters, holding it tightly with both hands; he hadn't even noticed June take it down from the shelf and pass it to her sister. June noticed Sam's reaction to what May had just said. The expression on his face had changed from a look of compassion, to deep sorrow. His eyes were now showing deep pain, and he cupped his hands one in the other, his fingers pressing hard into his own skin.

"One month after Megan died," – and every word she spoke now was clearly torture for her, her face unable to disguise her anguish – "we received a letter from April informing us about Megan, and asking could we take care of Penny for a while." May turned to look at June, and then Sam. "April put Penny on a plane, and we picked her up from the airport. We were hoping to see April again, but she didn't come. After that, neither Penny nor we received any further contact from her. Then we got word a few weeks later that she had died." (Sam found himself leaning further and further forward in his seat as the story unfolded.) "The inquest concluded that it was natural causes, but we knew April died of a broken heart. There was a letter in her belongings addressed to June and me. She wanted us to raise Penny, and said that she was sorry, and that she loved us . . ."

May started to sob quietly, turning her head away from Sam. June looked across at Sam, seeing the same look of anguish on his face, the loss and loneliness in his eyes. She had seen that look many times before in Penny's eyes as a child. *But why yours Sam?* she asked herself. *What links you to her pain? What bond do you think you share? What painful history do you have that makes you feel hers?* She wanted to know, but knew she must keep these thoughts to herself for Penny's and Sam's sake – for the time being anyway. Suddenly June remembered what Penny had told her soon after she first met Sam, that she felt as if they knew each other. Penny and she had had a laugh about it. *Maybe some how they do*, June thought then, not in a physical, flesh and bones way, not even in a spiritual way, but maybe they had met at a junction in their lives . . . Did Sam know when, and why?

June turned to look at May, taking the picture from her hand. She stood up, as usual her hip causing her pain and discomfort.

"You see, Sam," she said, as she put the picture back, "our concern is for Penny. She's very much her mother's daughter. She has the ability to be a great stage actress, but she holds herself back – and we know it's because of what happened to her mother and Megan. She has monstrous self-doubt, and doesn't cope with failure, that's why she hides behind her facade of being a mouthy madam. But those of us who love her, know she's anything but, and can cry like the best of us. Penny knows Toby is no good for her, but she's playing with fire just as her mother did. We drove April away by trying to tell her about her lover, and we don't want to do that with Penny."

June reached for Sam's hand and looked straight into his eyes.

"They say the eyes are the gateway to your soul," she whispered, with a tearful smile. "You will look after our girl, won't you, Sam?"

He then knew she had seen the pain in his own eyes. He put her frail hand to his lips, and said, "Don't worry, I'll keep an eye on her, that's what friends are for."

"So, you're going to have a lodger," Sam said to May, trying quickly to lighten the atmosphere. He felt emotionally drained; goodness knows how the two sisters felt.

"Good, she asked you," May replied. "But you're not our lodger, Sam, you're our friend, and friends don't charge friends," she stated, seeing him shake his head in response.

"Alright, alright," he smiled, "but I'll do the dishes."

It was now late afternoon, and Sam was preparing to go back to his hotel when May rushed over to him, overexerting herself like her sister and sounding short of breath.

"Ah, there you are, Sam." She placed the house phone in his hand. "It's Penny, dear," she whispered, with a look of excitement on her face.

"Thank you, May," he said, giving her a quick peck on her cheek.

"Hello, you!"

He heard Penny laugh at his greeting.

"Are you ready for another all-nighter, Sam?" she jokingly asked.

"Canapés or meatballs?" he asked.

She then laughed even louder, knowing exactly what he meant.

"Oh, meatballs, Sam, definitely meatballs."

"Well, count me in then!" Sam cried enthusiastically.

"Sam, could you be a love and make your way to my place? We're going by car, and it'll be a nightmare to pick you up in the city on a Friday night."

"Don't be silly," he told her in a stern tone of voice. "I won't hear of you going to all that bother. What time do you want me?"

"Six thirty, and bring your toothbrush, you can stay the night in the spare room at my place."

Surprised at her offer – although it wasn't a problem for him – he felt he should at least query her decision to ask a man she had only known for a few months, and only met three times, to stay over.

"Are you sure?" he asked her in an inquisitive tone, intending to sound flattered by her offer, yet questioning.

"Don't be an ass, Sam. If I didn't trust you, I wouldn't suggest it, and I certainly wouldn't agree to you staying at my aunties, now would I?"

Shit! he thought, *I may have pressed the wrong button this time.*

"Point taken. So, where are you taking me?" he asked.

"School. You're going back to school. That's all I'll tell you."

His mind conjured up all sorts of places and answers, but none of them seemed plausible, so he gave up.

"OK, boss lady, you win."

"Good, I'm glad you know your place," she informed him with a loud laugh. "Now you'd better go if you're going to be here on time."

Chapter 15

The Reading

Ah this is what I need . . . a hot bath and peace and quiet, Penny thought as she stepped into the water; but then her phone beeped. It was a text from Sam: 'Tux or T-shirt?' She smiled. *Tux,* she thought, and then laughed – *no, that would really piss him off when he saw where they were going.* 'T-shirt', she typed, and slid into the water.

Penny was on the phone to Toby when Sam arrived at her door, and when she opened it she quickly gestured to him with a finger across her mouth – ssshhhh! – and then pointed to her lounge. He had no intention of eavesdropping on their conversation, so walked into kitchen, helped himself to a glass of water and sat at the breakfast bar to wait for her.

"I'm so sorry, I forgot Toby said he'd ring me," she said when she joined him.

He could see she was nowhere near ready, standing in front of him in her pink and white fleecy bathrobe with a towel wrapped around her hair, and he smiled as he looked into her eyes.

"Sam, you're looking at my eyes, why? Are there bags under them?" She squinted her face at him.

"Someone recently reminded me that eyes are the gateway to the soul, and no, you don't have bags under them."

"Oh, don't bother looking for mine," she replied, in a throw away manner. "Some would say I have neither heart nor soul."

(She wanted to give him the impression that she wasn't bothered what people thought of her.)

"Waste of time having that devil-may-care look on your face," he retorted, gently, intending to defuse her attitude. "The woman I met on those steps showed me plenty of heart and soul, so, don't come that with me."

She smiled then, remembering the day, and knew he meant it.

"Sam, you bugger, you're distracting me, be a love and make me a coffee while I get ready. There's a beer in the fridge if you want one."

"A girly Mercedes," Sam said, surprised at Penny's choice of vehicle.

"It's not mine. I couldn't afford this. It belongs to a friend of mine who lives down the road. She's a fashion model, so when she jets off somewhere for a few weeks she lends it to me – and in return I get her theatre tickets for all the best shows."

She plonked her handbag in his lap and started the car.

"That sounds a fair exchange."

They stayed quiet as Penny negotiated her way through the traffic.

"Almost there," she said. "Have you worked out where we're going or what we're doing yet?" she asked.

"No, haven't a clue, I give in," he replied, watching her concentrate on her driving.

"OK. I'm taking you to a Shakespeare reading. I hope you'll like it."

She glanced at him.

"Thank you! I was hoping you would sometime!"

He said this to make her feel happier, but he couldn't help thinking that between her and her aunties they were perhaps overwhelming him a little with their passion for the Bard.

"We get a good crowd, you'll like it," she said enthusiastically, aware it would be a new experience for him.

He had been to a Shakespeare play with Annie many years before, and had now finished reading *The Tempest*, but tonight he would see his friend, the consummate professional, doing what she loved: performing Shakespeare to the masses. He felt a sense of humility; he knew of her pedigree and would, at last, see a glimpse of her abilities.

They arrived at the church hall of a small village, some thirty miles outside of London. Penny took Sam's arm and guided him past an elderly lady at the entrance who was taking money from those arriving to see her perform.

"OK, I'll shoot off, get yourself a good seat," she said. "Oh, and by the way, get me some raffle tickets. See you in the interval!"

At the far end of the hall was the stage – *more like a black box*, he thought – approximately ten feet wide and nine feet deep. It had three stools placed upon it.

The number people at the venue impressed Sam. All the chairs where taken and it was now standing room only. The audience was a mish-mash of young and old, from early twenties to pensioners.

"Oh bugger, I haven't filled in a request slip," Sam said, quickly asking someone who looked like one of the organisers.

"Here you go, fill this in and give it to the guy who collects the slips," he told Sam, as he studied the list, looking at five quotes from Shakespeare's plays and three sonnets.

"'No more than two from each section'," he read, but he didn't have a clue.

"Are you Sam?" asked a young man in his early twenties who he had seen collecting the slips.

"Yes, I am," he answered.

"I'm Patch. Penny said you were here somewhere. So what do

you think? Not a bad turn out by the looks of it." He put his hand out to accept other people's request slips. "Let's have yours, Sam. Which ones have you chosen?"

Sam felt slightly self-conscious, aware he was a novice with regards to Shakespeare; and he didn't want to embarrass Penny.

"It's a bit potluck, I'm afraid, I'm still on the first rung," he admitted.

Patch made a strange gesture with his head, making him look shifty.

"What makes you think this bunch know any more than you?" he asked quietly. "Tell you what, Sam, if her aunties are helping you, just keep reading their books," he said, walking off. He disappeared through a door by the 'stage'.

Penny came out first, followed by Ahmed and Patch, and applause broke out as they did. Penny and Ahmed sat on their stools, while Patch informed the audience about the evening's performance.

During the first part of the evening, Penny and Ahmed read passages from *King Lear*, *Timon of Athens* and *Midsummer Night's Dream*, interspersed with sonnets. Patch verbally drew the audience a mental picture of the various scenes.

To Penny, reading Shakespeare was no different to a musician playing a composition of one of the great masters – Beethoven, Handle or Mozart – as she could interpret the tone of how the words should be spoken and in what context. To her audience, it was music to their ears.

In the interval, Sam could see her talking to Patch, pointing in his direction.

"Hi, Sam, so what did you think of us then?" she asked, grabbing a chair and sipping from her bottled water. She was bubbly and pleased with herself, in her element.

Sam thought of Annie, and the similarities between her and

Penny: both women loved to express their art . . . the art of expression. For Annie it was to interpret what was in an artist's mind – why he chose a particular colour or brush stroke, for example – and she painted her students a picture to illustrate. For Penny it was a passion to enlighten her audience about the Bard, to delve and explore his life's work.

"Impressive," Sam answered. "I thought I had an idea about what it would be like, but I was totally wrong."

She listened to him, detecting emotion in his voice, and she could also see it in his eyes, and she knew why that was: Shakespeare's words had pierced his soul, and he was conscious of it.

"The second half isn't as long, and has some beautiful sonnets, plus lines from *Romeo and Juliet* . . . even a total brick-head knows that one," she said, looking at him, her face slightly screwed up. "You know those sections you selected on the sheet of paper?" she asked.

"Yeeess . . ." Sam replied, slowly, curious as to why she'd asked.

"Well, I've got it."

"Oh, have you? I'm not sure if that is good or bad."

"I'll show them to May and June. They can use them to decide what book you should read next," she said, giving him a studious glance. "I've got to go . . . got to have a pee," she whispered, disappearing back towards the stage.

At the end of the second half, Sam waited while Penny sorted herself out, watching all the other people drift away.

"Sam, I'm Ahmed," said the rakish-looking man in his thirties. "She won't be long, she's having her usual spat with Patch."

Sam wondered what sort of mood she'd be in when she returned; he didn't have to wait long.

"Right, Sam, ready?" she asked, pointing towards the door.

"Sometimes I wonder why I do this. How am I supposed to work with someone who gets his facts wrong? If June knew what he was like, she'd bend him over her knee."

Sam was intrigued to know what June had to do with it.

"Have you calmed down now?" he asked, with a stern tone.

"Yes. Sorry, I was angry with Patch, not you."

"Well, I gathered that. But I was wondering what the connection is between June and Patch?"

"Ah, June . . ." she replied. "Well, she used to mentor him in his early days. He's given up acting now to become a school teacher instead, and just moonlights doing this. He's a nice guy, but he makes mistakes. He thinks no one notices, but they do – I do!" she said, sounding frustrated with him.

Sam decided not to pursue the subject any further.

Chapter 16

The Magic Carpet

Once home Penny cooked them omelettes. Settling down on the settee after their meal. She noticed in the corner of lounge something he had brought with him.

"What's in the box?" she asked, picking it up and giving it a slight shake. "Is it for me?"

"What do you think?"

"Oh! I hate surprises! What is it?" she said, sounding like an impatient teenager.

He pointed towards the settee.

"Sit down and I'll show you," he said, as he removed the item from the tatty cardboard box and placed it on the floor by her feet.

"It's a foot spa! Bloody brilliant! Thank you so much," she cried, her face aglow with gratitude.

"Here, read the instructions and get the wine. No better still, get the wine and then read the instructions, while I put some water in it," he told her.

"This is so brilliant, this is great, this is just what I wanted!" she enthused.

"There you are, madam." Sam filled the foot spa with warm water from the kettle. "I'll get you a towel."

"They're in the airing cupboard, top of the stairs." She lowered her feet into the water, letting out a low moan as they were submerged.

It was obvious to him that she was pleased with it, but there was still something else to do.

"This is great. *Now* what are you doing?" she asked, watching him crawling on his hands and knees behind her settee.

"Have you not noticed? It's not working, you silly bugger," he said – adopting one of her favourite words – "I'm trying to plug it in!"

When he emerged, her eyes were closed, her mind a thousand miles away.

"Myyy god, this is lovely," she proclaimed, as the spa water bubbled to life and an expression of sheer pleasure spread across her face.

She opened her eyes to gaze at her feet, and then reached over to the box. She removed a glass bottle.

"What's this? Is this what I think it is?"

"That's a new bottle of massage oil," Sam informed her.

"Great! You said I should have my feet massaged with sensual oils, didn't you? Do it for me later, please?" she asked, her face brimming with joyful expectation.

"Sorry, hun, I want to . . ." he said, shaking his head as he watched her happy smile disappear and turn to disappointment.

"Why not?"

"Because it would be wrong for me to do so," he replied, pausing while he thought about what he was about to say next. The last thing he wanted was for her to get the wrong end of the stick. "When I massage a woman's body, even her feet, with sensual oils, it's akin giving her a magic carpet . . . the sheer pleasure takes her mind and body to wherever she wants to go, and it's not for me to take you there, is it? I'm sorry."

He hoped he hadn't offended her; but she was transfixed by what he had said, momentarily fantasising about what it would be like.

"Aw, go on, Sam. Just one toe, my little one, please?" She wanted to sample the magic carpet experience he was denying her!

"Especially the little toe?" Sam was pleased that she sounded more disappointed than dejected, but added, "Like I said before, that's for Toby to do, not me."

She huffed at his remark.

"That's a joke. The only thing he knows about oil is that you cook chips in it." Realising she wasn't going to get her way, she put a cushion behind her head and lent back. "Bliss. I'm going to sleep down here tonight with my feet in the tub." She turned to look at him. "Thank you, again." She sipped her wine.

"So where is your man at the moment?" He decided it was wise to ask, but he didn't dare think what Toby would make of the scene if he walked in.

She leant forward and starred at her feet.

"He's in Tenerife on a stag party with his cousin. He's back Monday," she said in a very matter-of-fact way.

"So, you've got a wedding to go to?" he asked, watching her splash her toes in the bubbling water.

"Yes, in two weeks' time . . . deep joy," she replied, making no secret of the fact she wasn't enamoured with the thought. She took another *large* mouthful of wine, followed by a long sigh. "Don't get me wrong, I love Newcastle, I've been there loads of times and it's a great place, and the people are lovely – well, most of them – but Toby's family are a nightmare," she said. "Toby and I went to his sister's wedding last year. I heard his mates ask him things like 'Is she a good shag?' and 'I bet she's minted?' – crap like that."

And Don't Forget the Roses

As Sam listened he noticed her relaxed face became strained.

"Later I found out that his brother, of all people, sold some photos of me at the wedding to the local paper, the little shit," she continued. "I know I sound like a snob, but I don't want to associate myself with cretins like that."

Hearing what she was saying, Sam felt for the first time since they'd met that he wanted to hug her, to let her know he was her friend and would protect her from such people.

"No, you mustn't think that about yourself," he told her, firmly. "Who wants to be treated like a piece of meat?"

"Too bloody right, I'm no man's piece of meat." She noticed Sam was looking at her very intently. "You're not still trying to find my soul are you?" She gave him a look as if to say *You're wasting your time.*

Then he told her something, un-aware of its impact.

"Many years before I met Annie, I was going steady with this girl who I had been going out with for almost two years. I thought I was besotted with her, so we got engaged." Sam stopped to sip his wine; he could see Penny was listening to him, in between splashing her feet and taking large mouthfuls of her wine. "It wasn't long before I realised I didn't want to get married," he continued. "I loved her but couldn't see myself *marrying* her," he said, diverting his gaze from looking into her eyes to staring at her feet.

"So, what happened?" Penny asked, intrigued.

"Oh, she dumped me. Can't say I was heartbroken, though. It wasn't until I met Annie that I found out what real love felt like."

Penny wasn't quite sure what he was trying to convey.

"So, are you saying Toby may be having second thoughts about getting married?"

He looked straight at her, with a frown on his face.

"No . . . *you are.*"

Her pupils suddenly dilated, and her face became ridged and tense, red with rage.

"Who the hell are you to make an assumption like that? You've got no right!" she yelled, making him realise he hadn't only touched a nerve, he'd severed it!

"I apologise if I spoke out of turn, that wasn't my intention. I just say it as I see it," he replied, his tone of voice restrained, trying not to sound argumentative or aggressive.

"Well, you need to get your bloody eyes tested!" she replied, tersely. She took a deep breath and then breathed out slowly, looking back down at her feet.

Sam stood up.

"Where the hell do you think you're going?" she asked, angrily.

"I think it would be best if I left, don't you?" he said calmly, his face deadpan.

"Oh sod this, fill up our glasses and sit down Sam."

He stared down at her, pausing for a moment before he replied. "That depends," he answered.

"Oh yes . . . depends on what?" she asked.

"As I said, I apologise for hurting your feelings, I really am; but a please wouldn't go amiss."

Her eyes flashed in response to his request, but she knew he would go, and yes, he had angered her, but she also knew he didn't have to put up with her shouting at him . . . he wasn't Toby!

"Sit down, please . . ." she asked, now sounding conciliatory. She patted the cushion next to her.

He stood there, studying her expression, expecting it to be one of disappointment and annoyance with him. But strangely he saw only loneliness in her eyes, as if she had no one, not even Toby.

He sat down and put his hand on her arm. She moved her head from side to side, as if relieving the tension in her neck. He didn't say a word. He knew she hadn't finished with him yet. He had seen it all before with someone else, and had learnt not to fuel their moods by talking, so he just watched and waited.

"I can feel your eyes on me, Sam." She couldn't help but wonder how the hell he'd worked out that she was having second thoughts about marrying Toby, but she was livid that he had. "It makes me sad that I raised my voice at you," she said.

"I should go, Penny. We can talk tomorrow."

He started to stand up again, but he couldn't because Penny put her hand on his leg and pressed down, wanting to stop him. An angry moan of resignation escaped her lips.

"Yes, you're right, of course," she said, with a look of acceptance. Sam assumed she meant about his leaving, but then she continued, "It was great for a while, after he asked me, then reality set in, and to tell you the truth, I'm not sure if I know what love is." She shrugged her shoulders. "We argue, or to be truthful . . . I argue. He can be such a knob at times, but that's not to say I want to end it. To be honest, I can never see myself being . . . tied down. I really can't. I hope our relationship will continue. Toby is a lovely guy – well, most of the time. Recently he seems to be different, though, strange even. Maybe he's getting cold feel as well?"

Reaching over to take the empty glass from her hand, Sam could see she seemed lost in thought. Then those thoughts tumbled out of her.

"Toby talks about us having kids, or to put it another way: he expects me to put my career on hold, then have a foetus rolling around my womb for nine months, and after that be at its beck and call for the rest of my days." Her tone now challenging, as if she wanted Sam to know that that was the line she would not cross for any man. She lifted her head and turned to him, and continued, "Sorry, but that's not me. I know you must think me a cow, but that's how I feel." Tears now ran down her face. Sam reached for the box of tissues on the side table and handed her one; he didn't say a word.

"Well, Mr Know-it-All. Do you think I should tell Toby?"

"That's for you to decide. But lots of couples spend the rest of their lives together and never get married because they say marriage changes people. The thing that has changed here is that you're finally being honest with yourself."

Penny could see the pensive look on his face as he spoke, sensing he didn't want to hurt her feelings anymore as he continued.

"I've always believed friends should speak the truth to each other as it is a mark of the strength of their friendship. And they should remain friends, and value that honesty. I cherish this quirky, new friendship of ours," he said, feeling a lump in his throat as he remembered how they met and why. "Sitting on those steps I was calm, but was at my lowest . . . the lowest I've been for many years . . . and yet for whatever reason, I find myself here."

She gave him a gentle smile, and wondered what it would take to make him angry, really angry. She had been impressed with his self-control when she blew her top.

"If I told my friends, Sam." She stopped and corrected herself. "My *other* friends . . . how we met, and why I trust you as if we've known each other forever, they wouldn't understand."

"I often ask myself that same question," he said, aware of why she felt puzzled, almost mystified by the whole thing.

"The strange thing is, Sam, I don't give a toss what people think about our friendship." She paused, took a deep breath, and then asked, "Tell me what it was like when you fell in love with Annie."

He responded with a big smile. "Distracting. She was so distracting. Every day at work or away from her – especially at night – she was always on my mind."

And Don't Forget the Roses

"'*Like a jewel hung in ghastly night*' – that's from a sonnet about a man who longs for his beloved. '*Weary with toil, I haste me to my bed, the dear repose for limbs with travel tired; but then begins a journey in my head, to work my mind, when body's work's expired. . .*' It's one of two of my favourite sonnets. If someone recited it to me, in its entirety, I would surely know he loved me; but I wouldn't necessarily love him!" she laughed. "But I would know he loved me!"

"Is it ever on your request list?" he asked.

"Now and again, but no one ever picks it."

"So, which is your other favourite sonnet?"

"Sorry, my turn to say no. I won't tell you. I've promised myself I'll only ever recite it to *my* beloved."

"So you've recited it to Toby?"

"No, I haven't," she replied, with a frown, looking at her feet again. "They must be all shrivelled up by now!" she suddenly said, indicating her feet, wanting to change the subject now that Toby's name had been mentioned again. She lifted her feet out of the water to inspect them. "No, all good, I'll keep them in for ten more minutes."

"Well, I'm off," he told her, feeling the strain of the day had caught up with him. "What time will you be up?" he asked.

"Not before ten. Do you have any thoughts about tomorrow?"

Sam made his way to the hallway.

"I'll be gone by ten. I've got to get some bits for your aunties' place."

"Tell you what, if you can be back here by 11.30, come shopping with me, and we can get your stuff at the same time. I've got a girly night tomorrow tonight here, so I have to get some food in."

He blew her a kiss.

Chapter 16

"See you tomorrow. Sleep well," he replied.

Knocking on Penny's front door, Sam saw her next-door neighbour's curtain move and a face appear at the window. He waved at her, just as Penny opened the door.

"Who are you waving to?" she asked.

"Some old lady. She watched me leave earlier. Goodness knows what she must be thinking."

"Oh that's Sissy, she's a darling. Bloody Toby stuck his fingers up to her once. There was no need for that, she's harmless. Come into the kitchen and have a cup of tea, I'm not quite ready yet."

"There's something I feel I must say about last night," Sam said, as he followed her through to the kitchen. "I awoke this morning feeling quite ashamed of myself. So I just want you to know how sorry I am for distressing you," he said.

"You silly sod. It doesn't matter, really it doesn't. I had to realise the truth, it's no big deal. When you went to bed, I thought about our conversation and actually felt better about Toby and me. Our talk brought clarity to a conundrum I've subconsciously been wrestling with for a while." She sighed deeply. "It just means I won't marry him. So no, Sam, don't feel bad about what was said. Some pills are hard to swallow, that's all, and that's the end of it." She was very matter-of-fact in her tone.

"Do you still plan to go to the wedding?"

"Sadly, no . . . poor May and June will be going down with a bad tummy bug, so unfortunately I'll have to stay behind and care for them. Never mind, eh!" She grinned at Sam, who couldn't help but laugh; they laughed together.

"I was going to buy you some roses to say sorry."

She looked at him with surprise, and said, "That was a lovely thought, but I wouldn't buy roses at London prices! Did you buy Annie roses?"

"No, we had a rose garden," he told her, unaware at that

moment of the unfolding significance of the flower in their friendship.

Chapter 17

Trust

"God, I hate driving in London. Did you see that motorcyclist? Bloody kamikaze." Penny was clearly agitated.

"I wouldn't have minded getting on the Tube from your place, you know that," he said, as they made their way through the weekend traffic. "I carried that foot spa of yours halfway across London, so I'm well able to carry a bag of shopping!"

"Finished?" she asked.

"Might be."

"What are you like when you're angry, Sam?" she asked, still wondering about the night before.

"I'm not the Sam you know anymore," he replied in a low voice.

"I hope I never piss you off."

"Don't be silly," he said reassuringly. "I like you far too much for you to piss me off that badly. I'm only not Sam when I'm with people I don't like; but I like you, so you're safe with me."

"I always feel safe with you."

She knew that to be true, but still couldn't understand why. She didn't fight it. She liked and trusted him and enjoyed his company, so why conjure up a doubt that doesn't exist?

"Don't ask me why," she then said, "but if there was one man on this earth who I knew would protect me, it would be you."

He didn't reply to what she said, and she wasn't expecting him to, but from the depth of her soul she knew he would – he didn't have to confirm it.

"So what are you doing tonight?" she asked, thinking of him on his own, which was partly why she agreed that he should stay with her aunties when he came up to see them.

"Catch up on my reading, plus speak to my girls – it's been a few days," he said, and then laughed as he thought of something. "I told Harry's wife I'd fix her kitchen window for her. Apparently, when it comes to DIY, Harry's as useless as a bottle of wine without a corkscrew!"

Penny laughed, but said, "You mustn't let them take advantage of you, Sam."

"I don't mind at all. Over the last thirty years all I've done is push and push, and take and take. I don't have to do that anymore. Now I can do things I want to do, and help people I want to help. If Annie's death taught me anything, it's not what you can't take with you, it's what you leave behind."

"Christ, you've done it again, you've made me cry! You're going to cost me a fortune in mascara, you bugger." She wondered why he always made her so emotional.

"Sorry."

"So, when am I going to meet those young ladies of yours?" she asked, wondering if they were like him.

"I tried telling Maggie about you once. She asked me what I did after I left the National Gallery. So I told her I met this beautiful young woman, and took her for a picnic in the park. She didn't believe me, she just laughed. All she said was 'Are you sure you weren't dreaming, Dad?'!"

"You poor thing!" she replied. "Wait till I meet her, I'll tell her it was all true! Tell you what, next time Archie has another of his parties, invite them up. Arch always has good-looking blokes there. It'll be fun for them."

"And for you, too, I expect?"

"God no, I've got Toby, he's enough," she said, and then thought *and you, Sam.*

Chapter 18

The Cross

June was talking to Betty from next door as Penny drove up.

"Hello, dears! I'll go and put the kettle on, give me something to take in."

"No, you won't. I'll bring it all in. You go ahead," Sam instructed her, as he picked up the shopping from the boot of the car.

"You're not bullying my aunties, are you?" Penny asked, smiling at him.

"Of course!" He cracked a smile back.

Inside May was carrying the tray of cups of tea in to the lounge as June appeared from upstairs carrying a shoebox.

"Penny, dear, I've been sorting things out in your old bedroom and found these. Can you tell me if you want any of them?"

Penny sat down next to Sam on the settee, taking the box from June and resting it on her lap.

"God, that takes me back. Look at this, Sam – a Blue Peter badge!" she laughed, rifling through the box. "These wrist watches can go, they're broken."

Sam could see a silver Celtic cross pendant in the box and picked it out. *This is pretty*, he thought, silently reading the inscription on the back: *To my Spanish eyes, love Mummy.* He handed it to Penny, who stared at it for a few moments.

"It's nice, isn't it? Shame it's broken. That can go."

Sam was surprised at her speedy decision and he reached for her hand.

"Hold on, if I repair it would you wear it again?"

"Fix it first, then I'll see," she replied. Her face was filled with emotion.

He put the pendant safely in his jacket pocket.

"What else do you have in there?" he asked, wanting to distract her.

Penny knew he'd read the inscription and wondered if she'd be upset by its presence. She also realised her aunties may have of told him of her sister and mother. She looked at him with an inquisitive stare.

He knew she was wondering if he was aware of her early childhood, and he gave her a small smile – which made her want to smile back – and she knew right then that he knew.

"Old rings and earrings mostly," she replied. "Oh my god! A Wham badge!" Penny declared, holding it up to her breast. "I'll give it to Archie."

Sam laughed at the thought of Mr Dapper in his Savile Row suit exhibiting such a trinket.

June and May watched the two of them laughing and joking about the contents of the box, and then June whispered to her sister, "Look at those two. They're like a couple of kids."

Penny showed him an earring.

"I really liked these, but this pearl has fallen off, look. Can you work your magic on them? They used to be May's."

"I'll bring them back next time I'm up. Anything else?" he asked.

"No, that's all." She looked at the time on the mantelpiece clock. "I have to go. I'll drop you back at your hotel."

"No, you won't. I may not know London as well as you, but I know that my hotel is in the opposite direction to your house. I'll walk."

"Are you sure? I don't mind."

"These bones of mine need their exercise, besides, I'm not ready to go yet, I have to sort some gear out for tomorrow," he said.

"Don't keep them up late! I know what you're like," she said, winking at him. She then hugged her aunties and left.

June walked up to Sam and smiled at him; but he knew even in the relatively short time he had known her it wasn't just a smile . . . she was thinking, wondering.

"Have you noticed, dear, that Penny's always in a good mood and happy when she's with you?"

Not last night! Sam thought.

"I know exactly why that is, June," he replied. "We don't make demands on each other. We've become good friends, but Penny has her own life with Toby, and I have mine. We don't need anything other than friendship."

"Well, it's just lovely to see her happy, dear. With Toby we can never tell if she's happy or not."

Sam knew it wasn't his place to say anything about Penny's relationship with Toby, and had no intention to; besides, he'd said more than enough the previous night!

"Penny's an intelligent woman, she's knows her own mind," Sam concluded, sensing that if he didn't end this conversation she would try to tease more information from him. "I must sort things out for tomorrow, or I won't get anything done."

Chapter 19

Aaron

June was busy in the kitchen preparing lunch when Penny arrived.

"Hi!"

June turned around to see her standing by the kitchen door, taking her coat off.

"Hello, dear, you're early! I'll put the kettle on."

Penny watched June filling it up from the tap Sam had repaired and thought of their new handyman.

"So, where is he?"

"Who, dear?" asked June, knowing exactly who she meant, but loved to play games.

"Your fancy man, June, who do you think!"

"Sam? He's gone, dear." June could see Penny was surprised.

"What do you mean gone?" she asked, with a frown, as June walked past her into the dining room to prepare the table for lunch.

Penny was just about to follow when she caught site of Sam in the hallway.

"Hi, babe," he smiled.

She looked at him with utter confusion.

"June said you had gone?"

"Oh? I expect she meant gone next door. I've been repairing Betty's window, remember?"

"June, you bloody mischief-maker!" she shouted.

She heard a cackle coming from the dining room.

"No wonder Toby calls her a witch," she muttered. "Too much *Macbeth* in her early years, I reckon." But she managed to raise a smile. "Hello, Sam. Sorry. These buggers always manage to wind me up somehow."

He stood back and gazed at her and said, "You've got that fabulous dress on again. You look wonderful."

"I was wondering if you would notice," she replied, giving him a twirl as she did the last time she wore it.

"I may have said something earlier, if you hadn't had a face like thunder at the time."

God, you've got beautiful eyes, he thought.

"So how did your girly night go?" he asked with interest.

Suddenly Penny's eyes became larger and sparkled brightly.

"My mates love you! Three of them want to take you out on a date!" she laughed.

"What? Why?" he asked, in disbelief.

"I got your foot spa out and that was it, they all wanted to have a go. They all said that not one of their blokes would ever think of getting them one."

"So how many of you were there?" he asked.

"Five of us. You should see the state of my carpet – it's soaking!" she replied, as she laughed again.

"Well, give me their names – the three who want to take me out, that is," he said, looking at her straight-faced.

Penny's face took on the expression of a child who had a toy and didn't want to let anyone else play with it.

"No! No, Sam! You're my friend. I'm not sharing you with them. Besides, they're all high maintenance. I'm not cheap, I know . . ." she admitted, "but they'd cost you both arms and both legs." Then she kissed him on his lips, utterly surprising him. "They told me to give you that."

He grinned, and then let out a sigh.

"What? Only one! I thought you said they were four of them."

She looked at him sternly, and replied, "Don't push your luck, Sam Farmer."

After lunch, as had become the routine, they all retired to the lounge for coffee.

Penny sat on the settee and tapped the cushion, gesturing for Sam to join her. As he did, she moved so that she could put her feet on his lap.

"There you go, you know what to do," she laughed.

May looked at him with surprise.

"Don't let her get away with that, Sam! Tell her to rub her own feet."

He turned to see her fluttering her eyelashes at him.

"I've got two daughters who work the same ploy, and it doesn't work for them either," he said, looking at her sternly.

Penny put on a sad face, withdrawing her feet.

"Sorry," she said, with a conciliatory smile.

"Ah, go on, put them back," he said, relenting.

Penny grinned and wriggled with excitement, whispering, "Thank you."

"Well, Sam, I honestly thought you were made of sterner stuff!" exclaimed May.

"Don't worry," he replied, "when I've done hers, she can do mine."

May let out a little giggle, noting the childish banter going on between them again.

Hearing his intentions, the look on Penny's face was anything other than compliant!

"If they're anything like Toby's, you've got no chance! Come on, Sam, you're slacking," she giggled.

Sam just rolled his eyes, and slowly moved his head from side to side.

"Penny, you little madam! You shouldn't encourage her, Sam, she'll expect you to do that all the time when you're here!" June said, as she walked in the lounge.

"What a good idea, I didn't think of that," Penny replied with a chuckle. "Oh, Auntie June," she said, twisting her body around so that she could see her auntie. "Tell Sam the latest news about the American, Aaron, and the play he's writing."

June looked over to him, resting her bottom on the arm of the settee and putting her hand on Penny's shoulder.

"I believe you've already met Archie? He's a dear isn't he, but a bit of a naughty boy at times."

"Yes, he bloody well is," Penny agreed. "You should have heard what he asked Sam!"

June smiled, not at all amazed by Archie's antics; she'd known him too long to be surprised by anything he said or got up to.

"Archie brought Aaron here to seek our advice about a play he's writing," she said. "The man is very sweet and polite, isn't he, Penny?" Penny nodded, and June fidgeted about on the arm of the settee, trying to get comfortable. "He's writing a new version of *Taming of the Shrew*, Sam, but he's very shy. He's more like a boy in a man's body, and with a rather strange demeanour: extremely tall, but with huge hands and a huge head."

"He is very sweet. There's something about him which is so likeable," Penny confirmed. Then a veil of exasperation came across her face. "Bloody Toby called him 'Herman'," she said, casting her mind back to when she was first introduced to Aaron, and how he seemed to have willed information out of her about Sam. It seemed strange at the time, and it still did, that Aaron, a man who'd she only met hardly half an hour before, was interested and asking questions about Sam, a man she had met by accident.

"That's not fair of Toby to say such a thing," May retorted, determined to fight Aaron's corner. "Some of that young man's writing shows ability far beyond his years, and with guidance he could produce a script worthy of any theatre in the West End, or Broadway for that matter."

"Well said, dear," replied June, determined to have her say too. "He may be from the back end of nowhere, but he's read all of Shakespeare's works – all of them! – and committed them to memory. Can you believe that? The *entire* Bard's original works! If only for his perseverance in his writing, and love of Shakespeare, May and I have agreed to give him our council," she said, forcing herself to her feet. "I think Archie is having another one of his soirees in two or three weeks' time, dear. I'm sure Aaron will be over here by then."

"Brilliant!" Penny sounded thrilled at the prospect of Archie having another one of his parties. "Tell your girls, Sam, and they can stay with me and you can stay here," she said, near bursting with enthusiasm.

Sam gave her a cautious stare, and then tickled her foot.

"Sam, you bugger, don't do that! I almost wet myself!" she screeched. "Please, Sam! Stop! It would be lovely to meet Sam's girls, wouldn't it, May?" she asked, her eyes so bright they almost blinded him.

"I'll ask them," he replied, well aware Maggie and Estelle wouldn't turn down an opportunity to party. "Are you sure you want them to stay with you? What about Toby? It might be awkward for you . . ." He hardly knew Toby, but the little he did know he wasn't impressed with.

Penny sensed he was apprehensive, and knew he wouldn't be happy if his daughters stayed with Toby there too. They may be all grown up, but they were still his little girls. She wanted to placate his fears.

"Don't worry. If Toby's up I'll get him to stay at his mates, and if he comes, too, he can meet us there. Happy with that?"

"That sounds OK. What do you think May? Do you think I should trust this woman with my girls?" he asked, knowing May would need no prompting to cause a bit of mischief.

"Well, dear, they could always stay here and you stay at Penny's. I'm sure Toby wouldn't mind."

"May, don't stir it, and that goes for you too, Sam Farmer," Penny warned. "Well, you two, I'm going home," she then announced. "I'm up early tomorrow.

Sam gave a restrained laugh in response to her auntie's suggestion, laid Penny's feet aside, and left the room.

"Where's Sam gone now?"

"He's gone to get his coat, dear. I think he plans to walk you home," June replied.

"Oh does he?" Although pleasantly surprised at his intention, she still fancied teasing him. "I seem to remember his hotel being in the opposite direction to my home . . ." she said, just loud enough so that Sam would hear.

Chapter 20

The Eyes

Back at home in his cottage in Devon, Sam reached into his jacket pocket and retrieved the pendant Penny had reluctantly given him to repair; he was puzzled by the inscription on it – *To my Spanish eyes, love Mummy* – so he phoned June to see if she could cast any light on it.

May answered, but because she had become very emotional when they'd spoken about April, he felt it might be better to speak to June. May kept Sam talking for several minutes, mostly about the weekend he had just spent with them and Penny, before finally handing the phone over to her sister.

"Hello, dear, lovely of you to ring," she said, slightly surprised to hear from him so soon.

"Hi, June," he said softly, "just a quick question . . ."

"Yes, dear, what is it?" she asked, having no idea what he wanted to know, but was sure it concerned Penny.

"June, this pendant of Penny's . . . why 'Spanish eyes'? Penny has beautiful hazel eyes, not the traditional dark brown eyes of the Spanish."

"You're right, they are beautiful, aren't they." June paused before she spoke again. "What colour eyes do I have, Sam?" she asked.

He tried to remember.

"Hazel eyes, June, like Penny's." He wasn't sure where this was going.

"That's right, dear. And what colour eyes does May have?" Her question was now direct and lacked her normal softness of tone.

Sam became concerned he was digging too deeply and had offended her. He racked his brain trying to remember the colour of May's eyes.

"Brown, June, dark brown."

"Yes, dear, that is correct. April's eyes were hazel." June paused again.

Sam closed his eyes to concentrate on the information she had given him: *Penny's are hazel, June's are hazel, April's were hazel, May's are . . . dark brown. Oh God, I'm such an idiot*, he thought.

"I'm so sorry, June, I have been very insensitive. The pendant was Megan's, wasn't it?"

"Yes, dear, that's right. April gave it to Penny the day she died."

Sam heard a quiet sniffle, and her voice had a tremble to it.

"June, I'm so sorry if I've upset you, it wasn't my intention, I hope you know that."

"No, don't feel bad, dear. It's the only item of Megan's that Penny kept. She used to wear it all the time . . . and then one day she stopped. It was hidden away until Sunday," June continued. "May and I are pleased you persuaded her to keep it, and that you'll repair it for her."

Sam couldn't bring himself to ask any more questions; he knew only too well that some memories should remain in the past.

"Thank you, June, for telling me. I'll get it cleaned and repaired, and hopefully one day she'll wear it again."

"We'll be pleased if she does," June replied, but Sam detected an air of doubt in her voice, as if she didn't hold much hope of Penny doing that.

He ended the call, promising to phone again over the weekend.

Chapter 21

The Birthday

Now late afternoon, Sam was busy in his garden, splitting logs to feed the insatiable appetite of his open fire, when two very attractive young ladies arrived unannounced.

"Hi, Daddy! Happy birthday!" they said in unison, in sing-songy voices.

Hearing them was a sweet sound to his ears, and light-headed with excitement, and totally surprised by the sight before him, he rushed forward open-armed to greet his daughters.

"So, how long are you here for?" he asked, beaming a smile at them.

"Till tomorrow, Dad," Estelle replied, as she stood back and took a look at her father.

"But can we party tonight, Daddy?" asked Maggie, kissing the side of his unshaven face.

Knowing his curvaceous daughter had a zest for having fun, he laughed, taking both his daughters' hands and leading them back into the cottage.

"Well, if we're going to party, let's make it the pub – they do good food and we won't have far to stagger back!" he told them, still grinning with the joy of seeing them again, especially on his birthday.

"You're not going out like that, Dad! Go and get cleaned up!"

Estelle demanded, her tone and posture reminding him of her late mother.

While Sam showered, his girls sat on his settee chatting away and putting his birthday presents out.

"Your phone's ringing, sis," said Maggie.

"No, it's not mine, it's Dad's," Estelle replied, picking it up from a small side table next to where she was sitting. "Penny . . . I wonder who she is? Do you know a Penny?"

"No," Maggie replied, shaking her head. "Do you think he's got himself fancy woman?" she giggled.

"This is *Dad* we're talking about!"

"Who's Penny, Dad?" Estelle asked, watching him walk down the stairs into the lounge.

All shaven and showered, both daughters looked at him with inquisitive expressions on their faces.

He smiled, but said nothing.

"Come on, Dad! Do tell! We're busting to know!" Maggie cried, walking over to her him.

He knew then that it was as good a time as any to tell them.

"Sit down and I'll tell you," he replied.

With Maggie and Estelle either side of him, eager to hear what he had to say, he was reminded of when they were little girls and they would snuggle up beside him and he would tell them a bedtime story – except it wasn't a story he was going to tell, it was the truth, and he felt apprehensive to whether they would believe him.

"Ever heard of an actress by the name of Penny McCain?" he began. (*God*, he thought, *what if they've never heard of her?*)

The sisters looked at each other, trying to think who she was.

"You know her Mags . . . she's the one who's shagging the hunk who plays that Geordie detective, remember?"

Sam was shocked to hear her course language, and his eyes did not disguise his displeasure.

"Sorry, Dad," Estelle uttered, glancing sheepishly at him.

"He's called Toby, and he's not a hunk, he's a knob, but don't tell her I said that."

Estelle's eyes widened.

"What do you mean, Dad?" Maggie pulled at her father's arm wanting to know more. "Are we going to meet this maid of yours?"

Sam laughed at Maggie's calling Penny a 'maid'. She had no intention of hiding her Devon roots, and why should she?

The genie was well and truly out of the bottle now, and he knew he had to explain.

"Yes, you are going to meet her – in about three weeks' time, if you're free, that is? You've been invited to stay at her place and go to a celebrity bash."

The look of disbelief on their faces was wonderful.

"Dad, you sly old fox! How long have you known her?" Maggie asked.

"Remember when I went to London with Mum's ashes? And remember I told you I spent the day with this beautiful young woman in a park?" Neither of the girls answered. "You didn't believe me, did you? Well . . . it was Penny."

Maggie lowered her head, as if in shame, and peered out at him under her eyelashes. She felt embarrassed because she had doubted him.

"Does the maid know I didn't believe you?" she murmured.

Sam didn't say anything, just nodded.

"What's Penny like, Dad?" Estelle asked, keen to know more about this new woman in their father's life.

"She's lovely, very sweet, and a very talented actress. We've become good mates, that's all. No strings, just good pals."

His daughters were now dumb-struck at the thought of their father taking them to London to be guests of his new friend.

"Our old dad mixing it with celebs, how cool is that, sis?" said Maggie excitingly.

He smiled at her, but he shook his head.

"Most of them are in a different world to us, but some of them are very lovely – and just wait until you meet Archie, he's a great laugh! You'll like him Mags. And I think you will too, Estelle, he's an interesting 'personality'!"

Both girls laughed at that.

"Right, you two, when you're both ready . . . it is my birthday, remember, and I'm getting thirsty!"

Later on in the pub he told them more about Penny and her barmy aunties, and how it was they who had roused the interest in Shakespeare in him. They listened, fascinated, and were genuinely happy to see their old dad with a smile on his face.

Penny phoned again when they got home, a little worse for wear, and after he'd said his goodbyes, both girls talked to her for what seemed liked ages. He kissed them goodnight and wandered off to bed. It had been a good birthday.

Chapter 22

No Time to Sleep

Sam ticked off the date on his wall diary.

Come on, Sam, you old fart, get your finger out or they'll start the party without you, he thought, knowing the opening of his new letting agency office in Bristol was running behind schedule. He'd decided to change his plans and make a detour on his way to London. He had planned to go up a day early on his way to May and June's, and collect his new suits and shirts on the way. He dialled their number.

"Hi, June, it's Sam."

"Hello, dear!" came the welcome reply. "Everything alright, dear, you sound rushed?"

She was right, he was, and that was the last thing he wanted to be.

"June, I can't make it up today, I've got to go to Bristol this morning," he said, apologetically. "I'll stay over in Bristol tonight and then get an early train up tomorrow. Hopefully I shall be with you by lunchtime. Sorry to mess you about."

"Oh that's perfectly alright, dear, don't concern yourself," June soothed, fully aware that he owned a busy company. "You just turn up when you like, dear." She then told him her news: "Penny phoned earlier. She's so excited about meeting your young ladies, and so are we," she said, hearing him laugh.

"Those girls of mine have cost me a small fortune this week.

They cried 'Daddy, we're skint and we want new dresses, help us!'"

"You can't take it with you, dear, now can you?" June said.

"You're right, but at this rate, I won't have any left to leave behind!"

The remainder of the day was taken up with meetings with builders, meetings with landlords, interviewing staff and piles of paperwork. It was gone four in the morning by the time he slumped onto his hotel bed.

"Good morning," June said, standing in the kitchen as May walked in, still in her nightdress as usual.

"Have you heard from Sam today?" May asked, filling up the kettle for the first of many cups of tea she'd drink throughout the day.

"No, dear, not yet, but it's still early. I don't expect he'll arrive before midday," June replied, putting on her apron. "We must ask Penny what her plans are for Sunday lunch, dear. If Sam's daughters come, plus Toby, that will be seven of us and we'll have to get some more food in."

"Seven for lunch!" May exclaimed. "I can't remember the last time we had that many people around our table!"

June smiled, and then became a little more subdued.

"Toby . . . it won't be any trouble feeding that man . . . he'll have beans on toast I expect," May chuckled.

"There you are, governor."

Sam took his change from the taxi driver.

"Hi, honeys, I'm home," he shouted as he let himself in.

The sisters were in the lounge, resting after their lunch.

"My god, Sam! Have you seen the rings under your eyes? When was the last time you slept?" asked May. She patted his cheek in a caring way.

"Hello, May. Do I really look that bad?" he asked, as he removed his jacket. "It's been a hectic couple of days, but I'll feel a lot better after a cup of tea."

"I'll get you a cup. You sit down," May told him, as she headed in the direction of the kitchen.

"No, he won't," June said adamantly. "I tell you what you're going to do, Sam. You're going to get yourself to bed and we'll *bring* you your cup of tea. Have you eaten? No, of course you haven't. I'll make you a sandwich." She sounded very concerned for his well-being. "How do you think Penny and your girls would feel if you ended up dead on your feet?"

He looked at her, but was too tired to respond with any objective argument, so he just gave her a smile of resignation as he ran his fingers through his hair.

"Don't let me sleep too long, June."

She walked over to where Sam had laid his new suits over the back of the settee.

"You go on up, I'll hang these up ready for you. We'll bring you a cup of tea and run a bath for you at five. Now off you go," she said, with her hands on her hips. She sounded like a sergeant major on the parade ground!

"May, dear, be a love and take Sam's tea and sandwich up to him."

May returned a short while later, still with them in her hand.

"He's asleep already, dear," she said. "I've brought his phone down in case it rings and wakes him up."

June smiled at her in agreement, saying, "Good, he needs his sleep."

And then as if by fate his phone rang.

"Oh my," May said, as she pushed it into her sisters hand. "You answer it, June, go on, quickly."

She hadn't used this type of phone before. She'd used Penny's, but Sam's was bigger and different. She remembered seeing him swiping the screen with his finger to answer it.

"Hello, Dad, is that you?"

June spoke very quietly, and put her hand over it, thinking it would mask her voice.

"It's one of his daughters, dear."

"Well speak to her, you fool!" spouted May.

"Hello, dear, it's June, one of Penny's aunties. Your father is asleep, poor dear, he was so tired when he arrived so we made him go to bed."

Estelle listened to the unfamiliar voice.

"I'm Estelle, his daughter. So Daddy's gone to sleep? We keep telling him to slow down, but he never listens."

May was trying to put her ear to the phone as well, so she could listen in on the conversation.

"So where are you, dear?" June asked.

"I'm at the station waiting for Maggie, my sister. She's on another train. I've just phoned her and she'll be here in twenty minutes," Estelle replied, thinking it sweet that her dad had two elderly ladies looking after him. "Dad told us a lot about you both. He said you're very sweet and kind."

June felt a bit taken aback by Estelle's relay of her father's kind words.

"Oh dear! I'll have to speak to him about saying nice things like that! We have a reputation to keep!" June replied. She heard Estelle giggle.

"I better go, June. Maggie said she'd phone me before the train gets in."

But before they said goodbye, Estelle told June how to end the call on her father's phone.

And Don't Forget the Roses

"Well, what was she like then, do tell?" May asked impatiently.

"Be a dear, May, and put the kettle on, and I'll tell you all about her. My hands are killing me."

"Sam, dear, time to wake up. It's five o'clock and May's running you a bath," June said gently. Sam was still tucked up in bed, fully clothed. "There's a cup of tea for you here."

He opened his eyes and rubbing them with the palms of his hands.

"God, I needed that. What time did you say it was?"

"Just past five. Penny phoned. She said your girls have arrived safe and sound, and they're getting on like a house on fire."

That made Sam smile. His girls could be a handful together, but with Penny thrown into the mix too!

"Your suits and shirts are hanging on the back of the door, dear," June said as she left the room. "We've ironed your shirts again, they were a bit creased. Must say your suits look awfully good. And . . . oh yes, I almost forgot . . . Penny said, 'Don't let the bugger go back to sleep!'" She chuckled to herself as she walked out of the bedroom.

After his bath and shave, Sam prepared to get dressed. Which suit though? The blue pinstripe, or this beast?

"May! May! Come and see this handsome man in our lounge! Honestly, if I was Penny's age I'd marry you tomorrow!" said June, brushing Sam's suit jacket down with the flats of her hands.

"June, careful darling, your arthritis," he told her.

"Don't fuss so. We have to make sure you look your best for your ladies, now don't we," she said sternly.

He felt very comfortable in his new suit, but it took him ages to fix his bow tie. He leant forward and kissed June on the cheek.

"I hope I get one of those, Sam! After all, I did cook brunch!" said May, taking her place in the kissing queue.

"Doesn't he look smart, May! I like your patent leather shoes, all very coordinated, dear. Archie will be impressed. He likes men to dress well. So many don't even bother to wear a tie these days."

Glancing at the clock, Sam noticed it had just passed six thirty and he had to be at Penny's by seven.

"Well, ladies, do I pass muster?" he laughed. "Because I've got to be off. Madam will kill me if I'm late!"

The sisters cackled loudly on hearing Sam call their niece 'madam', a term of endearment they found amusing, especially coming from Sam.

"Yes, you'll pass," June said. "Now be on your way!"

Chapter 23

Tunnel Vision

Arriving outside Penny's House, Sam could hear laughing and loud voices coming from inside even before he rang the doorbell. He listened for a few moments to identify who was the nosiest. Maggie! He'd recognise that laugh anywhere!

Penny was upstairs getting herself ready when she heard the door.

She called down the stairs, "Could one of you be a darling and answer the door, it's probably your father."

Estelle opened it, still wearing her bathrobe.

"Hello, Dad!" she said joyfully as he walked in and kissed her.

The air was heavy with perfume, but one fragrance stood out above all – Maggie's.

"Bloody hell, Dad! You look the dog's bollocks!" she laughed, as she topped up her glass of wine.

He smiled and rolled his eyes.

"Thank you, Mags, for those kind words." He gave her a big hug. He looked at the vision of beauty before him in a red crepe off-the-shoulder dress and said, "You look stunning in that dress, my darling." Maggie did a little curtsy and giggled, thanking him. He noticed Estelle had disappeared. "Where's your sister vanished to?" he asked.

"Oh, they two are still getting ready, she's gone back upstairs. Would you like a glass of wine, Dad."

They two! He smiled to himself. You can take the girl out of Devon, but you can't take Devon out of the Maggie.

"Yes, my darling, a glass of wine would be lovely," he replied.

"Tell you what, Dad," Maggie said, grinning, "that maid is really lovely. We haven't stopped laughing and talking since we arrived, and she thinks the world of *you*. She's been asking us what you were like when we were younger and things like that." It made her happy to think that her father was making new friends and rebuilding his life after the loss of her mother.

Sam could hear voices coming down the stairs and Estelle entered the room, making a beeline for the glass of wine Maggie was holding out in her hand for her. She was the taller of the girls, with a figure that would grace any catwalk, and she looked stunning.

"My god. All this beauty in one room! How can a man sustain such an assault on his senses?" he cried.

Estelle smiled, and the dimples in her cheeks became more pronounced. She was wearing an emerald-green satin dress, which complemented her complexion. Sam was so proud to be their father, and told them how their mother would have been so happy to see them in their finery, all dressed up with somewhere to go.

He then heard someone behind him clearing their throat in a manner as if to say *I'm here, Sam*. He turned around to see Penny standing a few feet from him in a stunning silvery-blue taffeta halter-neck dress. Her hair was arranged in a French knot that exposed her bare shoulders and elegant neck. Suddenly he felt as if the oxygen in the room had been sucked out and he gasped for breath. The expression on his face was beyond description, but in his eyes Penny could see everything she needed to know. He walked over to her and kissed her cheek, a tender peck that treated his lips to the pleasurable experience of her soft skin. In that second, Sam remembered the first time he'd set eyes on her and, like then, she had accentuated her natural beauty and skin to perfect effect rather than plaster her face with make-up.

"Hello, Sam." She smiled at him, a gentle, welcoming *I'm happy to see you* smile.

"So what do you think?" she asked, giving him her now customary twirl.

As Sam gazed at the beautiful woman inches from him, he couldn't even blink, it was as if he had tunnel vision . . . all he could see was her.

"What do I think?. . ." His voice was gentle. "I think that if Toby doesn't fall at your feet and tell you in his first breath how beautiful you look, he needs his head examining."

Penny moved nearer to Sam, so close he could feel her sweet breath on his face.

"What makes you think I did all this for Toby?" she asked softly, and then turned to look at the girls and winked.

"Be careful, Penny," Estelle said. "At Dad's age, all this excitement could be bad for his blood pressure."

"OK, I see, we're a gang of three now are we?" he said, smiling. "With you three beautiful women in my charge, Estelle's probably right about my blood pressure!"

Penny inspected him up and down with an approving eye.

"James Bond move over! You look very handsome, Sam," she declared. "Now take your jacket off!" she ordered. He hesitated. "Go on, take it off," she repeated with an air of authority in her voice.

He now felt a sense of *deja vu* come over him. He looked at his daughters and said, "The last time she said something like that, we were standing in a park in broad daylight. Then she proceeded to undo my belt and pull my shirt out and rearrange me, so to speak."

"So she should, Dad," Estelle replied. "It's not cool for men to wear shirts tucked in these days, except with suits."

"Put your arms out," Penny said, and then proceeded to remove his cufflinks. "Maggie, be a dear, in my bag over there, there is a small box. Can you bring it to me, please?" He watched, feeling like a spectator of his own life. "Right, Sam, you bugger," she said, sounding cross at him. "You never told me it was your birthday." Then she picked a pair of cufflinks from the box and fitted them to his shirt cuffs. "There you go. Happy birthday." She placed a small birthday kiss on his cheek.

He inspected the silver cufflinks, each with a cream porcelain square top with an inscription written in the glaze.

"Go on, Dad, what do they say?" enquired Maggie.

He looked at Penny, his smile holding back the temptation to frown. She could see he was touched with the gift she had given him.

"It's Shakespeare . . . a few words from *Richard the Second*."

He nodded his head, and then they listened as he recited more of the words from memory, his gaze never stirring from Penny's eyes: "'*This royal throne of kings, this sceptered isle, this blessed plot, this earth, this realm, this England. . .*'"

As he finished, his face became smeared with two shades of lipstick as Maggie and Estelle kissed him, watched by Penny who clapped her hands, impressed at the way he recited the words to her.

"OK, you lot, you've had your fun," he said sternly. "Haven't we got a party to go to?"

Chapter 24

Tease

As the taxi pulled up outside Claridge's Hotel, Mayfair, the doorman welcomed them, assisting Maggie and Estelle out of the car, followed by Penny. Sam paid the driver, and once they were all inside they were ushered through to Archie's private party.

"There's Archie, talking to a waiter," Penny said, quietly sneaking up on him, whispering in his ear, "Hello, Arch."

He quickly turned and cried with boyish excitement, "Penny, darling!" He air-kissed her, cheek-to-cheek. "You look fabulous, sweetie!" He then looked at Sam and his daughters as they joined them. "Farmer, my dear friend!" he gasped, clasping both his hands around Sam's. "Are these two beautiful women your daughters?" he asked, taking Estelle's and then Maggie's hands in turn and placing a kiss upon them. "Of course they are, how silly of me! This one has your proud stance!" Archie said looking at Estelle, still holding onto her hand. "And this creature definitely has your eyes; full of mischief and passion," he observed, with a puppy-like smile.

The girls giggled in response to Archie's flattery. Penny put her arm though Sam's, and they watched as Archie, his arms now around his daughters' waists, escorted them into the venue.

"Looks like you're stuck with me," Penny informed Sam, with a faux forlorn look.

"Yes," he sighed. "Looks that way." He shot her a smile, but he could see her looking around for Toby. "Any sign of him?" he asked.

"No," she muttered, "I'll ask Arch if he's here yet."

He noticed she had a strained and pensive look on her face, rather than the look of a woman searching the crowds for her beloved.

They mingled amongst the other forty-plus guests. Waiters were milling around with drinks and canapés. Sam remembered being introduced to many of them on the earlier occasion they'd met.

"Sorry, dears, had to greet Sir Richard, and just introduced him to Aaron," Archie said, returning, minus Sam's two daughters.

"Have you seen Toby, Arch?" Penny asked.

"Yes, sweetie, he's over there." He pointed in the direction of a small lounge area. "He's holding court with some lovelies." He finished off the remains of his glass of brandy. "He said to tell you to go over when you arrive," he added, knowing all too well what Penny's response to that statement would be. She now looked distressed, and Sam noticed that her whole body seemed to tense.

"Oh did he?" she replied, unhappy at being told what to do by Toby. *The shit*, she thought.

Sam put his hand around her waist and gave it a gentle squeeze. He knew she wasn't happy, and the last thing any of them wanted was a showdown between the two of them tonight.

"Come on, Sam, I promised your girls I'd find them millionaire boyfriends," she said, trying to appear up-beat, but her eyes betrayed her anxiety.

Nearly forty minutes had passed when Sam noticed Toby heading towards them.

"Your man is on the way," he said, as he started to remove his arm from hers.

And Don't Forget the Roses

"What are you doing?" she asked.

"Toby's coming," he replied. "If I was him I'm not sure if I would be pleased to see my fiancée with her arm linked with another man."

"Does it bother you that I'm holding your arm?" she asked.

"No, but it bothers me you're teasing him and using me to do it."

Penny knew he was right, and then sighed, saying, "I'm sorry."

"Hello, pet," Toby said, moving forward to kiss her. She turned her head, leaving his lips in mid-pout.

"You've met Sam, haven't you?" she said, making sure *she* got the first salvo in. "So what do you think of my dress, hun?" she smiled.

Toby stepped back and looked at her as she made a pose for him.

"It's alright, Pet, nice colour."

Penny's smile disappeared, and her eyes filled with anger.

Toby turned to speak to Sam. It was clear he was agitated because he was there.

"Would you mind if I talked to Penny, private like?" he asked.

Sam nodded, and gestured with his hand and said, "Not at all. I expect you've got a lot to catch up on," giving Penny an overly long kiss on her cheek.

Who's teasing who now? she thought, raising a small smile. He wandered off the find his girls.

"I'll catch you later, Sam," she whispered.

Toby moved to stand directly in front of Penny, a large glass of white wine in his hand.

"What's that all about, pet, you holding his arm and letting him kiss you like that? You can see the old man fancies you," he said, as he tried and failed to kiss her for the second time.

She grabbed his arm and moved to an area a few feet away, giving them a little privacy to talk.

"Don't say that about him," she said in a tense, muted voice. "He doesn't fancy me, he's just a very good and kind friend."

Toby laughed.

"Why? Is he gay? Has he turned? Is he one of Archie's stable mates?"

Penny wasn't at all pleased to hear a friend of hers, any friend of hers, being spoken about in that manner.

"Toby, wind your sodding neck in. I won't have you speak about him, or any other friends of mine, like that," she said, her eyes burning into him.

"Sorry, pet," he said, showing her his boyish smile, and he then succeeded in placing a kiss on her cheek. "So, what are our plans, pet?" he asked, acting as if Penny's annoyance with him was just playful banter.

"To meet up with Sam and his girls. It would be rude of us to just walk off and leave them . . . besides, I'm hoping to see Aaron again," she said, smiling and acknowledging people she knew.

"What? That Herman Yank?" Toby said jokingly, grinning and thinking she would find his comment amusing. He moved closer to her, instinctively putting his hand around her waist pulling her to him.

"Give me some bloody air, Toby," she demanded, trying to wriggle free. She had a look of sheer exasperation on her face. "Who do you think you are? I invite people for the weekend to meet you, and invite you here to Archie's party, and all you can do is take the piss out of Aaron. Do you not realise that it's because of talented writers like him that I'm inspired to be a better actor, and you would be, too, if you had any pride in your craft." She gave him a sorrowful gaze, at a loss as to why the Toby she fell in love with was not standing in front of her tonight.

"What is wrong with you, sweetheart?" she asked when he didn't reply, again puzzled by his attitude. "You didn't even bother to dress smartly. Some of the people here are in suits that cost thousands of pounds, and yet here you are in black jeans and a scruffy black shirt. You never used to be like this, did you?" She frowned deeply, not bothering to hide how despondent she felt. "Come on, let's find the others and get some food."

Estelle was deep in conversation with a tall, handsome actor when Penny and Toby joined them.

"Jack, honey, keep your grubby hands of this beautiful young lady," she said.

"Hello, darling," he replied, greeting her by pecking her on both cheeks. (He looked at Toby and wondered what she saw in him.)

She introduced Toby to Estelle, and along with many men that evening, he was entranced by her elegance and stunning green eyes. He wasted no time in showing her all the charm and charisma that Penny had in recent times thought he'd lost, and had been missing in their relationship.

"Where's your father, sweetheart?" Penny asked Estelle, who at five-foot ten-inches without shoes was as tall as her father, and with her three-inch heels could easily see over the heads of fellow guests.

"I think he's over there with the strange-looking American and Archie," Estelle replied, pointing to a side lounge.

"Toby, I'm sure you wouldn't mind entertaining Estelle while I catch up with Aaron," Penny said.

She kissed the side of his face, feeling that after his earlier antics he didn't deserve the pleasure of her lips on his.

Penny had no trouble finding Aaron – she just followed the

sound of the low, booming laughter coming from the direction of the lounge.

"Aaron, great to see you again. No, don't get up," she said. "I'll sit next to Sam. Move over you," she said, shuffling up next to him on the Chesterfield sofa.

Aaron was elated to see her again, remembering how she'd helped him on his last visit.

"Hi there, ma'am, Penny. Sure is nice to see you again," he said, putting his huge hand out to greet her. "Me and Sam here have been talking about your aunties," he continued, looking very thoughtful. "They sure sound like characters," he said, raising a broad smile, making the skin on his face tighten and stretch over his broad and pronounced cheek bones.

"Ah, I wondered what the raucous laughter was about. Those aunties of mine can be buggers at times," she said. She looked at the glass in Sam's hand. "What's that you're drinking?" she asked, reaching over and taking it from him.

"Single malt, so go easy," he replied, watching her as she put the glass of whisky to her lips, closing her eyes as the liquid aroused the senses on her pallet. He put his hand gently on the top of her arm, keen to tell her the news, "and Aaron's informed me he's finished his play and is ready to see your aunties again." He removed his hand.

She turned and glanced at him as if to say *Don't take it away, please.* He could see in her eyes that it wasn't to tease Toby this time, but for comfort, and instinctively he knew Toby had upset her again.

"So, you've finished it already, have you Aaron?" she asked, impressed with the pace he had worked. "I'll tell them. They'll be happy to see you."

Aaron beamed his infectious smile at them both. She could sense that Aaron was happy to be in her company, and then she felt a strange sense of comradeship between the three of them, like a three-piece jigsaw puzzle being put together for a reason.

They continued to talk about the play for over half an hour, until Archie returned with Maggie; shortly afterwards Estelle and Toby joined them too. Archie had arranged for a buffet to be served and they ate, people drifting home afterwards; most of the other guests had left by midnight.

Toby sat down next to Penny; Sam was at the bar drinking tequila slammers with Maggie.

"Dad, can I tell you something?" she asked, looking around the bar area, making sure no one could overhear their conversation. "You're right about Toby, he is a knob, isn't he?" she said knocking back her tequila. "He doesn't deserve her. She's just like you said: sweet and very beautiful."

He nodded in agreement.

"I think what I actually said was '. . . she's very sweet and very talented', but you're right, she is beautiful too," he replied, remembering how she had left him gasping for air earlier that evening.

"She certainly makes your pulse race, don't she, Dad," she replied with a cheeky grin. She leant forward to give her father a loving kiss.

"I may be in my fifties," he replied, "but I still know a beautiful woman when I see one. I'm looking at one now." He put his hand up to the barman for another round.

"Archie's a love, isn't he? Did I tell you I already knew him; well, knew *of* him really. I spent a couple of days at his stud farm in Dorset before I graduated, but I never got to meet him until tonight."

"I might have known you two would hit it off, especially with your love of horses!" he laughed, watching her knock back another tequila.

"I could do with one of those," said a familiar voice.

"Hello, babe. You OK?" he asked, seeing the troubled look on Penny's face.

She stood next to him and linked her arm through his, breathing a deep sigh.

"No, not really," she replied. "Toby's drunk again, and the sod made a couple of sly remarks at Aaron. Archie's getting his driver to take him back to his mate's flat." She was clearly angry with him.

Sam watched Maggie gently run her hand up and down Penny's arm to comfort her.

"Never mind, maid," she said, giving her a broad smile, "the nights still young."

"Well . . ." Penny replied, now sounding livelier. "Archie thought we could go to a club in Soho." She shot Sam a mischievous look. "Or do you need your beauty sleep?" she asked, undoing his bow tie and top button for him. "There you go, Mr Bond," she said.

He gave her a suave smile. "Thank you, Miss Moneypenny," he purred. "Oh, I think I can hobble on behind. What do you reckon Mags? Soho?" he asked.

"Bloody hell, Dad, that's a no-brainer, me and sis – we're up for it!"

Sam never got to his bed that night. It was approaching four thirty by the time they got back to Penny's house. Penny didn't want him scaring her aunts and offered him the settee or the floor, and blankets. There was no point arguing, and he was too tired, so crashed out on the settee.

Chapter 25

Pizza

"Good morning, Sam!" said June, seeing him enter the kitchen. "I take it you all had a good evening? I was wondering if you would stay over at Penny's . . ." she mused, putting the kettle on.

"I was up by six. I didn't manage to get much sleep, so thought I'd walk here to clear my head. I needed to," he replied, stretching his arms above him, touching the kitchen ceiling. "I thought I'd have a shower and some breakfast, and then make my way back to wake the buggers up. Sorry, June . . . that's my phone ringing."

Sam took the call in the lounge and paced up and down while he listened. When he walked back into the kitchen, his body language and facial expression did not bode well for a happy weekend.

"June, I have to get myself back to Bristol. My manager's father has sadly died, so now I've got builders standing around not knowing what to do, and we open on Monday. I'll have a shower, grab some gear, and be on my way." He shook his head and frowned. "Bugger! I was looking forward to spending time with you all."

His mind was now whirling around like a top, trying to get his priorities in some sort of order as he showered. He then packed his bag and was about to head downstairs, when May entered his bedroom.

"Good morning, dear."

"Hi, May. June told you the news, I take it?" he asked.

"Yes, dear, but you're not leaving yet, you're having breakfast first, and don't argue, come down when you're ready," she said.

Eating his breakfast as ordered, he was quietly pleased that they'd made him some; he knew he wouldn't have much time to eat once he got to Bristol.

"When the girls come around for Sunday lunch, you make sure those minxes do the washing up," he told June as she topped up his cup of tea. "It's probably a good job I won't be here listening to five women yapping away hour after hour, it would probably make my ears bleed!" He took a bite of his toast.

"We're sad you won't be here, and Penny won't be happy, I'm sure."

"She'll be fine. She'll be having too much fun with my girls, I expect!"

"I don't think that's true . . ." June replied, knowing he was pulling her leg. "I'll tell her you said that!" She put her hand on his arm, and said softly, "Don't overdo it, dear, or we'll send Penny down to sort you out."

"'*She is a wasp, he had better beware her sting*'," he replied.

June hooted with laughter.

"My, my, Sam, your Shakespeare is certainly improving! I'll tell her you compared her to Katherine the shrew."

Sam gave her a look of horror.

"Oh God, don't do that! She'll get Maggie to do something nasty to me!"

When Sam was on the train he called Estelle.

"Hello, sweetheart, it's Dad. Are you out of bed yet?" he asked quietly.

"Hi, Dad. Me and Mags are sitting in bed with Penny. Have you seen the size of it? You could have some serious fun on this!" said Estelle, giggling down the phone.

And Don't Forget the Roses

"Can you put Penny on, darling?" he asked, listening to girly screams of laughter in the background.

"Hi, Sam! Are you still at my aunties' or are you on your way here?" she asked, sounding happy and buoyant.

"Sorry, but I'm on train to Bristol. My manager has had to go on compassionate leave."

"Oh no! That's not fair! I'm so sorry. We were planning what to do tonight."

She told the girls the bad news. Penny knew there wasn't anything that could be done; after all, he did have a business to run.

As when he was last in Bristol, he worked late into the night, and it was Sunday afternoon before he had time to phone Penny's aunties.

"June, it's Sam. How are you coping? It sounds like mayhem!" Once again he could hear laughing and general pandemonium in the background.

"Hello, dear," she replied. "We're having a wonderful time. Your girls are a credit to you. I've never laughed so much in years. Do you want to speak to Penny? I'll get her, dear."

As he waited for Penny, the decorator approached him.

"Give me five minutes," he told the impatient man.

"Hi, Sam, it's *Katherine* here . . ."

Oh shit, he thought. *June told her!*

"Hello, babe!"

"Don't babe me, you bugger, *a wasp am I*," she replied.

It didn't take him long to realise she was just having fun with him. He knew if she was truly angry she would have replace the word 'bugger' with 'bastard'.

"Those aunts of yours would get two stones fighting, besides, I have a soft spot for Katherine, she's a marshmallow really."

If that doesn't do it, he thought, *then nothing will*! He was relieved to hear her laughing down the phone!

"OK, Sam, you've pressed the right buttons, I'll forgive you this time."

"Thank you. I'll sleep better tonight now." (*If you do get any sleep*, she thought when she heard him say that.) "By the sound of all the commotion going on, you're having a great time without me. Is Toby with you?" he asked, hoping the answer would be *no*. (He could hear her telling May to be quiet as she could hardly hear him.)

"No, he's gone to watch the rugby."

Sam could see the impatient decorator pacing up and down still waiting to speak to him.

"Sorry, I've got to go, I'll call you in a couple of days. Tell the girls the same."

He ended the call feeling depressed; this wasn't where he wanted to be.

As promised, he texted Penny first before calling: 'Hello, babe, are you Penny today or Katherine? Sx'.

She laughed when she read that, realising this would be the private joke between them from now on. They talked for nearly an hour. She told him how much she loved his daughters and that they could stay with her anytime, and that Archie had treated them to dinner at the Ritz on Saturday night. He was envious; all he'd had was a pizza.

Chapter 26

Masterpiece

"I thought I heard the front door," said June, taking Archie's coat from him.

"Hello, sweetie!" he replied. "I hope you don't mind me just dropping in like this, unannounced, but I do need to speak to both of you."

Archie, as on most days, was wearing a pinstriped suit and cravat, with a silk handkerchief tumbling out of his breast pocket; flamboyant to some, but with his wealth he could afford to have impeccable (albeit slightly eccentric) taste in clothes.

"Come through to the lounge, dear, I'll put the kettle on."

It wasn't long before May came downstairs from her afternoon nap to catch up on events and hear all the latest news; the one thing the three of them enjoyed was a good gossip. They had known Archie since he was born, and they knew he didn't just pop in on friends without a good reason.

"So, why are you here, Archie dear, is it about Aaron's play?" June asked, making an informative guess it was in response to Aaron's recent visit to them.

Archie held the sisters in high regard for what they had achieved in their lifetime. You didn't get honoured with an OBE, or be made a Dame of the British Empire, without having the respect of your peers. They had dedicated their lives to the Bard – for them Shakespeare had no equal – and if ever they gave their approval to a performance or to a writer's script, people took note.

Archie sat on his own on one of the settees. May sat on the other. June stood up to one side, her old hip once again giving her discomfort.

They observed him rolling his hands, looking tense and nervous. With their skill at observation, it gave them the upper hand when it came to assessing a state of affairs unfolding in front of them; an advantage they wouldn't hesitate to use mercilessly to their own benefit, and Penny's, if it concerned her.

Archie sipped at his Earl Grey tea; the sisters preferred the supermarket's 'Best Buy', but always made sure they had his favourite brand in for when he did call.

"I've spoken to Aaron, and as you rightly stated June, this is about his play. The lovely man is over the moon with your praise," said Archie, looking directly at her. "Do you really think his play is a masterpiece of modern interpretation of the *Shrew*?" he asked.

They both replied in unison: "Yes!"

"Without a shadow of a doubt," confirmed June. "There are a few areas which require alteration, of course – mostly to the pace and tone of certain sections of the script – but other than that, it's an outstanding piece of writing," she exclaimed.

Archie leant back into the settee, sprawling a little.

"Don't do that, Archie dear, it doesn't become you," said May.

"Sorry, darling," he replied, with a polite smile.

"An actress dreams a script like that will come her way," she said, sounding slightly envious towards the lucky actress who would play the leading lady. She then glanced at her sister, giving her a slight wink. "Tell you what, June, whoever they get to play Katherine has to be a cut above the best, don't you think?"

Archie was listening intently.

And Don't Forget the Roses

"That's the reason I've come to see you both," he said, not sure which of the two ladies to look at first, his head going from left to right as if he was watching a tennis match as he spoke. "Aaron has had a lot of interest from producers and directors about the script . . . even from Sir Richard."

"That's fantastic, dear," replied June. "He would be a worthy producer, and I expect Aaron must be elated with the prospect."

Archie now looked sheepish and forlorn, and started fidgeting in his seat.

"Aaron has made one stipulation," he said, and then he sat forward, pulling at his shirt cuffs. "He dearly desires the play to have its premiere in London, but insists that unless he gets the actress *he wants* to play Katherine, he'll take it back to America . . . and you know what would happen then . . . whoever gets to produce it will probably choose some Hollywood has-been and ruin it."

For a few moments nobody spoke, and then Archie looked up and said, "The actress he wants is Penny. He's very insistent about that. It's Penny or no one."

June turned to look at May. They were clearly ecstatic at the thought of their niece being given the role. But what he didn't know was that the sisters were several pages ahead of him.

"That's fantastic news, Archie, have you told her?" asked May.

"No," replied Archie, shaking his head. "There's a problem. I'm sorry to have to say this . . ." He fidgeted some more before taking a deep breath and saying, "None of the producers want to have her as Katherine."

"Surely not! She's perfect for the role. How can they say that?" June cried, not expecting to have heard of such disregard towards her niece.

May got up from the settee and stood directly in front of Archie.

"What about Sir Richard? He's well aware of her abilities," she asked.

Archie now felt enclosed and uncomfortable with her looming over him, and June looking at him like the teapot would fly in his direction at any moment.

"He says that due to his position on the Arts Council, he couldn't involve himself," Archie replied, tersely. "No one wants her for the part, and I feel as badly as you. I love that woman as much as you do. They say it's because she doesn't stand out like a lot of other actresses. It's all to do with bankrolling, believe me, I've tried. You know what they say about her? That she's afraid of her mother's shadow . . . and yours." He knew his words would cut them like a blunt knife and tear at their emotions, for this was a woman they'd raised like she was their own daughter. He felt tears prick his eyes.

June turned and smiled a rather knowing smile, which was received by May with an accepting nod and a quiet, "Yes, dear."

June now rested herself on the arm of Archie's settee and took hold of his hand.

"Oh do stop snivelling, Archie," she said, and then used her considerable acting skills to her advantage. "Do you really think our angel could do this, because we do?" she asked, watching him wipe tears away from his eyes.

"Of course I do, she's a bloody McCain, isn't she."

"Well, then, that's settled. We will fund the production, May and I. We know how it works; God, don't we know how it works," she replied.

Archie look perplexed.

"You haven't got that sort of money?" he said. "We're talking hundreds of thousands of pounds here. No one will lend you that amount . . . you're too old, too high a risk." (He clearly thought it was a preposterous idea.)

And Don't Forget the Roses

"We'll mortgage this place. It's Penny's when we go anyway. You know what these properties are worth. They go for a king's ransom. For Christ's sake, we're just down the road from Knightsbridge. No. We won't have any trouble raising the cash," said May as she leant over to Archie and kissed his cheek.

"No!" he countered. "No! I won't allow it."

He ran his fingers thought his hair, now sensing a pincer movement on him by the sisters.

"It's not your decision, Archie, and if she fails – which she won't – we'll live out our days in an old people's home in Southend," May declared forthrightly.

"No!" he replied again, sounding more desperate. "If Penny found out she'd be furious as hell, and wouldn't agree!" (He was now panicking at the thought of what they planned to do.)

"Then we won't tell her, will we, Archie dear?" said June, mentally turning the screws on him. "Now go and tell Aaron you've got the finance." She looked directly across at May and winked.

Archie stared at the floor. Then he sat back in the settee knowing he'd been out manoeuvred.

"OK, you two scheming witches," he said, letting out a long sigh. "I give in . . . I'll bankroll her."

May gave June the thumbs-up sign behind his back as she kissed him.

"There you go, Archie dear, now, don't you feel better?"

"Penny hasn't said yes yet," he informed them.

June put her hand on Archie's shoulder.

"Leave her to us. She'll do it."

Chapter 27

The Cottage

Penny and Sam hadn't spoken to each other for a while. She had been to Portugal on holiday with Toby, and since her return her acting commitments had been many, and what with Sam's work load . . . The occasional text had been sent to keep in touch, but nothing of any particular length or detail. Then one Friday afternoon he got a call from her out the blue.

"Sam, it's Penny."

"Hi, babe," he replied, pleased to hear her voice, but for no apparent reason he suddenly felt something was wrong. "Everything alright?" he asked in a casual tone.

"Everything's fine, Sam," she replied, sounding relaxed, putting him at ease. "Are you at home for the weekend?"

"I am. I've got nothing planned. Why?"

"Do you fancy having two gorgeous women stay with you?" she asked, waiting attentively for his reply.

"Yes! That would be lovely," he laughed. "Who are they?"

"You know one of them – she's called *Katherine* – and her friend Suzie."

"Really? So no Penny, then?"

"Oh, she might turn up later, Sam. Depends what mood Katherine is in," she said.

He laughed again, and she realised she had missed that laugh.

And Don't Forget the Roses

He won't be laughing when he hears what I have to tell him, she thought.

"Looking forward to it immensely," he replied, and he meant it.

"That's great. Thank you. I'm looking forward to coming down, but I'm sorry it's at such short notice."

"No problem. So where are you?"

"Cardiff. I've been here all week. We're getting a lift to Bristol, and then we can get a train to Exeter. Would you be able to pick us up?" she asked.

"Of course," he replied. "Phone me when you're on the train. It'll be wonderful to see you again."

"Could we possibly use your washing machine also? We've been living out of suitcases for a week."

"No, sadly, uz yockles still wash our clothes in the stream . . ."

"Sam, you bugger! I almost believed you!"

"Is it OK if you two share a bed?" he asked.

"Of course it is," Penny answered.

Sam swept through the cottage, tidying up, getting the bedroom ready, and even preparing cottage pie for their evening meal.

He had just stepped out of the shower when Penny called to say they were on the train, and that they were packed in like sardines. He quickly calculated how long he had before they arrived at the station, dressed, and jumped in the car. This was a new experience for him, having Penny stay, and he hoped she would like the cottage. *Who wouldn't?* he thought.

Glancing in the window of the florist at the station, he saw what he was looking for. He then went to wait on the platform.

"Hello, ladies," he said, as Penny and Suzie walked up to him. He placed a single red rose in Penny's hand, and gave her a welcoming kiss on her cheek. "And this one is for you," he said, as he gave the other rose to Suzie.

"That's so nice of you!" she replied, beckoning him to lean forward so she could give him a peck on the cheek.

"Hey! Keep your greasy hands off him, Penny laughed, with a mock glare. "I saw him first!"

He led the way to the car and opened the doors for the ladies.

"This wouldn't look out of place in Knightsbridge!" said Penny, feeling the leather seat and scanning her eyes around the interior of his top-of-the-range Range Rover Evoque.

"You like?" he asked.

"Oh yes. But get a red one next time; white is so plain. Can I drive it?" she asked, showing him big, child-like eyes.

"Can't see why not; but let's get home first, I've got a meal waiting."

Penny seemed happy enough on the journey to the cottage, but sometimes during their conversation her mind was obviously elsewhere.

"How did your holiday go?" he asked.

She took a deep breath, and replied, tersely, "It didn't."

Sam realised then why she was distracted.

The sun was low in the early September sky as he drove through the five-bar gate and up the gravel driveway to the cottage – he'd deliberately left it open to save getting out of the car.

"Here we are, ladies, home sweet home," he said, opening the rear door for Suzie, and then the front passenger door for Penny; but she was already out of the car.

"If I'd known you were going to do that, I would have waited!" she said.

"Well, don't be in such a hurry next time," he replied.

Penny stood there smiling, admiring his home with its light pink washed walls and small box-sash windows.

"Wow, Sam! It's a chocolate box cottage! I can't wait to see inside," she said, sounding impatient and excited. "Come on!"

"Is she like this with you, Suzie? Nag, nag, nag?" he asked.

Both girls laughed.

They made their way to the small stone porch that was encased in ivy, intertwined with jasmine.

"There you go, madams," he said, opening the heavy oak ledge and brace door for them. It led directly into a small timber-framed, panelled lobby, and then into the spacious lounge and dining area.

"Suzie, look at this room! Isn't it lovely. Oh, Sam, it's wonderful," Penny said, making her way across the oak flooring which was scattered with Persian rugs. She gazed up at the exposed ceiling beams, bent and twisted with age. "Now that's what I call a fireplace!" she then cried. "Are you going to light it? Go on, please light it?" She looked admiringly at the large wrought iron fire grate and the copper pots and horse brasses. "All I can say is wow!" She felt like she'd been transported back to when Shakespeare himself was alive, and knew she wanted to come here again and again. Suzie agreed wholeheartedly that it was a fabulous fireplace.

"I'll sort you two out first, and then I'll light it, he replied, smiling.

Penny then collapsed onto the large, comfortable sofa with its off-white linen covers and soft cushions.

"Oh my god, I've died and gone to heaven," she uttered, kicking off her shoes and stretching out. "I'm going to sleep here tonight, sod the bed," she sighed. "Suzie come and sit down. It's so comfortable."

Sam was happy that she liked his home.

Chapter 27

"Come on, you two, I'll show you your bedroom," he said, putting his hand out to Penny. "Do either of you want a bath or shower before you eat?"

"I could do with a shower, Sam," Suzie said.

"I fancy a nice bath," Penny replied, following Sam to the bedroom.

"And a large glass of your favourite wine, no doubt," he added with a laugh as he led them up the open-tread stairs to the landing.

Penny gasped when she saw the bedroom. "Just when I thought it couldn't get any better!" she said, as she walked over to the bed. She then laid on it, bouncing up and down. "Maybe I will sleep up here tonight after all!"

Sam stood in the doorway and pointed to the bathroom.

"There's a separate shower and bath, and the loo is in there as well."

Suzie stood by the window and looked out over the garden.

"Have you seen the thickness of these walls, Pen?" she observed.

"In some places they're over two feet thick. It makes the place very cosy," he told her.

Penny opened the wardrobe doors and inspecting the contents.

"This is your bedroom, Sam?

"It is," he replied.

"So where are you sleeping?"

"I've got a futon in the spare bedroom. I use it when the girls come down and stay."

"I feel bad turfing you out of your own bedroom," Suzie said.

"Don't be," retorted Penny. "He lives a life of luxury when he stays with my aunts. Don't you, Sam?" she replied, and her hazel eyes shone at him, temporarily hiding the sad thoughts going through her head about Toby.

"Right, I'll go and get your wine, and by the way, you can put any clothes you need washing in there." He pointed to a round wicker basket in one corner of the bedroom. He opened one of the drawers. "These belong to the girls – they should fit if you want to put them on," he added, handing Penny two pairs of pyjamas.

He lit the fire as promised, and he could hear laughing and all sorts of commotion going on upstairs as he did so. He then went to the kitchen to finish preparing their meal.

Suzie was the first one down, with two empty glasses in her hand.

"Hi," she said as she put the glasses on the worktop next to the Belfast sink.

"Fancy a top up?" he asked. He picked up the bottle of wine.

"No thanks, Sam, water will be fine for me."

"Madam still prettying herself is she?"

Suzie laughed. "Penny thought she was the bloody Queen of Sheba in that bath of yours!"

Sam smiled at her. Like Penny, she was probably in her early thirties, but she was shorter in height and petite, with short, spiky bleached hair.

"Are you an actress as well?" he enquired.

"No, I'm a make-up artist. I've been working on location with Penny." She leant against the kitchen doorframe, looking into the lounge and watching the shadows form around room as the flames flickered and darted. "I've worked with Penny many times over the years. Some say she's hard work, but she's lovely really . . . and she often talks about you," she said, speaking quietly, knowing that Penny was walking around upstairs; they could hear the old floorboards above their heads creaking.

"Oh does she?"

"So, it's nice to meet the face behind the name."

"Well, I hope that what she's said about me hasn't disappointed you." (He wasn't sure if he felt embarrassed or flattered that Penny talked about him.)

"Oh no, Sam, Penny always says how very charming and kind you are."

The floorboards creaked again and they heard Penny making her way down the stairs.

"You're not chatting Suzie up, are you, Sam?" Penny asked, smiling and taking his glass of wine out of his hand.

"Fat chance of me chatting up anyone with you around." Suzie laughed at that. "I thought you'd gone down the plug hole, you've been so long!"

"Sorry! It's your fault anyway."

"What have I done now?" he asked, showing them to the dining table, bottle of wine in hand.

"It's that lovely bath of yours. Once you get in and turn on the spa pool thingy, you don't want to get out. It feels like I've been pummelled all over, but I'm so relaxed. Can you fit one in my place?" she asked, giving him a cheeky, little smile.

"Can't see why not."

"Great! I'll do some voice overs to pay for it!"

"I didn't know I was so hungry. That was delicious, thank you!" said Penny, as Sam picked up her empty plate.

"Would you consider marrying a woman who couldn't cook, Sam?" asked Suzie.

"At the moment I've got no intention of marrying a woman

who can cook, but I'll bear your thought in mind," he replied, seeing Penny give him a piercing look over the rim of her wine glass.

"What about Katherine?" Penny asked.

"Oh yes," he said, with a deep intake of breath. "I forgot about her."

"Who's Katherine? Your girlfriend?" Suzie asked.

Sam turned to Penny, knowing she could carry off the ruse; she was an actress after all.

"No," he replied. "She's an old lady we know who keeps an eye on me from time to time."

"She's younger than you, Sam," Penny quipped.

Sam found it hard not to laugh, and said, "She can be a bit *waspish* at times, but it's all an act as she's kind-hearted and caring really. She certainly was to me when I needed a friend," he said.

Penny's eyes flickered, but her face remained still.

"She sounds a bit like you, Pen," said Suzie.

"Yes, you could say there is a resemblance, don't you think?" Sam replied, and the three of them broke into sudden laughter.

"OK, ladies, coffee or more wine?" he asked, gathering the plates.

The log fire was roaring and it was late by the time Penny dived onto the settee.

"Ah, this is so comfy," she said, curling her legs underneath her and snuggling a cushion to her chest. Sam sat at the other end, and Suzie sat on a cushion on the floor, warming her feet by the fire.

"Don't you get lonely living here on you own?" Suzie enquired, craning her head to look at him.

He didn't need any time at all to consider the question, as the answer was easy to give.

"No, not at all," he replied softly, reaching across to the small side table for his glass. "Most of my life I've been in the company of someone or other, mostly women, and especially my two girls – and they're not what you would call 'stealthy'! Penny could vouch for that, couldn't you, hun?"

"They are gorgeous. Full of life and great fun to be with. Not like their *I vont to be alone* father," Penny replied, putting on a deep German accent.

Suzie stood up, taking Penny's empty glass from her hand.

"You don't have a telly, Sam," she noted, topping up Penny's glass with wine, and hers with water.

"I've got one – it's in the garage somewhere – but I can't be bothered to set it up. Thanks to madam, here, and her two lovely aunties, I have better things to do." He looked across at Penny, who seemed to be distracted by other thoughts again. "They're trying to educate me in the works of Shakespeare," he said. "Her aunties say the more you read, the easier it gets, so that's why I don't use my telly."

Penny took the cushion she was holding and laid it across Sam's lap, resting her legs over it. He knew exactly what she wanted him to do.

"See what I've got to contend with? She treats me as her servant!" he said, rolling his eyes.

As he put his hands on her feet and gently manipulated them, she let out a long sigh.

"God, he's good at this. I'll tell what else he's good at – which two little birdies told me," she said, closing her eyes and savouring once again the enjoyment of his hands on her feet. "Music. You're a bit of a musician, aren't you, Sam?" She smiled at him and waited for a reply; but he didn't speak, he just gave her a studious look. "Apparently, our Sam here plays the piano and guitar," she continued.

Sam stayed quiet, deciding to let her have her fun.

Suzie turned to him with a look of excitement, and said, "Oh, I love the guitar! Have you got one here?"

Penny, without hesitation, quickly answered her question: "Yes, he's got three of them in his spare bedroom."

He looked at her with enquiring eyes; there was only one reason she knew that!

She gave him a sheepish look.

"I had a nose around while you two were chatting in the kitchen," she confessed, sheepishly.

He looked at her sternly, but a hint of a smile played across his face.

"Actually, I have two guitars and a banjo," he replied.

"Can you play something for us now? Please?" asked Suzie.

Sam shook his head and then downed the remainder of his wine.

"What the girls didn't tell you is that I can't play in front of people. I freeze, lose my concentration," he said.

"The girls said you play the piano with them!" Penny said.

"Yes, that's true, but that's because they're sitting next to me, and I'm not looking at them. If you were on the other side of a door, that would be fine, but if you were to watch me . . ." he said, shrugging his shoulders, "I can't play a note once I see you, I'm buggered. If you want to hear me, you'll have to stand in the garden. Sorry."

"Fear not, my sweet Sam, help is at hand," Penny declared, swinging her legs off his lap. "I'll teach you to overcome it. It's just like stage fright, pure and simple. Lots of actors have a similar problem, and it takes time and concentration and practice, that's all. Trust me." She looked so animated in the firelight that he had to smile. "We'll have you playing in the Royal Albert Hall in no time. Go on, Sam, try it?" Her eyes were now wide open, and her passion shone into the room.

"I'll give it a go, but I can't promise it'll work with me."

"There are very famous actors – household names – who have suffered stage fright. I sure as hell know that if they can control it, you can." Penny squeezed his arm. "When I come down on my own, we'll get started. Honest, Sam, it's doable, and just think how pleased the girls will be!"

"Have you ever had stage fright?" he asked her.

"Good God, no. Never," she replied without hesitation.

She sat back down and snuggled up to Sam. For a time none of them spoke. He could see his guests were getting tired. Penny was falling asleep on his shoulder – partly due to the amount of wine she had drunk – and Suzie was lying by the fire.

"Right, ladies, get your arses up to bed. I'll tidy up here," he said softly.

They said goodnight and wandered off upstairs.

Sam pondered Penny's offer of help as he tidied up. He smiled. She was bound to nag him, but maybe it would be worth it . . .

He was up and dressed by six thirty and sorting a few things out around the house.

About eight thirty, he knocked quietly on their bedroom door. He waited a few seconds and then went into the room with their coffees. They were both still asleep. Penny was lying on her side, her hair all ruffled on the pillow, and he couldn't help but gaze at her for a few seconds; Suzie was nowhere to be seen – all he could see was a shape of a torso under the duvet. Putting his hand on Penny's shoulder he gently rocked her.

"Wake up, sweet pea, it's a lovely day," he murmured.

She stirred and rolled onto her back, opening her eyes slowly.

"What time is it?" she asked, pushing herself up onto her elbows. He rearranged the pillows for her, noticing she was wearing Estelle's sky-blue satin pyjamas.

"Its eight thirty, hun," he told her, watching as she combed her fingers through her hair.

"Did I hear you call me 'sweet pea'?" she asked.

Sam nodded and smiled.

"There's nothing sweet about me first thing in the morning, Sam, you'll have to wait another couple of hours at least." She raised a sleepy smile and then turned to look where Suzie should have been. She lifted up the duvet, and said, "Hi, Suzie, wakey, wakey."

"Penny, take a look at Sam, quick!" Suzie urged – Sam was splitting logs in the garden – "Not bad for an old man, eh!" Some of the guys you hang around with would most likely chop their own foot off if they tried to do that," she laughed.

Penny leant out of the opened window.

"*O Romeo, Romeo, wherefore art thou Romeo?*" she called.

Sam looked up to see them waving at him, still in their pyjamas, and waved back.

"I take it you slept well?" he enquired as she sat at the kitchen table for breakfast.

"I can't believe how quiet it is here, and dark. I got up in the night for a pee and walked into the wall twice!"

Sam laughed as he drew himself a mental picture of her feeling her way around the bedroom in the dark.

"If you look in the draw next to the bed, you'll find a small torch. Sorry, I forgot to tell you that!"

"In answer to your question," she replied, "yes, I slept like a bloody log, thank you. I didn't want to get up, I was so cosy.

I can see why you love living here, it's so quiet and peaceful. I envy you," she said, looking around, still taking in how lovely the cottage was with the farmhouse-style kitchen and floor laid with large slabs of slate worn and marked with age.

"Well, there's no need to, you can come and stay any time, you know that," he said refilling the kettle, knowing how Penny liked her mugs of coffee in the morning. "No Suzie yet?" he asked.

"She's on the phone to her chap. She's pregnant, but he doesn't seem too happy about the prospect of being a dad. Poor thing, she's in a bit of a state, she's worried he'll cut and run," she answered, very quietly, certain he knew that that's what her father had done when he found out her mother was pregnant.

"It sounds like you've taken her under your wing, that's very good of you."

"That's why I brought her with me, otherwise I would have come down on my own . . . you don't mind, do you?" she asked.

"Don't be daft." He shook his head. "I think it's very sweet of you to support her. I know only too well what it's like to have a friend like you when your life is at a crossroads, don't I?" She smiled, but somewhere behind her eyes he saw unrest again. "So. Breakfast," he stated. "Fancy a boiled egg straight from next-door's chickens?"

"Yes, please," she replied; but now sounding cheerless, she reached out her hand for his to hold. "But first I want to apologise for being impolite when you enquired about my holiday with Toby."

"Look, you don't have to apologise to me, you know that."

"I do," she replied adamantly. "You're the one person whom I feel I can confide in and not be lectured . . . and by that I mean my aunties."

Sam turned his head towards the door as he could hear the timbers of the stairs creak, telling him Suzie was on her way down.

"Tell me later," he replied, and Penny nodded. "Good morning, young lady. Boiled eggs?"

"I thought as the weather looks good, I'd show you the delights of Dartmoor," he said, noticing Penny staring at him, her eyes intense, like a child busting at the seams to ask a question. Sam gave her a knowing smile and then sighed, "Yes, OK, you can drive," he declared.

Penny shot out of her chair, rushed over to him gave kiss on his cheek, crying, "You see, Suzie? This is what I mean when I say he's lovely!"

"Why do I get the impression that my girls have been giving you lessons on how to get around me?"

She laughed and winked at him.

"They've given me a whole armoury full," she replied.

Suzie giggled. It was so lovely to see these two people – who wanted nothing more from each other than untethered friendship – relaxed and enjoying each other's company.

"Sam! I forgot to say thank you for washing and ironing our clothes. We should have done it, really," she said.

"It's no problem. I expect my lovely daughters neglected to mention that sometimes, no, most times they visit, I do the same for them . . . and always do."

Penny, who was eating the last of her bread soldiers, turned to Suzie and said, "It's a pity we can't bottle him. We'd make a fortune: a washing, cooking tour guide."

"You haven't got off that lightly," Sam informed them. "You two are doing the washing up, even with those nails, and I haven't got any Marigolds!"

After breakfast, as promised, Sam let them experience the delights of Dartmoor with its alluring, rugged landscape of protruding granite tors, and ponies and sheep grazing free. Penny drove them across the moor to the highest pub on Dartmoor – the

Warren House Inn – for a coffee, and then on to Postbridge for a walk around the twelfth-century clapper bridge. They sat by the riverbank, absorbing the tranquillity and views across the moor.

Later Sam treated them to lunch at the East Dart Hotel, and later still he drove them back to his cottage. Penny commented how the shafts of light reaching down through the clouds onto the moor, changed the landscape with a constant palette of colour.

Sam could only agree: it was beautiful, nature at it best.

"God, I'm wacked, it must be all the fresh air. I'm going for a bath and I may be in there a while," said Penny, heading for the stairs when they got back.

"Just before you disappear," he said, as she stopped and twisted around, not intending to alter course for her soak. "I was hoping you could pop down to the pub with me. There's a young lady there and I would like to introduce her to you."

Her face showed indignance to his request and she grumbled, "Oh, Sam, must we? I was hoping to sit by the fire in my jammies and just relax."

"Do this for me, please? She goes to bed at six," he asked, disappointed with her selfish attitude.

Penny now felt cajoled, and said, "Oh, go on then, if it makes you happy."

Sam walked up to her, put his arm around her waist and gave her a squeeze.

"It will make her happy," he said quietly.

"Hello! What's all this then?" said Suzie, jovially from the top of the stairs, seeing Sam with his arm around Penny.

"Don't get too comfy, hun, he's dragging us out again!" Penny said, and rolled her eyes and sighed.

"Christ, Penny! The way you're going on, you'd think I'd asked you for sex!" Sam snapped, pulling his arm away.

"Well, at least I wouldn't have to go out," she snapped back.

"It's nearly four thirty," he said, ignoring her comment. "If we get there for five, we'll be back by six and you can have your bloody bath then. I'll sort out a light supper and then we can all chill out in front of the fire, OK?" he said, frustrated with her egotistic attitude. "We'll take the car as that will save time walking."

God, woman, you can be a selfish bitch at times, he thought, as he walked into kitchen to see what food he had.

Suzie took hold of Penny's arm.

"I think you've pissed him off, Pen, he's not happy with you at all."

"That's his problem," she griped. "It's no doubt some spotty kid he promised an autograph to."

"Come on, we'd better go, you don't want to be late having your bath, now do you?" Sam called up the stairs a few minutes later, putting on his jacket.

He was stony-faced when they got into the car and drove in silence to the pub. When they arrived he asked them what they'd like to drink, and then pointed towards the lounge and suggested they go and sit in there.

"It's nice in here, isn't in, Pen?" Suzie said, trying to make small talk.

"I suppose so," Penny sighed, sounded utterly disinterested.

Suzie could just see Sam at the bar, and watched his face break into a beautiful smile as he bent down and crouched on his knees.

"Penny . . ." she whispered. "You need to see this."

Penny reluctantly turned to look.

They watched as a little girl in a party frock, with a pink silk scarf wrapped around her head, appeared from behind the bar, her face devoid of any healthy, natural colour. She saw Sam and made little steps towards him, very slowly. She then put her arms around his legs and hugged him. He pointed in the direction of Penny. Standing up he took her hand as they walked towards her, again with small, slow steps.

"Emily," he said in a quiet voice, "this is the friend I told you about."

Penny looked at the little girl. *Oh, Penny, you stupid selfish cow; you should have known he had a good reason to drag you out*, she thought, gazing at the waif of a child. Her heart ached when she saw the young girl standing in front of her.

"Emily, may I introduce Miss Penny McCain."

Penny glanced at Sam, and the expression on his face – which she read loud and clear – indicated that he wasn't happy with her.

"Penny, may I introduce Miss Emily Stagg."

Penny held out her hand, and then ever so gently took Emily's outstretched hand in hers. It was as fragile as a tiny bird and she feared the bones would break. She smiled at Emily, her senses numbed.

"That is a really nice name," Penny smiled.

"Thank you," Emily said quietly, and then her face lit up as she smiled back at Penny.

Sam could see Penny had tears in her eyes now.

"Would you like to sit next to me?" she asked.

"Oh yes please! But can I get my scrap book first to show you?"

"Yes, I'd like to see that, very much," Penny replied, raising a remorseful smile at Sam.

Emily then turned to Sam and held her arms out to him. He bent over and gently picked her up, carrying her through the bar.

He returned a few moments later with their drinks. He could see they were both wiping their eyes with tissues.

"Sam, I-I feel like shit . . . and I deserve everything you must think about me," Penny stammered.

"So you should be. Do you honestly think I sit at the bar telling people I know this actress and I'll get you an autograph if you buy me a pint? I thought you held me in higher regard than that," he said, making his feelings clear to her. "All I wanted was to make that little girl's dream of meeting you come true, that's all." But then he softened, seeing it from Penny's perspective too. He put his hand on hers, and she moved closer to him. "I've got no right to be angry, though," he told her. "You weren't to know. I should have told you about Emily before we came out, but you were so dismissive."

"I'm so sorry. I know I'm a selfish cow at times," she said, frowning. "I'm annoyed with myself for questioning your motives, I really am."

"I can see you are," he replied. "Just make sure you're her bestest friend before we go."

"I will, Sam, I promise."

Emily returned, carried by her mother Sue.

"No more than ten minutes, Sam," she told him, her face etched with concern for her daughter.

Emily sat between Penny and Suzie and showed them her scrap book.

"These are pictures of you that Sam gave me, and I cut these out of magazines," she said proudly. "You are very beautiful."

They talked like they were old friends, Penny not letting go of Emily's hand. Penny looked across at Sam, realising he had done something for Emily that no other person had been able to do, but also that he had done something for her: he had removed the mask she hid behind, but not only removed it, he had torn it off, exposing the emotional rawness of the person she was behind it.

"Come on, young lady, bed!" said Sam, gently. "Mummy said 'ten minutes'." He picked her up again, cradling her in his arms. "Say goodnight to the ladies."

Penny stood and kissed her pale, soft face, mesmerised by the dark blue eyes that smiled with love and gratitude.

"When I come back, I'll bring some more pictures, I promise," she told Emily, and waved goodnight as Sam carried her back to her mother.

She was numbed by what she had just experienced, and sat back down, lost in thought.

"I felt so bloody ashamed," she finally said. "I was beginning to believe he brought out the best in me. Now I've let him down something rotten, haven't I?"

"Well, from where I was sitting, it looked like two lovers making up."

"Don't be so stupid. It's nothing like that with us, we're just very close . . . good mates . . . very good mates. Sam certainly doesn't want a relationship. He's only just lost his wife, poor darling, and I've got enough to cope with, with sodding Toby," she replied.

But she knew Sam had made her feel bad about herself for all the right reasons, and she fell silent once more.

"Here you go, ladies," said Dave, the landlord, as he brought them another round of drinks. "These are on the house from me and Sue." He then chatted for a while about Emily and Sam, and how they had taken to each other since Sam had moved to the village.

Penny made room for Sam on the bench seat. He could see Emily had climbed into her heart, and knew exactly what she was experiencing: she was listening closely as Dave spoke lovingly about their daughter, and then he left Sam and his guests alone with their thoughts about their little angel.

"She's lovely, isn't she?" Sam asked, taking a long breath.

"She's very brave," Penny said quietly.

"She's amazing," Suzie whispered, her hand on her tummy.

"Emily's been fighting something or other since she was born, but the cancer has taken its toll on her. You wouldn't think she was eight, would you?" he said, dividing his gaze between the two women. "Each day that she wakes up is a blessing for those who know her." He cleared his throat, choked with emotion. "She should be in hospital, but she so badly wanted to be at home with her brother and sister . . . she's only here for the weekend." He paused again, composing himself. "The doctors were concerned about infections, but they know that's the least of their worries now . . . Emily won't see Christmas."

Penny could see the anguish in his face as he spoke those words, and put her hand on his; but his hand wasn't the warm gentle hand she was used to, it was now clenched hard like a piece of iron. His emotions were raw.

"Suzie and I should cook something, Sam, it's not fair on you," Penny said, seeing how drained he was when they returned to the cottage.

But to be honest, none of them felt much like eating.

"I'm going to bed," Suzie said. "I need to give my man a call." She gave Sam and Penny a kiss. "Thank you, Sam, I've enjoyed today very much." She made her way upstairs.

"Why don't you go too? You look worn out," Sam said, as he looked across at Penny.

"No, I'd really like to sit here and relax with you," she replied, quietly.

Sam put more logs on the fire and then turned all the lights off, except for the lamp on the small table behind them. He topped up her glass of wine, and then settled himself back down, staring into the flames.

"What are you thinking?" she asked, softly. "You've been staring at the fire for ages."

She could see from the expression on his face that he was deep in thought.

"I was thinking of Annie, our little Emily, and your sister Megan," he said, still absorbed by the flames.

Penny only a felt slight twinge of surprise; she had already realised that her aunties must have told him about Megan and her mother. But she wasn't concerned; she felt her past was safe with him, although she still didn't know why.

Sam moved his head from side to side, loosening his tense neck muscles.

"Are you alright?" she asked.

"Fine, thank you," he replied, and then still gazing into the fire, decided to confide in her. "Annie . . ." he said, letting out a heavy sigh, "there were times when she wasn't an easy person to live with. She was very moody – the girls described her as 'living with a hand grenade' – and she would rant and rave; but other times she was sweetness personified." Penny listened intently, realising he was telling her something deeply personal to him. She knew that in the relatively short time they had known each other, the trust she felt for him flowed both ways. They had an unstated rule: I talk, you listen; you talk, I listen.

"Her mother was apparently the same," Sam continued, "so I put it down to something hereditary. When the girls were in their teens, as most parents do, she'd say things like: you're not going out looking like a slut or trollop if they had their skirts up to their arses. Maggie was the worst for that – she still is – but that's Maggie," he said, quietly chuckling to himself as he thought of her. "Estelle was the one Annie made a beeline for. She was constantly insulting her and putting her down. I think it was because Estelle is so much like her: naturally beautiful, and with the same passion for beautiful things . . . I could go on and on. But Estelle's not moody like her mother was. Oh she has a temper alright, they both do, what women don't?" He turned and looked at Penny and then smiled as she gave him a sheepish look, knowing he also meant her.

He stood up and stretched his back, and then put his hand out for her glass.

"No more for me," she said.

"Is there anything else I can get you? Something to eat?"

"No, Sam, I want for nothing," she said contentedly.

He went to the kitchen and poured himself a malt whisky with a dash of water – his favourite.

"Now where was I?" he said, sitting back down. "Yes . . . I begged Annie to get medical advice for her terrible moods, and she was put on medication. It helped, but she was still 'Hand-Grenade-Annie'. After she was diagnosed with a brain tumour, she changed almost overnight. Maggie noticed first that something was wrong when they went into the post office and Annie thought she was in the hairdressers, and as time went on she became more and more confused and insecure.

"She yearned for love – not physical love, but child-like love; the love Dave and Sue have for Emily. When she went blind, it was hell for her, and as the tumour spread, she was no longer Annie. I promised her she wouldn't die in hospital – that was the first promise." He looked at Penny. "You know what the second one was?"

Penny noticed that when he spoke about Annie it was with a thoughtful frown, but very little emotion. Then suddenly his face became strained and taught, and his breathing heavy and irregular.

"The other day, when I gave Emily those pictures of you, it was as if it gave her a reason to wake up the next day. Sue came up to me in the bar, after putting her to bed, and said Emily wanted to tell me a secret. So I went upstairs and sat on a chair next to her, and she started to tell me."

He closed his eyes for a moment, and then continued with his story.

"Emily was lying on her side, holding on to my thumb. She spoke very quietly, as if she didn't want anyone else to hear except me. She looked up with those lovely blue eyes and said, 'When I was in hospital the other day, a nurse told mummy that Peter, my friend, who was sick like me, had gone to fly with the angels." Sam was struggling to hold back the tears now, but he needed to have self-control as there was a reason why he wanted to tell the story to her.

"Emily thought that sounded like great fun, and then the little darling asked me, 'Do you think I'll be allowed to fly with the angels, Sam?' 'I know you will," I replied, softly. She drifted off to sleep then, still holding my thumb. I stayed there, just looking at her. Eventually. . ." Sam let out a billow of air, "Sue came up and tucked her in. She said, 'I take it Emily told you about flying with the angels?' Sue was smiling at me, almost a joyful smile, and then said, 'Emily's looking forward to that." Sam finally succumbed and felt tears trickle down his face. "The little darling . . . I don't think she realises what flying with the angels means." He looked directly at Penny. "Or does she?"

Penny moved nearer to him and took his hand in hers.

"Wouldn't you like to think that Megan had dreams like that?" he asked.

He stood up and walked over to a cupboard, opened the drawer and took something out, and then sat back down next to her. Penny didn't say a word in reply to his question, but he could see she was deep in thought. He had in his hand a small, plain gift box.

"One of my tenants has a son who suffers from a form of autism.

He was one of Annie's students and he's brilliant at jewellery and design, so I gave him your pendant to see what he could do with it." Penny stared at the box in his hands, unsure how she would feel when she saw the pendant again. "He's cleaned it, and it has a new silver chain, but this is the clever bit . . ." he said as he removed the item from the box and showed it to her. "You see this clasp, slide it thought there, click that, and now you have a beautiful brooch."

He passed it to her, and she gazed at it, moving her fingers over the cross, caressing it.

"I hope you will wear it to remind you of Megan . . . and perhaps Emily; but it's up to you."

They both had tears in their eyes now.

"Look at me," she whispered. "Crying again."

"That's because we share the same pain, you and me," Sam replied.

"What do you mean? she asked, but his eyes had glazed over – he clearly did not want to talk anymore. "Maybe we should just leave it at that," he said.

Penny was surprised, startled even, by his reply.

"Sam, you've just put up a barrier, why?" He turned away from her. "Don't look away, please. If there's something you can't, or won't, tell because it's too painful for you, that's fine, but don't put up barriers, Sam. We trust each other, right?"

He tuned his head to look at her again, took a deep breath, held it, and then breathed out slowly.

"Like you, I feel a sense of trust. I know I can tell you anything." Penny could now see Sam was trembling and instinctively held his hand again. "Something happened in my family many years ago. Not even the girls will talk about it, and I've buried it deep inside me – it was the only way I could survive." She realised that the pain he was talking about now was different to the sorrow he felt losing Annie. This was a pain that had scarred his heart and memory deeply. "I have a feeling that one day I'm going to have to tell you," he said slowly, puzzled as to why he felt that. "But not yet, I'm sorry."

She brought his hand up to her lips and kissed it.

"It's a good job we're only friends," she whispered. "If we were any more than that our emotions would be red-lining all the time – they're high enough now!"

She put the pendant back in the box, and placed it on the floor by her feet. She then snuggled up to him and rested her head on his shoulder. He could feel her hair against his face and the fragrance of her shampoo – his shampoo.

They didn't speak for a while, and then Penny murmured, "Thank you for getting the pendant repaired. I will wear it, I promise." She sat there with him, her head still resting against his shoulder. "When Megan was ill, Mummy was always with her, or with the doctor, or at the hospital – sometimes for days on end – and it seemed I was always on my own. Granny, or someone else, would pick me up from school – not my mum – and look after me. At weekends I would stay in my bedroom, and I always felt so alone. I was jealous of her Sam. Sometimes . . . sometimes I wished I could be ill like Megan, so that Mum would spend time with me. I was young. I didn't know what leukaemia was. I feel so guilty about that now . . . so guilty it haunts me . . . but I knew very little about such things. Do you want to know why I stopped wearing the pendant? I felt ashamed that I actually wanted to be ill like my sister. How awful does that sound? I hated myself for thinking that!"

He turned and kissed the top of her head.

"It's horrible to lose a sister, no matter what the reason, but you learn to live with it and you can't turn the clock back."

Penny thought about what he had just said. It was as though he had just implied that he once had a sister who was also dead.

Oh, Sam, she thought, *what have you just told me?* But she knew if he wanted her to know, he would tell her one day.

They sat for quite a while, until Penny was almost asleep.

"Come on, you, get yourself to bed," Sam whispered.

"You too."

Chapter 28

Christmas

"Good morning, Sam!" Penny cried, bounding into the kitchen, followed by Suzie – who was looking at the clock on the wall.

"It's only 8.30. . ." he replied, hesitantly. "I wasn't expecting you two to be up for another hour yet."

"Well, it's good to keep you men on your toes, besides, we've got a busy day ahead," she said, getting a saucepan from the cupboard to boil some eggs. "We've looked on my phone, and the trains run every hour or so going to Paddington. So, we thought we'd get a 3.30, 4.00-ish train. Or . . ." she said carefully, smiling at him.

Sam smiled back at her.

"Or . . . or what?" he asked. Penny shrugged her shoulders, fluttering her eye lashes at him. "Go on . . . or what?" he asked again, with a puzzled expression.

She looked at him from under her eyelashes again, and indicated the car parked outside with a little movement of her head.

He looked sternly at her then gave an exasperated sigh.

"Oh, go on then."

Penny punched the air with success.

"*Yes*! Thank you!" she cried, as she kissed his cheek. "You don't really mind, do you?"

"Well, just to piss on your fireworks, madam, I'd planned to drive you back anyway. I've already phoned June to say I'll stay the night, so there you go, Miss Clever Clogs."

Suzie observed the two of them carrying on, knowing that despite Penny saying that their friendship was just friendship and nothing more, she'd never seen her so happy and relaxed.

"God, you two are acting like a couple of newlyweds," she laughed.

Sam gasped with surprise, and replied, "Now that's not funny, Suzie . . . a man my age shouldn't suffer a shock like that."

"Well I thought it was funny, in a twisted sort of way," Penny smirked, and then asked if he would mind terribly if she borrowed the car, oh, and also if they could find some eggs to take back for the aunties; she knew they'd enjoy them.

Sam handed over his keys to her, asking, "Are you going to tell me why you need the car?"

"*NO*, I'm not. Just be at the pub at midday, and don't be late."

When Penny went to leave, Sam noticed the brooch pinned to the collar of her coat . . . she would wear it for her sister for the rest of her life.

When Sam arrived at the pub, he could see his car in the car park, but no sign of the girls. Dave shook his hand, and then asked him what he wanted to drink.

"Fruit juice . . . I'm driving," he replied, still scanning around the bar and restaurant area, now beginning to fill up with walkers coming off the moor and passing Sunday trade. "So, what's up? What's the big secret? You *must* know!" he asked.

"Sorry, Sam, can't say – Sue will have my balls."

He was sitting at the bar when Suzie appeared,

"Hi there, Sam! Penny told me to take you to the table, and

to wait there," she said with a giggle, looking very pleased with herself.

Walking into the restaurant area he could see a waitress putting the finishing touches to a table – which was laid out differently to the other tables. It was early September and the days were still long and warm, but this table looked like it had been set for a Christmas party! Crackers and party poppers and cupcakes of all shapes and sizes where placed upon it. The sight before him bewildered Sam. And now he could hear the sound of Christmassy music filling the air!

He turned around towards the bar. It was then that he saw a most wonderful sight: a young lady with long wavy blond hair, tied back with a pink ribbon which matched her pink and white flowing party dress. Her rosy complexion and wonderful blue eyes were accentuated by beautiful pale blue eye shadow, and her normally pale lips were glowing with a soft pink lipstick. Sam gazed at her through tearful eyes. Emily was walking slowly towards him wearing red, shiny, patent leather shoes. Penny and Sue where either side of her, holding a hand, helping her walk her tortuous steps. As she walked up to him, Sam knelt down on bended knees, and took her little hand and gentle placed a kiss upon it. His heavy heart lightened when she smiled the most beautiful smile he had ever seen.

"What a beautiful princess you are," he said, briefly looking up at Penny. He then whispered in Emily's ear, "I see you brought your ugly sister with you."

Her frail body trembled as she giggled in response.

"I heard that, Sam, thank you!" Penny said; but she smiled as she said it.

Emily's party only went on for one hour, as that was all she could manage, but for that hour she lived the life of a young child not drained of energy by disease. They created a microcosm of normality that was almost fantasy, not to corrupt or con, but to allow a little girl to dream that if she closed her eyes, she really was a princess.

They enjoyed a delicious lunch before their journey back to London, and then Suzie took Emily upstairs to gently remove the make-up from her delicate skin. It was a while before she came back down.

Chapter 29

The Villa

"Sam, would it be OK for Suzie to drive the car to the cottage, and then you and I can walk back?"

Sam checked the time.

"Yep, that's fine, it's a lovely walk and it'll help clear our heads," he replied, but it didn't take him long to realise it wasn't going to be a relaxing stroll back.

Penny handed the car keys to Suzie, and then took Sam's arm; he knew there must be a reason for her wanting them to be alone.

She didn't say a word for the first five minutes. Then she stopped and turned to look at him with a face that seemed to show little emotion.

"Toby's contract for the next series isn't going to be renewed," she stated. "He's being written out. I had an idea that was going to happen, bush telegraph and all that." She let out a long, forlorn sigh. "He wants to move in with me." She started walking again, still holding on to his arm. "There something else, Sam, about him, but it's private, and it must stay between you and me. You're . . . the only person I can tell." She started crying quietly.

Sam had no idea what she was going to tell him, and wondered what the man had done to her. He pulled her into a hug, and put his hand gently on the side of her face.

"Shit, I'm am actress, I should be able to control my emotions!"

she sobbed. "This is your fault. I always seem to let my barriers down when I'm with you," she said with a sniffle. "This place feels like Shangri-La for me. I know I've only been here three days, but I'm genuinely sad to be leaving. I hope I get the opportunity to come back."

"You make it sound like this is your first and last time here?" Sam still wondered what she was about to tell him. He was now worried too.

"You asked me about our holiday," she said in a subdued voice. "Toby and I, in recent years, have always rented a small villa by the beach in Portugal. We'd just chill out, eat in nice restaurants, catch up on our sex life and just enjoy each other's company away from work."

Sam had made a point of never enquiring about their relationship, and until now she had never discussed intimate details about it.

"He said he'd booked the same place as before," she continued, "but he hadn't. This time it was a much larger villa, and four of his mates were there waiting for us, plus two girls – two rather stupid girls in their twenties who called themselves actresses/models. My heart sank. I was so looking forward to our time alone together, to try to rekindle our love for each other – well mine for him, anyway – and hopefully move forward from there.

"I won't repeat what I said to him – you know what comes out of my mouth when I'm pissed off, especially with him – but I was so disappointed and so bloody angry. Toby said he had it all worked out. Our bedroom was at the far end of the villa, away from the pool where the others were; but we didn't have our own patio, and the sodding room was facing north. I was so upset that all I wanted to do was get the next plane back home, but Toby persuaded me to give it a try.

"It was horrible, absolutely horrible. His mates were drinking all day by the pool, and the girls were parading their tits all over the place. I had no idea which guys they were with. The noise coming from their bedrooms was ridiculous. I've got nothing against being vocal when having sex, but it was like having a running commentary, and it was practically non-stop – in between the drinking that is."

Penny walked to the hedgerow and picked a couple of blackberries.

"It's been years since I've done this!" she said as she inspected it for bugs and then popped one into her mouth. "They're delicious!" she cried, before continuing. "Do you know what that bastard said? He said I was a prude and that I should relax. He then buggered off to the patio with his mates to drink." She closed her eyes. "Listen to that, Sam . . . peace and quiet . . . so different from London.

"Anyway, I went to our room. I'd been asleep three or four hours when I woke up. I was hungry as I hadn't eaten since breakfast. Toby wasn't in bed, but I really didn't care where he was. It must have been about ten o'clock at night. The bloody bastard – sorry, but I really have to say that now because I hate this bit because I think my future with Toby, if ever there was one, ended right then.

"As I said, I was hungry, so I walked into kitchen to see what food there was. I thought I could hear Toby's voice, so walked to the door leading to the pool area. All I could see was Toby, but he was laughing, sitting at the patio table on his own. I couldn't believe my eyes at what I was witnessing! He was chopping out lines of cocaine, Sam! I had no idea what to do. What the hell was I supposed to do? I still don't know what to do."

"Are you asking me for advice, or thinking out loud?"

"Thinking out loud. I know what I should do, and I'm glad you're not saying much . . . you don't need to . . . I know what you would say."

They were almost at the cottage now.

"While I was watching Toby destroy his, and our, life, I realised he must have been completely out of his head, because he didn't even see me. Then one of his buddies came into view, completely naked, and I heard him say, 'Go on, Toby, your turn.'" She turned to Sam. "It answered the question of why he's changed so much over the last year. I ran back to our room, packed my suitcase and left. I walked in the dark to the village, got a taxi to the airport, and booked the first available flight home."

Sam felt rage engulf him, hearing what Toby had put her though. All he could think of was teaching him a lesson for betraying Penny's love for him. He was also struggling with long-buried memories of his own, which had now surfaced.

"I ended up in Birmingham," Penny said, "and got a train home. I haven't spoken to him since; but he texted me, and I'm seeing him tomorrow night. I guess I'll have to take it from there." She leant against the top bar of the gate and looked out over the fields. The light breeze and the walk, and being able to talk to Sam so freely, had freshened her senses, and she was beginning to come to terms with her situation.

They were just about to walk the last few metres to the cottage, when Penny stopped and stared directly at him.

"This is no good, I can't sit next to you in the car all the way home and not know what you're thinking. Please tell me what you're thinking?"

Oh no, Sam thought, *I really hoped you wouldn't ask me that.*

"What do you want me to say?" he asked sadly. "I'm not going to tell you what I think you should do, or say. Toby is your business. He's your private life, separate to our friendship – and I'm sorry if that sounds harsh, but he's not my problem. But if you want to make him my problem, that's a different kettle of fish . . . I'd protect you from him, you know that."

Penny was startled by his bluntness. It wasn't quite what she'd expected. But she preferred his honesty, rather than hollow words.

"I've said of you before, Penny," he continued, "that you seem to like being a hard, selfish Katherine-type. But watching you over the past two days, with that angel of a little girl, I saw the true Penny: a woman with love and compassion in her heart . . . and nothing will make me change that opinion of you."

If anyone has love and compassion in their heart it's you, Sam, she thought as she considered what he'd just said.

"I've no doubt you will show Toby the same," Sam said then. "Even if you may not love him in the same way you used to, and even though he has hurt you, I think you still want to help him, for old time's sake." Sam held out his hand for her to hold.

"They say everyone deserves a second chance, but I'm not sure if I agree with that when it comes to Toby."

"You now know what drugs do to people, if you didn't before . . ." His face was suddenly hard. "I've seen drugs rip the heart out of families, and innocent people get dragged into the nightmare that drugs cause. If there was any advice I could give, it would be this," he said, and there was no easy way to say it: "Toby has betrayed you, but he has everything to lose, including you. Don't be surprised if he betrays you again, despite what he may promise."

He could see her pupils dilating as the jolt of his words registered in her brain.

They walked slowly up the drive to the cottage.

Chapter 30

The Meeting

Back at the cottage, Penny and Suzie collected their belongings and put them into the car.

"I don't want to go, Sam, I really don't," Penny said as she stood in his lounge. "I would hate it if I never came back, and I'll miss this room." She ran her hand over the back of her favourite settee.

"I'd like to think you'll miss me," he replied, with a small smile.

"That goes without saying."

He walked off into the kitchen, returning moments later.

"There you go, but don't have any wild parties if I'm away," he said, placing a spare front door key in her hand.

"Sam, are you sure?"

"If I wasn't sure, I wouldn't give it to you, now would I? Besides, you trust me with your aunties . . . But I have the feeling you've got the better deal!" he said, and they both laughed.

The drive back up to London was uneventful. Penny and Suzie slept for a while, and Sam thought of Penny and the situation she'd now found herself in. Penny didn't suffer fools gladly, and Toby was one of the biggest fools he had come across in many years.

He dropped Suzie home first, but didn't stop at Penny's for a coffee. He could see she was worn out from thinking of her forthcoming confrontation with Toby. By the time he got to her aunties' house, there was a meal waiting for him; Penny had phoned them to say he was on his way, which he considered very thoughtful as he too was tired now.

He chatted to May and June and told them about their weekend, and about Penny's new bestest friend, Emily.

They didn't tell him their news concerning Aaron's play, and they didn't plan to until after they'd met with Penny – a meeting that Penny knew nothing about.

Sam was soon to bed. It had been a long day.

"Where the hell is Archie?" May asked as the sisters prepared lunch for their guests.

"They're here!" said June, opening the door to Archie and Aaron. "Aaron, so pleased to see you back," she said. "Please, do come in."

"Sure is nice to be back, Miss June," he said, beaming one of his room-filling smiles at her.

Archie was standing behind Aaron, lost in the shadow of his huge frame.

"Archie, dear, there you are, no use hiding."

"I wasn't hiding, June," Archie murmured, adjusting his creamy-yellow cravat with blue dots, and checking it in the round, oak-framed wall mirror. "Just no room to swing a cat in this hallway of yours, sweetie." He was feeling more than a little tense.

"Well, come on through, both of you. We've prepared a light lunch."

"Archie! Aaron! What are you two doing here? This is a pleasant surprise!" Penny cried as she entered the lounge.

"I've invited them for lunch. I thought it would be nice to have a little get together," June replied. "Shall we go through to the dining room?"

Penny started telling them all about her weekend at Sam's cottage, but soon realised something else was lurking in their thoughts. Archie was clearly there for more than just a pleasant lunch and a bit of chit-chat, and he was fidgeting in his seat – which told anyone who knew him that he was nervous.

"Archie, what is the real reason you and Aaron are here?" she asked pointedly, her hazel eyes flashing at him.

"Penny, dear," June said, "Aaron has something to ask you. Go on, Aaron, ask her . . ."

"Ask her what?" said Penny, and her eyes widened as she scanned the group of people around the table. She realised she was right – this lunch date wasn't a chance meeting, and whatever the reason, it involved her. "Come on, is someone going to tell me what this is all about? Aaron?" she asked, her voice now tense. With everything that had happened in the last few days and weeks, she was in no mood for games.

Aaron picked up the briefcase that was close by his side, opened it and placed a large folder on the table in front of her.

"This is part of my script for my play, which is all but finished," he told her, his eyes full of excitement, but full of gentleness too. "Miss Penny," Aaron continued, "I know people laugh at me, at the way I look and sound, it's always been like that, but I don't care if I'm different. I feel different because I sense things in people, and sometimes when I speak to someone they inspire me to write. When I came over here, my dream was to meet these two kind ladies . . . some Americans just want to see your tower of London–" he said.

Archie chuckled to himself. "These two ought to be in there," Archie sniped, obviously referring to May and June.

"But my dream wasn't to see your tower, it was to meet the McCain sisters," he continued, "and when Archie here introduced us, you were so kind and genuinely interested in me and my writing, that I sensed truth in your interest, like the guy you were with last time we met." He looked directly at Penny.

"Toby?" Archie quickly asked.

But Aaron shook his head. "No, not that guy, the other guy . . . Sam."

Penny bristled at the mention of Toby's name, and then softened when she heard Sam's.

"He's a nice guy, and he said such lovely things about you and your aunties. I can also sense that you like him very much and trust him."

Penny felt moved and slightly embarrassed at his sentiment.

"Yes, Aaron, he's a good friend of ours," she replied, glancing at her aunties. "But I'm pretty sure we're not here to discuss Sam.

"You're right, Miss Penny, ma'am, I apologise. I'll tell you why I'm here. When I wrote this adaption of *Taming of the Shrew*, I wrote every word with one lady in my mind to play Katherine."

The sincerity in his eyes told her who that person was, and she felt a cold shiver run down her spine as all eyes turned to her.

"Oh no! You can't be serious! What makes you think I can play her?" she asked. She was totally shocked.

"I believe you're the *only person* who can be Katherine," he told her, his voice resonating around the room. "It's you, or no one. It's your play," he said, putting his huge hand out and pushing the script over the table towards her.

Penny looked across at her aunties, her face pale and bemused.

"I take it you had a hand in this?" she asked. "What did you do, put a spell on him to remove his common sense? And as for you, Archie, what about you? What was your role in this conspiracy?"

"He's putting up the money, dear," May replied.

"Really!" Penny snapped. "Well, if that's true you need your bloody brains tested. I know what they say about me, Arch. I'm not stupid or deaf. It's why I don't get many roles in the West End, let alone lead roles. And now you think you can just waltz me on stage and producers will come running because that dear, deluded man over there has written a brilliant play?" Penny now felt pressurised and cornered. She had been saving her anger for her meeting with Toby, but had now let it out early. "Now, let me guess, which producer did you show the script to?" Penny was burning a hole in Archie's face with her eyes. "How about Albert Steinman? He's a Bard man! I bet the blood ran out of his face when you told him I was to be the leading lady, didn't it?" Penny paused to draw breath. "My dearest Archie, this is a non-runner, you know that, even if I were to agree." She shook her head passionately from side to side. "No, Arch. It will not happen," she spat, venom rising in her blood.

Archie moved his chair and stood up, and started preening himself, pulling down on the leg seams of his trousers and then tugging at his shirt cuffs, making sure they extended out from his jacket by an inch. Not until he was content with grooming did he speak: "When you have quite finished, sweetie, I'll tell you something. Yes, you're right, the producers whom I have spoken to won't put their hands in their pockets to back the play. And when I told these two witches that I can't get backers, they cornered me to agree to back you myself, and reluctantly, and with great trepidation, I agreed."

Penny felt deflated at hearing this truth, but Archie was now smiling. He was happy, even elated.

"Don't you understand, sweetie, you're a McCain through and through. You had all of us mesmerised by your zeal. Oh yes, you're Katherine alright, and I will back you whatever it costs if you can reproduce venom and passion like that on stage. And when you do, there will be a whole lot of pissed off producers who missed the boat."

Once again, all attention was on her.

"Please, Miss Penny, please say yes?"

The intensity of Aaron's words bounced off her skull. Penny looked at her aunties and breathed a heavy sigh. "Who will be stupid and tough enough to direct me? I'm not easy to cope with at the best of times."

June could feel May's hand under the table squeezing hers.

"I will, dear, I will."

Penny's face once again displayed pure shock.

"No, June. It's been nearly twenty years since you last directed. You're seventy-four now . . ."

June looked directly at Aaron. "Will you allow me to direct your play?" she asked.

Aaron bent down and kissed her cheek, and answered, "Miss June, it would be an honour."

June then turned to Archie.

"Archie, dear, will you bankroll me? Yes or no?" she asked in a no-nonsense tone.

Archie was well aware of June's renowned directorial expertise. He also knew she didn't take passengers, and demanded that her actors work hard – very hard – to achieve perfection. Suddenly he felt sorry for his dear sweet Penny. She may be June's niece, but June wouldn't show her any favours.

"Yes. I will back you to the hilt," he said simply.

There was silence around the table for a few moments, before Penny exploded, "No! This is all wrong! I'll not be talked into this!" She looked at her dear Auntie June. "For a start, my dear aunt, you are in no fit state for the physical stresses of directing a project like this. You need a new hip, and you can hardly pick up the kettle because of your arthritis." She took June's hand. "Let's be sensible about this, please. I'd love you to direct me, you know that. Your mind is as capable and sharp today as it was thirty years ago, but your body isn't. I would be so worried about your health if you were to do this." She smiled softly at her. "The producer should find a director to direct me, and who Aaron could also work with."

Penny then turned to look at Archie and said, "And you, you lovely, silly man, you're a theatre critic, not a theatre producer. Find a producer who is willing to put his reputation on the line, and I'll promise you all one hundred per cent of my abilities, heart and soul." Her brain was now whirling like a top, trying to comprehend the task she had agreed to.

Then she looked at Aaron and quietly said, "Yes, I will be your Katherine." And tears of joy suddenly ran down her face. "I just hope you stupid bastards know what you're letting yourselves in for."

Archie hugged Penny.

"Don't worry, sweetie, I'll make it happen, you leave it to me." He held out his hand to Aaron. "It looks like we've got ourselves a play to put on."

"Sure have."

Penny arose from her chair and checked the time on her phone. *Shit*!

"Archie, sweetheart, I have to get home to see Toby. Could you drop me off on your way?"

Her mind was spinning. She had been very stressed about the showdown with Toby, now she had to accept the realisation that her long-time dream of being a leading lady in a West End play might well be coming true.

Chapter 31

After the Showdown

Penny opened her front door for Toby to leave. As he walked past her, they hugged, and Toby kissed her; he could sense that her embrace was restrained. He left without saying a word. They had been talking for over three hours, and had agreed a way by which they could hopefully rebuild their damaged relationship. But first she had to sleep.

The text message from Penny arrived at 07.30am the following day: 'Hi, Sam, need to see you. Px'.

'Am in Bristol today, be with you early evening, don't tell your aunties, I won't be staying. Sx' he replied.

'Thanks, I'll cook a meal. Px'.

Penny arrived home shortly before 6.30pm after a long of day of rehearsals. No sooner had she kicked off her shoes then her doorbell rang: it was Sam.

"Hi, Sam," she said. "Sorry I just got in myself." He could see she looked and sounded tired. "Want a beer? I'll cook something to eat." She opened her fridge door. "Shit, I've got sod all, sorry, Sam."

She turned to look at him, and he could see in her eyes that she looked lost, and that even her smile seemed forced.

"Come here," he said, and put his arms out.

As she felt them close around her she burst into tears. Sam didn't say anything, he just held her while she sobbed. He wished the people who thought she was insensitive and uncaring could see her now: the victim of a man who she thought loved her.

After a minute or so she pulled herself away from his hold.

"That bloody man tried to dictate to me what I should and shouldn't be doing," she blurted. "I'm sorry, I know you said this is not your problem, but I just need to tell you what happened, because it involves you."

"Really?" he replied. "OK, but firstly, let's get organised, then you can tell why this involves me. Where do you keep your takeaway menus?"

She pointed to a cupboard to his left. "In there. Just to the side of the plates."

"You choose what you'd like," he told her, putting the menus into her hand.

"I'm not really hungry," she answered, her face a combination of anger and hurt.

He inspected her collection of wines, remembering what she had once said about being high maintenance: the labels on the bottles made it quite clear they were more than just your average supermarket's offer of the week.

"Red or white?" he asked, and then turned to her. "I would say you're in a red mood, and in reply to you not being hungry – I bet you haven't eaten a good meal since the one you had at the pub."

Penny reached to a cupboard for two large wine glasses and watched as he poured, and gesticulated as if to say *Fill it up*!

"I've not come here to watch you get pissed, have I?" he told her. "Now go and have a nice long bath. I'll order the food for an hour's time, and then you can tell me what the problem is."

"That's easy! Toby's the problem!" she replied, trying to hold back a yawn. "And a bath will be lovely and it'll wake me up a bit," she said sounding melancholy.

"I promised the girls I'd phone them, and they'll keep me talking for ages, so just relax, there's no hurry."

"I'd like to talk to them, too, but tell them to phone me this week, and give them my love." She disappeared up the stairs.

"Sam, sweetheart, wake up," she said. "You poor love, you must be worn out with me dragging you up here at a moment's notice. I feel bad about that now."

"Don't be," he replied, and then stood up to stretch his bones. "Is the food here?"

"No, not yet, but in the meantime a top up would be nice – or a half top up," she asked.

Sam replenished their glasses. Penny removed the towel from her head and her wet hair fell over her shoulders. She sat down, putting her hand out to pick up her brush in one hand and take her wine in the other.

"Not enough hands," she smiled.

"Stand up," he told her.

She looked at him, slightly amused. He then he sat down on the settee and put a large cushion on the floor between his legs, gesturing with his eyes for her to sit on the cushion.

"Go on, sit down, I'll dry your hair."

She smiled, knowing that with two daughters their daddy would have had lots of experience in drying a girl's hair. She put her hand out for her wine and sat down. She then felt his fingers on her head as he ran them through her hair, strong and firm. She was enjoying the pampering he was giving her, and for a short while she pushed aside the reason why he was there.

"Sam, the doorbell, sweetheart."

Sam paid the delivery boy for their takeaway and they settled down to eat. Penny then took their empty plates to the kitchen and returned with another bottle of wine.

"Toby sees you as a threat," she announced. "He didn't say that exactly, but that's what he was implying."

"Yes, I can understand that. He's wrong, but I understand his concerns."

"When he came here yesterday, I demanded the truth from him," she said, not looking at him but watching her wine swirl around the inside of her glass as she moved it with her wrist. "At first, he denied using cocaine, he said I was mistaken; but you know me, Sam. Remember when we first met and how I kept badgering you about your bag until you told me? Well, I was like that with him – perhaps even more so.

"He eventually owned up. He said it wasn't a habit – but he would say that, wouldn't he? I felt he'd insulted my intelligence. I asked him if he took other drugs. I didn't state any drug in particular, but as far as I'm concerned, if you take any drugs you're a stupid idiot." She bent down to look at her feet. "I should have brought down my foot spa, never mind." Sam could see her eyes were full of tears again. "Look at us, you and me . . . I know I've said it before, but I always feel safe with you, even now when I'm feeling vulnerable because of Toby. I know you don't see me as any more than a friend . . ." But as those words left her mouth, she felt strangely remorseful that she'd said them. "He said I'm naive for trusting you." She searched his face for a reaction to Toby's accusation: there was none.

"The last thing you are is naive," he told her. "You've approached the situation you have found yourself in exactly like I would have done: you've put distance between you and a potentially career-destroying scenario. You know as well as I do what would have happened if the press had got wind of you being around drugs, and Toby would have taken you down with him. How you handled that – by leaving – showed presence of mind, not naivety. And I'm glad that as your friend you trust me enough to talk to me like this."

He could see that she took that comment to heart.

"We've talked about our friendship before, at length," he said. "I know you trust me in a way most people can't understand – Toby included. Your aunts understand our friendship. My girls do too – and they think the world of you, incidentally. We don't love each other, but love to be with each other, and I'd define that as a loving and deep friendship, wouldn't you?" he said as he reached for her hand. "But I make no bones about what I'm going to say next . . . sometimes I look at you, and I'm blown away by your elegance and charm. I'm only in my fifties after all, and with one of the most beautiful creatures on God's earth holding on to my arm, I would be worried if the old male hormones didn't kick in now and again. . ."

She listened and watched him smile at her; she knew he was speaking from his heart, but she wondered why she felt a tinge of sadness at his words.

"I won't do anything to jeopardise this friendship of ours, and you know that," he added, emphatically. He then frowned. "Besides, there are two elderly ladies across town who would most likely turn me into frog if I did anything to hurt you."

Penny laughed out loud at that.

"Not forgetting the other two: your lovely daughters! Us girls stick together, despite blood being thicker than water and all that, and Maggie would certainly have something to say. We're the gang of three, remember?" She sipped her wine, and then said, "I've never doubted your trust and friendship, Sam, and those who do only want to be in my shoes."

Neither of them spoke for a few minutes, until Sam broached the subject of Toby again.

"OK, Penny, you didn't ask me here to buy you a Chinese meal, did you? What else is there?"

Penny unlinked herself from his arm – she'd almost subconsciously put it there a while ago – and then curled her legs under her. She took a cushion and held it against her breast, almost as a comfort, or as defence . . .

"I also asked Toby if he'd had sex with those tarts. He stayed there for the rest of the week, after all, and my guess is that he did, either because he wanted to or was out of his skull – but I'm convinced he did." She turned her head away and looked into her glass. "The bastard said he didn't, but his eyes told me otherwise. I've known too many men in the past who have lied to me not to recognise another one.

"He told me he was sorry and then he said something which I though was a bit cheap . . . that some of his problem was *my fault*. He said that since I met you, when I wasn't working, I was always with you." Penny raised her voice. "I'll be damned if I let him put me on a guilt trip. Our problems started way before I met you. I couldn't let him get away with that."

She was still hugging her cushion tightly to her, shaking her head in utter disbelief. "Well, the up-shot of it all is for him to get a blood test, lay off the drugs completely, and move back to London. And *no,* Sam, before you think it, or say it, I won't be letting him move in with me, and he's got no chance of getting back into my bed for a very long time, if at all. He wants to rebuild our relationship, and for me to learn to trust him again, and like you said – I will stand by him whatever my feelings towards him are now. Thinking about it, I did tease, didn't I, when I was you? But that was because he was behaving like a dick."

"Yes, you're right," Sam replied. "You did, and I didn't feel good about it either, you knew that; but he's lucky a man if despite what he's done to you, you still want to help him. Just be careful, and remember what I said about betrayal." His voice was now full of foreboding; he couldn't help it.

"You'll still come up and see my aunties won't you, Sam? And chat on the phone?" she whispered. "We can still see each other from time to time, can't we? But it may not be a good idea me taking you to readings with me anymore. I'll miss that." She then gave him one of her child-like, mischievous smiles. "But it'll have nothing to do with me if Archie invites you to another of his soirees again, Mr Bond."

He laughed at her description of him, but felt sad that they wouldn't see so much of each other.

"Would it be OK for me to stay at the cottage when you're in Canada? I'd really like to see Emily again." Sam shot her a look. "On my own, Sam."

He knew really that she wouldn't take anyone there. "You have your key, and you know where I keep the car keys," he replied.

The gratitude and relief in her face was instant.

"Sam, we've drunk another bottle of the red wine!" she said, holding up an empty bottle. "Right, what else was there?" She frowned. "Oh yes! Aaron wants me to be Katherine."

"I know."

She flinched, surprised at hearing him say that.

"How do you know? Who told you? My aunties?"

Sam smiled and shook his head, and said, "It was Aaron. When I met him at Archie's bash, he told me then. I think his words were: 'It has to be Penny, or no one'. He's a very nice and sincere chap." Sam stared straight at her. "Is it going to happen?" he asked.

"I don't know. Most of the money-men won't touch me because they think I'm not box office material, so Archie is trying to put it together. We'll see . . ." she replied, her eyes now heavy.

Seeing her yawn was enough for Sam to realise it was time for him to leave.

"Well, madam, it's about time I left."

"No, Sam. You're staying here."

"No, Sam is leaving," he replied. "I'll quickly tidy up the

kitchen, and then I'm off. I've already booked into a hotel and need to be away early."

"I'll phone you tomorrow," she said, throwing her cushion aside and preparing to stand up. "Christ, my bloody legs have gone!" she teetered, and she put her arm out to steady herself.

"I'll be up again in ten days en route to Canada . . . and I'm sure we'll bump into each other," he smiled. Looking in to her eyes, he could see she was done in. "Get to bed woman!" he ordered.

He tidied up, as promised, and called goodnight as Penny made her way up the stairs. He then let himself out and walked the short distance to his hotel. It was a cold and rainy September night, but he was pleased he'd made the trip up to see her.

Penny awoke the next morning to the sound of her alarm ringing in her ears; she instinctively reached out an arm to silence it. Her head was banging. She lay on her back and recalled the previous night. She went through what they had said to each other and felt a lot happier. Like Sam told her, Toby was her problem, not his, and talking things through with him had given her strength. She realised she was a stronger person than she thought – certainly strong enough to deal with Toby, and definitely strong enough to take on the challenge of Aaron's play.

Penny smiled to herself. *Sam already knows that, the bugger*, she thought, now aware that he understood her more than she had given him credit for.

Chapter 32

The Last Time

"This place costs me more to park than my suits do," Sam said to himself as he parked his car at the hospital.

He'd promised Emily he would visit her before he left for London. As he walked into the paediatric ward, he was met by a nurse who showed him the private room where Emily was.

"Hello, princess," he said, ever so quietly.

Sue was sitting on a chair next to her. He could see Emily was connected to various monitors and an IV drip. He handed Sue a small package.

"This arrived from Penny," he informed her, smiling into her tired face.

Emily was awake but didn't speak. She looked at him and smiled with her beautiful blue eyes. He felt a lump in his throat, and he wanted so much to hug her like he used to when she was home at the pub.

"She's very tired, Sam, you'd better not stay," Sue whispered.

He bent over and gave Sue a kiss on the cheek.

"Give that to the princess from me and Penny."

Back in his car he sat there for a while; he had a terrible feeling that that would be the last time he would see her.

Chapter 33

The Letter

"Hi, ladies, I'm home," Sam called as he let himself in at June and May's house.

"Sam, we were beginning to get worried about you, dear, it's gone nine," May said, as he entered the lounge. They were sitting next to each other in their nighties and dressing gowns.

"Sorry for worrying you. I phoned you a couple of times, but you were engaged for quite a while, so I gave up in the end."

"Oh, that was Archie," June replied, and then turned to her sister thinking she might say something she shouldn't; Sam detected the slight hesitation.

"So, has Archie any news about getting the production up and running?" he asked.

"Well, yes and no, dear. Archie thinks he's got the theatre and a producer. We should know more by next week."

"That sounds promising. I should imagine those sorts of things don't happen overnight, do they?" he asked.

"Archie, as you may know, dear, likes to hide behind a mask so that people can't always see the true man." June spoke with an air of confidence; if anyone knew him inside out the sisters did. "He's no fool. He's his father's son, and when his father said he would do something, by God he would do it. Archie will get our girl on that stage. You can put your money on it – or in Archie's case, put his money on it."

Chapter 33

Sam removed an envelope from the inside pocket of his jacket.

"Talking of Archie, could you make sure he gets this letter," he instructed. "I was going to post it, but wasn't sure if his secretary opened his mail. It's private, so I'd rather only Arch read it."

June was very curious as to its contents.

"Of course, I will, dear. I'll give it to him personally, don't you worry."

"So, does Penny get to have any say on who will direct her?" he enquired. "I haven't got a clue how it all works."

"No, Sam, she doesn't, not in this case. Ordinarily, if Penny was interested in auditioning for a particular part, she would most likely know the director, or know of him and whether she could work with him, or he with her, and decide appropriately."

"But, Sam," said June, joining in on the conversation. "Most actors don't have the luxury of picking and choosing; their main concern is paying their mortgage. Don't worry, dear, Archie will come good. He'll make sure the producer will get the best director he can, or he will have us to answer to."

"I have no doubt you two will have a say it, no doubt at all," Sam laughed.

Sam set his alarm for 3.00am, and had time for a quick shower before his taxi picked him up to take him to the airport.

He was in the departure lounge for first class waiting to board, when a text message buzzed on his phone: 'Hi, Sam. Toby neglected to tell me he's appearing in pantomime in Manchester, rehearsals start soon. I can't believe he's done that. So much for trying to rebuild our relationship. Have a safe flight. Text me when you get there. Px'.

After an eight-hour flight, it was another thirty minutes before Sam cleared Arrivals. He could see Oak waiting for him. This giant redwood of a man stood at six feet and four inches tall, and was standing there in his well-weathered hide hunting coat. Even at fifty-nine years old he could still bang heads with the best of them; he was the best of them. Suddenly Sam felt vulnerable. He remembered what Oak had said when they'd last met at Annie's funeral: '*When you come over, you'll be in my world . . . we treat people different there.*'

"Hello, Oak," Sam said. "Well, I've made it . . ."

He shook Oak's hand, but neither of them smiled; they had a mutual respect for each other, but friends? No. They had a long way to go before they could ever call each other that.

"Hi, fella," Oak replied, and his deep voice resonated from his huge, muscular frame, and Sam couldn't help thinking that his straight back and broad shoulders gave him an intimidating air.

Oak took one of Sam's bags from him and turned for the exit, saying, "Come on, we have fair drive yet. I've got a place just outside the town, we'll stay there tonight." He led the way to his vehicle.

"So where is home these days?" Sam asked.

"Simcoe, a town not far from Lake Erie," Oak replied.

"Oak, I was wrong! I saw you as a Dodge man, not a Land Rover man," he said as they reached their transport.

"Hell, no!" boomed Oak, his voice echoing within the confines of the multi-storey car park. "Where I take her you wouldn't want a fancy RV." He laid his hand on the Land Rover's bodywork and then gently tapped his fingers on the chassis. "We've been together a long time, me and her. She's not pretty, but she ain't let me down yet."

Sam could see he had true affection for his beaten up ex-military vehicle; it was people Oak had trouble with, and Sam knew he was entering the lion's den. Both men had deep scars on their hearts due to what had taken place years before, and both knew it was time to build bridges.

"This old lady of the road, does she have a name?" Sam asked, as Oak lifted his suitcase into the back of the vehicle.

"Canda calls her 'Ali'," he replied.

Sam smiled, and said, "Canda . . . why am I not surprised she thought of the name?" he said as he remembered that as a child she was always putting names to everything.

The evening had set in by the time they arrived at Oak's home as the journey had taken over two bone-rattling hours. They didn't talk too much on the way, but that wasn't because they didn't want to, it was because they couldn't hear each other – Ali's engine had made sure of that.

"You go on in, fella, I'll bring in the bags," Oak said, opening the rear hatch of Ali.

Sam walked inside.

"Hello, Uncle Sam!"

He set his eyes on a woman in her late twenties, and then he felt his eyes moisten with emotion, and his voice quiet and strained as he replied, "Hello, Canda. Wow, look at you – you look just like your mother."

Canda was standing three feet in front of him with her arms open, waiting to hug her uncle. As they embraced, memories of her mother come flooding back to him. He kissed her cheek, and then stroked the side of her face with his fingertips.

"You even have your mother's lovely soft skin."

Canda smiled and then grinned at him, "Isn't that the sort of thing to say to Penny, Uncle Sam?"

He raised his eyebrows in surprise, and asked, "OK, which one was it? Maggie?"

She laughed, and her beautiful brown eyes sparkled in the light.

"No, it was Estelle. She told me all about your Penny. She

sounds lovely, and I think Estelle is staying with her this weekend," said Canda, seeing her uncle slowly shake his head.

"Those girls are proper mischief-makers," he said as Oak walked in with the bags.

"Come on, Canda," he said. "Let the fella go and sit down. I think Ali has taken her toll on him!"

Canda had prepared a meal for them and it wasn't long before Sam began to relax. It was gone 10.00pm Ontario time, but his body was thinking it was still late afternoon. Sam looked around the room; it was sparse, as if it wasn't lived in.

"Here, Sam." Canda passed him another can of beer and one to her father, and then sat down next to her uncle on the settee.

"I've texted Mags to say you've arrived, but she hasn't got back to me yet," she said. "She told me about the famous Shakespeare sisters. I've got DVDs of Shakespeare's plays with them in. Mags said they're like two aunties to them."

Sam laughed; he felt tempted to tell her that they were more like two scheming, mischievous witches! Canda was an English teacher at the high school, and had taken a natural interest in the sisters.

"Do you remember the time when Auntie Annie took Mum to London with her?" she asked, eagerly wanting to tell him what she knew about the people they met.

It was then that Sam began to nurture thoughts of fate and coincidence. Events from the past were so often brought into the present.

"Your memory is so good! I don't remember that?" he said, reluctant to leapfrog back to the time before their lives irreparably changed.

"That's because you were always busy," Oak said, his look stern.

And Sam was transported to the days when he was always

elsewhere, rather than being at home with his family, and he felt he was being studied by Oak, his piercing green eyes looking as if he were prey he wanted to hunt.

"So, Oak, what have you got planned while I'm here?" he asked, expecting him to say *I'm going to give you a twelve-hour head start, and then I'll come after you*! But he didn't, he looked directly at Sam and gave what he interpreted as a smile.

"I only stay here when I'm in town. I spend most of my time at my lodge by the lake. I reckon we could stay there a couple of days, show you around, sort out our gear, and then take you north and head for the Hudson."

Sam had done some homework before he left and he knew Hudson Bay was the other side of Ontario.

"That sounds great," he said. "I'm looking forward to seeing 'your world', as you once described it; but please don't tell me we're going in Ali?" he laughed.

Oak laughed too – a sound that was old and rusty, like it wasn't used very often.

"Hell, no . . . floaters," he said, noticing Sam didn't have a clue what floaters were. "Float planes," he explained, "but you probably call them sea planes."

Sam nodded his head in acknowledgement.

"We'll get one from here at Lake Erie," he said, "then onto North Bay on Lake Nipissing, spend a few days there. I've got some deer to check on, and then see what the weather's doing."

Sam realised that everything in Oak's world had to be planned because of the harsh environment he worked in – and loved.

"It's the beginning of our fall now," Oak told him. "Your autumn. I think this is the best time of the year to see this country."

Sam turned to Canda, and then nodded his head towards her

father. "Well, I'm hardly going to argue with him, am I? I know he's got a hunting rifle!"

They laughed at that, but later that night while lying in his bed, he thought about what Canda had told him about her mum and Annie visiting London, and particularly who they'd met . . .

Stranger things happen at sea, he thought, *or do they*?

Chapter 34

End of Holiday

All too soon his stay was over and he was back at the airport. He genuinely felt sad saying goodbye to Oak, who had shown a side of him Sam thought was lost forever – and a country he was already looking forward to coming back to.

He arrived back at Heathrow around 10.00pm, but his body told him it was 3.00am, and he felt pretty wrecked. As he walked out into the airport foyer, he couldn't believe his eyes.

"Hello, Sam," Penny said, smiling. He looked at her slightly dazed, but he was so happy to see her. "Please, no hugging," she whispered, and then asked, "Which one's got my present in?" with a giggle.

"Oh bugger! I knew there was something I forgot to get!" he told her.

"Sorry about the hug, but there are a few photographers around. One has already said hello to me, and asked who I'm meeting."

They walked to the car park, chatting about his trip, and Penny came to a halt next to Sam's car.

"If I didn't know better, I would say this is my car?" he declared, as he looked at her.

She unlocked it and opened the rear door for him to put his bags in the back, and then she walked up to him and stood so close that their bodies touched. He could see she was trying to compose herself, but for what reason?

"I'm sorry, Sam, I thought I could tell you without crying." She put her arms around him.

"What about the photographers?" he asked, his face clouding over. "What is it?"

"Sod the photographers, Sam," she replied. She was about to answer him, but she could see in his eyes he knew.

"Emily . . ." he whispered.

"Yes, sweetheart, she's gone to fly with the angels."

Her body trembled and he held onto her firmly, hearing her sob. He cupped his hand around her head and ever so gently kissed it, feeling her hair against his face.

"She's at peace now, at peace . . ." he murmured; but his heart ached with sadness for his little friend.

"I know," she replied, in a quiet, tender tone.

"When did she pass away?"

"Last week. Dave and Sue said not to contact you as they didn't want to upset you while you were away. Her funeral was yesterday, but I went down the day before. It was well attended, so very sad, but so lovely. Her ashes are going to be placed in the church graveyard next to the pub, Sue said she would like the idea of being close by."

She stopped crying, and they got into the car and pulled away.

"Are you worried I might put a dent in your baby, Sam?" she smiled.

"No. It's insured anyway. Besides, only people matter to me, you know that." He had to admit she looked good driving his car. "So, what's with picking me up then?" he asked.

"Well, I drove back up this morning and thought you might like to stay up here till Friday. It's only a couple of days after all."

(Sam instinctively knew she had planned something then.) "I could go back down with you for the weekend, the final rehearsals for the Noel Coward review I'm in are on Monday and Tuesday, and then we open on Wednesday . . . what do you think?"

What do I think? he thought. *I know what I think: I'm tired and would have preferred a good night's sleep before I had to think.*

"What do I think?" he said, taking a deep breath. "I think 'Toby', that's what I think."

Penny didn't turn to look at him, but said, "I thought that would be the first thing you'd ask. We've been trying hard to sort our differences out. We've been out a few times together, but he's pissed about not being tucked up in bed with me. I'm sorry if this sounds crude, but I'm not going to drop my knickers for him just to save our relationship. I told you he'll be in Manchester over Christmas, didn't I?" She stopped at a set of traffic lights and turned to Sam. "Do you know what that bastard has gone and done now? He's only arranged to go to Tenerife again on another bloody stag night. He's off tomorrow, so he won't even be here for the opening night of the play . . . the shit."

Sam just listened and said nothing; he'd learnt that from living with Annie and being the sounding board for her many rants, which, in fact, were far more severe than Penny's.

"I'm really trying to be conciliatory towards him, I really am, but when I asked Toby about supporting me, do you know what he said? He said he couldn't let his best mate down. But what about letting me down?" She drove along the row of mews and parked outside her auntie's house and switched off the engine. Sam heard the click of her seatbelt un-do and whirl as it retracted, but she made no effort to leave the car. Instead she turned to Sam, her voice now quieter but still filled with anger. "I've told him that while he's on the piss, and having a jolly good time with his mates, to give our future together some serious thought, and I'll do the same." She frowned then and looked Sam straight in the eye. "Just to be straight about this, I'm not using you to get at Toby. You're too intelligent, older and far too streetwise to let that happen; besides, you know I wouldn't do that to you."

"Thanks for the 'older' part."

Penny had to chuckle at that.

"I know it seems selfish of me, considering you've only just got back, but . . . I just needed my friend," she said, and she shrugged her shoulders.

Sam yawned, and then said, "I couldn't think of a nicer way to spend a weekend, but can I get some sleep first?"

She now felt terribly guilty for telling him her woes and keeping him from his bed.

"I'm sorry. I can be an inconsiderate bitch at times, can't I?"

"Yes, you can, but a lot has happened recently, with Toby and Emily, and like you said, we're friends. Pick me up when you're ready to head to the cottage."

"Thank you. Thank you so very much. I won't come in. If they're still up they'll keep me talking for ages, and you need to sleep."

Chapter 35

The Lie

Sam spent the next two days getting over his jet lag, contacting his two daughters and hearing all the gossip from the two aunties. He also made phone calls to his office and Emily's parents.

On Friday, he had to go out.

"Sam, you've got your nice suit on, where are you off to, dear?" May enquired.

"Archie. He's invited me to have lunch with him."

She was busting to ask what the lunch meeting concerned, but Sam wasn't entirely sure himself, so was glad she didn't ask. Sam was aware Archie had found a producer to put on Aaron's play; perhaps it was to do with that . . .

"He's sending a car," Sam added. "I should only be a couple of hours or so."

Arriving back at the house later than he hoped, he found the sisters in the lounge. He knew he had to tell them something about his lunch date with Archie, but he couldn't tell them the truth, not yet, so he decided he'd have to lie.

"Well, that was useful," he said, making himself comfortable on the settee opposite them.

"Really, dear, in what way?" June asked, looking directly at him.

"I asked Archie for a favour. I'm looking to open an office in Reading. There's a letting agent already up and running there

– London-based – and they want to sell up. (He thought that sounded convincing enough.) "I asked Archie if he could use his business contacts to check them out."

"Well, dear, what did he say?" she asked.

"Keep away from them, was his advice," he replied. "They're being investigated by the fraud squad."

June didn't say a word; she just smiled politely, giving him the impression that she didn't believe a word of it.

"So, there you go, that saved me a few bob," he said, as he got up from the settee. "I'm going to change. Madam is on her way."

Sam was having a cup of tea with the sisters when Penny arrived.

"Hi, Sam, you look better for the rest," she said, receiving welcoming kisses from her aunties.

"You're looking very lovely, dear, and happy," June told her.

Penny smiled a beaming smile back at her, and replied, "That's because I am happy. Rehearsals have gone well, and I'm going to have a nice quiet weekend with my friend here."

"Be a dear, Sam, there's something I need you to do for me before you both go," June said. "I need something from the top of my wardrobe. Could you get it for me?"

He looked at her; he knew she'd just lied to him too.

"Yes sure, lead the way." He turned to Penny. "Won't be long, hun," he said with a wink.

"Close the door, dear," she said, with authority in her voice. "Right, Sam, you know damn-well I didn't believe a word of that rubbish about Reading, so why don't you tell me the truth, especially if it concerns Penny," she demanded.

He realised the ruse was up, and didn't want to tell her, but he also knew there were no flies on June. She would keep him there until he told her.

"It concerns Toby," he said in a quiet voice. "He's been misbehaving. Penny's aware of it, and she has told me herself that all is not well, but it seems that other people now know, and it's going to get messy." Sam took her hand and felt the tremble. "Archie wanted me to know, that's all. The three of you are as dear to me as my girls, you know that, and I was just trying to protect you – for the time being. I knew you didn't believe me, but I had to say something. I think May believed me, so can we keep it that way?"

June now had alarm etched on her face.

"So, what's the idiot been up to?" she asked, sternly.

"Sorry, June, that's not for me to tell. Penny is the person you should ask."

"Are you going to tell her what Archie told you?"

"Yes. She needs to know so that she needs to protect herself from him."

"That bastard of a boy. We told her he was trouble. It's history repeating itself," she proclaimed, sounding anxious and angry.

"Not if Archie or I have anything to do with it. You'll just have to trust us," he told her; he knew that like their niece, June and May did trust him.

"I won't say anything about this, dear."

Letting go of her hand, he turned to walk away.

"If we don't go down soon, June, Penny will think we've been carrying on up here."

"You go, I'll follow," she replied. Normally she would had chuckled to herself at the thought of carrying on with Sam; now humour was the last thing she had on her mind.

Penny was sitting next to May on the settee, chatting away about the play.

"Right, I'm all ready when you are," he informed her. "Can I have the car keys? I want to put my bags in," he asked.

She reached into her bag and tossed them over to him. "I want them back, I'm driving," she told him.

"Penny, dear, I forgot to ask Sam if he's coming up on Wednesday to see the play," June asked, on her way back into the room.

"I don't know. I'll have to ask him. It's a bit cruel to drag him up from Devon every five minutes."

"Never mind, dear," June replied. "If he can't come, Archie is taking us anyway."

"Are you ready to go, dear?" May asked. "I think Sam is waiting by the door. At least it's not raining for the drive down."

They said their goodbyes and set off.

"How long did you say you're coming down for?" Sam enquired. (He'd seen a large suitcase in the back of the car when he'd put his own bags in.)

"Well, I thought that as you said I could come down anytime I liked, it would be a good idea to keep some clothes there, instead of living out of a suitcase all the time." She turned her head to look at him. "You don't mind, do you?"

"Concentrate on the road!" he told her, but Penny could hear him laughing to himself. "God, it's a good job I love you!" he replied.

"Do you? Really?" she asked, in a giggly, girly sort of way.

But Sam had started searching through the CDs in the glove compartment; he was sure he'd left something in there.

"If I do love you, I have a feeling it's getting less each day," he said with a sigh, wondering if she had anything to do with its disappearance.

"How much do you love me?" she laughed. "If it was based on a dozen red roses, how many roses do you think I'm worth?"

She may have been laughing, but he realised her question was due to the hurt she was feeling because of Toby, and his answer needed careful consideration. He knew she needed to know that there was at least one man in her life who felt some resemblance of love towards her, even if was a platonic love.

He leant over and put his hand on the back her seat and breathed in the fragrance of her perfume.

"What are you doing?" she asked.

"I'm working out how much I love you," he said, turning to sit back properly in his seat. "Considering you already have the keys to my cottage, and my car . . ."

"Go on, Sam, tell me! Please?" she asked, smiling with anticipation.

"I suppose I love you three-roses-worth; but you have to share that with your aunties," he told her, endeavouring to sound stern, but failing.

"Oh no. I'm not sharing your love with them. They can have their own roses, thank you!" she cried. "Sam Farmer loves me three-roses-worth. Hmm. I would have settled for two, Sam, but three? I'm a lucky girl. Aren't you curious how many roses I love you by?"

"No, not really," he responded. "Just seeing you happy in my company is good enough for me."

She felt strangely humbled by those words, unable to remember being in the presence of a red-blooded male who wanted nothing more from her than her company.

"Do you know, soon after we first met, I told Auntie June about the feeling I had about you, about how I thought we'd met before. She reckons we must have been lovers in a past life," she told him with a giggle. "If we were, I bet it ended in tears," she added. "That's the story of my life when it comes to lovers."

As much as Sam was enjoying this light-hearted banter, he knew he had to tell her about his conversation with Archie.

"I had lunch with Archie today . . ." he tentatively broached.

"Did you? Did he tell you how the play is progressing?" she asked.

"Yes, he spoke of the plans in great detail. By the sound of it you should be opening mid to late May next year," he continued. "I don't know about you, but I'm getting excited." He noticed a sign for a lay-by. "Pull in at the lay-by coming up and I'll tell you what else he said."

He couldn't see the expression of intrigue on her face in the dark, but he could visualise it clearly.

She pulled over.

"OK. What else did he say?" she asked, curiously; but when he reached over to hold her hand, anxiety spread across her face.

"Penny . . ." – there was no point beating around the bush – "one of the girls who was at the villa in Portugal with you has sold her story to a newspaper: how she spent a week on holiday with a well-known actor." Sam looked at her face, expecting to see anger, but it wasn't there, instead was a look of resignation; perhaps she had guessed something like this was bound to happen sooner or later. "You don't need me to tell you the rest, do you?"

"How did Archie know? No, don't bother to answer that, there isn't much that goes on that Archie doesn't know about." She reached for her bag and searched for her phone. "Do my aunties know?" She searched for Angie's number and hit 'call'.

"Yes and no," he replied, not really wanting to explain.

"Angie, its Penny . . ."

Penny explained what had happened with the call on loudspeaker, and Sam was surprised at how calm she was.

When she ended the call, she asked, "Should we turn around and go back?"

"No. You need time to think things through. You love the cottage and you'll be amongst friends."

She let out a sigh. "Thank you. I hoped you'd say that."

He took a deep breath. "I'd better tell you the rest of my conversation with Archie."

"OK. . ." he continued, "you know far better than me how shit hits the fan where celebrities are involved; but like Angie said – you're the innocent party in all this. The press will be camped outside your place when we get back, you know that, but Archie has arranged all the transport you need to and from the theatre."

Then he gave her one of his cheeky grins, making her realise he had something up his sleeve, something pre-planned.

"Sam, what are you up to?" she asked.

"Not me. Maggie."

"Do tell!"

"Mags has taken a week off work and will stay at your place from tomorrow to keep an eye on it. The only people she'll let in are Angie and Archie, no one else; I'm not even sure she'll let me in! Is that OK by you?"

"Sure, yes, you organised this? For me? Thank you. I can't see anyone trying to search my rubbish bins with Maggie around."

"You know how it works, Penny. This girl has sold her story; the other might decide to do the same. Soon after, Toby's so-called mates will want to get in on the act. After that, it'll be Toby's turn. 'Damage limitation to save his career' Archie calls it, and he reckons Toby will get a good PR man and do a kiss and tell on you. You already said he felt threatened by our friendship."

"Toby wouldn't be as stupid as to involve you."

"Archie thinks he will. That it will be something like: 'My fiancée became infatuated with an older man, blah-blah'–"

"No!" she cried. "He shouldn't involve you! It's wrong! I'll have to speak to him!"

"No, you don't," Sam said sternly. "I don't care a toss what he says about you and me, and you shouldn't either. Think about it – who will it hurt? No one except Toby himself. Your aunts will support us, and like Archie and the girls, they will serve Toby the contempt he deserves."

"I'm so sorry. Maybe you should stay away until it all blows over," she said, concerned he might get pestered by the media.

"OK. Turn the car around and I'll take you back."

He could see that what he had just said had surprised her as she frowned.

"Alright, let's go back then," she replied.

"Sorry, that was cruel," he said, seeing her close to tears. "Do you really think I would do that, you silly bugger?" he asked. "It's hard for us, let alone other people to understand our friendship, but my three roses are a lot love and friendship, don't ever forget that, and if I hear anymore silliness, I'll take one off you. . . come on, change places, my turn to drive."

Chapter 36

Scars from the Past

Arriving at the cottage just before 10.00pm, Penny quickly climbed out of the car.

"What's the hurry?" Sam asked.

"I'm busting for a pee, Sam," she told him, disappearing inside.

Women . . . especially this one, he thought and laughed out loud.

"If you light the fire, I'll cook us something," she said, when he hauled their bags in. "I've brought food enough for tonight." She started taking ingredients out of a carrier bag.

"Don't worry, hun! I'll carry your bags upstairs for you."

"Will you, Sam? That's sweet of you," she replied, giggling, without bothering to turn around to acknowledge his sarcasm.

Soon they were sitting together on the sofa, eating their evening meal on their laps and enjoying the warmth of the roaring fire.

"When I came here on Monday, on my own, I didn't have a clue how to light your fire, so Terry next door kindly lit it for me and showed me how to do in the future," she said. "They're a lovely family, aren't they?"

He had to agree, but as he observed her relax he couldn't help but feel worried for her. Next week her whole world was going to crash in on her – and all because she'd loved and trusted someone. And once again his own memories of the past rose to taunt him.

And Don't Forget the Roses

The next morning Penny awoke to muffled thuds coming from the garden outside. Repositioning her pillows to sit up, she listened to the sound. She let her mind wonder as she looked at the thick, whitewashed walls, and tried to imagine what life would have been like two hundred years before. She climbed out of bed and walked to the window; Sam was splitting logs again, and she watched him for a while. *Cup of tea, that's what he needs*, she thought.

Sam walked into the utility room and removed his sweat-soaked T-shirt. He threw it into the washing machine, unaware Penny was in the kitchen. She turned and smiled at him, and then the joyful look on her face turned to horror and she put her hand across her mouth, starring at his torso, transfixed at the sight in front of her. She slumped down onto a chair.

"Oh, Sam . . . who . . . who did that to you?" she gasped, her eyes wide.

He stood less than two feet away from her. He knew she would be shocked – most people were when they saw his scars – which was why he'd deliberately hidden them from her, but he knew it was only a matter of time before she would see them.

"It looks like a piece of modern art, doesn't it?" he said, smiling, intending to make light of them.

A series of slashes and zigzags ran from his chest to just above his belly button.

"Don't joke. Who did this to you?" she asked again, anger now in her voice.

"Put the kettle on while I get a shirt," he replied.

"There you are, I've done you some toast too," she said, trying to raise a smile; but it felt wrong after what she'd just seen.

"Thank you," he said quietly. "I was on a cargo ship in Indonesia," he told her, spreading honey on his toast. "Two of us were on our way back on board when we got mugged by a bunch of youths. I was only twenty-one at the time, but these were just kids. When it came to scrapping, I'd always been good with my hands *and* head, so I knocked a couple of them over – my mate, had run off by then, leaving me alone at the party, so to speak – but I then got arrested for assault, and the locals who jumped us pressed charges; they said it was me who started the fight."

Penny stood there motionless, listening to every detail.

"The police put me in a holding cell on my own while they decided what to do with me. Then, for a laugh, they put me in another cell with three nut-jobs. There was one particular man, who, because I wouldn't kneel down or bend over for the other two – you know what I mean by that? – he thought he'd have some fun with me in another way. How the hell he got a cutthroat razor in there, beggars belief . . . but it could have been a whole lot worse . . . at least he didn't cut my dick off," he shrugged.

"How can you make light of it, Sam?" Penny asked, shocked by his devil-may-care quip.

"I have no choice. What is done is done. I have to live with it, live with these," he replied, putting his hand to his chest. "Once the police realised they'd ballsed up, I spent the following two months hidden away in an army hospital, and then I was sent home; well, more like deported."

Penny shook her head in utter disbelief. The thought of what he'd been through brought home to her what sick-minded people there were in the world.

"What did the girls say when they first saw them? Do they know what happened?"

"When they were young they used to sit on my lap and count the stitch holes . . . they'd lose count after a while. He also carved his initials, too, but they didn't spot them. The guy who did this to me knew what he was doing, and he could have spilled my guts all over the cell floor, but he didn't."

"That was considerate of him. I-I'm lost for words, Sam."

"Ha, that's a first," he replied.

"Don't say that. I just don't know what to say apart from . . . bastards," she said sadly.

They spent the morning in Exeter, and Sam bought Penny a pair of walking boots for Dartmoor. He then popped into his office, before heading back to the cottage, via the pub, to see Sue and Dave.

As they talked of the loss of their darling daughter, Sue gave him something that belonged to Emily: a porcelain angel.

"She would want you to have this, Sam," she smiled. "To remember her by."

Penny held his hand, feeling his anguish.

And later on, after they'd eaten, he spoke again of the fight. He hadn't discussed it with anyone, for years, but somehow he felt he needed to. Penny sat quietly, watching the flames as he talked.

"When those lads attacked me, and I fought back, do you know what hurt me the most? The betrayal. The guy who was with me, Henning, he was my friend – or so I thought – and we'd known each other for a couple of years. He was a big chap, well capable of looking after himself – and me. My dad had drummed into me that you never turn your back on your friends, and some would say I was naive to rely on anyone. I should have run away myself." He looked at her. "The reason I'm saying this is because I want you to know that I won't run away. You've got a whole lot of shit ahead of you, and I'll be there for you."

"I know, Sam, I know," she whispered, resting her head on his shoulder.

That night Sam realised that Penny had begun to invade his mind and his every thought, and that he was starting to care for her very, very much – and that scared him.

"Just don't fall in love with her, there's a good chap," he said to himself as he dropped off to sleep.

The next day, after lunch, they prepared to leave for the drive back to London.

"Sam, did you get my eggs from Terry?" Penny asked, putting her handbag on the front passenger seat.

"Yep," he replied. "But before we leave, I've got something for you," he said, leading her back into the kitchen and handing her a phone. "This is for you. I've always got a spare in the office in case I lose mine or it gets stolen. The reason I'm giving it to you is obvious really: the fewer people who have your personal number the better, especially Toby."

"Sam, you're a love," she told him as she turned it on. "I'll put you in first."

"I've already done that. Look under 'R' for Rose."

She looked puzzled, but then moments later started laughing.

"You bugger! But I like that!" she said, blowing him a kiss.

As they drove away from the cottage, Penny looked out of her side window.

"You know I'm sad you won't be coming to the opening night of the play," she said. Sam didn't reply. "That gate could do with a coat of paint," she then said, as they passed through it.

Sam stopped the car.

"Do you want me to paint it before or after I come up and see the bloody play?" he asked.

She smiled and then mouthed, "*Thank you.*"

Chapter 37

Messages

Sam dropped Penny outside her house and then quickly sped off. Maggie was at the door to let her in.

"Hi, Mags," she said, so relieved to see her. "I'm so grateful you're here. What's it been like?" she asked.

She walked to her front door and knelt down, peeping through the letterbox to see who was out there . . . it all seemed quiet, but then sudden flashes of light appeared from nowhere.

"Bastards," she muttered.

"It's been like this all day. I was tempted to open the door with just my bra and knickers on, just to give them something else to talk about, but I don't think Dad would be too happy," Maggie laughed. "Come on, come away from the door. Don't pay any attention."

"Christ, your dad would go spare!" Penny pulled a torturous face, imagining Sam's reaction to that. "I don't think his sense of humour would stretch that far!" She looked at Maggie – a young, intelligent woman, who lived life to the full, but within the confines of propriety. *Not like the two sluts who helped Toby destroy our relationship*, she thought.

"There you go, all your new and old friends have left you messages," Maggie said, holding a very large amount of A4 paper in her hands. "I told them you'd get back to them tonight." she said, showing no emotion on her face as she put the mass of paper down on the table in front of Penny.

"You're joking," Penny cried, and then realised she was having her leg pulled. She let out a sigh of relief. "Christ, Mags, I almost wet myself!"

"Sorry, maid, couldn't resist it!" Maggie laughed.

"You're definitely your dad's daughter! He's always winding me up!"

"Don't take it personally, we all love you, you know that," said Maggie.

Listening to her kind words, and remembering what her father had said – '*my three roses are a lot of love*' – made her realise that included Maggie and Estelle, as well as Sam.

"OK, let's read these messages, but firstly a glass of wine," she said, looking at her wine rack. "Mags! Where has all the wine gone?"

"Ah yes," Maggie replied, looking sheepish. "Well . . . um . . . Angie and Archie came around last night and we ended up opening a few; but not to worry, he's coming around later with a couple of cases of your favourite."

Penny pulled a disgruntled face as she endeavoured to remove the cork from her last bottle of wine.

"Well, I hope he won't be long, because this one ain't going to last very long, is it!" But she laughed as she said it.

"I'll phone Arch to remind him, besides, I've asked him to bring a couple of bottles of my tequila. I'll be buggered if I'm going to be holed up here without my tipple."

"Here's to an absent friend," Penny said, raising her glass, and handing the other to Maggie.

"Do you mean that dad of mine?"

"Yes," she replied. "The poor love drove me up here, but now has to spend the rest of the evening with my aunties getting the third degree about Toby. I'll phone him later to see if he's still sane."

"Talking about Toby," Maggie said, as she fumbled through the sheets of paper, "he's phoned loads of times."

"You didn't tell him I was with your dad, did you?" she asked, panic in her voice.

"No," came the reply, and that one syllable put her fears at ease. "I told him you were well pissed off and won't speak to him. He asked me if you were here, so I said yes, and that you were listening in on the call."

Penny raised her glass of wine to her.

"Well done, Mags, one to us. Do you know everything that happened on holiday with Toby? Did your dad tell you?"

"No, Pen, I only know what Archie told me. Apart from that, I know bugger all. You should know my dad doesn't tell tales," she replied.

"I know he wouldn't, but I wouldn't have minded if he had. So, you obviously don't know what that bastard put me through?" she asked.

Maggie shook her head.

"Come on, I'll give you the full script, word for sodding word."

Sam spoke to Penny and Maggie by phone for over an hour that evening, and they filled him in on the latest developments. As Archie had predicted, the newspapers and internet where having a field day with Toby's drug taking and sexual exploits, and photographers continued to arrive outside her home, waiting like vultures in case Toby turned up.

As promised, Sam went to the opening night of the Noel Coward review Penny was appearing in, but on his own, and he stayed in the shadows: Archie had got him a seat in the upper circle, away from peering eyes. Penny knew he was up there and supporting her, but it was hard for them both. And that night, back at her aunties' house, he started to miss her, and not being able to be with her openly saddened him.

Chapter 38

Another Showdown

Maggie had agreed to leave the house while Toby was there, but she wasn't happy about it. She had become protective towards Penny, as her father was, but she knew their meeting had to take place in private. Penny had had the presence of mind to dictate where and when she confronted him the last time, and now she had to do it all again. She had decided to talk to him in the kitchen; the lounge was too cosy, and the bedroom was definitely out – now and forever. She knew the first thing Toby would do was open the fridge and get himself a can of lager, so she removed them. Instead she got a coffee mug ready for him, and water for herself. Her aunties had always advised her to drink water, lots of water, especially before a performance; it hydrates the brain, they told her.

Her phone rang.

"Penny, it's Toby, open the door, pet."

She could tell by his tone that he was already stressed. *Good*, she thought, and then smiled as she put the final touches to her make-up. By the time she was ready to open her door to him, he had been outside her house for several minutes in the full glare of the press and photographers, and he felt vulnerable and stripped naked by all the attention. She put her eye to the spy hole in the door – which had been fitted earlier in the week – and grinned.

"My turn," she muttered with glee.

She hadn't agreed to the meeting with him without giving it

a lot of thought, planning her every move as if she was acting out a scene in the theatre. Penny knew she had what her aunties considered the McCain's aptitude: timing! She wasn't going to be rushed; she would dictate not only the pace, but the mood too. She'd put on a pair of skin-tight, electric-blue leggings, black velvet shoes with three-inch heels, and a cream cashmere sweater. Her hair was tied back, showing her elegant neck, crying out to be petted. She applied just enough make-up to extenuate her hazel eyes. Although approaching her mid-thirties, she knew she still had what it took to turn heads. Her beauty spoke louder than any words, and she wanted Toby to be speechless and to think she had dressed like this to please him. *How wrong he was going to be.*

She stood behind the door and opened it, allowing just enough space for Toby to walk through, but so that she wouldn't be seen by anyone outside.

"Well, pet, thank you for that, I would have brought have sandwiches if I'd known," he said, clearly furious at having to wait.

She smiled at him, a nice polite smile, and then leant forwards for him to kiss her and be intoxicated by her perfume; his favourite perfume.

"Hello, sweetheart, come through," she said entering the lounge. She pointed to the settee. He took off his coat, scanning the beautiful woman in front of him. "Sit down, babe, I'll put some music on."

She walked over to her stereo, turning her back on him and then leaning forward to pick a CD. (She chuckled to herself as she thought of the look on Sam's face when he couldn't find his CDs in the car.) She was in no doubt that Toby was gazing at the perfectly shaped bottom in front of him, which hid little from his imagination.

Turning to look at him, she could see he was now comfortable, even showing signs of arousal: his guard was *down*.

"Come on through to the kitchen," she told him in a soft tone, gesturing with her head.

He stood up, but looked disappointed that they wouldn't be sitting next to each other on the settee.

"Whatever you say, pet," he replied. He immediately headed to the fridge to get a cold can. "Ah, no lager, pet?" he said, seeing she was instead making him a cup of coffee, her eyes not looking in his direction.

"Sorry," she told him, stirring his coffee, the teaspoon making a clinking sound. She passed it to him as he sat on the stool on the other side of her breakfast bar. She took the stool opposite him, and slowly unscrewed the lid from her bottled water. She took a small mouthful, and placed the bottle silently back onto the worktop. She folded her hands into her lap, out of sight. "I had a bit of a party last night . . . been too busy to get to the shops," she finally said.

She sat there looking at him, her face now empty of the smile she'd had a few minutes before. Toby now felt uneasy; he needed her to continue the tenderness she'd shown him when he arrived. He put his right hand out on the worktop towards her, in a gesture for her to hold it, but she didn't. Sipping his coffee, he frowned.

"I don't know what to say, pet." He said the words in a boyish tone, as he looked appealingly into her eyes.

Penny breathed in through her nostrils, filling her lungs with air, and then slowly breathed out.

"You're an actor, Toby, you should have rehearsed what you wanted to say before you came here."

Then he realised that this was all a set-up to snare him, and to give him a false sense of security. He could also see her eyes were now wide open and had the look of Medusa about them.

"What do you want me to say? I'm sorry? I screwed up?"

His body language had changed from being relaxed, to a

typical macho stance: his shoulders were arched back, he sat more upright on the stool and his open hand of a few moments before was now clenched.

"To tell you the truth, anything you say won't wash with me anymore. At first I was prepared to give you the benefit of the doubt, to try and salvage our relationship, but once that slut had spewed the beans on you and your buddies, my love for you died."

Toby sat there, trying to appear nonchalant.

"You don't really believe all that bollocks, do you, pet? You know what the papers are like. They flower everything up to sell more copies. It's her word against mine, anyway, and it's not true – any of it."

A thin band of sweat had appeared across his top lip, and down the side of his temples.

"The truth is, Toby, that *is* the truth, isn't it?" She got off her stool and walked over to a pile of newspapers by her back door, removed one and then sat down again. She rustled through the pages, looking for the article she wanted, and then without looking at him began to read from it. Her voice controlled, clear and crisp: "'*Toby walked to the edge of the pool. We were all skinny-dipping when he shouted: "That frigid bitch has pissed off!"*'." She looked at him coldly, and then continued to read from the paper: '*Toby was out of his head on cocaine. He told me that he bought a king-sized bed for his girlfriend, Penny McCain, and always fancied doing a foursome on it with her.*" Again, she looked at him coldly. "Did you really?" she asked. "'*He hated her aunties - who he called 'the soap queens of Shakespeare'* . . . do you want me to carry on?" she asked, pushing the paper towards him. She then put her hands back in her lap.

Suddenly he swept his forearm across the worktop, sweeping the paper and his now empty coffee mug onto the floor where it smashed into several pieces. He glared at her with anger in his eyes.

And Don't Forget the Roses

"So why all this dressing up if you planned to dump me?" he growled. "I bet you were put up to this by that old fart. I always thought he fancied getting into your knickers. I don't know who to feel sorry for, you or him."

She calmly got off her stool, and without replying slowly reached into a cupboard for her dustpan and brush. She placed it on the worktop in front of him.

"You see all this?" And she ran her hands down her body, from her breasts to her thighs. "This body, my love, my trust – all this was once yours. But for whatever reason – and I actually don't give a shit what that reason is – you made a conscious decision to throw all that away, to throw me away. I wanted you to realise what you've turned your back on." She fixed him with a look that turned his blood cold.

"And as for Sam," she said, as he desperately tried to look away, "do you know what he said to me? That you're my problem, not his, and he's right, because if you were his, and believe me when I say this," she said, moving her face nearer to him. "Sam would rip you limb from limb. Don't be fooled by his gentle demeanour, or because he's almost twice your age. He's experienced things in his life which would give *you* nightmares." Her heart was now pounding in her chest as she thought of Sam and his scars. She could smell Toby's breath on her face, stale from drinking beer shortly before he arrived, and it only added fuel to her quiet rage.

"Well, pet, if you're finished like, I'll go. I've got better things to do than get lectured by you."

Penny thought it strange that he hadn't put up much of a fight to save their relationship, and she concluded that cocaine was more important to him now than her.

"Yes, Toby, go. But before you do, I want you to know that I've packed your clothes and other belongings into boxes, and I want them out by the end of next week – and that includes your sodding bed." She raised her arm in the direction of the front door.

He turned to her and smiled. "Do I get a farewell kiss for old time's sake, pet?"

"No, Toby, and I'm not your pet anymore," she replied, calmly, noticing he had the gall to look surprised at her refusal, as if he thought kissing her might change her mind. She stood behind the door as before, closing it with a slam. She stood there for a few moments, gathering her thoughts.

Chapter 39

The Secret

"May, dear, where have you put Sam's Christmas card? I don't want him going without it," June shouted up the stairs to her sister. "What are you doing up there anyway?"

May walked to the top of the stairs and looked down at her sister.

"I'm doing exactly what you asked me to do, dear. I'm making up his bed, and as for the card, it's where you left it. June, your memory is terrible these days."

"Yes, May, if you say so, but where is the card?"

May decided to go downstairs to find Sam's card herself in the end. June was now talking to someone on the phone.

"It's Penny," she mouthed.

"Here it is, June," said May. "I found it exactly where you left it, dear." She placed the card into June's hand.

"Thank you, dear," June replied, taking it into the dining room to sign. May followed on behind.

"So, what did Penny want?" May asked.

"It was about Sam's girls, dear, and the meal at the Dorchester. She also asked if we could check his suit and shirt are clean and pressed."

"She's so much happier now she's got that horrible Toby off her back," said May, putting Sam's Christmas card into the envelope. "Do you know, June, I don't think I've ever seen her so relaxed."

"So why do you think that is, dear?" May gazed at her sister, giving thought to what she had said, and then she suddenly pulled out a dining chair and sat on it as if her legs could not hold her a moment longer.

May smiled, and June gave her a pixie-like grin back.

"It hasn't dawned on her yet, and we won't tell her or Sam, it's up to her to realise for herself. Do you think Sam is as well?"

"I don't know, May. If he is, he's doing a good job of hiding it."

"Well, I think he is. When you see him with her, how can he not be?"

"It's best we don't say anything to either of them, don't you agree?" They both chuckled like naughty girls with a secret. "Go and get his suit, May, and I'll run the iron over it."

Sam arrived just before lunch.

"We haven't prepared you much for lunch, dear. Penny said you're off out with Archie to the Dorchester, that will be nice for you," May said, as she put Sam's mug of tea on the table.

"Thank you, May." He put his hand on hers, giving it a gentle squeeze. "It's nice to be back. I have your book with me."

May sat down at the table opposite him, thinking about the conversation she'd had with June earlier.

"I hear you won't be here for Christmas or New Year, dear? That's a pity." There was genuine disappointment in her voice.

"Unfortunately not," he replied. "It seems to be lambing season at the moment. Between my two offices I've got four members of staff either having or just had babies, plus staff have booked time off, so I'm covering over Christmas. I've got two days off, though, but then I'll be working right through the New Year, till I go to Canada."

"What's this about holidays, dear?" June asked, coming into the room and removing Sam's plate from the table.

"He was just saying he'll be on his own over Christmas and New Year, dear," May told her.

"That's not quite right, May," he said, correcting her. But he knew from past experience that when they said something slightly askew there was always a reason for it. "The girls are coming down on Christmas Eve for three days, and I'll be in the pub New Year's Eve – what more would a man want?"

But a look passed between June and May. *Yep*, he thought, *these ladies are definitely up to something.*

As usual when Sam arrived at Penny's for an evening out, he could guarantee that no one would be ready on time, either his daughters or Penny – or so he thought.

Sam stood outside Penny's front door for nearly two minutes before she opened it.

"Where are the girls?" he asked when she finally let him in, wearing her bathrobe. "It's unusually quiet!"

"They've already gone, Sam. Wait in the lounge, I'll be down soon," she shouted, running back up the stairs.

"Do as you're told, Sam, Her Holiness has spoken," he muttered to himself.

He looked through her music collection to wile away the time, noticing something rather familiar . . .

"The crafty minx. So that's where they got to," he said, shaking his head.

He heard Penny calling and went to the foot of the stairs. What he saw took his breath away. Penny was standing on the half-landing in a deep-red, off the shoulder evening gown. Her hair was tied back into a stylish chignon, and she wore the pearl earrings Sam had repaired for her.

"You like?" she asked, her voice soft and alluring, her smile seductive. She could see he was mesmerised by her.

"Oh yes, wow," he replied, his pulse racing. "You look so beautiful." He made a little circular motion with his forefinger, indicating that she should do one of her customary twirls. She indulged him. "Can I breathe now?" he asked, holding out his hand for her.

She walked down the final few steps to him, and as she moved towards him, the urge to take her into his arms and kiss her soft, perfect lips consumed him; but he knew that was a fantasy too far.

"Come on, Sam, let's party," she whispered, planting a slow kiss on his cheek.

They arrived at the Dorchester by taxi, walking arm in arm into one of the cocktail lounges where Penny had arranged to meet Archie, Estelle and Maggie. Sam then stopped in his tracks, bemused but vindicated; his earlier suspicions had not been unfounded!

"The sly buggers, I knew they were up to something," he said as he was greeted by May and June.

"Hello, Sam," said June. "We thought that as you're not here for Christmas, dear, we'd have a little party. Isn't that so girls?"

He turned to Penny, and then looked at the smiling faces around him, including Archie's.

"Five beautiful woman, and only two men; I don't know if this is bliss or purgatory," he laughed, his heart lifted by the sight of these new and dear friends, and his beautiful daughters.

Back home at his cottage in Devon, Sam sat alone in his kitchen and looked through the photographs he had taken of the party. He scrolled through pictures of Archie, Estelle and Maggie, and

And Don't Forget the Roses

Penny's aunties, but mostly of Penny in her wonderful evening gown. There was picture after picture of her looking so happy. Sometimes she posed playfully, pouting her lips or looking demur; in others she just smiled right into the camera, her eyes bright.

It can't go on like this, he thought, *you're going to have to pull your reins in . . . you mustn't fall in love with her.*

Chapter 40

The Accident

Christmas came and went. Sam then concentrated on his business, resisting the temptation of going up to London earlier than planned to see Penny. He was determined not to let his feelings cloud their friendship. In mid-January, he flew back out to Canada, spending most of his time with Oak tracking deer in the winter snow and enjoying lots of skiing. Arriving back at Heathrow, Sam was half expecting Penny to greet him – he knew she'd left the play a week before – but she wasn't there, Archie was.

Walking out of Arrivals, Sam could see him waving his arms around; but he wasn't smiling, his face was gripped by tension. Trepidation flowed through his body as his mind conjured up terrible thoughts.

Sam shook Archie's hand. It was hot and clammy.

"Archie, what's wrong?" he asked. There was no room for niceties.

Archie was trying to be calm, but Sam knew Archie didn't do calm when he was stressed.

"She's alright, Farmer, just a bit banged up," Archie replied, his voice a higher octave than usual. "She was on her way to pick you up, sweetie . . . to surprise you. The police say another car pushed her into the central reservation." Archie was speaking so quickly he had to stop to draw breath. "I've seen her. I took June and Angie with me. We got her into a private room, away from prying eyes."

Sam could feel himself getting emotional.

"Where is she, Archie?" he asked, trying to keep his composure.

"She's in Bristol Hospital, sweetie. The doctors say she has concussion and cracked ribs."

"When did this all happen?" he asked, running his hand over his un-shaven face.

"Three days ago," Archie replied. "Penny told us she'd stayed at your cottage for a couple of days on her own, relaxing. The doctors say she should be able to be discharged tomorrow. I've arranged a car to pick her up and bring her back up here."

"Cancel it, Arch, I'll pick her up. She can come home with me. I'll look after her. She loves the cottage, and she can rest and heal in peace and quiet."

Archie could see he had already made up his mind, and was relieved.

"To tell you the truth, Farmer, we were hoping you'd say that. May and June are worried that she won't look after herself the way she needs to be, or that 'friends' will come around to pry."

Archie opened his navy cashmere overcoat and pulled out his canary-yellow handkerchief from the breast pocket of his suit, pinched the corner, and with a flick of the wrist the satin material opened up like a flower bursting into bloom. He dabbed the corners of his eyes, showing Sam a tearful smile.

"She's got a lot of bruising on her face, Farmer. We don't trust any of her so-called friends – they might put a picture of her in that state on the bloody internet. Remember, a lot of her friends were Toby's friends, and still are. We want her to be safe and out of the way of bloody lenses." Archie took hold of Sam's hand.

"Penny told me how you looked after your dear wife when she was ill. I'm sure she will be a walk in the park compared to that."

Sam smiled at him and then let out a quick laugh.

"Ha! Whatever that woman is, Archie, she's anything but a 'walk in the park', you know that! But yes, I'll keep her safe, you have my word."

On hearing that, Archie wrapped his arms around Sam and hugged him.

"When she speaks of you, Farmer, her face lights up with joy. I'm confounded as to why she says she doesn't love you, because I do." Suddenly Archie put a hand behind Sam's neck and pulled his head forward, kissing his cheek.

Sam smiled, putting his hand to his face. "I think we've just had our photo taken, Arch."

"Good," he replied. "It might make that stupid woman jealous and come to her senses."

Sam didn't talk to Penny's aunties for very long. They knew he was tired from travelling, and like them, he only had Penny on his mind. He told them that he'd get an early train to Bristol, and en route arrange for a hire car to be waiting at the station when he arrived.

Lying in his bed, trying to get some sleep, Sam kept whirling Archie's words around his mind – 'I'm confounded as to why she doesn't love you' – and he couldn't decide whether he was happy or sad about that. Perhaps he'd lost his touch? Perhaps it was for the best . . .

Chapter 41

Safe

Arriving at the hospital, Sam walked into the foyer. He knew the ward she was on, but first he went to the reception desk and asked to speak to an administrator, aware there must be photographers or reporters skulking around to snap her; he was going to do his best to spoil their day. He then spoke to the ward sister, and was shown to Penny's room. June had phoned earlier to tell them he would be collecting her.

"Is it OK to go in?" he enquired, after receiving a curious look from a female doctor – an Asian lady in her late twenties.

"Are you a relative?" she asked, her eyes looking him up and down.

"Sort of. I'm her partner, Sam Farmer."

He hated the word 'partner' – to him it sounded too business-like. Girlfriend or wife, that's what he knew, but he thought it wrong to call himself her boyfriend, especially after what Archie had told him.

"Sure, go in, you can take her home now. I've told her everything she needs to know. Just make sure she gets plenty of rest," she replied.

Sam smiled and entered. Penny was dressed and sitting on the edge of the bed, her hands resting flat on top of the bedding as if she was trying to take the weight off her body. As he walked over to her she slowly turned her head to look at him, and then turned away.

"Sam, don't look at me, I'm a mess." Her voice was quiet and strained.

He had seen facial bruising many times throughout his life – in some cases the result of his own handy work – but to see Penny's head and face bruised and battered upset him deeply. *Come on, Sam, be strong for her, you've done it before*, he thought.

"I've come to take you home, sweetheart." Penny glanced at him and smiled with her eyes; he could see she knew what he meant by 'home'. "A hospital porter is going to wheel you to a tradesman's entrance. I'll see you there."

You poor darling, how I want to hold you in my arms and tell you you're safe now, he thought, his heart aching to hold her and care for her.

Sam reversed his car into a service area and waited for her. He kept looking around, noting every person around him or in the distance, as the last thing he wanted was to be cornered by the media. He could see Penny tentatively walking towards him, aided by a nurse, and opened the passenger door for her.

"With those sunglasses, you look like a movie star," he whispered, taking her hand and helping her into her seat.

"That's so not funny," she replied in a breathless voice as he carefully leant across her to connect the seat belt.

"OK, hun, are you ready?" he asked as he prepared to drive off.

"No, I'm not," she said forlornly, and then reached over and lifted his hand off the gearshift and held it. "I broke your car, Sam, I'm sorry."

He turned in his seat to look at her, his eyes not hiding the truth in his words. "Not half as sorry as I would have been if I had lost *you*." He couldn't see her eyes due to the sunglasses, but he noticed a tear run down her face from behind them.

No sooner had Sam parked outside the cottage, than Penny was trying to get out of the car and inside.

"Don't tell me, you're busting for a pee?" he asked as he jumped out of the car and ran around to help her.

"No," she said, with the tiniest smile. "I just want to be back inside and safe."

Once inside, she dropped her handbag on the floor and lay down on the settee, curled up like a child trying to hide from a cruel world.

"I'll light the fire for you shortly."

He brought all the bags in from the car. He saw that she had fallen asleep and was lying peacefully, despite all the pain her body was feeling. Sam covered her up with a blanket, and then phoned her aunties to tell them she was with him at the cottage, and safe.

Penny opened her eyes and watched the yellow, blue and red flames lick around the burning logs, the heat of the fire warming her body. Sam was sitting at the other end of the settee and her feet were snuggled up against his leg.

"How long have I been asleep?" she asked, her throat dry and sore.

"A couple of hours," he whispered, passing her a glass of water. "I'll run you a bath, if you like. You can have a nice long soak, and then I'll make you some soup."

Penny looked at him and wondered if this was how he looked after Annie, tending to her every need, day after day. She knew in her heart that he wasn't looking after her for fun or for adulation; he wanted to get her well and only that.

Sam was running her bath when he heard her calling for him; a pitiful 'help me' call. He entered her bedroom to see her sitting on the edge of the bed, wearing only her panties and a T-shirt. Her breathing was shallow, and she was trying to catch her breath, as slowly as she could, not wanting to expand her ribcage more than necessary. She turned her head to look at him as he entered the room.

"Sam, can you help me?" she asked in a pained voice. He could see the agony etched across her face as she tried to control her movements. "The nurse helped me get dressed and put this bloody T- shirt on, and now I can't get it off."

He stood in front of her, deciding what to do.

"Which side hurts the most?"

She put her right hand on her left side. He knew she wouldn't be wearing a bra, as that would be the last thing she'd want on with cracked ribs.

Sam gave her a reassuring smile and said, "I know it won't be easy, sweetheart, but try and relax your shoulders for me."

She fixed her eyes on his face as he lifted her T-shirt, slowly working it upwards and over her breasts. He lifted her right arm and gently moved her elbow against her ribcage, and then carefully tugged the fabric over her bent arm, over her head and down her left arm.

"There you go, now you can say you've been undressed by Sam Farmer," he smiled, helping her into a bathrobe.

"I was thinking the same thing myself," she whispered.

"Now go and enjoy your bath, there's no hurry," he said.

You naughty girl, Penny, I do believe you enjoyed that, she thought.

"Thank you for looking after me," she told him, as he tied the robe for her. "Am I being a good patient?"

"No," he replied, "you talk too much. Now go and have your bath."

"Good morning," he said, as he pulled a chair out for her. She was still in her pyjamas, and there was no hiding the pain she was in – even with the medication she was taking, her every breath was measured, every movement considered. "Fancy some porridge and a moat of warm milk?" he asked.

"Yes, please. Thank you. And thank you for all this . . . for looking after me . . . you don't have to, we both know that."

She could see by the expression on his face – a look that she had come to know well – that she was talking rubbish again: he wanted to look after her.

"Any more dumb questions?" he asked.

"Yes, how can I wash my hair?"

After Penny had finished her breakfast, Sam brought towels and shampoo and conditioner.

"Come on then, madam," he said, "the salon is now open." He put a kitchen chair up against the Belfast sink. "We'll give it a go, but if it's too painful, we'll try plan B," he told her.

"What's plan B?" she asked.

"That's where I take you outside and throw a bucket of water over your head."

Over the next three weeks, Penny slowly recovered. The bruises began to fade from her face, and her ribs slowly healed. Sam drove her up to Dartmoor a few times, to get her out of the cottage and to encourage her to stretch her legs, but sometimes they just sat in the car and watched the ponies gather around them. Angie came down and stayed a couple of nights, and at other times he drove her down to the pub to see Sue. She would sit in the kitchen out of the glare of the prying public, and Sue told her that if Dave found out that any one of the locals had told the media she was there, he'd bar them from the pub, and all their family.

"Where did you come from?" Sam asked, surprised, as Penny placed two mugs of tea on the table; he'd not long dropped her off at the pub and was curious as to why, and how, she was back so soon.

"I'm not disturbing you, am I?" she asked, as he sat back in his chair.

"No, not at all," he replied. "I take it Sue dropped you back from the pub?" he asked.

"No, she didn't, I walked."

"That's good to hear," he said, pleased to know she was getting about more on her own.

"Sam . . . I know dozens of people in my profession, you know that, but I can only think of a few who I can honestly say I trust, and you know who they are," she said.

"So where is this leading?" he asked.

She sighed as she began to explain, "Walking back from the pub, I bumped into an elderly couple who I had chatted to in the bar one night – before the accident – and they said how nice it was to see me up and about again." She paused to sip her tea. "Alice – I think that's what she's called – she speaks a bit like Maggie, and she said to me, 'Don't worry, maid, we won't tell anyone you're down 'ere.'" She gave Sam a thoughtful stare. "I just think it strange that I trust more people here, who I don't really know, than anyone I know at home – my other home," she added, with a giggle.

He was so pleased to hear the positivity in her voice, and the fact that she considered the cottage home; but he knew she'd have to go back to London at some point, and so did she.

Chapter 42

The Surprise

A couple of days later, he left Penny at the cottage – he had to go to Exeter on business – but promised to bring her back a surprise.

Good, he's gone for a couple of hours, Penny thought, and popped in to see Sam's next-door neighbours.

Returning before lunch, as arranged, he walked in to his lounge.

"What the hell is all this all about?" he asked loudly, cracking a smile and more than a little confused.

He made his way to the foot of the stairs, where he could see Penny on the landing.

"Hi, Sam. Is there a problem? I heard you shout," she asked, her face showing little emotion.

"Well, yes, there is actually . . . I was wondering why my lounge is full of bloody teddy bears and dollies, plus lots of other funny-looking things?"

"They're your audience, sweetheart."

"What do you mean – audience?" Then suddenly he lowered his head as it dawned on him. *Oh no*, he thought. Then he looked back up at her. "No . . . not today, babe, please?" he implored.

"Yes, today, babe. Now! Well, almost now, but I want to know what my surprise is first."

"God, woman, you're the works sometimes."

Penny linked her arm around his and said, "Come on, Sam. I said I'd help you get over your stage fright, didn't I? Well now is as good a time as any, isn't it?"

"OK, if I must; but what do you want me to do?" He sounded exasperated. "And don't think that the lounge is going to look like that all the time," he added.

"That depends on you, Sam, and how long it takes to get over your problem. Besides, I think they're sweet."

"Take them back with you then! Anyway, where the hell did you get them all from?" he asked.

"The children next door. They said to tell you, you can only borrow them, you can't keep any! Is that clear?"

"I'll try not to get too attached to them, honest."

"Good, that's sorted," Penny replied, trying not to laugh. "Now, where's my surprise?"

"It's outside," he said, taking her hand, and leading her to the front door.

"Sam you've got another one! And it's red this time!"

He could tell from her voice she wasn't enamoured by it, but he wasn't expecting her to be.

"I'm not driving this one, not after what I did to the last one," she told him, with a look of trepidation on her face.

"It wasn't your fault, you know that, but this isn't your surprise," he said, pointing to the number plate, which was covered over with a piece of cardboard. "Go on, take it off." She looked at him suspiciously. "Go on, take it off," he repeated.

"Sam, you silly man!" She cried. "You shouldn't have!" Penny walked back to him and kissed his lips.

"That was nice," he smiled. "Do I get another one for the rear plate as well?"

"Don't make me laugh! You know my ribs still hurt," she replied, slipping her hand into his. "ACT 1 – wow! – thank you. I've always wanted a private plate. You're too kind to me."

"It's for your birthday. The girls found it on the internet and thought we should get it for you. And until you get you own car, we thought we should put it on mine," he said.

"OK," she said, with a sigh. "I know I've got to get back on the horse sometime, but not yet."

"I was going to suggest going for a drive this afternoon," Sam replied. "But looking at all my new friends in there, it'll have to be tomorrow now."

Chapter 43

Distraction

Penny explained how she was taught by her aunties to blank out what was going on around her, literally anything that wasn't relevant to what she was doing.

"Playing your guitar is like acting out a scene on stage with another actor," she told him. "It's about timing and concentration, Sam, timing and concentration – just like reading music. The audience don't exist. You blank everything else out." She could see the anxiety on his face as she was talking.

"Can't I just close my eyes?" he asked.

"No Sam, don't be silly. If actors did that, you'd have them falling off the stage every five minutes!" Penny did her best not to laugh. "You go and get started. I'm going for a bath, and I'll have the door open so I can hear you play. But I will come down, so do what I said: concentrate."

Penny was lying in the bath for a while before he started to play. She turned off the jets to listen to his music. *What a waste*, she thought. *If only others could enjoy hearing you play.* She relaxed to the sounds rising from the lounge as they resonated around her.

Sam had been playing on and off for nearly an hour when Penny came down, in his bathrobe, again, and instantly he lost his concentration.

"Why did you stop?"

"I missed a note, I'll start again," he told her, inhaling the fresh, clean smell of her body – which distracted him even more.

"What do you mean, start again? If you make a mistake, you carry on; you don't stop and start over."

He realised helping him wasn't a task she planned to take lightly. Her professional attitude to getting it right wouldn't allow her to cut corners just because they were friends. She had become his director and wouldn't give up on him until they'd conquered his problem.

"Just imagine if I were on stage and ballsed up a line. Do you think I'd ask the audience, and the rest of the cast, if it was OK if we started again? No, I couldn't do that; I'd have to carry on regardless and just hope that they hadn't noticed – and to tell you the truth, most of them don't. If you miss a note, don't stop, just carry on. I couldn't tell that you'd missed a note. And as for distraction – I told you to concentrate and blank everything out. Now try again, I'm going to make us a cup of tea," she said.

He watched her sashay away, making his bathrobe look like Haute Couture.

"God, Sam, no wonder you can't concentrate," he muttered.

Time after time he kept getting distracted, and time after time Penny kept repeating the same words, until they both decided they'd had enough for the day.

"I'll tidy up here and cook us something," she said.

"No," he insisted, "you should be resting. Put the babies to bed, and I'll cook."

Chapter 44

Why Don't I?

"Your bruises are fading nicely, aren't they?" he observed, a couple of mornings later.

The Penny of old was reappearing from the mask of un-natural colour. She put her hand to her face and tenderly patted her skin.

"I thought I'd try some make-up later," she replied, smiling.

"I suppose we'd better start to think about getting you back home," he said. He watched her frown at him; the same look his daughters used to give him when they were younger, when they didn't want to go to school. "Stand up. Let's have a look at you," he asked, gently lifting up the side of her pyjama top. Her stomach and ribs were still covered in bruises of all colours: purples, reds and shades of yellow. She heard him sigh. He'd seen her injuries many times while she was here, but it didn't make it any easier for him. "Could you force yourself to stay here for at least another week?" he asked.

She looked disappointed, and asked, "What? Only one week?" She appeared to show no enthusiasm at the thought of going back to London.

"No, I said at least one week, but it's up to you. I'll take you back tomorrow if you want to go," he told her. "But personally, I wouldn't risk it. You've still got a lot of redness on those ribs, and I still hear you wince in pain at night when you're asleep."

She again observed genuine concern on his face for her wellbeing, which filled her with a calmness that was alien to her.

And Don't Forget the Roses

She knew she wasn't going anywhere soon. He wouldn't take her back until she could look after herself.

"Really the decision is yours, isn't it?" she asked. "But I don't want to be a burden on you."

Sam rolled his eyes and shook his head, and again gave her that look of his.

What's holding me back from being in love you, Sam Farmer? she thought. *Because at this moment, I don't want to be anywhere else than here with you.*

"You know what this means, don't you?" she asked.

"Yes," he replied with a huff. "Those bloody teddy bears have to stay."

Over the following days, he continued to divide his time between running his company from his laptop and phone, and caring for Penny – but he did his office work mostly late at night when she was asleep so that he could spend the time with her. Lying in bed one night, he recalled one of Shakespeare's sonnets where he spoke of being '*weary with toil*', and he knew, despite his growing love for her, he would still have to do his upmost to suppress it for the sake of their friendship. But it wasn't getting any easier.

Chapter 45

The Gift

"Well, it's time to say goodbye," he said, as he stood in her kitchen and drank the remainder of his coffee.

Penny was standing very close to him, and tears were running down her face.

"It's going to be strange not seeing you every day, Sam," she whispered. "I'm missing you already . . . isn't that what they say in the movies?" He gently hugged her; not his normal goodbye hug, but a long *I don't want to let go* hug. "Go on, you'd better go, I need to stop crying." Again, she was forced to question why she'd miss him.

"I've got something for you before I go," he replied, and went out to the car. He returned with a flat parcel approximately three feet by two feet. "There you go . . . something to look at when you're feeling homesick. But wait till I've gone before you open it."

There wasn't really anything else to say to each other, it had all been said over the previous two days as he'd helped her settle back in. He'd stayed with June and May, and had run her around in the car to buy groceries and visit them. They both knew they had their separate lives to live, interspersed with living in each other's.

Penny waved Sam off, and then walked into lounge with her present, hastily removing the paper. She instantly recognised the scene and instinctively put her hand across her mouth in surprise, her eyes again full of tears. She rested the watercolour painting of his cottage on the settee, and stood back to admire it. She then sent him a text message: 'It makes me feel as if I'm there. Px'.

'You are, look closer. Sx' he replied.

She gazed again at the painting, and there she was, sitting under the leafy shade of the willow tree in his garden, wearing the red polka dot dress she liked to put on for him.

Playing his guitar without the teddy bears, or Penny, seemed a little strange to him now, considering that less that than month before he couldn't play a note if anyone was in the same room as him. After all the stress and endeavours on her part to get him to overcome his stage fright, he no longer had anyone to play to, and no one he wanted to play to. He then chuckled to himself, thinking he should have kidnapped one of the teddy bears.

He stood up and set his guitar on its stand and then went to draw the curtains. He briefly looked out of the window to his driveway. It was now late February, and the days were slowly getting longer; he could see the shadows of the setting sun over the flowerbeds. The green shoots of spring were pushing their way up and out, like fingers searching for the light and the warmth.

His thoughts drifted back to the few days before he took Penny back to London. She had planted a selection of mixed bulbs around the rose bush where Emily's ashes were laid to rest in the church graveyard. They were in clear view of Emily's bedroom, where Sam and Sue had watched her. He recalled what Sue had said: 'I always leave a window open so that her spirit can come and visit us.' Like her, he missed the little angel. His thoughts were then interrupted by the sound of his phone buzzing away; he instinctively knew it was Penny.

"Hello, hun. I'm pleased it's you." His voice sounded far away.

"Hi! Everything OK? You sound subdued?" she asked, full of concern.

"Yes, fine. Funny . . . I was just thinking of you and those bloody teddy bears." He heard her laugh.

"Ah, you poor dear, you're missing them, aren't you?" She laughed again. "The reason I phoned is that Archie has asked me if you would like to come up on Thursday. He's having a get together with some of the cast, and he thought you would like to meet the producer and directors. Would you like to come? Go on, Sam, can you come? Please? Aaron will be there as well."

Sam needed time to think. He knew Archie wouldn't drag him up to London just for a nice chit-chat and cocktails – there must be something else.

"I'm not sure if I can make it," he replied. "I'll phone you back. Let me check my diary, sweetheart."

He then realised Archie's possible motive for wanting him to meet them. *Very clever*, Archie, he thought. *You don't trust them, do you? But who is it you don't trust? The producer? The director? And you know if you don't, then I won't. Christ, Arch, what are you getting me involved in?'*

"Are you coming?" she asked in anticipation.

"Yes, I'll be up Thursday," he told her, with a sense of trepidation.

"That'll be great! Thank you, Sam. And . . ."

"Yes," he replied, knowing her all too well – there was certain to be something else.

"Will you be coming by car and staying the weekend? I hope so, because the reason I ask is that Patch and Ahmed have asked me to do a reading with them, and it's possible it'll be the last one I do for a long time . . . if at all." She paused in case he wanted to say something, but he didn't as he knew she still hadn't finished. "And as I haven't got my friend's car to use," she continued, "I'll have to use the Tube, or . . ."

Here we go again, he thought, *the word 'or' . . .*

She could hear a muffled sound coming from the phone, and knew it was him shaking his head and laughing.

"You're such hard work at times, woman. It's a good job I love you three-roses-worth, isn't it!" he said. "For a moment there I thought you wanted to drive the car drive through Knightsbridge to show off your number plate."

"Yes! We can do that on Saturday! That would be brill!"

All the time she was talking to him, she was gazing at the painting of the cottage that was now hung on the chimneybreast opposite her. She was imagining she was there, snuggled up in Sam's bathrobe in front of the open log fire, listening to him play the guitar, instead of being back in London. She was still perplexed about her feelings for him. She remembered how she once felt about Toby: she thought she had loved him, totally loved him; but that had ended when he betrayed her. But she missed Sam when they were apart, and she yearned for his company. She liked to keep things tidy in her mind, and this was turning into a bit of a mess.

Chapter 46

The Elephant

Sam could hear the sisters chatting away in the kitchen, and neither June or May seemed surprised to see him.

"Hello, you two!" he said, giving each of them a kiss. "Sorry I've called unannounced, but I was hoping we could have a little chat."

"Certainly, dear, we'll sit at the table, that'll be better for June's hip," May smiled.

"Well, dear, this is all very intriguing," said June.

He knew he would be sitting there for a month of Sundays if he didn't get the ball rolling; but he hoped it wouldn't be a wrecking ball.

He politely smiled at them, and sat there for a few moments to settle himself. He placed the flats of his hands on the edge of the table.

"I keep having this nagging thought as to why Archie has invited me up here to meet the people involved in Penny's play," he said. He paused to study their reactions; the obvious downside being that they were both accomplished actresses, and they could lead him a merry dance in facial expressions if they so wished. "Archie is fully aware I am a busy man at the moment, and that I'm still trying to catch up on some projects I shelved while I was caring for Penny. Now don't misinterpret that, because if she still wanted to stay with me, she could for as long as she needed to."

And Don't Forget the Roses

He noticed they were glancing at his hands to see if they were shaking, or fidgeting; but he knew they weren't.

"So, I'll get to the point," he continued. "Archie wouldn't ask me up here unless it was important, and you wouldn't tell him to get me up here unless it was *very* important. Further to that, Archie wouldn't draw breath without getting permission from you first if it concerned Penny. It's only fair, and correct, that I'm aware of the facts and that whatever this is, I go into it with my eyes open."

Sam took his hands off the table and rested them on his legs, and waited.

"People can be such *twats* at times, can't they?" May sighed.

"That's a very gutterish comment coming from you," he gasped, shocked at her choice of language.

"I said that because it's about taking people at face value, dear," she replied. Her gentle tone only added to Sam's bewilderment as to why she'd suddenly spoken so crudely before. "We accepted you, and you accepted us on face value, is that not so?' she asked. "To you we could have been two elderly little ladies who wouldn't say boo to a goose, let alone use foul language." She then showed him an unscripted smile; one that he could see wasn't fake, but that only added to his general sense of unease. "We all have a façade, dear, don't we; but behind that facade we can be quite different on the inside." He could sense that she was trying to reach into his soul, pulling and tugging at memories he would never want to disclose to them. "But on the inside, we have memories, don't we? . . ."

He now began to feel uneasy and realised that the letter he had entrusted June with to pass on to Archie, and the subsequent information gleaned from it – that could open a Pandora's box of nightmares for him – had most likely been opened and read by the sisters. Sam knew Archie had received it, as they'd discussed it over lunch the last time he'd been in London.

"This all has to do with betrayal, Sam," June told him. "By people we thought of as friends, people we trusted. You know all about betrayal, don't you?" she asked, pointedly." She saw his jaw clench and his posture stiffen as if he were preparing himself for more verbal punches, punches that for Sam seemed to be thrown below the belt.

"Yes, June, I do," he answered, taking a deep intake of air. "I know only too well about betrayal, and obviously, you know that."

She now placed her hands flat on the table, and heaved herself to her feet, wincing as she rose.

"God, this bloody hip is going to be the death of me," she muttered, and then shuffled her way over to him. "Please don't be angry with Archie, dear. This isn't about you, it's all about Penny."

"What?" he responded, as anger flashed in his eyes, revealing a deep darkness. He looked straight at her, his voice now low, as if coming from the pit of his stomach, and said, "She hasn't tasted real betrayal, though, has she? Toby's indiscretions weren't the type of betrayal which makes you want kill yourself, betrayal that haunts you, and regret that tears at your soul for the rest of your life."

He looked across to May, who knew he was off balance, disturbed by memories that were screaming at him from his past.

"We cried for you, Sam, and for those lovely girls of yours, we truly did." She reached out her hand to him in a gesture of solace. "Is Penny aware of what happened?" she asked, softly.

"No, and there would have to be a bloody good reason why I would re-live the worst days of my life," he said. June put a glass of water in front of him, and he took a mouthful.

"Do you believe in fate, Sam?" June asked, her voice full of compassion.

"If you mean was it fate that Penny and I met, and that for some inexplicable reason our pasts are somehow linked, and we've been drawn together for the benefit each other? Then, yes," he replied.

"Oh, sweet man, how life can be so cruel to the nicest of people."

"If you know all about me, then you'll know I wasn't always nice by any stretch of the imagination." There was remorse in his eyes now.

"Yes, but people do change, don't they, dear."

"I like to think so. I've tried to," he answered.

May rose from her seat and made her way around the table to sit next to him.

"Sam, you were right," she said, "June and I did ask Archie to invite you up here, because we need your help." A look passed between the sisters; a look that had been honed over a lifetime and one that spoke volumes. "We realised when Archie couldn't get backers for the play that something sinister was going on behind Penny's back. Those who call themselves producers and directors – and whom Archie approached – betrayed her. They said, amongst other things, that she lacked commitment. Utter *crap*, dear," she hissed.

May was again showing a side to her that was seldom seen. The sisters knew that in order for him to have any idea of what was transpiring, they had to open a portal into *their* past.

"You forget, dear, we were young and excitedly free ourselves once, and along the way, like Penny, we made a host of life-long friends; but we also made enemies. Those who are still alive are like elephants: they never forget, and we think it's one of those persons who is behind this. He wants her to fail as an actress, but we can't understand why that is. Maybe it's because she's a McCain . . . but we're determined to find who he is and why he wants to stifle her career. And it's up to those of us who love her, dear, to stop him and protect that lovely young woman."

He listened to her intently, and realised that up until now he had been an outsider, on the periphery of their world, but now they had drawn him in, and he knew why: because of his agonising past. They knew he would fight tooth and nail to protect Penny from that kind of torture.

"How do you know, May? How do you know it's one of your elephants?" he asked, trying to separate fact from guesswork. "And what makes you sure it's a man?"

"Because whoever it is, dear, he's been around as long as us. And it's a man alright, a man with influence," said May, and for the first time he could detect vulnerability in her, a helplessness.

"When we read through Aaron's script," June said, watching her sister, "even before he told us, dear, we could tell by the way he'd structured the dialogue and scenes that Penny was shouting out from the pages."

"And we'd be buggered if we were going to let the *bastard, whoever he is,* screw it up for her!" retorted May, angrily.

"Your language is as bad as Penny's!" Sam cried, and the sisters laughed loudly.

"Where do you think she got it from in the first place, dear?" May chuckled, winking at him.

Sam had to laugh then, but he was unaware that his analogy of the wrecking ball was already in motion, not swinging indiscriminately, but wheeled by someone who had more than just Penny in his destructive sights.

Chapter 47

The Pond

"Come on, madam, the car's waiting,"

Sam was trying to get Penny out of the door on time, but as usual she was delaying their departure. He looked at himself in her full-length mirror, and admired his black trousers and blue shirt and blazer.

"Very smart, Sam, now get out of the way," she said, as she shimmied past him in white jeans and Ralph Lauren heels. "Do you like my blouse? I bought it in Exeter. I like the dots, don't you? D'oh, silly me, of course you do – you love my dotty dress!"

He shook his head.

"Sam, you're shaking your head! You no likey?"

"I don't know if you're making me feel younger or older, sweetheart, but how can any man not likey you?" he laughed.

"Have you forgotten what I told you when we first met? You're as old as the woman you hold!"

He had to smile; to hold Penny would be wonderful.

Even before Penny was out of the car, members of the public and photographers were swarming around the barriers, hoping she would stop and talk, or at least stop and pose for a picture; but this was Archie's party and he wasn't going to have his leading lady standing on the pavement for the happy-snappers. She took Sam's hand and they were ushered into the venue by Archie's staff, then onto the obligatory red carpet for the benefit of the official photographers – all vetted by Archie for maximum publicity. Penny smiled and posed, aware of Sam putting his hand around her waist and holding her close. She rested hers on his, coupling herself to him, demure and relaxed in his company.

Archie hastily made his way over to greet them in a sky-blue suit and garish, bright yellow polka dot cravat. He greeted them with his normal aplomb and excitement, but Sam soon realised Archie was trying to hide something from him: his embarrassment. Penny left them to catch up on events, while she nipped to the ladies' room.

"I'm sorry, Farmer," said Archie, nervously. Sam smiled, perplexing him further. Sam knew when it came to business, Archie was as ruthless as they come, but the supposedly harmless elderly ladies could work him like a ventriloquist's dummy. "You know what they're like. It's impossible to hide anything from them. I am sorry for being part of their deception," he said, waiting for Sam's friendly demeanour to change; it didn't.

"There's nothing to be sorry about, Arch, it was dumb of me to give them the letter in the first place. I should have remembered what they're like, and realised they'd probably steam it open," he said, shaking his head in amusement, thinking of those two seemingly harmless ladies and their antics. Even if they had made him go back into his past, he found it hard to think of them in any other way than just a couple of scallywags.

"Oh they did, Farmer. They had already read it by the time June handed it to me. I'm sorry, I should have told you."

"Archie don't beat yourself up over it. As far as I'm concerned, the matter is closed." He then put his arms around Archie's shoulders and pulled him close, giving him a hug and then a little peck on the cheek. "Maggie told me to give you that," he said, seeing Archie's boyishness return at the surprise of getting a kiss from him – even if it was at the behest of his daughter! "There is one thing you can do for me, if you want to make amends . . ."

"Anything, sweetie," replied Archie, eager to please his friend.

"Put your hands in your pockets and get that bloody woman a new hip. You wouldn't allow a dog to be in as much pain as she is."

Much to Sam's surprise, Archie sniggered and said, "If she were a dog, I'd have her put down."

"Have who put down, Archie?" Penny enquired as she brought Sam's drink over to him.

"Anaesthetic, sweetheart," Sam said quickly. *Shit, that was close*, he thought. He turned to Archie. "Archie is going to pay for June to go private and get a new hip, aren't you, Arch?"

"Really, Arch? You're such a darling!" she cried, throwing her arms around his neck, and giving him a huge kiss. "Come on, Sam, I didn't come here to stand in the foyer all night." She took his arm, and as they walked away she looked at him curiously. "How the hell did you get Archie to agree to that? I've been badgering him for months!"

"I don't know, maybe he loves me," he replied, giving her a cheeky grin.

"Don't! I'll get jealous," she laughed. "But thank you."

They strolled arm in arm into the imposing function lounge with its royal-blue flock wall covering and crystal chandeliers hung from ornate Edwardian ceilings. Waiters were serving canapés and succulent oysters, all washed down with the best French champagne.

"There's the play's producer," Penny said, pulling at his arm excitedly as they made their way over to him. "Come on, I'll introduce you."

He wondered to himself if this was the elephant man, or just one of the herd? If Penny hadn't been with him he would have asked some searching questions – *polite*, searching questions, but questions nevertheless – and watched to see if there was hesitation upon replying, or an animated response.

Sam shook his hand. *This is good, someone with a firm grip at last*, he thought.

The man was taller than Sam by a couple of inches, and older, in his mid to late-sixties. They looked each other straight in the eye, not to see who turned away first, but to survey; both men knew that first impressions tell a lot about a person.

"Sam, this is George Dawson," Penny said, and he gave her a polite peck on each cheek. "George, meet Sam Farmer."

Sam soon began to realise by the tone of their conversation that George Dawson was intent on seeing the play through; Penny was his Katherine, no ifs, no buts, and Penny was obviously happy introducing him to everyone, from fellow cast members to stage hands.

He noted that she rarely let go of his arm. It was as though she was swimming in a pond, and wasn't sure what was lurking in the water with her and he was her raft.

"So, what do you think of George?" she asked later, mingling amongst the other members of the cast.

"Early days, sweetheart," he replied. "He seemed sincere," he added as she passed him another glass of champagne stealthily removed from a waiter's tray.

"Archie said he's old-school and knows the theatre world inside out. Auntie May knows of him as well, she said he–" She stopped mid-sentence as she recognised a friend of theirs. "Sam look, it's Aaron!" She pointed to her right, with her glass in her hand. They made their way across the room.

"Oh, he's talking with Art and Max," she said excitedly. "You'll like Max, he's sweet."

"So, who are they?" Sam quickly asked.

"Aaron!" Penny cried.

"Hi, Miss Penny," he said in the softest tone he could manage; but it still made the champagne ripple in their glasses. He bent over almost double to kiss her, and the two people either side of him had to move out of the way as Aaron's head filled the void between them. "Hi there, Sam!" he said with a huge smile.

Passing his glass to Penny, Sam put his hands out to him, knowing the best way to greet Aaron was to grip his hand with both of his, like he had a wild beast in his grasp, and hold on!

"Hello, big man," he replied, with a wink.

"Sam, this is our director, Arthur Grainger, but we all call him Art, and his assistant director, Max Saunders."

Again, Sam studied both men, listening and observing. During the ensuing discussion, he felt a trace of an attitude from one of them – similar to Toby's when they'd first met – and that he was being made to feel in the way; an outsider.

Archie appeared, holding onto the arm of a large, stocky, bearded man in his forties.

"Hello, Sam, nice to see you again!" boomed Peter Tillson, giving him a mighty hand shake. "Did you know, Sam, old boy, I'm the poor bastard who's got to joust with this old slapper here?" He laughed a mighty laugh.

"Tilly, you sod. Don't take any notice of him, Sam, he's just scared he's met his match," Penny said, blowing him a pouting kiss. "So, when did you two meet?" she asked, trying to remember, knowing she must have been with them at the time.

Sam shook his head and smiled at her and said, "Memory of a goldfish, sweetheart, haven't you." And then watched as she buried her head in her shoulder. "Last summer – in Soho? Chinese restaurant? Getting home at four in the morning?" he added, with amusement. She looked none the wiser. "And the girls say my memory is going," he whispered in her ear, to which she giggled.

As the evening wore on, she introduced him to everyone she thought he would be interested in meeting, but it was getting late and Penny had other plans.

"Guess what I'm thinking?" she asked, closing her eyes.

"Meatballs?" he suggested.

"Ah, you bugger! Got it in one. Come on, let's go," she laughed, turning in the direction of the foyer.

Sam stopped and beckoned her back.

"Hold on, Penny, let's take Aaron with us; he was looking a bit overwhelmed earlier with all the attention."

She agreed and Sam went off to find him.

They arrived at the restaurant only to see that members of the cast had beaten them there, and others turned up as the night progressed. Aaron enjoyed the company of his two friends, and the cast, and ate a colossal plateful of meatballs. They consumed many bottles of wine between them. Sam could see and hear that Penny was happy and relaxed, not only with him, but with her fellow cast members. As he watched her laugh and joke with everyone, his mind drifted back to when she had confided in him that she had been anxious as to whether she had that extra something – the difference between a good actress and one who has no peers, one who could turn a good play into an outstanding one – and he remembered telling her that it was already a brilliant play, with a brilliant Katherine.

He also recalled the conversation he had with June and May regarding the elephant man, and Aaron's deliberate adaption of Shakespeare's play. They had played Katherine in many guises themselves over the years, but Aaron's play, they told him, was like the reinvention of the wheel: every other adaption after his would have an Everest to climb to surpass it. He wondered why someone was contriving to deny her a role that was so obviously hers, and what further lengths he was prepared to go to. One thing that was apparent to him was that whoever he was, he was clearly ordering others to do his dirty work whilst keeping his anonymity.

"Come on, home," Penny suddenly said, interrupting his

thoughts. "We've got things to do tomorrow, or is it today?" she said, giggling. She stood up, a little unsteady on her feet.

By the time they arrived back at her house – after dropping Aaron off at his hotel – she was already asleep, her head resting on Sam's shoulder in the back of the taxi. Sleepwalking her into her bedroom, he rolled back her duvet, and watched with a smile as she crumpled into bed. He removed her shoes and pulled the duvet back over her. *If she wants me to undress her, she'd better think again*, he thought, and switched off the light.

Chapter 48

How Many Roses?

"Good morning." Penny kissed his cheek and then ran her fingers down the side of his face. "Oooh, you need a shave!"

"I thought the unshaven look was all the rage?" He wondered what her reply would be. He knew there would be one, but in what form would it come he didn't know. A short, off-the-cuff, one-liner? or a considered, but cutting response? He didn't have to wait long.

"Sorry, sweetheart, you're knocking on sixty, the grey bits around your chin don't look very sexy," she said bluntly.

Ouch! I don't like that, he thought, turning away from her.

"Sorry, I should have said fifty-three," she said, trying to catch his eye, with a consolatory smile.

"That's even worse, thank you," he replied, knowing she didn't mean to hurt him, but her words did touch a nerve. "Now you're saying I look old at fifty-three!"

Oops, maybe I've overplayed it a tad, she thought.

"I didn't mean to say that, you definitely look younger than your years, but only after a shave ..." she giggled, relieved that he laughed too; he knew exactly what she meant.

"Come on, Sam, I'm ready!"

"This is a change, you having a pop at me!"

Sam watched her checking her reflection in the mirror as he pulled on his shoes.

"What do you think? Good enough to take out in daylight?" she asked.

"You look lovely, as usual," he informed her with a heavy sigh. "Maybe you should walk in front of me . . ."

"Why?"

"Well, you don't want to be seen with a fifty-three-year-old man like me, who looks nearer sixty, now do you?"

Her face suddenly changed, and fear shone in her eyes – as if she was suddenly scared she had offended him so much that she wouldn't see him again.

"What's all this about, you silly thing?" he asked.

"I'm sorry. I don't know what came over me. I looked at you and I sensed something. Call it a woman's intuition, but I suddenly felt very scared and sad."

"What?" he asked, sounding surprised at her statement. "Like I'm going to hurt you?"

"No, you silly sod! I-I felt worried that one day we may not be friends anymore." She walked back into the lounge, sat down on the settee and stared at the painting of Sam's cottage.

He followed her in, sat down next to her and held her hand. Her eyes were transfixed on the picture.

"Do you know what I do when I'm stressed or feeling down?" She smiled a slow smile. "I imagine I'm walking up the driveway and then though the door, and that I'm closing it behind me."

"Then rush upstairs for a pee, I expect," he said, as he moved her hand to his mouth and gave it a tender kiss.

"Real shit goes through my head sometimes, doesn't it?"

Sam thought that perhaps she did sense looming storm clouds that could test their friendship, but one thing she wasn't aware of was his love for her – and he was having trouble keeping it at bay.

"Ready to try again?" he asked, as he stood up, still holding her hand.

"Yes," she said quietly. "Pull me up then."

The remainder of the morning was spent shopping at the supermarket. Sam insisted on stocking up on food for her; he knew that as from Monday rehearsals for Aaron's play would be starting in earnest, and combined with other commitments, her days would be long and tiring.

On the way home, they called in to see Suzie and her new baby, Emily.

"Look at her, Sam, isn't she beautiful?" Penny whispered, cradling Emily in her arms, her joy of holding the new life to her bosom filling the room.

Suzie smiled and glanced at Sam. She had never seen Penny like this, neither of them had; but then they hadn't seen her with a baby. She'd only ever said she was utterly devoid of the maternal instinct that most women have; but Sam saw, just for a moment, the sad and negative thoughts she held onto about motherhood dissipate as she cuddled Emily; maybe Penny would be able to leave the past behind.

"Your turn," she said, gently passing the precious cargo to his less than willing hands.

"God, I'd forgotten how light these things are!" he smiled, touching her doll-like fingers and gently stroking her fine hair.

It was Penny and Suzie's turn to look on with quiet amusement.

"There's mileage left in you yet, isn't there?" Suzie remarked, giving Penny a mischievous glance.

And Don't Forget the Roses

"Sam how many roses do you love me by now?" she asked in the car.

Sam turned the radio down. "Why?"

"Well, considering I've already written off one of these and you trust me with this one while you are in Canada again," – she indicated the car – "I just thought you must love me more than three roses, that's all," she replied, looking at him thoughtfully; but there was an air of despondency in her tone, as if it was important for her to know that he loved her, even in an abstract, platonic, counting roses, kind of way.

He looked at her, wondering what to say by way of reply, not wanting to show his true feelings for her.

"Well, I suppose it's been a while since I gave you those three . . ."

"Sam, now you're being cruel, you must love me a little bit more, surely? Don't you?"

Then he wondered if the feelings she'd had earlier had scared her more than he realised. He also then thought about Toby. He'd said he loved her, and then betrayed her. Maybe she thought his love for her was fanciful, not real, that it wouldn't be strong enough to hold at bay the woes she sensed looming ever closer.

"Don't you think three are enough?" he answered. (Perhaps she would suggest she needed another one?)

"I'd hoped I would be up to at least four by now, but considering I wrecked your car, and called you old . . . I wouldn't be surprised if I didn't have any left at all." She picked at a thread on her coat.

"OK. Well I love you five-roses-worth now, and if you can manage to pick me up at the airport without trying to kill yourself again, I've got another one for you," he replied.

"I would have settled for four, you know that," she replied, with a big smile. "*Hell,* what if it got to twelve? What would we do then?"

"I wouldn't be too concerned," he replied, trying to reassure her. "I'm a twenty-four-roses man, so we've got a long way to go before I max-out on love for you."

Two dozen roses. I can never imagine a man loving me that much, she thought.

"I thought I'd take June and May down to Brighton in the car, you don't mind, do you?" she then said.

"Yes, I do! I'm not having those two slashing my leather upholstery, thank you!" His reply was terse, and accompanied by an intimidating glare.

Penny looked at him and laughed.

"That's good, Sam! Ever thought of becoming an actor?" She grinned at him, leaning forward so that he could see her face.

"Oh go on then, but tell them *no chewing gum in the car*!"

"Yes, dear."

"And no boyfriends. I don't want any backseat hanky-panky either."

"Theirs or mine?" she asked. Then she thought, and said, "Actually, why would I need a boyfriend, Sam, when I've got my very own Mr Grumpy?"

Chapter 49

The Mantle

"Sam, while I'm cooking the meal, have a look in my document case behind the settee, it may interest you," Penny called from the kitchen, as he loaded *his* CD into her stereo system.

He lifted the very large black leather case onto the settee beside him, and un-latched the strap, causing it to open into a four cavernous segments like a concertina.

He peered into the various sections – filled mostly with A4 paper in various colours – and removed one. It contained schedules and days of the week written across the top, and had boxes entitled 'Run Thru', 'Scene with Leads', 'Scene with Casts', etc. There was sheet after sheet of schedules, some with times and places penned into the various boxes, and one which contained a short sentence that told him there was still a lot of sweat and toil that lay ahead: 'Move to Theatre'.

He took great care to put the sheets back in the correct order. He then lifted a mound of paper onto his lap, bound together with two brass brads. The script wasn't as thick or as heavy as he had imagined, but it didn't detract from the reverence he felt towards it. The name of the play – *Katherine* – was printed on the front. He ran his fingers around the edges and across the top, feeling and caressing it like it was a priceless work of art – which to him it was, as he knew this bundle of paper would propel Penny to the pedestal he felt she so richly deserved to be placed.

"This is nice music, isn't it, Sam?" she said, drying her hands on a tea towel as she stood in the archway joining the kitchen to the lounge. "I listen to it when I'm concentrating on learning my lines." She was pleased to see him engrossed in her play.

"It's Mantovani, sweetheart," he replied, deeply studying the script.

"It's very nice. Easy on the ear. Is it yours?" she asked, in a manner that implied she already knew the answer to that question.

"It used to be . . . until you swiped it from my car." He looked at her, eyebrows raised.

"Really . . ." she said, giving him a devil-may-care look back. "Then it's a good job I took it, isn't it, otherwise you may have lost it in the accident." She gave a little laugh, and turned back into the kitchen, saying, "Five minutes."

Chapter 50

Canada

"Hi, fella," said Oak, as they shook hands. "Welcome back."

Sam was pleased to be back, and was looking forward to being out in the wild, open spaces and forests again. It would give his mind a break from all the chicanery that was closing in on Penny – and drawing him ever closer to her. He walked up to Oak's trusted Land Rover, Ali, and laid the flat of his hand on the bonnet as if to say *Hello again*!

"That's a waste of time, fella," Oak smiled. "She'll rattle your bones as she always does, whether you're nice to her or not."

But Sam actually felt some affection for the 'aluminium box with a wheel in each corner', as Canda described her.

"So, where are we off to this time?" he asked, eager to get his hiking boots on.

"It's your turn to teach me," Oak informed him, with the regular, stone-hard expression he used when he had no intention of fully answering the question.

Sam had no idea what he meant, but once they arrived at the marina at New Dover, the penny dropped. A couple of minutes later he found himself standing on a pontoon looking at a sturdy thirty-two-foot sloop.

"Hi, Uncle Sam!" Canda called from the cockpit. "It's been a long time since you took us sailing!" She held up two cans of beer, a beautiful smile on her face.

Over the next six days, Sam and his crew – Oak, Canda and her brother Jake – sailed across Lake Erie, brushing up on old skills he had not used for many years. They anchored at night in bays and inlets, and enjoyed barbecues and beer on the shore. During their time together, Canda tried to draw memories of her mother from him, about the times when they use to go sailing together, and Sam realised who had encouraged her: Maggie and Estelle.

But all they wanted was for him to lay that ghost to rest, and forget about the events that changed their family beyond comprehension. He wanted to do it, not just for his sake, but for Penny's too. He knew their friendship was now more than he expected. There was a trust, an honesty that was so precious to them. Penny, he felt, had laid hers to rest – that of her deep sadness about her mother and the childish jealousy she had once felt towards her dying sister – but Sam had turned his into a secret; not even his daughters, and certainly not Penny or her aunties, were aware of all the facts. But all he wanted, like Oak and his children, was a life with no secrets.

Relaxing at Oak's lodge on his last night, Sam was once again sitting on the veranda overlooking the lake, drinking a few beers and reading.

"You certainly haven't lost your enthusiasm for that Shakespeare guy, have you?" Oak observed. "What are you reading now? That must be the second book you've read while you've been here."

Sam turned the book to one side, to see how much he had read.

"Yes, I must admit I can't seem to put him down. This one is a book of his sonnet's . . . or poems to you," he replied.

Oak handed him another beer, and then took the book from his hand, stretching out his arm to read from it, struggling to see the words without his reading glasses.

"'*Weary with toil I haste me to my bed*'," he read. "Da!" Oak spouted. "If that fella was weary, he should have got his ass out on the lakes, got some fresh air in his lungs, not run to his bed!"

Sam laughed at Oak's interpretation of the words.

"It's about a man who's missing his woman, Oak, and how he can't get her out of his head, day or night."

Oak sat back in his chair with a look of curiosity on his face.

"So, you're feeling like that about that woman back home, are you? That Penny of yours?" he asked, chucking a curious look in his direction.

Sam drank his beer, knowing Oak would keep looking at him like that until he got a reply.

"No, not me, sorry, you got that wrong," he replied, and then stood up to look over the lake. He watched the ripples forming across the water, caused by the light breeze coming from off the shore.

Oak, with book in hand, and reading glasses now firmly in place, continued to read, occasionally glancing over to look at Sam.

"'*Intend a zealous pilgrimage to thee. For then my thought from far where I abide*'." As Oak finished reading, he looked sternly over the top of his reading glasses at Sam. "Do you want me to read more?" he boomed, and he put the book on the table next to him.

"So, what do you expect me to say? That I'm in love with a woman who is young enough to be my daughter?" he replied, as he pulled two tins from the six-pack. He passed one to Oak, and then leant against the rail and stared at the reflection of the moon glistening on the water. "It wasn't meant to be like this. I thought I could handle it, handle her." He didn't sound like himself as he continued, "You know what I was like in the old days. God, I would have chalked her up by now and moved on, but she's different . . . when I'm with her I become the Sam I thought I'd lost when Annie died. But how can I be her friend – a friend with no ties – if each time I see her all I want to do is pull her to me and make love to her?"

"Got any idea how she feels about you?" Oak asked, as he suddenly stood and relieved himself over the side of the veranda."

Sam then let out an untimely laugh.

"Watch it, fella! Quit your laughing! It's not that small!" Oak laughed too.

"Sorry! You reminded me of Penny when you did that."

Oak looked at him in bemusement, and asked, "Why? Does she piss over the side of the veranda as well?"

"No! It's just that she drinks a lot of water, and you can guarantee the first thing she does when we get to the house, is shoot upstairs for a pee."

"Jesus, you've got it bad haven't you," Oak replied, seeing the sudden look of pure affection spread across Sam's face. "So, what are you going to do about her?"

Sam let out a heavy sigh.

"To be honest, I haven't got a freaking clue. I've let her into my life, and I like her being part of it. Maybe she'll meet someone and cool it between us . . ." he replied, shrugging his shoulders. "Find someone nearer her own age. I'm pretty sure she doesn't love me."

"How do you know?"

"The truth is, Oak, I don't, but I'm scared to find out either way. Maggie and Estelle keep dropping hints that she's more than just fond of me, but considering what those girls' love lives are like, I take that with a pinch of salt!" He turned back to look over at the lake, and wondered if that was what he really wanted – for her to find someone else. "I try to keep my feet on the ground by telling myself this old dog has had his day, but I have a feeling it can't go on like this for much longer."

Oak smiled at the back of the man in front of him.

"If you want to run away and hide, fella, you could always move over here, we seem to get on OK now. Give it some thought. The offer's there if you want to."

Sam felt humbled by Oak's offer, considering that at one time all Oak had wanted to do was kill him for what happened to his wife. He also knew that the reality was he had to help protect Penny from whoever was trying to destroy her career, only then could he have a bare-knuckle fight with his heart; but he wasn't sure who he wanted to win.

Chapter 51

Another Lie

Sam smiled broadly as he set eyes on Penny standing by the barrier. He'd told Oak he would be having a good talk to himself when he got home, but it was to no avail – he was in love with her.

"Hello, babe," he said as she stood there, her arms open for a hug from him.

He wrapped his arms around her and gave her a big kiss on the cheek.

"So, have I still got a car?" he enquired as they walked out of the airport terminal.

"Yes, she's still in one piece."

"Pleased to hear it," he laughed. It was so good to see her. "Are you able to come to the cottage for the weekend?" he asked.

"Sorry, I can't," she sighed. "I thought that I might be able to, but I can't, not this weekend."

Oh my god. What have I just done? she thought, in shock. *I've lied to him! I've lied to Sam. Why? What possessed me to want to lie him?* Suddenly her mind was in turmoil. She'd been looking forward to him being home so much, and so wanted to spend the weekend together, but now she'd broken the special bond between them about being honest and truthful to each other. *What the hell have I done?* she thought again, showing him a forlorn smile, trying to disguise her disbelief at her own lie.

"That's alright," he replied, as she unlocked his car. "I know you've got a lot on your plate. It's a shame, but never mind." He turned away so that she wouldn't hear his sigh. *Maybe it's a blessing in disguise to see less of her*, he thought, trying to counter his disappointment.

He observed she was subdued once they got inside the car.

"So, what is it you have to do this weekend?" he asked her, trying not to sound displeased or disappointed with her.

She didn't reply to his question, and Sam sensed she was troubled.

"I'm done in, Sam, I'm going to bed. It's been a long day," she finally said, standing in her hallway.

"That's alright, babe. I'll just get my things and be on my way."

He felt like picking her up in his arms and carrying her upstairs and tucking her into bed, but instead he just kissed her cheek and said, "Speak to you tomorrow."

As he went to leave he noticed a cardboard box in the hallway – it was packed with provisions she'd obviously intended bringing to the cottage. His mind went into overdrive. If she hadn't been planning to go with him, why would she have packed a box of food and . . . two bottles of her favourite wine?

Penny closed her bedroom door. Normally she would leave it ajar, but this time she wanted to lock herself away. She walked over to her bed and removed the small suitcase that was lying on top . . . ready for the weekend. She lay there in the dark, knowing Sam was most likely wondering what had happened, and if he had done anything wrong.

Why? she thought, again. Why did I suddenly feel I had to lie to him? *He's always been the perfect gentleman – gentle being the operative word – and never made me feel threatened or vulnerable, so why*?

She slumped down onto her settee in the morning and looked at the painting of the cottage and wept.

"What is going on inside my head?" she shouted, as she let out a cry of frustration and anger, a growling sound more akin to an animal than a cultured woman. "It's not as if I'm never going to see him again or go to the cottage!"

She stood up and walked into her kitchen, and then stared at the gift box on her worktop. There was a note attached. Her hands started trembling with apprehension, and a chill ran through her body. She read:

'My dearest Penny.

I hope you are feeling better after a good night's sleep. You may not have realised, but it's nearly a year to the day since we became friends after that fateful day when you crashed into my life. I have left you the rose I promised you, which I hope will bring luck, (as if you need it) to you and Katherine. I had hoped to give it to you at the cottage but brought it with me in case you couldn't come.

I know you actors say, 'break a leg' as a term of good luck, but I will say - may the wind fill your sails.

Love Sam xx'

"Oh, Sam, you lovely man," she cried. "I did forget. I'm so sorry, sweetheart."

She wiped tears away from her eyes and reached over for a knife, gently folding back the top flap and opening the tissue paper to reveal the gift inside.

"Oh!" she cried. "Oh my goodness!" She took out a single, twelve-inch, filigree silver rose. Each delicate petal was enamelled in a vibrant red, and she sat mesmerised by its beauty; it was the most precious thing she had ever held. "It's so beautiful," she whispered, and fresh tears filled her eyes. She wished he could have been there to see her open it; she wished she hadn't ruined his day, and his weekend; she wished she could pick up the phone and tell him how ashamed she was.

Chapter 52

The Truth

Reaching for his towel after stepping out of the shower, Sam looked in the mirror and stared at his face, pulling at his jowls.

"Definitely passed your sell-by-date, old man," he muttered. He detected Penny's scent laced into the fabric of his bathrobe. "And definitely too old for her," he declared, picking his phone up off the bed.

He headed for the kitchen for something to eat, checking it for messages as he sat down at the table: four missed calls from Penny.

"Hi, hun, what's up?" he asked, when she picked up. "Sorry I missed your calls – I was in the shower. Everything alright?" he asked in a matter-of-fact voice; he did not want to sound too eager or excited on hearing her voice after the disappointment of the night before.

"Hello, Sam. How are you?" she asked, her tone sheepish.

"Fine. I was about to cook myself something. Why?" (*God, you do that a lot, don't you, Sam: answer a question with a question*, he thought, realizing how nice it was to hear her voice again.)

"Well . . . if you can pick me up from the station in an hour, or . . ." – that word again – "actually its forty-five minutes now, I'll treat you to a meal at the pub." She waited for his reply, her brain blanking out the surrounding chatter of all the people around her in the carriage. Conversely, on the other end of the phone, she could have heard a pin drop.

"No," he replied. He paused to gather his thoughts. He heard her draw in breath and then a slight sniffle – was she crying? "How about I pick you up, cook you something and you treat me to a meal tomorrow?"

"That sounds even better," she said, so quietly he could hardly hear her.

"I'll be waiting for you at the station. That'll give you enough time to stop crying, you silly bugger."

Penny walked towards him at the station, but her feelings of joy at seeing him were restrained. . .she knew she had to fall on her sword and tell him why she lied.

"Hello again," he said, smiling, taking her travel case but not giving her a hug or a kiss – which she noticed and missed. She put her arm through his, as was her way; but instead of resting her hand on his forearm, she gripped his sleeve. He glanced at her while he was walking; she was a million miles away. He'd seen that look before – when he drove her back to London to have her final showdown with Toby – and little did he know that she was once again rehearsing her lines in her mind, word for word, only this time *he* would be the recipient.

"Sam . . . before we go on, I-I have to tell you about last night," she said, her heart thumping. It was making her breathing irregular, which was in turn making her more anxious. Years of training in self-control seemed to have abandoned her. "Please. Turn the engine off. You need to turn it off because you may want to put me back on the train after what I have to say." Her voice was trembling, and as Sam was about to answer she said, "No, Sam, don't say a word, please. I just need you to you listen, and then you can say whatever you like afterwards." He frowned and nodded in acceptance. She didn't look at him, instead she picked at her fingernails, making a clicking sound which he found irritating and distracting, but he could see she was a bag of nerves so he didn't stop her, he just allowed her to talk.

"Last night when I picked you up, you asked me if I would be coming with you to the cottage, and I said *no* because I was busy with other things to do." She was still struggling to control the tension she felt, but knew she had to carry on. "Well, I lied. In fact, my bag was packed all ready to go, to the point that I was going to suggest picking it up and that I'd drive us down last night." But when I opened my mouth I lied, and I don't know why."

Sam was totally surprised by her revelation. He hadn't considered that she might have lied to him, he just thought she had changed her mind; but he didn't respond, he just did what she asked and listened.

"I didn't intend to, but I did, and for the life of me I don't know why I lied, it's such a mystery to me," she said, as she studied his face, trying to read any reaction to what she was telling him. "I didn't have any reservations about seeing you again, or coming to stay with you, and I'd been looking forward to seeing you for days. I've been trying to work out why my mouth said something completely different to what I was thinking." She stopped to fumble in her bag for a tissue; she wasn't crying, but she knew there was a good possibility she was going to before too long. "When I went to bed, I couldn't sleep. I asked myself if warning bells were ringing about my feelings towards you. I've lied to people before, loads of times, mostly men, but I intended to. And you probably lied to Annie over the years, as it's what people do. I say things which aren't true, I'm paid to, that's my profession I'm an actor after all, but I shouldn't do that in real life. I–"

Sam put his hand on hers, and said, "Take a breath, sweetheart," alarmed to hear her stress manifesting itself in her voice. He leant over and opened the glove compartment, removing a bottle of water he had brought with him. He twisted off the top and handed it to her with a reassuring smile. Taking the bottle from him, she showed no acknowledgement for his kindness, instead he watched as the expression on her face changed from nervousness to deep sadness.

"This is where it's awkward for me, but I have to say these things, Sam, and for you to hear them, it's not going to be easy. . .

"I've asked myself if I'm in love with you, and I don't feel that I am. I'm thirty-three, not some young virgin experiencing the first taste of womanhood and love, and I think I'd know if I was, don't you? I have feelings for you. I care for you. If I didn't, I wouldn't have travelled all this way to tell you all this, and I wouldn't have felt like shit for lying to you. I'd like to think you have feelings for me . . . do you?" She suddenly stopped and realised she had said something very dumb. "That was a stupid question, wasn't it? I know you do. You wouldn't have rushed up to London to support me when things went tits-up with Toby otherwise. You're a good listener, and how you cared for me in that loving way of yours after my accident, when I was at my most vulnerable . . . I'll never forget that." Then out of the blue she felt light-headed as she remembered how he undressed her, and the all-too-brief sensation of euphoria that flowed through her at his gentle yet manly touch.

"I even thought about control – whether you've ever tried to control me or dominate me – and the answer to that is definitely no. I've been with men who've tried to do that, and you are the complete opposite. I think it's more me who tells *you* what to do, but I'm a woman, I'm allowed to, aren't I?" she asked, giving him an uneasy smile. She then looked down to see he was holding her hand again and felt comforted by his strong hand as she wrestled with her nervousness.

"I'm not stupid or naive enough not to realise I'm in the company of a man who probably hasn't made love to a woman in a very long time, but when I see you looking at me, when I'm all dolled up, I see a man with pleasure and delight on his face – and yes, desire too – but that's what a woman wants a man to feel. You once said to me that as a man you'd be worried if you didn't feel desire for me, even if we are just friends. I don't do it to tease you, you know that, I like to look nice for you," she said, speaking quietly and sincerely. She knew she had to be articulated and truthful . . . their friendship was at stake.

"That day I finished my relationship with Toby, I told him he had me, body and soul, which I now realise *was* a lie." She huffed and then screwed her eyes up in thought. "He had my body, but not my soul – I never trusted him with that. Which brings me on to us.

"Our friendship has been on quite a journey so far – since I crashed into your life, as you so perfectly put it. It would be sad if it ended here, almost a year to the day when we first met. It was the trust of a stranger – a man who I had never met before – that had brought me here, *us* here. It's that bloody word *trust* again, and how that word seems to haunt me, like it was planted in my brain. One major difference between you and Toby is that I *do* trust you with my soul."

Penny hoped she hadn't made a fool of herself by speaking her mind. She felt relieved that Sam had let her speak, but still she uttered a deep sigh as she continued, "And all I can say is that I'm sorry and I apologise for yesterday, and . . ." – the tears now arrived – "any amount of roses I may be given throughout the remainder of my life will *never* have the same impact on me as your single, filigree rose. It is the most beautiful thing I have ever been given, and I will cherish it forever."

He released her hand and sat back in his car seat, holding on to the steering wheel.

"Finished?" he asked, with that look of his which told her their friendship was as strong as ever.

"No, Sam, I hate you."

"Well, that's a pity, coz apart from the fact you talk too much, I think you're rather sweet."

"You're such a bugger. You're supposed to say you hate me too!"

"Ah, but I don't, and if I said that it would be a lie, wouldn't it? Now put your seatbelt on," he said, starting the engine.

Lying in her bed that night, going through the events of the previous twenty-four hours, Penny felt elated that in the morning she'd be waking up in the cottage she loved, and seeing the man she felt deep affection for. She then realised that since her split from Toby, Sam had become the only man she wanted to spend time with.

Sam sat on his settee playing his guitar, giving thought to what Penny had said, and then looked up to see her standing in front of him in her pyjamas.

"Sorry, have I kept you awake with my playing?" he asked.

"No. I couldn't get to sleep anyway, so I thought I'd keep you company. You don't mind, do you?" she asked.

He shook his head and patted the cushion next to him. He then picked up his glass of whisky and offered it to her.

"Thank you," she murmured, so quietly, as if she didn't want to disturb the serenity of the moment. "I'm getting a bit of a taste for this, aren't I?" she smiled.

"Yes, I've noticed."

"You were deep in thought when I came in the room. What were you thinking?"

"I was thinking about everything you said earlier," he replied.

"Sorry, I've upset you, haven't I?" She looked instantly worried.

"No, not at all." He took the glass from her and topped it up. "Your honesty and frankness reminded me of what Annie used to say. She'd always say that telling a lie was easy, but telling the truth was easier because you'd done the hard part – that of being truthful to yourself." He rested the guitar on his lap. "Annie would have admired you for what you did today," he told her.

She felt humbled at what he had said, and content that after all the turmoil caused by lying to him, she had done the right thing. She laid back as he started to play again, listening as his fingertips pressed and petted the strings, teasing, stroking, picking, making his guitar resonate to his bidding. Penny closed her eyes and opened her mind to his sweet music, enticing her imagination to wander and dream, to paint a vision in her subconscious. She felt honoured that he was now able to play comfortably in front of her.

After a while he stopped, placed his guitar back on its stand, and put another log on the fire.

"I imagined I was on a beach with the sea lapping over my feet when you were playing. There was a woman in a small sailing boat waving, calling out to me, she kept saying *'Awesome, awesome'*."

"What colour was the sail?" he asked; his voice had changed and sounded tense.

She looked hesitant, not sure whether to answer him. She sensed the scene she'd drawn for him meant something so much more than just a dream.

"Pink, Sam, bright, girly-pink." She smiled a hesitant smile.

"God, did we have some arguments over the colour of that bloody sail," he said dreamily.

"Who do you mean by *we*? Who's *we*?" she asked, feeling her pulse quicken as she waited for his answer. Every second seemed like twice that, three times that.

"Ruth . . . my sister," he told her, looking sad at the mention of her name.

She then knew the significance of her daydream, and that it was now for her to be by *his* side as he endeavoured to let light enter the deepest reaches of his memory where only darkness resided.

She had worked out for herself that perhaps he'd had a sister, but when he came close to talking about her, he couldn't, until now. She instinctively moved closer to him, and he put his arm around her waist and held her close, feeling the tenderness of her body through her pyjamas.

"Tell me about Ruth," she said quietly, as she slipped her fingers between his, not wanting him to let go of her.

"You would have liked her," he replied, in an upbeat tone. "*No.* You would have *adored* her. Imagine my two lovely girls wrapped up into one beautiful woman, and how wonderful that would be." He felt strangely excited and happy to be talking about her again, after all the effort over the years to keep her a distant memory. "Our dad taught us to sail and bought us a racing dingy. God, we were good!" All the good memories flowed back into his mind, but he knew that this lightness would be followed by the darkness and the nightmare that lay there-in. "When we were out in our boat, we always seemed to know what the other was thinking. We had no need to shout instructions to each other, we just sailed and had fun." He stopped to drink his whisky, and draw breath. "In the sailing club, they called us The Awesomes." (It was now Penny's turn to draw breath.) "You want to know why? Because we were just about unbeatable! We'd crew with other people from time to time, but together we were the real deal. They were great times." He offered her his glass, but she declined.

"She'd always call me her big brother, as if I was older than her. I always felt curious when she said that."

He could see a brightness in Penny's eyes, as if she somehow knew what he was about to say, and then tears.

"She may have called me her older brother, but in fact she was older than me by over seven minutes." He leant over and kissed her face, and then whispered to her, "Your tears are our tears, for Megan and Ruth, our twin sisters."

Penny started to sniff as she dried her face with the sleeve of her pyjamas.

"I'll have that drink now," she said.

I've never known a woman cry as much as you, especially one who likes to think she's a hard bitch, he thought, as he handed it to her, and a man-sized tissue from the box on the coffee table.

"We did have an elder brother – Sidney. Ruth called him Sid. He was nine years older than us. I remember Mum saying, 'The two times your dad got me drunk, I got pregnant!'" He paused while he ran his fingertips over her thumb, feeling the smooth, perfectly manicured fingernail.

"Rose-red," she said. "I put it on before I came down, to remind me of that beautiful rose you gave me."

"I'm glad you like it," he replied, as she put his hand to her lips and tenderly kissed it.

"I loved it, you silly sod. What woman wouldn't? Now don't start me off again, tell me about Sidney."

"Sidney, he was a very clever, His brain got up early and went to bed late, if you know what I mean. He was always thinking. Once we played a board game and Ruth won . . . he didn't speak to her for a month. It was as if he thought he had control over us. He couldn't hold down a job for too long, as he never fitted in. I suppose these days you would call him a sociopath, and unless he was the centre of attention he became very moody.

"Sometimes I would go up for a weekend to Birmingham – where Sidney was living. He seemed to be doing OK for himself: nice flat, new BMW. He always had plans and deals in the pipeline. Sometimes I'd lend him some money to help him out. I never got it back, though. I didn't expect to really, and anyway, he was my brother and I loved him," he said, clenching he jaw as he thought of him, his eyes showing anger. Penny could feel his hand tightening his grip on hers; he was hurting her.

"Sam, you're hurting me, sweetheart," she said.

"Sorry, babe, bad thoughts," he replied, suddenly letting go. "When I was at sea, and after I left, I was buying properties, doing them up and selling them. I then started to rent some of them out. I was getting a pretty good portfolio together. I had the opportunity of investing in a property deal, so, I did some research into it and all the information I received was enticing – you know the saying: 'This time next year . . .' Well, I went for it. I re-mortgaged everything – all my properties, even my own home – and I borrowed from the banks. I even sold my beloved sailing boat." He looked at her to see if she was listening, or even still awake. "Why don't you go to bed? I can tell you this another day," he said, thinking that perhaps she was bored.

"No, you carry on. I'll put some more logs on the fire," she said, not wanting him to have a reason to stop.

"In the end, I raised just over £400,000; but I was likely to get three times that back within a few years. Sidney became interested in the deal, so I told him that if he could come up with some cash, we'd go into it together. He invested just over £100,000, but, unbeknown to me, he had persuaded Ruth to put some money in as well. Oak, her husband, he wasn't at all pleased about it, but he trusted me not to risk my sister's money . . . some of it was what our parents had left her. So, the three of us formed a company."

"Oak is your brother in-law, yes?" she enquired.

"Yes, he is," he replied, as he put his arms straight up into the air and stretched, as if preparing himself for what he had to say next. "I'm telling you now," he continued, in a forceful, almost angry voice, "this was the worst time of my whole life, and some of it will upset you, and believe me . . ." He shook his head. "Are you sure you want to hear this?"

"Yes, I do."

"Sid . . . Sidney cleaned out our bank account and did a runner with all the money, every penny, over £670,000 all told.

"I was ruined, but my main concern was Ruth; she went to pieces, screaming and shouting and crying. She couldn't come to terms with what Sidney had done to us. I'd never seen her like that before. I tried to help her. I had a contingency fund – I've always had a contingency fund, just in case – so I gave it to her, £35,000, all of it, to help take the pressure off. My life was in meltdown by then. They say you know who your friends are when good times turn bad, and suddenly I didn't have any – they disappeared into the ether.

"Annie took the girls to her mother's in France, while I tried to come to terms with it all and see what I could salvage. I felt so betrayed and bewildered as to why our own brother stole from us. Then one afternoon, Ruth phoned me. She wanted to talk, so I arranged to meet her at my home; but when I turned up, her car was there but I couldn't find her."

Suddenly he started to take deep, long breaths, and Penny watched him with concern. In and out, in and out, he gasped, his breath almost becoming a pant as he tried to compose himself.

"I opened my garage door to put my car away . . . and . . . and, there she was." His eyes became dark and lifeless; the black hole of his soul had opened. "She'd hanged herself in my garage."

Penny cried a high-pitched whine and she put her hand across her mouth.

"I managed to cut her down," he told her, now crying nervously, wiping the tears away with his hands, his body shaking with the energy of the dark memories and anger that consumed him. "I was screaming for help like a child: *'Help me! Help me!'*- but no one came. I held her in my arms, my lovely Ruth, my sister, my twin, and I tried to revive her . . . then I felt a pain in my heart that has never left me. We always said that being twins, our hearts beat for each other. I felt I had failed her, that I'd let her down . . . I-I was late meeting her, you see." Sam stared at Penny, his face distorted with anger and remorse.

"Do you know what I was doing while my darling sister was killing herself? Do you want to know? I was screwing another man's wife. I couldn't keep it in my trousers in those days. I think I spent more time in someone else's bed than in mine."

Penny couldn't move; she was distraught, horrified and deeply moved by his words. It was her turn to listen, and she looked at Sam as if to say *It's OK to carry on.*

"A couple of days later, I was sitting at home, feeling sorry for myself. I'd lost my sister, my brother, my wife and children were abroad, and I was just about to go bankrupt. Then, to cap it all, I had a visit from the police. Apparently, Sidney was a known drug dealer in the Midlands." It was at this point that Sam's voice turned to pure venom. "He'd sold our sister's life for drugs," he spat, "and I have to live with that. Every day. *Every single day.*

"You actors act out your plays, and speak your sonnets, displaying all those feelings of emotions, betrayal and treachery; but you can't truly express them until you *experience* the pain and hurt and betrayal yourself, feel it tearing into your very gut . . . the same feelings that are running through my body right now.

"Do you know what Annie called me?" he asked then, almost spitting out the question at her. "She called me a 'nasty piece of work' for betraying our marriage vows, and she was right – I was bastard to everyone. I was selfish and arrogant, and it was no wonder Oak wanted to kill me. I should have realised Sidney was capable of stabbing us in the back.

"So, I learnt to harness that hurt, betrayal and pain, and use its emotional energy. I worked every sodding day and night, year after year after year, to pay off my debts – with interest. Annie came home and stood by me and supported me, and I never looked at another woman again after that. Things were never the same between us, though; we had our good moments, of course, but with her ever-present temper and my previous womanising, the damage was done. I still loved her dearly, though, she knew that.

"When I had finished, and didn't owe a penny to anyone, I tried to put the past away in the depth of my soul forever, but the memories never went away. I'd like to think I became a better person for it, but that's up to others to decide . . ."

They sat there for a few minutes, letting only the crackle of the fire take centre stage. She moved a cushion and rested her head on his lap.

"Go to bed, sweetheart, you're done in," he said, as she made herself comfortable.

"I want to be here with you," she whispered.

He could feel her weeping as he rested his hand on her head and ran his fingers through her hair . . . like it was the most natural thing on earth to do.

Chapter 53

Only You

"Time to wake up, sleeping beauty," he said, bending over her with mug of coffee at the ready. "I want to take you somewhere."

"Christ, Sam! What time is it? It's still dark!" She was barely able to keep her eyes open, but she sat up, taking the coffee from him, making a whining sound as though she was in pain. "I'm not going to object this time. I just hope it's bloody worth it!" she told him. And then she remembered her behaviour about meeting Emily, and how obstinate and indifferent she'd been to his request. She had learnt the hard way that he wouldn't ask her to do anything if it wasn't important to either one of them.

"Get dressed, and don't bother to tart yourself up, no one's going to see you," he told her, smiling.

He went to the kitchen to make them a flask of coffee.

"So, where on God's earth are you taking me at this hour?" she asked him a few minutes later.

"I'm taking you to my special place to watch the sun rise," he replied. "It's called the Cheesewring. I love to see the beginning of a new day from there, it's like . . . watching the darkness of the past being pushed away by the light."

"Wow! That is profound! Where is it?" She yawned and tied her hair into a ponytail.

"This place looks eerie," she said, and Sam let out a ghoulish sound as he watched her put on her walking boots with the light from his torch.

"You'd better not wander too far from me if you're scared. Have you not heard of the Beast of Bodmin Moor?" he asked, shaking the torch about.

"Oh yeah. I'm really scared now," she replied, with a smile.

They headed onto the moor, keeping a safe distance from the fence that protected walkers from the sheer drop into the disused granite quarry below. The well-trodden path led them to the stones. Stopping to admire them as they came into view, silhouetted against the faint light of the approaching sunrise, Penny was amazed.

"They look like giant, flat beach pebbles all piled on top of each other, don't they?" she said, as she looked for a place to stand to admire the dawning of the new day.

They stood together, near one of the many boulders partially imbedded in the terrain around them that offered a sense of proportion to the huge, precariously balanced Cheesewring stones. From the east, the glow of the sun rose from the horizon, shimmering behind the cloak of mist that lay low over the distant landscape. Neither of them spoke as they watched the sphere of molten heat spill out its glowing, liquid flame, on its journey to its azimuth.

"I'm so pleased you dragged me up here. Thank you," she said. She slipped her hand into his, bedazzled by the creation of this new beginning, this new day . . . the light of day in which she would finally realise her true feelings for him. "Did you bring Annie and the girls here?"

"Yes, once or twice, but only in the day time. You're the first person I wanted to share the sunrise with," he replied. He turned to see her wiping tears away from her eyes again. "What's up with you now, babe? You're not having one of your strange moments again, are you?"

"Sometimes I despair at you, Sam Farmer. You look after me more than most men are capable of, you give me such wonderful treasures – your friendship being one of them – and then you wonder why I cry when you say such heartfelt words to me."

He was unaware how the passing of the night had cleared away the fog that clouded her feelings towards him. He opened his arms to her, and she responded to him like she always did – and hugged him back.

Strolling back to the car, absorbing the views and the ruggedness of the moor, with wild ponies grazing just feet from them, she wondered if *he* was at odds in his mind now about their friendship and his affection towards her.

"Sam?" she asked.

"Yes," he replied, taking a photograph of her on his phone to send to his daughters.

"Have you ever thought that maybe us meeting wasn't an accident?" she asked, posing for the picture.

"Why do you ask?"

"You reminded me that it's a year ago today since I crashed into your life, and in that year so much has happened to me, good and bad," she said. "In that time, you've been there for me, *always*, like my knight in shining armour." He gave her that look of his, again, a smile laced with the look of humorous disbelief. "I know, Sam, I know," she said, laughing. "That makes me the silly maiden who talks too much."

He drove them back home for breakfast, where she spent the remainder of the morning, it seemed, chilling out in the bath. As promised, she treated him to a meal at the pub, and talked to Dave and Sue, arranging for them to see the play's opening night.

They spent Sunday quietly at the cottage, with Sam playing the guitar and pottering around the garden. He planned to take her back home by car, but this time she wouldn't hear of it, she knew he had a lot of work to catch up on, so she returned to London by train.

As they hugged each other farewell at the station, she smiled at him through tearful, hazel eyes, but this time was different – she knew exactly why she was crying.

And as he watched her go, he recognised an expression somewhat alien to her: that of wanting to say something and desperately trying to hold herself back from doing so.

Penny sat in the carriage, waiting for the train to pull out of the station, and looked at the pictures she had taken over the weekend – mostly of Sam on Bodmin Moor and of the sunrise. She remembered his words, that it was like 'watching the darkness of the past being pushed away by the light'.

It wasn't until later that day that she realised she felt something similar as she watched the dawning of the new day. She experienced a feeling of release, as if an entity had left her, releasing the shackles of her mind that had inhibited her from understanding her true feelings for him. She then knew, without a doubt, that she loved him – truly loved him. He was so different, so completely unlike any of the men she had ever been associated with before, and she felt euphoric. But with the euphoria came caution, a contradiction of emotions she at first found confusing; but then she knew why and knew what she should do: if fate had brought them together, then destiny hadn't finished with them yet . . .

Chapter 54

Betrayal

There was no hiding his pleasure now on hearing Penny's voice when they spoke by phone. More often than ever they found their conversations had no end. Then late one evening, a few days before he was due to go to London for Penny's opening night, he answered his phone, thinking as always it was her; but this time it wasn't, it was Angie, her agent.

"Sam, is that you?" Angie asked, with urgency.

"Yes, Angie, I'm pretty sure it's me," he answered.

"Sam, I've got no time for humour at the moment, and neither have you. How soon can you get yourself up here? We need to talk and as soon as possible."

"I can drive up tomorrow morning and be with you about midday, how does that sound?"

"No, I need you up here sooner than that. *Tonight*. And Penny mustn't know a thing about this, not until we've talked, is that understood?"

He was now under no illusion that Angie wasn't asking him, she was telling him, indeed summoning him. And why mustn't Penny know?

"I'd like to know what is so urgent?" he asked, politely. Unless it was an emergency, he didn't see why he had to drop everything and drive up tonight.

"I can't tell you over the phone, it'll take too long and it's complicated, and it obviously concerns Penny . . . and *you*. But that's all I'm prepared to say at the moment. I've spoken to her aunts, but I haven't told them too much. However, what I did tell them . . . well, May just said to tell you 'elephants never forget'. I have no idea what she meant by that."

"Oh shit!" Sam exclaimed.

He now had to think, and think fast. He had promised Penny he would never run away, and his love for her wouldn't allow him to, but this cloak and dagger stuff . . .

"OK. I'll leave in an hour," he said. "I'll be with you some time after midnight. Where do you want to meet?"

She could hear from Sam's tone that he wasn't happy about having to drive to London at such short notice without knowing why. She also knew from what Penny had said of him in the past, that he preferred people to be up front and honest with him, that he'd not be led by the nose, he wasn't that sort of man.

God, Sam, I hope you're as strong as Penny says you are, Angie thought, putting the phone down, and placing it with three other phones on her desk; two of them had flashing screens indicating incoming calls.

"Only two?" she muttered, "I'm surprised all four of you aren't rattling away."

From the basement car park, he pressed the elevator button to Angie's penthouse suite, wondering how big a stake she had in all this.

The elevator doors slid apart, making a muted *psssssst* sound which broke into the eerily quiet foyer. A surreal thought filled his mind: he was in the middle of one of the world's busiest cities, and all he could think about was how he missed the sound of birds, the wood pigeons and finches, and even the next-door neighbour's chickens. He realised he was well out of his comfort zone.

He heard the click-click-click of high-heeled shoes on a marble floor.

"Sam, I'm so sorry about all this," Angie said. She wanted to appear calm, despite the opposite being the case. "Plonk your bag in there, and then come on through to the lounge," she added, pointing into a bedroom.

He didn't bother to put the light on; he just dropped the bag down. He walked down a short hallway, admiring the craftsmanship of the carved solid oak doors. The lounge, like her private lift entrance, had marble flooring – white, with rich veins of red – and it gave the rooms a sense of warmth. He was overwhelmed by the view of the city stretched out before him.

"Christ, Angie, how much did this put you back? Two and a half, three million?" he asked, gazing with amazement at the Houses of Parliament to the left of the River Thames, and Lambeth and Westminster bridges in the foreground, and the London Eye on the opposite bank.

"Just under four, Sam; wonderful, isn't it? Mind you, you should see the size of my mortgage – it's what sends me to work each day!" she replied from behind him.

He stood at the wall-to-wall sliding glass doors, shaking his head with bewilderment at how a place, even with a fabulous view like this, was worth ten times the value of his tranquil cottage.

"Here you are, darling," Angie said, "a single malt with a dash of water – that's what Penny said you like."

He sat on one of the two huge, red leather sofas.

"Cheers," he said, raising his glass in Angie's direction. "Why do I get the impression that I'm going to need this, if not more?" he enquired.

Angie was standing by a cocktail bar, refilling a tall glass – almost to the top – with vodka, topped off with a minimal splash of Coca-Cola.

And Don't Forget the Roses

"Help yourself when you want a top up," she replied, ensconcing herself at the other end of the same sofa, kicking off her shoes and then crossing her legs under her. "Cheers," she echoed, and poured her drink into her mouth as if it was nothing more than water.

He had met Angie several times over the year he had known Penny, and she had told him how very clever with people she was, and that you underestimated her at your peril, so he thought it wise for her to take the lead and see where it took him.

"You do realise she's madly in love with you, don't you, darling, but she won't admit it," she stated, casually, as if she was telling him the time of day. "And I know you love *her*, don't you?"

He felt the inclination to look away from her, to hide his eyes, but he knew that's what she expected – to shy away would be to confirm the truth. Her straight talking challenged him, and he knew she was probing, feeling her way into his mind. He was also well aware of the chink in his armour: Penny, and Angie, had gone straight to it.

Sam gave thought to her assertion, realising she was the first person who'd openly implied Penny was in fact in love with him. But the two people who knew her better than anyone else – her aunts – never gave him cause to think he was anything more to Penny than her loving friend. Knowing May and June, so he thought, they wouldn't be able to contain themselves from telling him. He could feel Angie's eyes focusing on him, not taking any notice of his polite smile, but looking behind it, picking up on any involuntary signs, eye movements and facial expressions that might give him away. Angie certainly knew how to read a person's face; she didn't have to hear his reply to know the answer.

"Penny showed me the beautiful silver rose you gave her," she said, giving him an *I know something you don't* type of look. She then disappeared into her office and returned with her iPad. "That bloody woman had me driving all over London so that she could get a cameraman friend of hers to take a special picture of it; it looks like you can literality hold it in your hand." She showed him the picture on the screen. "She's put it in an antique silver frame, and now she takes it to the theatre with her every day for good luck." She looked Sam straight in the eye. "That rose wasn't just a gift, it was a token of your love for her, wasn't it?"

"Yes, I do care for her, deeply, I can't deny that. If I didn't I wouldn't be here at this godforsaken hour drinking an extremely fine whisky. And you may consider this, Angie . . . I'd like to think we're good friends, too, and that you realise I'm up here for you, too, so let's stop these mind games."

She knew the moment had come to tell him things he may not want to hear, and she wondered how he'd react. She hoped his love for Penny would be strong enough to accept that people make mistakes, and that he would continue his Mr Dependable status.

"Penny says you're a very private person, Sam, and I know she's confided in you about her past." Angie now positioned herself on the edge of the sofa, sitting upright, giving her an air of authority. Even with nearly a bottle of vodka inside her she showed no signs of fatigue. "There's something she didn't tell you, however, as she felt she didn't need to. Penny was once a very different person."

"Is that what this is all about? That some secret from the past is catching up with her?" Suddenly he stopped. Angie could see that his jaw and neck muscles had tensed. "Toby," he stated, simply, quietly.

"I'm afraid so, darling. Penny used to keep a journal. She said she hadn't written in it for years and had forgotten about it. It sounds like the bastard stole it from her house – probably when she threw him out. The poor darling, she's in utter despair . . . apparently, she was quite detailed about men she'd been with and–"

"Don't tell me anymore, Angie. I don't need to know about her past from you, do I," he said abruptly.

"No, you don't," she replied.

Sam walked over to the glass wall and stared out over the city of shimmering lights, pondering Toby's actions and what connection there might be with the elephant man.

"My contacts in the media say it'll all hit the fan tomorrow. Apparently, he's telling little snippets at the moment – not from her journal, but from their time together. I've been informed there's a lot more to come." Angie sighed. "Sam?" she said. He turned to look at her; he could sense her discomfort at what she needed to say next. "The silly woman let Toby take intimate pictures of her on his phone – you don't need me to elaborate – and it's all got horrible for her. The prick – prick being the appropriate word – has put them on the Internet, and now she thinks everyone is laughing at her; and to be honest, they probably are. And just when everything was going so well for her.

"Even Sir Richard Roddington offered her a peach of a roll in his latest production. Strange . . . he never showed much interest in her until she got the part of Katherine. Maybe word got out she was on the up. But if the play doesn't live up to its billing, Sam, because of Penny, she'll be finished as a serious actress. No one will touch her. The best she could hope for is some third-rate reality show.

"Tomorrow's papers will be full of Toby's crap, and I'm told he said things about you too – how you played mind games and controlled her like a dirty old man, and that their relationship ended because of your influence over her."

Sam's first instinct was to walk out of the apartment and try and find him, talk to him – Sam-style – but he knew that was pointless. He was in Toby's backyard and wouldn't have a clue where to look for him.

"We can't stop him from releasing his lies, I suppose?" he asked, his voice controlled; he didn't want her to sense the murderous anger he was feeling on the inside.

"No, darling. He's telling his side of the story about arguments he had with her concerning you and Maggie."

"Maggie? What the hell has she got to do with all this?" Suddenly his controlled anger rose. "The bastard better not have said anything about her! I'll break his scrawny neck! Can't we go to court and take out an injunction to stop him?"

"No. Archie has already tried, and failed."

Sam's heart pounded in his chest.

"I'll . . . I'll phone Penny later," he said. "I have to speak to her–"

"Sorry, Sam. She won't speak to you. She's too ashamed to talk to anyone, especially you. She's not sleeping and rehearsals aren't going well." Angie poured another very large amount of vodka into her glass, and held the whisky bottle up to Sam.

He put his hand over his glass, shook his head and said, "No more for me. I need a clear head."

He slid open one of the glass doors and stepped outside onto the balcony. The rush of the early morning air cooled and refreshed his face; but not his wrath.

"That bastard is out there creating havoc in our lives, and here are we, unable to do a thing about it," he said, as he looked at his watch, and back at the city. It was 4.50am. "Might as well watch the sun rise." He wished Penny were standing next to him, or better still, in his arms.

Angie moved to sit at the breakfast bar and switched on her laptop. She flicked through the day's newspaper headlines – and groaned. Sam heard her despair and joined her, sliding the door silently closed on his way back in.

"Well, that's it, Toby's arse is mine," he said, after reading over her shoulder for a few minutes. He was seething that no one, not even his daughters, were exempt from Toby's treachery. He read out loud: "'*Penny thought his daughter, Maggie, looked like mutton dressed up as lamb and felt embarrassed to introduce her to their friends . . ."'*

Angie jumped as his clenched fist pounded a single thud on the breakfast bar.

"No need to read any more, is there, darling," she said, closing down the screen.

"Penny didn't say those things!"

Angie watched helplessly as he tried to get a grip on his fury. She didn't know that there was one thing Sam could not stomach, and that was betrayal. She made coffee and poured them both a large mug, drinking hers in much the same way as she did her vodka – in large gulps.

"Look, darling, I have to disappear into my office for a couple of hours," she said. "I've got people to talk to. I'm not telling you what to do, but I suggest you go and speak to her aunties. We need to find out why Toby waited months to do this. It's odd. You'd think he would have gone to the press immediately."

"You're right, I will go and see them. I have a suspicion the old ladies know more about this than they're letting on. But first I need to pay a visit on someone else . . . elephants never forget."

Chapter 55

Truth Will Out

Sam didn't bother to pre-warn Penny's aunties he was going to call, he just walked in. The look on his face immediately told them he wasn't there just for a cup of tea.

"Sam, dear, you look dead on your feet, when was the last time you slept?

"Hello, June, I won't kiss you . . . as you say, I'm not in the best of conditions at the moment," he said, watching her wash up their breakfast dishes, and catching the whiff of toast and Marmite in the air – June's favourite. "Where's May?" he asked.

"She's next door, dear, with Betty. She won't be long. I'll put the kettle on while we're waiting for her."

June didn't engage in any small talk with him. It was clear Sam was in no mood for a light-hearted chat, and she had a good idea why.

When May returned, they assumed their positions at the dining room table: Sam seated opposite the two ladies. But this time Sam was not calm, he was openly shaking. He took a long breath. He was too tired to be anything other than blunt in his statements.

"I reckon I know who your elephant is, and now he's manipulating Toby like a puppet to do his dirty work. But I need you to tell me everything – and I mean *everything*. I spoke to Aaron and Archie on the way here and what they told me convinced me it could only be him, but I need you to confirm the man's identity.

As Sam continued, demanding answers from them, his eyes did not sway from the sisters' gaze.

"I know you thought you could deal with him, but it's got out of hand. You probably thought you could appeal to his better nature, didn't you? The only problem is, he hasn't got one, has he?"

"I didn't think he would go this far, just because of what happened almost forty odd years ago," May replied, her voice trembling with the realisation that a decision she'd made back then had returned to haunt her.

"It was you who said, 'elephants never forget', remember?" Sam replied. "Whatever you did to him, he's waited this long to settle old scores, and he's prepared to break the law to do it. If *you* don't stop him, he'll destroy Penny's life, and possibly her sanity, you must know that!" Pausing to catch his breath, he knew he mustn't hold back. Too much was resting on him to go soft on them now. "I don't know anything about the theatre world, but what do you think will happen to the reputation of the British theatre if he gets away with this? And what if the press get to hear the *whole* story? Have you thought of that?"

Sam stood up suddenly with a terrible cramp in his calf. He rubbed it as he hobbled about the room.

"When was the last time you slept, dear?" June asked again, worried for him. "Promise us that once we've talked, you'll go to bed while we sort this madness out."

Nodding his head in acceptance, he said, "He's going to run a bulldozer through our lives to achieve what he wants, and he's dragged my girls into it as well. I can't allow him to do this. I'm not going to let him or Toby humiliate them, or Penny, anymore. But you two have to take control. Whatever happened between you and your elephant, ends now." (He didn't repeat Maggie's saying, 'You don't mess with a Farmer' – he could see from their faces that they'd got the message.)

May, all be it reluctantly, told him everything he needed to know. Like Sam and Penny, she had hoped *her* past would remain in the past, but for the sake of her niece she gave it up to Sam. Then between them they put the pieces together; a plot of simmering revenge, want and betrayal.

"My god, Sam," May declared. "You would think the Bard himself had written this plot!"

June made a phone call to someone who was their spy at the theatre. It didn't surprise Sam to hear that their insider informed them there was yet another person being manipulated by the man from the ladies' distant past.

Sam then phoned Angie to update her, and she told him about Toby's PR people – who were paying the bills – and then he went to bed.

Angie relayed some more information to June, and then it was decided that Penny shouldn't be told until the next day – the day of the play's premiere.

"But who's going to tell her?" May asked.

"Who is the one person she listens to, dear?" June replied.

Chapter 56

The Spy

"Max, it's Sam. I'm almost outside your stage door."

Sam sat hunched in the taxi as he spoke into his phone; he didn't want to be seen. Angie had already forewarned him that the media had camped themselves outside the theatre, and with photos of himself now circulating the Internet, he wanted to keep as low a profile as possible.

"Here, keep the change," he said as the cabbie endeavoured to pull up as close to the door as he could, so that he could dive, superstar-fashion, out of the car – except he wasn't a superstar, and these weren't fans. . . they were, in his book, vultures!

"Phew, that wasn't fun," he told the assistant director, the spy in the camp, and shook his hand with a smile.

He had never been backstage in a theatre before, and was astonished at the frenetic activity going on around him. There was a strong smell of paint, and there were props stacked everywhere and acres of ropes. People scurried about in the stale air, and wafts of perfume and perspiration clung to their bodies. He noticed stepladders, almost at as tall as his cottage, propped precariously up against metal staging, giving the area a feel of a construction site.

"I'll take you up to the bar area, Sam, we can talk there. Too many ears around here," said Max, leading the way through corridors and behind scenery. He stopped to look around and listen, and turned to Sam and whispered, "We'll go this way. Art has got Penny on stage having a run through with Peter, and it's not going well for her. We'd better not let her see you – she's stressed out enough as it is."

He led Sam through the service passages to the front of the theatre foyer, and then up the emerald-carpeted stairs to the bar area. He was saddened that he couldn't see her. He wanted to give her support and encouragement, but he knew that wasn't why he was there; talking to her would come later. First, he had to speak to Max in private, and then deal with someone in the theatre whose agenda was contrary to her success.

Once in the bar's lounge, they sat on a red velvet bench seat and talked in detail. Max held nothing back, giving him the information he needed, plus something else; something that would certainly be a surprise to Penny, but not to her aunties . . . they already knew.

"OK, stay here while I see if Art and Penny are still on stage," Max said, and he scurried off.

Sam paced up and down, desperately trying to put the pieces of information given to him into context with what he already knew. He really wasn't looking forward to seeing Penny – which was a first – as he had to tell her things which were so outrageous and unbelievable that he thought May would have been better placed to tell her, but she couldn't, and Sam had got the short straw. But May and June had to deal with the elephant man, as they called him, and Angie was busy dealing with all the negative publicity engulfing Penny and him. Archie was in the law courts and, hopefully, this time would be able to stop the so-called elephant man in his tracks.

As for Sam . . . *What I wouldn't give for a nip of whisky*, he thought, aware that if he failed to play his part, Penny's career could be in tatters.

"She's gone back to her dressing room with Art," said Max, catching his breath, his face showing the pressure both men where under. Max knew it was now time for Sam to take over and bring the curtain down on Penny's nightmare. But before he could do that, he had to remove an obstacle first.

"We'll wait here. It's far enough away so they can't hear us. When Art comes out, he'll head for his office," Max whispered. He could see Sam was beginning to get restless and impatient, wanting to get it over and done with for his sake as well as Penny's. He flexed his neck, the way a boxer does before he goes into the ring.

"Christ, is that her in there shouting and screaming?" Sam asked.

But before Max could answer, he heard a quiet, "Hello, Sam," from behind him.

He quickly realised the voice was not Penny's, and as he turned around he saw a woman in her mid-seventies, who then reached up and clasped his face, squeezing his cheeks as she planted her lips firmly on his. After what seemed a millennium, she stepped back and took his hand, holding it as firmly as she could in hers.

"Give that to the beautiful woman in there, and tell her to get over it. Anyone would think she's the only person to be caught sucking a man's cock," said the elderly lady, in a cavalier manner, her face crafted with age. "Believe me, you lovely man, I've done a lot worse than that in my day! Ask her aunties, they'll tell you!"

He smiled at her in astonishment, and she disappeared as stealthily as she had appeared.

"Who on God's earth was that?" he asked, perplexed.

He noticed Max had his hand across his mouth, desperately trying not to laugh out loud.

"It's Penny's dresser, Mavis," he replied.

"What the fuck are you doing here?" a loud voice cried. It was Art. "She's too busy for visitors, and you've got no right to be backstage. I suggest you piss off!"

Sam moved forward towards him, and in one step reduced the distance between them to only inches.

"Let's see who's getting out of here, shall we," Sam replied, as he put his left hand out and pinned Art by the throat to the white painted brick wall behind him, rendering him unable to move. Sam knew from experience that you use your weaker arm to pin your foe down, thus freeing your stronger one to hit them; but he had no intention of doing so, he just wanted to scare the shit out of the man who was another part of Penny's nightmare.

"Right, you bastard, there's something you need to know . . ." Sam growled. "No one greets me like that and then wonders why I've got my hand around their throat," he said, glaring at Art, trying not to shout so as not to alert Penny – the last thing he wanted was for her to see him with his hands around her boss's neck.

Letting go of his grip on him, Sam gestured to Max to lead the way to Art's office, making sure he was within grabbing distance should Art feel inclined to do a runner.

On entering the room, Art rushed to the phone on his desk. He looked petrified that he may be in for more of the same.

"I'm not going to let you get away with assaulting me, you bastard," Art grunted, in a barely audible voice. He clutched his throat, and reached for the phone.

"Fine," Sam replied, not moving away from the door, "but if you intend to phone the police, I'd speak to George Dawson first if I were you . . . they're more than likely on their way for you." He then looked at Max, and said, "I'm going to speak to Penny now, and we won't want to be disturbed. A man will arrive, and he'll ask for me. Just tell him to wait outside her room."

He then returned his gaze to Art. Penny had taught him how to put his facial expressions into character, to display remorse or glee, for example, and it was a game they had often played – guessing what each expression was. Art had no trouble working out what was on Sam's face, his eyes gave it away: revulsion, sheer revulsion for what Art had put the woman he loved through.

"A word of advice," Sam said, as he pointed his finger at Art. "This guy who will call to see me, he will be here within the hour, and apparently, he's more of a bastard than me, so if I were you, I'd be long gone by the time he turns up . . . and I mean *gone*."

Sam had nothing further to say.

Chapter 57

Dressing Room

Sam stood outside Penny's dressing room, taking deep breaths and preparing himself for what he had to do. Once he turned the doorknob there was no walking away. He'd always promised her that he would never turn his back on her, and she knew he would adhere to his word, *always*.

He found her sitting at the dressing table, where moments before she had been resting her head in her hands, thinking things through after speaking to Art, and now all she wanted to do was be a million miles away.

The room was no larger than about ten feet by twelve feet, with another room leading off it – the loo he assumed. He reckoned his garden shed was bigger than this. The pale walls were hung with shelves that were full of colourful bouquets of flowers and cards sent by friends and well-wishers. A tangle of fragrances filled his senses: the sweet perfume of the flowers and the heaviness of hairspray and make-up. The dressing room's floor was covered in a short-pile carpet, the once dark green colour, now paled by wear and tear. A full-length mirror took up the only wall space not covered with shelves and pictures of previous residents of the dressing room.

"Go away, Sam. Not now, please. I don't want to see you." Penny's voice was abrupt, and she spoke to his reflection – which was illuminated by the bright light bulbs surrounding the dressing table mirror – but her eyes betrayed her real feelings.

Sam didn't speak.

"How the hell could you possibly want to see me, anyway, with everything that has been written about you?" she said coldly. "And the horrible things Toby said about Maggie. It's entirely my fault this has happened, all of it. It's best you go. I don't want you here. Please go, Sam."

He stood by the closed door and listened to what he had been expecting to hear. She had retreated into herself, just like she had done when she was a child when it seemed the world was conspiring against her. The Penny of old was raising her head again; the Penny who thought it was easier for people to dislike her than to love her. But she hadn't counted on Sam.

"No. I'm not bloody leaving," he replied, and in a tone that was as determined as hers, "and you know that." He spun her swivel chair around for her to face him.

She could clearly see the determination, and the care, in his eyes; a look she had seen many times before.

"We knew something like this would happen, didn't we? You even sensed it at the house, remember? I'm staying because we . . . no . . . *I* have a lot of talking to do, and with a bit of luck, you'll understand what all this has been about. And then maybe, just maybe, you will walk on stage in a different frame of mind than you're in right now," he said.

"I'm not going on tonight, Sam, I'm *finished*!" she shouted.

He walked to the corner of the room where he had seen a plastic folding chair. He sat down opposite her, reaching for her hands to hold in his.

"It was only a matter of time before Toby did something like this, wasn't it?" His voice was calm and, he hoped, comforting.

"That effin' bastard, Sam! I make no apologies for my language. He stole my journal, all the inner thoughts and secrets of a person I walked away from a long time ago." Her face was blank now, devoid of any joy, resigned as it was to humiliation.

"I know that, sweetheart. Neither of us are the person we used to be." He gently tugged at her hand as if to pull her out her low self-esteem. "You must ask yourself why . . . why has Toby taken so long to do this? And why today? He's probably had your journal since you threw him out months ago, so why now?"

"I don't know," she sighed, and reached for her bottle of water and took a mouthful.

"I know it's not easy for you, and what I'm about to tell you will seem far-fetched . . . even *I* had trouble taking it all in." His reassuring smile was as much to relax himself as her. "Ready?" he asked. She replied with only the slightest nod of her head.

"OK," he said quietly, and then took a deep breath and held it for a moment while he gathered his thoughts, knowing he had only once chance to get it right. "Toby did put all that shit out there . . . but he's being used as a pawn by someone else. Yes, he wanted to exploit his relationship with you and make lots of money out of it. He also wanted to play the sympathy card, but I doubt there's any sympathy out there for him now . . ." He paused.

"You have to keep asking yourself Penny, why. Why did Toby wait months to do this, and today of all days? It's because he was paid a lot of money just to keep his mouth shut until now, *that's why.*"

Penny sat very still, trying to use her already muddled mind to make some sense of what he had told in her.

"Are you telling me that bastard was put up to it? By whom?"

"Bear with me," he replied, aware he didn't have the time to tell her everything – her aunties would have to fill in the gaps at a later date. "You may have to help me with some of it. I'm a bit out of my depth with this theatre lark." He could see she was at last more attentive, and he needed her to be, because what he was about to tell her was akin to a who-done-it tale. But this wasn't make-believe. Yes, it was being played out in the theatre, but the players were real people, and the outcome couldn't be re-written.

Sam knew that every word he spoke from now on would be scrutinised by her, testing her trust and belief in him to breaking point.

"This all started nearly forty years ago, long before you were even born. Back then, your mother and her sisters where having the time of their lives: all the best scripts; the most eligible men to wine and dine them. But your Auntie May was prepared to use the one asset she possessed to open doors for her that her sisters wouldn't dream of using: her body. As she said, she picked her men carefully and discreetly: agents, directors – mostly directors – and the occasional producer."

Penny frowned at him then. After all, it was her Auntie May he was talking about, and she wasn't sure whether she was shocked or just numb with disbelief at what he was telling her.

"That's rubbish, Sam. She was never like that," Penny said, almost scornfully.

"Hear me out, please," he insisted. "May wasn't a slut, as she said, she utilised her assets to her advantage, and in her day, she was as ruthless as they come. You think you can be a bitch? May would have put you in the shade. But I know you're finding this hard to believe."

"Bloody right, I am," she snapped. "I knew she was a bit of a bugger in her day, but not like that, the naughty woman. But I still don't understand what this has to do with me?"

"Nothing, absolutely nothing, sweetheart."

"What do you mean *nothing*? What about Toby? You said yourself he's making money out of the hurt he's causing us."

"Like I said just now, he's being led by the nose, and you're just in the way. You're what the professionals call 'collateral damage'."

"What the hell are you talking about, Sam? It feels bloody personal to me!"

Come on, Sam, you can do better than this, he thought, realising his approach wasn't getting him anywhere.

"OK," he said. He thought about what May had said to him: 'Tell her the truth, don't hide anything for my sake.'

Penny got up to go to for a pee, and it was then that he saw the small photograph of himself placed against the mirror. He smiled with surprise. "At least it hasn't got darts in it," he muttered to himself, quietly.

"Sam, what is this all about? I'm so confused," she sighed, sitting back down.

"I know you are, but you'll just have to listen and concentrate on what I'm telling you. Did you ever hear May say, 'elephants never forget'?" he asked.

"Yes, loads of times. Why?"

"Well . . . May fell in love. Let's call him *the elephant man*. At the time, he was an up and coming theatre director. He was educated, charismatic, handsome – and very married. But she didn't care, she was in love, and believed him when he said he would leave his wife for her; but after a while, May came to realise that all he really wanted was to own her – his own McCain, a Shakespeare sister – and keep her as his possession, his trophy. May stopped getting the parts she used to get from other directors. They wouldn't touch her, he made sure of that – and he wouldn't even use her in his own productions." Again, he paused. But not to gather his thoughts. He knew exactly what he was about to say. "Then she found herself pregnant, but she knew already that their relationship was over . . . so . . . so, she had an abortion."

"My god," Penny whispered, her face full of anguish.

"She also, for good measure, told his wife of the affair. Boy! Did she take him to the cleaners? The now ex-wife took everything she could put her hands on."

"Good for her," Penny snarled.

"This is terrible. I'm not enjoying this one bit," he told her. He hated to see Penny angry because of what he was telling her. "Your aunties have asked too much of me," he added.

"Well, Sam, I don't want to hear what you have to say either, but I realise there must be a good a reason why you're telling me all this, so get it over with, will you please."

Sam wanted nothing more than to get it over with, but he knew it wasn't going to be that straightforward.

"May," he continued, "carried on with her career in the theatre, but a short while later she had to have a hysterectomy. So, her child-bearing days were over, and as the years passed, she began to regret the termination. Then one day, this little eight-year-old child turned up on her doorstep, looking all forlorn, lonely and unloved, with only half a mouthful of teeth . . . let's call her Penny, shall we?" He watched as she cracked a small, much welcomed smile. "Seeing this waif of a girl, May felt she could atone for her past, so she gave up her acting career and directed all her energies into bringing this child up and giving her a happy life, with the help of her sister, June. It didn't take them long to recognise a precocious talent in her for acting, however; after all, she was a McCain. And when you returned from university – a woman with life-skills and maturity – you joined the 'family firm' as they say, and then began to catch the eye of *the elephant man*, who by then was one of this country's most powerful and respected theatre producers and directors. He also had a great deal of influence in the theatre world."

Sam studied her face, and wondered how much more she could take; he was about to destroy her belief in the people she loved and trusted.

"As May said, 'elephants never forget', and he didn't, and although by then he was reconciled with May, he never forgave her for what she did, and when he heard all the rave reviews about your acting abilities, the last thing he wanted was another McCain taking top billing. And as the years went on, and his power and reputation grew, so his thirst for revenge on May grew." He faltered, not wanting to continue, knowing a life-long friendship would be destroyed by his next words. "You haven't asked me who the elephant man is, have you?" he said quietly, barely able to look at her.

"No, I'm scared to, for all I know it could be someone like Sir Richard—"

Immediately she saw him flinch.

"*No!* Not him! Please tell me I'm wrong! He's not only been a mentor, but like an uncle to me! Surely it's not him?" she cried.

"I know you've often wondered why you haven't been given any of the meaty roles in the theatre when, with your talent, you wouldn't even have worked up a sweat. But when he became chairman of some government-financed body that dished out funding to the theatres, he could control you as he wished, and he'd put subtle pressure on a director or producer who wanted to use you, then he'd toy with you so that you got some good parts and great reviews, and then nothing."

Penny then remembered how Sir Richard seemed to know all about her auditions and how she'd thought that odd, and how she unexpectedly she got a part in the Noel Coward play.

"He was wreaking his revenge on May through you, Penny, and like everyone else, you had to pay your mortgage, so you took on TV work and occasional film roles, but all the time he was pulling your strings, keeping you away from the theatre where you belonged."

"Were my aunties aware of this?"

"No," came his stern reply. "Your aunties didn't have a clue that someone had been manipulating your career for years. Don't you think that they would have dealt with him sooner if they'd known? It's only now, because of his lust for this play, that he's come out of the shadows."

"What do you mean 'this play'? What has the play got to do with him?" she asked.

"You met a man – Aaron – the strangest person we have ever had the pleasure to call our friend, and as Aaron said, he didn't write the play just for you to be in – he wrote it *for you,* for his friend; he wrote very word, every scene, for you. And when your aunties endorsed the script as a brilliant piece of play writing, they were unaware of the potential consequences. When word got out about the script, Sir Richard had to have it, and he was willing to go to any lengths to get it; but there was a problem: *you.* Aaron wouldn't agree to put the play on in London without his leading lady and friend, and the last thing Sir Richard wanted was for a McCain to play Katherine. And when Archie tried to get backers, they all ran for the hills. They said it was because you were impossible to work with, but really it was instigated by Sir Richard. That's when your aunties became aware that something underhand was going on. Their years in the theatre, and knowledge about how deals were done behind closed doors, sharpened their senses, but they were blinded-sided by him. They thought it likely it was someone from their past, but couldn't imagine it would be him . . . they even asked Sir Richard for help. And do you know he tried everything to persuade Aaron to dump you? But he kept refusing, again and again. Sir Richard even offered him £250,000, and when Aaron refused again, he doubled it to half a million."

Her senses were now in overload. She slumped down onto her dressing table and rested her head on her folded arms.

"Aaron's love for you puts my roses for you in the shade," he said, but he knew instantly it was a bad time to try and lighten the mood. "Sir Richard tried something else . . ." he continued, tentatively. "Archie became guarantor to other investors as a carrot who may be interested. He got George Dawson on board with his production company – who invested with options – but, and these are the bits I don't understand, so please be patient with me," he said. "Apparently, you hire a theatre for just a month, and then if the production goes tits-up, your liabilities are limited. You still have contractual costs incurred, but these are covered by the guarantor, i.e. Archie. Now if the play is a success, the producer has the option of extending the lease for the theatre or going elsewhere. Does that sound right to you?"

"Yes, that's how it works," she replied.

"Sir Richard bought into the option with George Dawson, and paid a hefty sum for it. You can't blame George, it was business, and he was lead to believe you would be going with the play; but maybe 'duped' is probably the right word to use. Then the plan was for the play to eventually move to Sir Richard's theatre for an agreed amount of time, or *run* I think is what you call it and, of course, Sir Richard would be head honcho." As he was talking he wondered what was happening beyond the dressing room door. Had Art, like Elvis, left the building? And had Sir Richard finally been written out as chief villain in the cast of characters hell-bent on destroying Penny's life?

"Sir Richard still had the same problem, though: *you*," he continued. "George's contract with Aaron stipulated you were the lead actress, but once it opened, you could be replaced due to illness, for example, but you couldn't be sacked – Aaron made sure of that. I'm not entirely sure how the contracts were written. You and Angie know more about these things than me, obviously.

"So now he planned to get rid of you, and at the same he saw the opportunity to demolish your career and credibility as an actress, and finally destroy your aunties' reputations – and all because you were a McCain." (He was tempted to think *all this over a play*, but he knew there was so much more involved than just the play.) "He knew they would never be able to go to theatres like the Globe again, due to the loss of face, and I would imagine that that would have finished them off, not being able to go to their beloved crucible. . . and his revenge would have been complete."

Penny grabbed a tissue from the box on her dressing table.

And Don't Forget the Roses

It was obvious to him she was deeply wounded by what he was telling her. He placed his hand on her shoulder, and then gently rubbed the back of her neck. He hardly wanted to continue, but knew she had to hear the whole sordid tale to the end.

"Sir Richard's stooges contacted Toby. Did you know that Toby used to go out with a niece of his?" he asked, gently.

"It seems to me I know sod all about anything, Sam," she replied, her head still lying on her folded arms.

"He pretended to take Toby under his wing, and Toby told him he had your journal and what was in it. So, Sir Richard got a good PR company to represent him, with the stipulation that none of the shit about you was to be released until yesterday."

Penny turned her head to look at him. Were there more tales of betrayal? Like verbal barbed wire, the more she heard, the more it cut into her soul, and she could hardly believe what she was hearing.

"Art was in the pay of Sir Richard, and his job was to undermine your confidence and gamble that you wouldn't cope with all the pressure he was putting you under, as well as all the bad press you would get, plus the pictures of you and Toby on the Internet."

"Have you seen the pictures?" she asked then, hoping he hadn't.

"No," he replied, firmly, probably a little too firmly.

"I'm sorry, I didn't mean to insult you," she said, putting a conciliatory hand out to him.

For a while neither of them spoke, and then Penny whispered, "I've told Art I'm not sure if I can go on tonight, because if I do I'll screw it up, I know I will." Her sad voice suggested to him that she had acknowledged her dream was at an end.

"And what did Art say?"

"He said I had to go on, but I can't, it's over."

"Art needed you go on, sweetheart, and when you did he would have had his fingers crossed that you *would* screw up, only then could he replace you. Actually, I don't think it was left to chance that you would mess up – he had something else up his sleeve, I'm sure."

"Why are you speaking of him in past tense, Sam?"

"I'll tell you that in a minute."

"How do you know all this? About Aaron, Sir Richard and that bastard, Toby?"

"I had dinner with Aaron, George and Archie last night. I've already been up here a couple days, staying with Angie, and then your aunt's. Angie told me everything; but friends don't pass judgement, they just want to help."

"I don't deserve your friendship, Sam."

"I was thinking the same myself," he quipped.

She gave a small smile.

"I've been watching you from afar. It sounds a bit melodramatic, I know, but we had to let the bastards show themselves, especially Sir Richard, but it wasn't until this morning that matters could be sorted out once and for all." He observed her frown; at least it wasn't a scowl.

"At the same time as I arrived here, Sir Richard was confronted by your aunties, Archie's lawyer and a representative from the Arts Council. He was finally exposed for what he was."

He then reached for a bag that he had kept out of sight, and passed it to her.

She peered into it and cried out with surprise and relief, "Oh my god, Sam! How did you get it back?" She clutched the journal tightly against her breast.

"Toby gave it back, well, sort of . . ."

"Please tell me you had nothing to do with that? I know you . . . you would have hurt him."

"You're right, I would have done, but Archie's boys beat me to him. Besides, May wanted him alive." He laughed; she didn't. "Your aunts also dragged him along to the meeting, and I think Sir Richard will have cleared his desk by now. Did you know June and May had a spy in the theatre?"

"*Spy*? Who the bloody the hell is that? One of the other members of the cast, I suppose?"

"No. Max."

"What the hell have they got on him to make him spy for them?"

"It's not what they've got on him, it's who he is – he's your cousin; your father's sister's son. The old ladies didn't know he existed until a few months ago, and it wasn't until Max was sorting through his late mother's private papers that he came across information that showed he was related to you, and as usual, your aunties used him to their advantage."

"The little buggers," she huffed. "So, what about Art? Is he still the director?"

"No. George sacked him and gave me the pleasure of telling him," he replied, with an evil glint in his eye.

"You didn't hurt him, did you?" she gasped.

"No, but he'll have a sore neck for a couple of days, that's all. Max is your boss now. From what you've said of him, he's done most of the directing anyway. You said yourself he's a talented man. How . . . how are you feeling?"

She was still cradling the bag with the journal inside.

"Numb. Ashamed. I don't know what to do I feel so betrayed."

"Well, it's over, and you know what you lot say: the show

must go on! And don't give me that look," he said sternly. "Do you remember when I told you about all the hate and disbelief I felt when Sidney betrayed me? And how I used the anger in me as energy to carry on when Ruth died? You must do the same sweetheart: use the anger you feel for Toby's betrayal. Take it on stage, and let it feed into every word you speak as you give the performance of your life." His voice cracked as he spoke.

She looked up and saw tears trickling down his face, as he again re-lived the anguish of that time and transferred the sentiment to her. She stood and put her arms around him, and together they found solace. She didn't think it odd to see him tearful; it was one of the many things that she loved about him.

"You make it sound so easy," she whispered, burying her head against his chest.

He pulled away, but held onto her shoulders, and said, "No, it's not easy. I said the same thing to a dear friend of mine once, who helped me to play my guitar in front of people, and do you know what her reply was?"

"What did she say Sam?" she asked with a sniffle.

"Timing and concentration, sweetheart, timing and concentration."

"OK, Sam, you win," she said with a deep sigh.

"No, you win. It's those bastards who have lost."

She sat back down, and looked at her dishevelled appearance in the mirror; she knew she had to get her act together – literally.

Sam opened the dressing room door and looked up and down the corridor; people were still toing and froing – with the exception of one man who was standing right outside in front of him. Sam shook his hand, firm and business-like.

"You must be Mr Farmer, sir, I'm James. I've been told by Archie to be at your disposal."

Sam scrutinized the young, muscular man before him. He was

in his early thirties, and dressed in non-descript, but tight beige jeans and a black, short-sleeved shirt; he was definitely one of Archie's men. He wondered what his previous profession, prior to becoming a minder, had been.

"Royal Marine?" Sam enquired.

"No, sir. Captain, Royal Artillery."

Sam smiled and nodded at him, then recognising the clipped tones of a private education.

"OK, James, no need for formalities. You can call me Sam, and Miss McCain, Penny."

He waited for a reply, but he realised James wasn't there to talk, he was there to protect. Sam knocked politely on Penny's door before he re-entered. She was re-applying her make-up, dressed only in her underwear and a bathrobe. Sam was used to seeing her like that from the times she had stayed at the cottage, and from all the times he had waited at her house while she got ready to go out, but it still made it difficult for him. She looked at him in the mirror, and realised that although he was fully in control, she was now finding it hard to supress her feelings for him. But the fear that history would repeat itself prevented her from admitting to those feelings.

"Hi," she said. "Where have you been?"

"When you've put some clothes on, I'll introduce you to the good-looking, young man waiting outside," he told her. "That's where I've been."

"Why wait? Bring him in."

"OK," he answered, putting his hand on the door handle.

"Actually no, Sam, no! I'm only joking. I've had my fill of young men, thank you," she said, slipping her legs into a pair of red denim jeans, wriggling as she pulled them up to her hips. "Be a love and pass me that blouse on the rail. No, don't, you're not my dresser, sorry," she said.

"I'll do it anyway," he replied. "I can think of worse things to be than being your dresser."

"You wouldn't want to be my dresser, Sam. I may be a pussy cat with you – mostly – but I still have my moments."

"Even with Mavis?" he asked.

"You've met her, then?" She looked surprised and pleased that he had. "She's an angel, isn't she!"

"Oh yes, I've met her alright," he replied, rubbing his cheek bones and doubting that an angel would have the vice-like grip that Mavis had. He watched as she checked through the clothes on the rails, lifting out each individual hanger in turn. "Are those the ones you're wearing on stage tonight?" he asked.

"Yes," she replied, pulling out one particular dress. "This is meant to be my party dress for the last scene. Bloody awful, isn't it? Art thinks it reflects my character's personality. Tweed?" She shook her head. "What I wouldn't give for a good, long soak in the bath right now," she added.

"Well, Art isn't here anymore, is he, and let's see what we can do about a bath," he replied.

Sam checked the time on his watch, noting she was almost ready to leave. He beckoned James inside.

"This is James, sweetheart. He's going to be your shadow and keep an eye on you."

Penny acknowledged him with a polite smile and then suddenly she reached out and slipped her hand into Sam's, like a little girl holding onto her father, her eyes uneasy.

"Don't worry, babe, you're coming with me. Archie's booked us in at the Dorchester, including my girls, so you can have a bath there. I'll make sure you get some peace and quiet," he told her.

"Thank you, that will be wonderful," she replied. "I'd love to see the girls too. I have to apologise to Maggie for what that bastard said about her. I didn't say those things, Sam, you know that, don't you?" She picked up her journal and handed it back to him. "When you get home, burn it, and then we can sit together again on the settee in front of your lovely fire. We know we've have put our pasts behind us, forever."

As James opened the door for her to leave, she giggled. Sam frowned, curious as to what she was thinking.

"You're definitely my knight in shining armour now, Sam. The knight who saved the silly maiden from the clutches of wicked Sir Richard."

He didn't reply to her; just smiled at her silly thoughts.

James led Penny and Sam from the theatre via one of the fire exit doors, and safely into a car and onto the hotel suite, where Maggie and Estelle were overjoyed to see them. Sam felt drained and exhausted, and wondered how Penny would conjure up the energy to go on stage and give the performance of her life. He knew she was a person of great strength, despite her lack of self-belief. She probably wanted to find a dark cave to hide in, and those bastards certainly had tried, and almost succeeded, to put her in one, but as he looked at her now he could see the determination in her eyes.

He left James outside the door in the corridor, and then headed to the cocktail lounge and treated himself to large single malt and a plate of sandwiches – courtesy of Archie's account. He instructed his daughters to phone him when Penny was ready to leave – which they did – and judging by the amount of giggling and banter he heard going on in the background, he doubted if Penny had managed to get her quiet soak in the bath; but maybe that had been just what she needed – a bath, yes, but some giggles with two friends as well. As he walked up to James, he could see a broad grin on his face.

"By the look of you, you've met my daughters?" Sam asked with pity in his voice.

James nodded.

"You poor man. They're going to be all over you like a rash. Think about the hardest situation you've had to deal with, and then prepare yourself for tonight when they let their hair down!"

He let himself into the room, knocking as he opened the door.

"Where's madam, then?" he asked, as Maggie tried to put a glass of champagne into his hand.

"Not just yet, Mags, I'll celebrate once the curtain's down," he politely told her.

"She's in your bedroom, getting dressed. She said for you to go in. I love you, Dad," she told him, her dark brown eyes speaking voiceless words. "And so does that lovely maid in there. Mum would want you to be happy, Dad," she said, her voice trailing off to a soft whisper. "Tell her . . . tell her how you feel. If you don't, I–"

Entering the bedroom, Sam had a broad smile on his face; Maggie's words were still ringing in his ears. He saw Penny standing by the bed in conversation with someone on her phone.

"Sorry, Sam, I was talking to Angie. I need her to get something special from home for tonight."

"Oh yes, what's that then?"

"Be patient, Sam, you'll find out," she said, intending to tell him as little as possible.

Sam could see from Penny's body language that she was a great deal calmer than when he'd found her sitting alone in her dressing room. The radio was playing and she was gently swaying her hips to the beat of the music. She turned and reached out her hands to him; he took them in his own.

"Angie and May told me how you rushed up here and went without sleep to help them sort this bloody mess out. I'm so sorry," she said, pulling him into her arms.

"Don't waste any anger you feel being concerned about me. You have to take it on stage with you, remember?" he said, placing a tender kiss on the side of her face. The sensation of his lips on her skin threatened to overwhelm him, but all too quickly was over. He had no idea she was struggling too.

"Can I tell the girls you kissed me?" she asked, and giggled.

Sam just took a deep breath, and then gave her that look of his.

It was time to go. Penny put her head around the door of the girls' bathroom to say goodbye to Estelle, who was supposedly having a relaxing soak – only to find Maggie had joined her, and they were both splashing around and drinking champagne, giggling like a couple of school girls.

"God, how I love those girls of yours," she said.

He walked over to the door with her, then stopped and turned, putting his hands on her waist. He then gave her another long and tender kiss on her cheek.

She already knew what he was about to say: although she wanted him to go with her, she realised it was now up to her to silence her critics and her so-called friends on her own. She put her finger across his mouth as he was about to speak, and he felt her nerves running through it onto his lips.

"No, Sam, you don't have to say anything. I know." He could see she was desperately trying not to cry again. "What's that you say? To wish someone good luck?" she asked.

He tenderly stroked the side of her face and smiled, like her trying to hold back the tears.

"May the wind fill your sails, sweetheart, may the wind fill your sails."

Chapter 58

The Show Must Go On

James quickly and efficiently leapt from his seat, opening the car door so that Penny could be corralled between her door and James's body, enabling him to protect her from the boisterous photographers now literally camped six-deep outside the theatre.

"Hello, boss," she said, acknowledging Max's ascension to director.

He gave her a polite peck on the cheek.

"Are we ready?" he asked, as they walked to her dressing room, taking in the maelstrom of activity going on around them. "By the way, I've sacked Amanda, so you've got no understudy."

"Max! Why?" she asked, stopping in her tracks. "Not her as well? Surely?"

"Sorry, but I'm not going to need her anyway, am I?" he replied confidently.

Max left her at the door with her dresser, waiting with her arms open to greet her.

"Mavis, you old tart, what's this about you accosting my Sam?" Penny smiled, not sure whether to feel sympathy for him, or envy at the thought of someone else having the pleasure of kissing him.

Sitting at her dressing table, she reached down into her document bag to remove the framed picture of Sam's rose, putting it in pride of place in front of her, and next to a picture of him she'd taken a long time ago. She thought of Toby and Sir Richard, repeating the words Sam had spoken: '*Take that anger and pain of betrayal on stage with you. . .*'

"Right, you bastards," she said under her breath, "So you want to see me fail, do you!"

Chapter 59

Curtain Up

"Sit next to me, Sam dear," May said, as she shuffled her way along the row of seats.

June was in front of her and could hear her sister chattering away like an excited child.

"Oh do shush, May," June demanded, her voice nervous and snappy as she made herself comfortable in her seat.

"Steady on, Auntie June, she's only excited like the rest of us," Estelle said, as she sat down next to her, reaching across to hold her hand, fully aware of the myriad of emotions the elderly lady must be feeling.

"I know, dear," June replied, with a smile laden with tension.

"Sam, how do you think Penny's feeling right now?" Sue asked.

"Right now?" he replied, turning to her, his voice quiet and tense. (He hoped that she wouldn't detect the nervousness running through every sinew of his body.) "She's probably wishing she was sitting at the bar with us lot, drinking a large glass of wine, I expect." (But he knew that wouldn't be the case. She'd be sitting at her dressing table, clearing her head of unnecessary thoughts, and then thinking to herself *timing and concentration . . . timing and concentration.*

He became distracted by competing fragrances hanging heavily in the confined space of the auditorium; perfume was worn with the intention to please, but some had a nauseating effect. It didn't take him long to detect a trace of white musk – after thirty years of having his home filled with its aroma because it was Annie's favourite. He recognised the strange quirk of coincidence that it was also one of Penny's, and she always chose to wear it when she was with him. *What are the odds on the two women I love liking the same perfume*? he thought.

The lights in the auditorium started to fade into semi-darkness, reminding him of his garden at home when, soon after the sun had set, the birds would have one last chatter before settling down for the night. Then suddenly all he could hear was his breathing, short and sharp, as the expectant audience went quiet and the curtain rose like a veil floating up into an endless ceiling. He could feel his temples throbbing with anticipation as his eyes scanned the stage for her, and then almost instantly remembered that it wasn't until five minutes into the scene that she would appear. He could see her leading man – 'Tilly' as he was affectionately called – with two other men on the stage. An actress who played Katherine's cousin Cleo, and her protagonist, was talking about Penny's character Katherine in a derogative manner.

Sam gazed around the auditorium, lit only from the spill of the spotlights illuminating the stage, and tried to look at the shadowy faces of people around him, many of them fellow actors and personalities from the world of entertainment. He wondered *had they come to revel in her success or gloat in what they hoped would be a glorious failure*?

After what seemed a millennium to him, the stage lights briefly dimmed to signify the end of the first scene, and then the lights returned and there was Katherine, sitting on a settee, wearing the tweed suit which he thought she was to wear in the *final* scene, conversing with Cleo. Sam had read a great deal of the script and was aware the interpretation of it would be down to the skill of the directors to mould it into a believable entity. He also knew that the audience would be led to believe that the play was set in the present, but it would soon become apparent to them that Aaron had cleverly dovetailed the era of the 1950s to create a bridge between social morals then, and the present time. Katherine yearned for those morals, particularly in a relationship, but she was such an unyielding and opinionated person that she believed there was no man who could pacify her. Peter Tillson entered the stage and the verbal jousting began.

By the end of the third scene she left the audience in no doubt as to what was to come.

The fourth scene began in the same tone as the third had ended, and she delivered her lines as if she had thrown away her script and every word she uttered was her own original thought. The tempo in which she spoke, her body language and breathing all synchronised to her every emotion, was breath-taking. She gave notice not only to her fellow actors, but the whole theatre, especially her dissenters. *She had become Katherine.* With venom on her tongue she divided her audience gender-wise, with command of them all. She argued and jested with such poise that at times the audience responded with laughter. She debated and teased. And both she and Peter Tillson's character probed each other's emotional defences, not for weaknesses, but for strengths. Scene after scene, the friendship forming between the two main characters ebb and flowed.

The second act ended with the intermission. As the audience rose from their seats, Sam detected debate and opinions forming in the minds of the audience. Sue asked a woman in the row behind her what she thought of the play: "Brilliant! What a bitch!" the lady replied, shooting the man beside her a spiteful look.

"Hey, Dad! Are you coming? Penny's got a surprise for you!" Maggie called, as she made her way to the aisle.

"Shortly, Mags. I'll wait for May," he replied, noticing May was crying.

"Come on, don't be such a wet, anyone would think you'd never seen her act before!" June teased, heading for the bar.

"Sorry, Sam, dear," said May, apologetically. "I know it sounds daft, but I felt as if April was up there. I closed my eyes and I could hear her, even feel her presence. Because she was my twin, I still feel her around me, maybe through Penny. I don't know, but sometimes I sense her. I'm sorry, I know you don't really understand."

Sam felt it inappropriate to tell her that he'd had a twin sister, too, and understood exactly what's she was going through. Taking her hand, he gently helped her to her feet.

"I know twins have a special bond, May," he said, and then he kissed her cheek. "I'm sure Penny would be happy to know you feel her mother here."

"Penny feels and senses things, too, Sam, even about you."

They started to make their way along the row of seats to the bar. They stood by the entrance, as it was crammed with people in pairs, or groups, or on their own waiting for someone.

"I can't see us getting in there, May, I'll bring our drinks out," he said, disappearing into the melee to make his way to where he knew Archie, June and his daughters would be. As he approached the bar he saw the back of a man who looked rather familiar.

"What the blazes?" he said, as the man turned around.

"Hi, fella!" Oak said, with a broad smile.

"Christ, Oak! This is a surprise!" Then from nowhere a bubbly female put her arms around him and kissed his cheek.

"Hi, Uncle Sam!"

"Canda! Two surprises!" he said, beaming with pleasure at seeing them both again.

He knew they couldn't talk in the crush of people around them, and wanted to take a drink to May. He explained what he needed to do to Oak and then made his way to the table where Archie had laid on champagne cocktails. He could see Estelle and

Maggie talking to Dave and Sue. *Give me the moors any day*, he thought, feeling a little overwhelmed by the heat and the crowd.

By the time he got back to May, Oak was already talking to her.

"Ah, so you found her. This giant of a man, May, is my brother-in-law Oak. I'm assuming he's introduced himself? Play your games with him and he'll feed you to the bears!" he laughed.

"No, ma'am, I wouldn't, that's all a rumour," he smiled, giving her a sly wink.

"Sam, dear, you mustn't give him the wrong impression of me – I don't play games!" May retorted with one of her particularly twinkly smiles.

The five-minute bell rang and people started making their way, very slowly, back to the auditorium.

As Sam settled in his seat ready for the final scenes, he considered the positive words and comments he had overheard from people around him in the bar, but he knew the chit-chat made little difference in real terms. Archie had made it clear to him that it didn't matter how much the general public liked a play . . . the critics always had the last word.

Seeing Penny back on stage, his tension returned. Watching her as Katherine – who now showed trust and benevolence towards her suitor as a sense of reverence prevailed between them – was both exciting and nerve-wracking. The penultimate scene depicted Katherine's engagement party, making the audience relax, but then Aaron took them on a rollercoaster ride as revelations were made that her fiancé was the father of Cleo's unborn child. Would Katherine revert to her belligerent ways? Aaron put the audience on a precipice, teetering, and kept them there while Katherine searched her soul, desperately trying to balance her moral compass with the fellowship of a man whom she had come to love.

As the play came to its conclusion, Sam became aware of a sense of *déjà-vu*: this tale seemed familiar to him in a personal way. As he tried to concentrate on the play, his senses were tugging at his brain, and then disbelief filled his body, as if he was seeing his reflection on the stage . . . what had Aaron done?

As he continued to watch, the surer he was. Aaron hadn't just written the play for Penny, he'd written it for them!

Sam could now see how Aaron had cleverly cloaked his and Penny's regard for each other within the script, with intimations of their feelings for each other played out right before his eyes! Then there was her nemesis, Toby, represented by Cleo – and a good helping of poetic licence. *Maybe I've read it wrongly*, he thought; but he knew he hadn't, and he hoped Penny hadn't worked it out – there would be hell to pay!

The final scene – Katherine's wedding reception – began. As Penny walked onto the stage, he could not believe what he was seeing.

"She's wearing your dress, dear!" May excitingly exclaimed, hearing loud *shushes* around her.

Katherine stood there, holding on to her husband's arm, wearing the red and white polka dot dress that Sam so loved to see her in. He then knew she had sent him a message. Not a veiled attempt to tease, but a bold and fearless message in front of hundreds of people.

The audience were in awe that Katherine, for the sake of love, had forgiven her husband for his past indiscretions. Then Cleo asked Katherine why she had renounced her moral beliefs for servitude. That's when Penny delivered her *coup de grace*: a master class in mesmerising her audience, confirming her as the supreme actress she truly was. She took Cleo to task, using each individual word – 'denounced', 'moral', 'belief' and 'servitude' – and then stripped them to the bone. She spoke with conviction and passion, humour and wit, leaving the audience in no doubt that her beliefs had *not* been compromised, but when love between two people is deep, you forgive.

With the sentiment and conviction of her final words hanging in the air, she left the stage, and the curtain came down for the final time. An eerie quietness came over the audience for what seemed an age, but was in fact just a few micro seconds, before an eruption of applause and verbal adulation filled the theatre as the audience rose to their feet with loud cries and cheers. Those who were not smiling were crying with joy, shaking their heads in disbelief that they had just witnessed a production that would no doubt be talked about for years to come. The curtain rose for the encore, and again the auditorium shuddered with adulation for the actors as they took their bow baring two: Penny and her leading man. They appeared from the wings moments later to a deafening admiration from the audience, *her audience,* and took their place centre stage. Penny then walked two spaces forward to take another bow.

Sam turned to look at May, who had tears freely running down her face, feeling every emotion possible.

"She's done it, Sam! She's done it!" May shouted, her emotionally charged voice barely audible over the noise. "In all my years in the theatre, I have never seen or heard such adulation! Look at her, Sam! Look at her! Wasn't she marvellous!"

"There's no one to stop her now," Sam replied. *Nor should there be*, he thought.

The curtain fell for the final time.

"Sam! Sam, dear!" called June, as she took hold of her sister's hand. "May and I are going to Penny's dressing room and then we'll be going home. Look after her, Sam, when we go, she'll be exhausted."

"Of course," he smiled.

"And Sam, bring Oak with you for lunch tomorrow," May then said.

"He'll be a bit tough to eat, May, he's more of a slow-cook

man," he replied, and May laughed. "He's got my niece with him too. Are you sure you've got room for all of us?"

"More the merrier! See you tomorrow, dear!" she said, showing him the side of her face for a farewell kiss.

Sam stood in the foyer watching the remainder of the audience leave the theatre, waiting for Angie to meet him, via a message passed on to him by Archie as he left with his daughters.

"Sam, just the man I'm looking for," Angie said, with a look of sheer relief written across her face. He noticed she was writing times and dates in a small notebook. "Penny's on Breakfast TV tomorrow morning at 9.00am, and she needs to be there by 7.30am at the latest." She gave him a sideways look; he knew instantly what she was asking of him.

"You've got to be joking! The woman has just had the worst, and the best, day of her life and you want me to drag her out of bed at some stupid hour? Can't you put it off for a couple of days? It's not fair on her. She's absolutely knackered."

"In normal circumstances, I would agree with you, but she has to show people that it's business as usual," she replied, now reading messages off her phone. "Also, it wouldn't hurt if you were seen with her. You know I'm right, don't you?" She knew he was trying to protect Penny, but Penny needed to do this. "I'll do a deal with you," she then said. "Get her there tomorrow, and I won't book anything in for her for the day after."

"OK, but I'm not going on TV with her; she's in show business, I'm *not*. Besides, the camera won't get my best side," he said, with jest.

"Wouldn't think of it, darling," she replied, giving him the type of look that he knew meant: she would if she could. "You head off to the party. I'll wait here for Penny, but make sure you have lots of lovely photographs taken of the two of you, and with those girls of yours, Sam. We'll make that prick Toby wish he'd never been born."

Chapter 60

The Big Mistake

May and June entered Penny's dressing room to find it packed wall-to-wall with members of the cast, and Max, all drinking champagne and celebrating the play's obvious success, trying to make themselves heard above the laughing and joking.

"Auntie June and May!" Penny shouted, as she saw them enter the room. "Right, you lot, bugger off and let me talk to my aunties and get changed!"

Penny looked happy but exhausted. They'd all congratulated her, but they knew from their own experiences in the theatre that it takes a while for it all to sink in after a performance as intense as that.

"I met Sam's brother in-law, Oak, dear," May informed her, as the room emptied. "A very charming man, and very rugged looking."

"The girls told us you asked him to come over as a surprise for Sam," said June, glancing at May. She then had a quick chat with Mavis, before she left the room, leaving the three of them alone.

"I'm looking forward to meeting him," Penny declared, sitting at her dressing table removing her stage make-up.

"I've invited them to lunch tomorrow, dear," May continued. "Should be fun. It's years since we've had such a full house. It's awfully sad to think his dear wife took an overdose, the poor man," May exclaimed, relaying the information she had gleaned from reading Sam's private letter to Archie; but she didn't realise she had just made a great error with her facts and choice of words.

Penny suddenly turned around and stared at May.

"Overdose? Who told you it was an overdose?" she asked, quite horrified at what May had just said.

"Well . . ." May replied, sounding hesitant and unsure. "No one. I just presumed it was an overdose . . . that's how most people commit suicide."

Penny stood up and held May's arms, just above her elbows, firmly. Her face wasn't hiding any emotion.

"You stupid woman! I suppose you don't know she was Sam's twin sister, *do* you?" she asked, angrily.

"No, we didn't," June replied. "Let go of May, Penny, you're hurting her."

"Hurting her? Do you realise how you've hurt Sam? You've made him re-live the past he so dearly wants to forget! And you've done it just because you can!" Penny was now shouting at them, angry in a way they had rarely witnessed. "She didn't take an overdose, she hanged herself in Sam's garage! He found her and had to cut her down. She died in his arms! Try to imagine that!" she cried.

She stopped to catch her breath, her heart now thumping in her chest. June and May looked shocked, and deeply saddened.

"He told me he's felt a pain in his heart every day since, which has never left him. I know that's true because it's the same pain I feel for Megan. And it's the same pain you feel for my mother, don't you? You both think you're so bloody clever, manipulating people and playing your games. I thought you loved Sam? So why treat him like this?"

June turned towards the door to leave, but May stood still, tears in her eyes.

"And while we're at it, as you're about to walk out of here with your nice, new hip . . . who do you think made Archie pay for that?" she asked, walking to the door to block their exit. "Sam would have paid for it himself, but he knew I would have ripped his head off! He's done more for you than you deserve, and this is how you repay him?" She stood there motionless gathering her thoughts. June reached out for her hand.

"We both now realise we have wronged him by speaking about this, and we feel ashamed, truly we do. We do love him. He's become like family, you know that, but we just got it wrong and we regret it."

"Sometimes I don't understand you. I just don't!"

But she put her arms out to them both as a gesture of unity. She was spent – emotionally and physically – and hadn't meant to get so angry with them.

"Please don't ask him anything else about his past life again, or discuss it with anyone. It *must* remain private, is that understood?"

They nodded and hugged her.

"We promise."

Chapter 61

The End of a Lie

Angie and Max tentatively entered Penny's dressing room, as if they were walking into a lion's den: they'd heard her raised voice.

"Sorry, you two," Penny said, sounding devoid of energy to speak. "God, they drive me mad sometimes. I need to get changed." Max raised his hand, intending to speak, but Penny continued, "All I want to do is go home and go to bed. I know I should be elated, but to tell you the truth, I'm shattered. My bones ache, I have a splitting headache, and I've got my period, so Max, what do you want?"

Max stood there, looking like a scolded schoolboy in the headmaster's office waiting for his punishment.

"Nothing really important . . . it can wait until tomorrow," he replied, nervously, smiling at them both – a quick, sheepish smile. He left the room.

Angie put her arms around her friend and held her as a mother would hold a child. She stood there for a few moments, wishing the day were over.

"I take it you heard all that?" she asked, slipping on a pair of jeans.

"Yes, poor bastard, it must have broken his heart."

"It made me so angry to hear them discuss such a personal thing so openly," she replied, inspecting the dark rings around her eyes.

"The way you were having a go at them, darling, it sounded like you were sticking up for the man you love. . ." Angie ventured.

"Don't be so bloody ridiculous. What makes you think I love the man? He's just a dear friend, and we care for each other, nothing more than that."

"My god, you can be a stupid cow at times. You say you're not in love with him? What utter rubbish."

Penny spun around on her chair, taken aback by her friend's unexpected outburst. She wanted to speak out, but she knew Angie – once she got a head of steam on, nothing would stop her.

"You talk about Sam all the time!" Angie continued, before Penny could speak. "You miss him when he's not with you. You've even hung the picture of his cottage on your wall. I've seen you cry when you look at it. And what about that bloody rose he gave you? You had me running you all over London because of it, remember?"

Penny felt paralysed in her seat, listening, knowing that every word Angie spoke was true.

"Who was the one person you wanted to care for you after your accident? God, woman! You say it's friendship . . . well, you're right, darling, it is . . . but with a huge dollop of love to go with it. Between you, me, and your aunties, we've had that poor man running up and down the country for us. If you don't love him, then stop behaving like you do. It's not fair on him. Do you want me to go on?"

"Stop. Please stop!" Penny shouted. "Yes, I love him. I love him more that anyone I've ever met, but only recently have I realised that," she said, trying to explain how she felt to Angie, but also to herself. "I know it sounds stupid, but I've felt as if I was being held back, that I was being tested to see if I was worthy to love him. It's fanciful, I know, but I couldn't help feeling it.

"After supposedly being madly in love with Toby, I wasn't sure what love was meant to feel like anymore. I've been so happy being with Sam, just being friends. . ." Her hands trembled as she spoke. "But something's happened inside me. As if for the first time my heart has been set free to beat for him. Whatever was holding me back has gone. But I'm so scared. All I'm really sure about is that I don't want to lose him.

"I'm afraid, Angie. All the men I've loved I've lost. If I lose Sam I'll die. Look how it affected my mother when my dad walked out on her. I'm afraid that if I show Sam too much of how I feel, or even if I tell anybody how I feel, he'll end our friendship. It'll scare him away."

"Try it. You might be surprised. I don't mean seduce him – you'd probably scare him, as he's not that sort of man."

"Oh, he used to be, Angie, once, a long time ago. Bloody men, they're the bane of my life."

"You don't mean that about Sam, do you, darling?"

"No, not him, he knows how to treat a woman. Well, he knows how to treat me. He gives me space; but the more space he gives me, the more I want to be with him. Ironic, isn't it?"

"Why do you think he gave you that beautiful rose?" Angie asked, not waiting for a reply. "He's wooing you, darling. I know he loves you, but like you he hides it, and I think, possibly, for the same reasons you do." She paused and then said, "I'm sure you wearing that lovely dress on stage tonight made him sit up and think, and that's what you wanted wasn't it?"

Penny sighed. There was no denying it . . . the answer was yes. She nodded, very slowly, and smiled, raising her eyes to her friend.

"Right, come on, you old slapper! Let's get you to the party! I've got other things to tell you," Angie said, aware that, like Sam, she wouldn't be happy about having to wake up early to appear on TV; but she hoped she would be pleased that Sam would be her alarm clock.

Chapter 62

Celebration

Sam put his phone away in his suit pocket as the taxi pulled to a stop outside the nightclub. This time the entrance to the club was more than a quick dash from a car door, as he had to walk twenty or so feet – not a great distance in normal circumstances, but when every inch of the pavement was lined by photographers pushing and shoving against the metal barriers, jostling to get the perfect picture, and asking why Miss McCain wasn't with him, it was a bit of a challenge. It was like running the gauntlet, but he couldn't run, he had to walk, casually, and smile and look pleased with all the attention he was receiving. Maggie and Estelle were there waiting for him, more than willing to oblige photograph – they knew they had to show a united front, not only for their father, but also for Penny.

"Where's Oak?" he asked, as his daughters linked arms with him.

"He's around here somewhere," replied Estelle, jigging around on his arm to the music that saturated every corner of the venue.

"Farmer!" Archie called out, waving to him, his trademark flamboyant dress sense as always a beacon for people to find him in a crowd. "So, where's our girl, then?" he asked. "I thought she'd be with you?"

"Evening, Arch," Sam smiled, shaking his hand. "She's with Angie. They won't be long, but she won't stay long either. When I saw her earlier, she was practically running on empty. How the hell she managed to do what she did tonight beats me," he replied.

George Dawson joined them, handing Sam a glass of single malt.

"Here, Sam, old chap, that daughter of yours commandeered me to bring it over," he said, just as Maggie appeared nestling herself between Archie and him.

"Thanks, George, you're a love," said Maggie, giving him a peck on the cheek, and one for Archie. "Dad, that maid certainly put on a class act, didn't she?" She then scuttled off to mingle.

Archie wasted no time replying to her question, vigorously nodding his head in agreement and saying, "Oh yes, she certainly did, and you should hear all the fantastic comments, Farmer, all of them, they can't speak highly enough of her and the play, sweetie."

"Talking of the play, Arch, where's Aaron?" Sam asked, looking around for him, knowing it wouldn't be too difficult to notice a six-foot seven-inch man – he was not exactly the proverbial needle in a haystack.

"Poor man," George replied, knocking back the remainder of his brandy, whilst at the same time gesturing to a passing waiter for a refill. "I think all this has overwhelmed him somewhat. He looks like he's been caught in the headlamps, poor old chap."

Sam wasn't surprised to hear that. Whenever he'd met up with Aaron, they'd always ensconced themselves in some quiet corner, out of the glare of the glitz and the glamour.

"He's with some hunk of a man, sweetie. I saw Maggie introduce them to each other, and then they disappeared somewhere," said Archie.

Sam laughed at the word 'hunk', and asked, "Big, rugged man wearing a tan suede jacket?"

"Yes, sweetie, that sounds like him," confirmed Archie.

"That's Oak, Maggie's uncle!" he said, letting out another hoot of laughter.

Archie looked pleasantly surprised on finding out who the stranger was, and did not hide his interest in him.

"Ah, so that's the mighty Oak," Archie replied, excitingly. "Tell me, Farmer, is it true he once broke a man's back by giving him a bear hug? That's what Maggie told me!"

"He's the last man you'd want to upset, Arch, believe me!"

Sam knew that although Oak was approaching his sixtieth birthday, if Archie had got him to track Toby down, all he would have got back would have been his head on a platter!

Peter Tillson then joined them with other members of the cast, including one particular elderly lady who again planted a passionate kiss on him.

"Our girl showed the bastards, didn't she, Sam!" Mavis said with a smile that lit up the room.

They all agreed that she certainly had.

Sam wandered off to find Aaron, and the hunk.

Oak stood up and gave Sam a welcoming handshake.

"Hi, fella," he cried. "Just been talking about you, and that lady of yours, with this guy here."

"You're a very clever man, Aaron Akkron," Sam said. "Shame you got the ending wrong though. It should have been that Katherine found a younger man and rode off into the sunset, leaving the old sod to live out his days in peace and quiet."

"I think that's the last thing Katherine wants her guy to do, Sam," Aaron proclaimed, uttering a deep, throaty laugh. "Besides, they love each other too much, don't they?" he added, sounding secure in the knowledge his assumption was correct.

He had come to like and trust Sam as a close friend, and had already told him that he sensed things in people that even they weren't aware of, like the first time Penny had spoken about Sam to him. He could see something in her eyes, a portal to her heart which Sam would eventually fall into.

Sam quietly chuckled to himself considering Aaron's statement, and Aaron peered at him, impressed at how quickly he'd worked out the inspiration for his play.

"Well, let's change the subject, shall we? I have a feeling I'm on a hiding to nothing with you two," he stated. "I'd just like to say, you wrote an amazing play."

Raising his glass to him, he saw Aaron look up, just as warm, soft fingers stroked the side of his face, sending a shiver of pleasure through his body.

The three men stood up to greet Penny.

"Sorry, guys," she said. "Please don't think it rude of me, but I'm not stopping too long."

They all knew she was exhausted and acknowledged her apology.

"Thank you," she mouthed to Aaron, who inclined his head and smiled his huge smile.

"And you must be Oak?" she asked, receiving a mini bear hug from him. 'Oooh, I could get use to that," she said smiling into his piercing his green eyes.

She sat on the arm of Sam's leather seat then, and put her hand on his shoulder.

She chatted for a while, and then whispered something in Sam's ear. They said their goodbyes and rose to leave.

James was waiting for them at a side entrance to the club, and made sure they got safely into the waiting taxi. Sam told him to stay at the club and enjoy himself; no doubt his daughters would keep him company!

"Sam, I'm so sorry," Penny muttered, shuffling herself as close as she could next to him and without hesitation slipping her left arm through his. "You should have refused. You're missing the party." She rested her head on his shoulder, and closed her eyes – and fell asleep instantly.

After a few moments he lifted her limp, warm hand and put it to his lips, feeling her soft skin. Sam then realised, more than ever before, the dilemma he had found himself in: his heart and head had started the inevitable fight. The question was, who would win? Should he confess to her the intoxicating love and passion which consumed him? Or put distance between them in the knowledge he may never see her again?

Chapter 63

Better Things to Do

As promised, Sam made sure she was up and ready to leave her house by 7.00am, impressed by how she had come through the previous few days. But despite that, he knew she would be a bitch to wake up – and she *was*.

"Are you coming? It'll be fun," she asked, as she took a bite of her dry toast.

"No, hun, I've got things to do this morning, I'll see you at your aunties' for lunch," he replied, which she interpreted as *I've got something better to do with my time, thank you.*

"Sorry if I've dragged you out of bed when you're tired, Sam, I really am," she said quietly, genuinely. "And what with all this other shit going on . . . I wish you could stay another day."

"I have to be in Bristol tomorrow morning, that's why I'm leaving today." He sensed that she really would have liked to spend some time with him away from the theatre and all the associated meetings and interviews. She looked tired, beautiful as ever, but tired. "Tell you what. I'm up again in ten days to fly out for Oak's birthday. I'll come up a day or so early and we can meet up, how does that sound?" he asked, glancing up at her kitchen clock. "You'd better be off. Your audience awaits, well . . . James is waiting anyway."

She smiled and got to her feet, picking up her bag. She moved to stand in front of Sam, and then reached up and kissed him on the mouth.

"You tenderly kissed my hand last night in the car, so I'm kissing you back," she replied in answer to his unvoiced question.

Bugger, I thought you were asleep, he thought.

"What am I going to do with you?" he asked softly.

"Well, when you've decided, sweetheart, let me know," she answered, placing her hand gently against the side of his face. There was a knock at the door: James. "See you later, Sam. I'll blow you a kiss on telly."

Chapter 64

The Love Letter

"Hi, June," Penny said, removing her coat and then placing it over the back of a dining room chair. "Where's May?"

"Oh, she's next door, dear. We haven't got enough room in our oven to cook all the food, so we've commandeered Betty's," replied June, looking up from a huge pile of potatoes Harry had peeled for them. "How did the interview go on TV, dear?"

"OK," Penny answered, clicking her fingernails on the worktop. She sounded vague and distracted.

"What is it, dear? You look troubled. Is it Sam?" June enquired, not wanting to sound too inquisitive after the dressing down she'd got from her the night before.

"Yes, it's Sam," she replied. She took a deep breath. "I'm in love with him," she said, with an air of resignation in her voice.

"Yes, dear, we know. We've been wondering how long it would be before you'd finally admit it."

Penny let out a sigh. She felt she was the last person on earth who realised her love for him was real.

"You've been falling in love with him since the very first day you met. I wouldn't worry about how long it's taken you to realise the fact," she continued, reading Penny's thoughts. "You loving Sam has been a journey of the mind, not just the heart. How unique is that?" she smiled kindly.

"I told Angie that I felt as if my feelings for him were being restrained, even tested. I've always sensed I felt something for him, but I thought it was just trust."

"That's because your deep friendship came first, and your trust is a wonderful part of that." June gently took her niece's hands in her own. "Maybe the reason you felt tested was because it's a love you had never felt or experienced before, or even expected. It wasn't for lust or gain. Falling in love with Sam has been like putting on your favourite coat: you enjoy the sensation, and you feel comfortable. The warmth and security you feel around him is because of that trust."

Penny smiled a dreamy smile as she remembered how she loved to wear Sam's bathrobe when they were snuggled up together in front of the log fire.

"May and I have never seen you so happy since you met Sam. Falling in love with him wasn't to be a *midsummer night's dream*, dear, where you are Hermia and Sam Lysander, and Puck puts the *love-in-idleness* juice on your eyes, and all of a sudden you're in love. No, you falling in love with him was more subtle than that; for you anyway, dear."

The tenderness in June's voice filled Penny's heart.

"But what of Sam? I don't even know how much he loves me . . . if he even loves me that way?"

"Oh yes, dear. That man loves you to distraction," June informed her. "'*Weary with toil I haste me to my bed*'."

"So why hasn't he told me?"

"Because he's a man, dear, not some young, flighty, love-struck idiot. Sam knows what being in love entails, and I can see in his eyes how his head is fighting his heart, more and more as time goes on. They say love is blind, and Sam may have closed his eyes to you loving him. How you get him to open them is for you to work out."

Penny helped herself to a glass of water to quench the dryness in her throat. Then the fog that clouded her thoughts, lingering in her mind, started to clear. She thought back to the night before when she'd worn her dotty dress on the stage for him, and how he had kissed her hand lovingly, thinking she was asleep. He'd kissed them before, but never with such tenderness. And then she remembered how earlier that morning she had returned the kiss far more intensely than any other kiss she had given him as friends.

"Angie persuaded Sam to stay with me last night, to be my alarm clock," Penny said, giving June a mischievous smile. "I have a feeling he's already sent me a message and I've replied to it." Her face lit up, realising they both had made tentative steps into the daylight of truth and their true feelings for each other. Tears of expectation formed in her eyes. "I wonder what Shakespeare would have made of it all? . . ." she mused, with a deep sigh.

June laughed in exasperation, and cried, "You of all people should know the answer to that!"

She disappeared into the lounge, returning moments later clutching an envelope in her hand. She passed it to Penny to read.

"Sam gave it to me to give to Archie. I realise I shouldn't have done, but I steamed it open and read it, but I'm not sorry I did. It's a love letter."

"Don't be so ridiculous, June, the last thing Sam is, is gay!" she retorted, scowling.

But June was smiling at her, and said, "But *it is* a love letter, dear, read it."

Penny quickly removed it from the envelope, and her eyes scanned word after word.

"The bloody fool!" she said, as tears once more trickled down her face.

'*My dear Archie,*

Please take this as a letter of intent. I have contacted my banks and have secured the sum of £400,000 to be made available to you in full, or in part, the purpose of which is obvious to you. I only ask for two things. Firstly, I would like it if Penny were not made aware of my intentions. I am not comfortable with keeping this from her, but she should be free to concentrate on her task ahead, and not be burdened with the weight of responsibility regarding the funding.

My second is that I do not wish to profit from Penny's inevitable success, only that any monies used are paid back to me within an agreed time of the opening date of the production. Any revenues above that of the original sum will be donated to a charity of my choice.

I have also given you access to certain information in order for you to know my motives are genuine, sincere and above board. Some of the information you will have access to is deeply personal to myself and my daughters, and I know you will respect their privacy, and prevent this from being made public.

You sometimes like to hide behind a façade of a court jester. The Archie I know is an astute and honourable man, and one who has become a very dear friend.

Your friend, Farmer.'

Clutching the letter in her hand, she stared at her aunt, unable to hide the fury running through every sinew of her body.

"I hope Archie didn't take his money! I'll be even more *bloody* furious if I find out he did! The stupid man! How could he? The last time he did something like this it almost destroyed him!"

"But that's what I call a love letter, dear," June countered. "When Archie read it he knew, like I did, that Sam loves you so much he will risk everything for you. And *no,* Archie didn't take his money; reading that letter shamed him, and it motivated him to find backers."

Hearing June's explanation made her realise that when it comes to love, even Sam could be as stupid as any man.

"Well, I'm keeping this, the bloody idiot!" she cried, and marched from the room.

Chapter 65

The Gathering

Penny tried to absorb what Sam had been prepared to do for her. Deep in thought, she was startled when a familiar voice brought her back into the present.

"Aaron, sweetheart, you've banged your bloody head again, haven't you?"

"Sure have, Miss Penny," he replied, stooping forward, trying to avoid hitting his head again, this time on the ceiling light.

He sat and they chatted.

It wasn't long before the rest of the guests arrived, baring one. Canda was soon deep in conversation with Aaron and Archie, while Maggie and Estelle helped their adopted aunties in the kitchen. Penny's attention turned to Oak, who was sitting on one of the settees like a fish out of water. She knew from what Sam had told her that he was at his happiest out in the open, not cooped up within four walls.

"Fancy a walk in the park before lunch?" she asked him, gesturing with her head towards the door.

His face lit up and he grabbed his jacket.

"Right, Oak," Penny said, putting her arm through his as they walked along. "Tell me all about him. Sam. The man only you know so well."

Penny felt the urge to run when she saw Sam's car parked outside the house when they returned.

"Sam's here, Oak!" she said excitedly, like a child.

"I should have known. He likes things like that, does Sam, not like my old Ali," he replied, looking curiously at the number plate. Penny had heard all about Ali and smiled.

"Sam's car. My number plate. He bought it for me for my birthday. Like it?"

Oak shook his head, and said, "Jesus, you two have got it bad."

Penny grabbed hold of his jacket lapels and then stood on tip-toe to kiss him.

"I can see why Sam likes you!" Again, Oak let out one of his rusty laughs.

She then ran up to the front door, feeling a girlish sensation of euphoria, her heart pounding heavily in her chest. Her eyes scanned the lounge for him.

"So, where is he?" she asked June. "And *don't* tell me he's gone, you're not getting me on that one again," she added, as Archie passed her a glass of her favourite wine.

"He's in his bedroom, dear, with Canda. They're looking through some of our books," replied June.

Penny found them surrounded by rare and valuable first additions.

"Hi, babe, you're back!" Sam said, putting his lips to her cheek.

She desperately wanted to hug and kiss him with all the love she could muster, but something told her to be patient. But it was not like the restraint she'd felt weeks before. This time her intuition was guiding her.

"Did you get everything done you wanted to do?" she asked, curious to know what it was.

"Yes, thanks, I've done something I've wanted to do for a long time," he replied as they headed down the stairs together, leaving Canda alone to absorb herself in the ladies' books.

The lunch party was enjoyed by all, with Penny's aunties the life and soul of the gathering, telling stories and anecdotes of their days in the theatre. Aaron couldn't stop laughing, his cavernous chuckle infectious to all, and he thanked everyone for making him feel loved and like he was a part of their family. Canda had a wealth of pictures taken with Penny and her aunties to show her English class back home in Simcoe, while Oak studied Sam as he would an animal in the wild, his body language and manner telling him he was happy and relaxed, knowing that he had made a potentially life-changing decision that Penny was unaware of.

And as for Archie, well, he was spoilt rotten. All of them knew that if it wasn't for him – even if at times he'd had to be cajoled – Penny's lifetime dream might not have been fulfilled.

Estelle and Maggie spent most of their time running around, trying and failing to stop June and May overexerting themselves.

Penny had a look of sheer delight on her face having her friends and family around her, people who cared for her and loved her, and she realised she was so fortunate to experience that.

Chapter 66

How Does it End?

"I'll run you home?" Sam offered, aware Penny was preparing to leave. Even the relatively short drive to her house would be a pleasurable indulgence before his lonely drive back to Devon without her.

"That would be lovely," she said.

"Sam, I want to ask you something," she said on the drive back. She sounded hurried, like she couldn't wait and needed the answer there and then. "Can you park somewhere?"

"OK. What do you want to ask me?" he said, turning off the engine, watching her as she clicked her fingernails again – a thing he had seen before when she was uneasy or nervous.

"Sam . . . how does it end?" she asked, her voice now wavering with nerves.

"How does what end, my darling?"

Penny was surprised to hear him use the words 'my darling'. He often called her 'babe' or 'sweetheart', and Archie called everyone 'sweetie' – which was his particular term of affection – and her aunts called everybody 'dear'. Angie sometimes called Penny 'darling', but for Sam to say, 'my darling'. . . She knew these were words he didn't use casually, and she'd only ever heard him call his beloved daughters that, because they were special to him. He loved them.

She felt the full force of those words combine with something

Oak had told her while out walking in the park; the something she needed an answer to. Now in a state of flux, Penny endeavoured to ask her question; the question she thought she would never need to pose.

"How does the story end . . . about the knight in shining armour and the rather silly maiden?" she asked, quietly.

"Oh, that story," he replied, taking her hands.

"Yes, Sam, that one. I'd like to think he sweeps her off her feet and takes her to his castle in Devon to live happily ever after; or does he board a plane for Canada, leaving the maiden, who talks too much, alone and heartbroken, knowing that the man she loves has left her?" She made no effort to hide the anguish in her eyes at the thought of that coming true.

"That's not a very happy ending, is it? Maybe that knight of yours has left the answer for you at home . . . an answer that speaks louder than any words," he told her, as he touched her lips with his. It was a gentle, cautious kiss; but he had no need to be cautious as she made no attempt to stop him, indeed her body juddered with excitement. She was also intensely curious as to what was at home, but she didn't want Sam to drive her home, not yet.

"Sam what have you done, you bugger?" she asked. "I know you! You've done something! What is it?"

Sam said nothing, but just smiled and started the car.

"There you are, madam," he said, checking the coast was clear of unwanted photographers.

"I miss you already, Sam."

Giving her another tender kiss, he knew it was neither the right place nor the time to express his true love for her. "I need more practise, sweetheart, I'm losing my touch," he said, with a small smile.

"That felt pretty good to me, but don't worry, Sam, you'll have plenty opportunity to practice when you come back," she replied, opening the car door to leave. "I love you!" she blurted as she got out of the car, aware that she could never retract those words, they were now his forever.

He was speechless, and watched her turn and blow him a kiss just before disappearing inside.

She was stunned. There in front of her was a sight she had not expected, but had only wished for. She frantically searched for her phone in her bag to text him, her hands shaking with exhilaration and happiness. 'Thank you,' she typed, 'I would have settled for twelve, Sam, you know that. I'm a lucky girl. Pxxxx'.

She inhaled the fragrance of her two dozen red roses, now realising what Sam had meant when he said, 'I've done something I've been meaning to do for a long time.' Lifting up the vase of flowers to carry into her lounge, she glanced at a greeting card resting against a jar of marmalade, laughing as she read the note. She opened her cupboards doors to realise that while she had been at the television studio, he had been out and done the food shopping for her. The note read: '*A beautiful woman like you can't live on love and dried toast alone! Sxxx*'.

Chapter 67

Delusional

As each day passed for Penny, it felt like being a child waiting for her birthday; but for her it was waiting to see Sam again. She knew from then on that not only would they be friends, but lovers too: a couple. But she was blissfully unaware that her road to happiness and contentment was still a long way off. . .

Entering her dressing room at the end of another sell-out performance, Penny was surprised to see Angie waiting for her.

"What is it, Angie? she asked. She felt as if an ice cube had been dropped down her back, and her whole body became chilled. "Is it Sam? God, don't say something has happened to him, please?"

"No, darling, he's safe and sound at home. I spoke to him less than half an hour ago," Angie replied, and Penny slumped into her chair, the sense of relief draining her of energy.

"Thank Christ for that."

"The reason I'm here, darling, is that Toby is causing problems for you again."

"Oh no. What's the shit done now?"

Angie scrolled through her phone and handed it to Penny. She quickly read the news item.

"What's wrong with the idiot? I haven't spoken to him for months? Now he's going around saying we've talked and agreed on reconciliation? The man is delusional!" Penny cried, staring at her friend and agent, exasperated with Toby's unwanted reemergence into her private life. "I take it you've told Sam about this? What did he say?"

"He's agrees with me that we have to take out a restraining order on him."

"No, I don't want to do that. Can't we get some pictures out there of Sam and me kissing and cuddling, instead? That should get into his thick scull that it's absolutely *over* between us!"

"I disagree. I'm worried that Toby doesn't know his own mind anymore due to his drug taking. He's on bloody breakfast TV tomorrow, no doubt planning to say you're together again. I contacted the producers, of course, and told them the facts, but they still want the man on. But you're right, darling, he is bloody delusional, and you need to take action against him now." But Angie knew that if Penny wouldn't agree to a restraining order, there was nothing she could do.

"Sam's back in a couple of days, Angie, he'll be my bodyguard," she said, wanting to erase Toby from her thoughts. "I've got a car picking me up every day, plus James is available at a moment's notice, so please, let's just leave it at that." She then had an idea. "Put me on the box! I'll tell everyone that Sam is the love of my life now!"

Chapter 68

Substance

Penny took her final bow to her rapturous, appreciative audience. With spirited steps, she made her way back to her dressing room with a sense that people around her knew that Sam was at home waiting for her. *No one* spoke to her; n*o one* got in her way. It was like the Red Sea had parted and her path to his arms were clear of obstacles.

As she headed back to him, her car winding its way out of the West End, she thought about how her mind and body would respond to being with him. The wealth of memories she had of men she had been with in her past all had one thing in common: *sex*. That's what she'd wanted from them, and that's what she got, but in all those relationships she realised, even with Toby, there was a missing ingredient: true passion. Not just a passion to have sex – like the passion for food or flashy fast cars – but the passion which engulfed your soul, like a substance flowing through your blood and every sinew of your being, unique and special. She tempered the temptation to revert to her past with equanimity. She knew this would be *her night, her day*, and she would remember it forever.

Chapter 69

You Haunted Me

"Hello, babe."

Sam was waiting for Penny in her lounge, his arms open for her to fall into.

"I'm grubby, sweetheart, let me have a quick shower," she replied, savouring the sensation of his lips on hers.

"OK, and I've brought you something from the cottage, by the way. Something which I thought you might want. I've put it on your bed," he said, handing her a glass of red wine to take with her.

Penny dabbed a light fragrance behind her ears and on her neck, but she didn't have to wear perfume when Sam was around, he had become her perfume and she wanted nothing more than to be near him to make her feel sexy and desirable. She recalled the times they had picnics at Dartmeet, sitting on the river bank where the East and West Dart Rivers converged to finish their journey together. She so hoped it would be the same for them.

"I can see us falling out over who gets to wear this!" Penny laughed, handing him the hairdryer as she sat on a cushion between his legs.

He laughed too as he watched her cross her arms as if to say *This bathrobe is now mine*! Then he treated her to sensual heaven, as her hair poured through his fingers like spring water off the moors, massaging her scalp, caressing her neck, a feather-like touch one moment, and then pressing down on her tired and tense muscles with the tips of his fingers a moment later. Her head swayed with the feeling of his warm hands teasing her senses. She moaned softly, her mind creating thoughts of what was to come.

"There you go, madam," he said, putting his lips to her head.

She turned and knelt in front of him, resting her arms on his legs, and her hazel eyes sparkling like multi-faceted gems.

"I've got something to show you," she told him, reaching into her bag and then settling herself on the settee, her legs over his lap.

She handed him an envelope . . . with his handwriting on the front.

"I wondered if that would turn up one day," he said, curious to know how it came to be in her possession.

"I know why you did this, but what if it had gone tits-up and the play flopped? A lot of them do, you know." She had been angry when she'd first found out what Sam had done, but now she just felt gratitude.

"I'm not a 'what if' man. I either believe in someone or I don't. Even if I hadn't fallen in love with you, I would still have done it." Sam looked at her with conviction in his eyes, but she had tears in hers. "Aaron gave you a chance to show everyone what a supreme actress you truly are, and I wanted to help you, that's all."

Those words wrapped around her heart, almost causing pain, and deeply affected her soul.

Sam took her glass of wine away from her and placed it on the floor, and she moved nearer to him. He felt the tremble of expectancy as he kissed her hands, lingering, lost in the fragrance of her soft skin. She looked into his eyes and saw something he had hidden from her until then: want.

"There you go, now you owe *me* a kiss," he murmured.

She leant forward, her mouth now only millimetres from his, and noticed his pupils dilate with anticipation. She kissed him, pressing her soft, moist lips onto his and then instinctively opening her mouth wider as the pleasure consumed them both. He put his hand on the back of her head, running his fingers through her hair, holding her there; but Penny had no intention of stopping or moving away from him, she was savouring every moment, pushing and moving her mouth around his, her breath coming in short gasps. Her fingernails scratched and dug into his scalp and neck.

Sam gently pulled her away, to see a satisfied smile on her face. He then kissed her lips again – a quick peck – to which she giggled.

"God, I love you so much," he whispered as he kissed her under her chin, and along the side of her neck to her ear lobe, and she arched her head back in delight to the lascivious pleasure he was treating her to. "So, what changed your mind from just being fond of me, to loving me?" he asked softly, not wanting to disturb the aura of bliss between them.

She laid down, rested her head on his lap and looked up at him.

"When we all had lunch at my aunties', I got there early and talked to June. I told her I was in love with you. She gave me that lovely smile that only old ladies can give, that kind, gentle, knowing sort of smile, and she said I'd been falling in love with you since the first day we met. How could that be? I knew I felt something that day – the feeling that I already knew you and trusted you, and I know I've told you that many times before – but my mind has been in turmoil over you for quite a while.

"But if you really want to know when I knew I loved you beyond any doubt, it was when you took me to watch the sunrise with you. I remember we were standing together as the sun rose, and I was holding your hand. I felt a sense of liberation, as if the fog had been pushed from my mind, freeing me to love you.

"I now know I love you with all my heart, and if you had decided to leave me and go to Canada, you would have broken it. . . So, what about you, sweetheart?" she asked. "I'll admit I found it hard to know whether your feelings for me were more than those of just a loving friend."

He combed her hair with his fingers, thoughtfully smiling at her.

"This morning, when I was getting ready to leave the cottage, I was in my bedroom, and as usual, I was thinking of you – I'm always thinking of you. '*Weary with toil*'. . . how those words have been my constant companion. I was recalling when you stayed with me after your accident, and how during the nights I use to come in to your room and check to see if you had enough water or put the duvet back over you.

"One night I stood at the end of your bed. I was listening to you wince with pain in your sleep. You have no idea how much I wanted to hold you in my arms and comfort you. Then I thought of Ruth and how I'd let her down, and how if I hadn't been late – because of my terrible behaviour – she may be still alive. And I thought of Annie and how badly I treated her with my womanising.

"I thought I could control my affection for you, that that would be the safest thing to do, but every time I saw you, you ended up deeper in my heart. Yes, I admit, I did think about Canada, but that would have been running away, and I don't know how to run away, do I? That's why I've got these bloody scars."

As he spoke, Penny realised what a monumental decision it had been for him to love her.

"I thought about how I loved you, and about my past, and I stood there and promised you that there wouldn't be a third time: I'll never let down a woman I love ever again.

"You know the girls love you very much, don't you?" he asked. "And as soon as they met you, it didn't take them long to realise my true feelings for you. We may not have known how we really felt about each other; they did though.

"Ha," he mused. "Maggie said that if I didn't tell you the truth about how much I love you, she'd tell poor Archie I'm gay! She said she'll do it to remind me how obstinate I can be."

Penny let out a loud laugh at that, and said, "Well, he's going to be bloody disappointed, isn't he, sweetheart!" When her laughter had died down, she whispered, "Sam, recite it to me, please?" She was desperate to hear the words spoken from his mouth.

He knew exactly what she was referring to, and he stood up and held out his hand, gently pulling her to him. He then spoke the words she had waited a lifetime to hear:

"'*Weary with toil I haste me to my bed.*
But then begins a journey in my head
To work my mind, when body's work's expired:
For then my thoughts - from far where I abide -
Intend a zealous pilgrimage to thee,
And keep my drooping eyelids open wide,
Looking on darkness which the blind do see:
Save that my soul's imaginary sight
Presents thy shadow to my sightless view,
Which, like a jewel hung in ghastly night,
Makes black night beauteous, and her old face new.
Lo! Thus, by day my limbs, by night my mind,
For thee, and for myself, no quiet find.'"

She stood there, supported in his arms, the expression on her face reflecting the fervour of the words he had uttered to her.

"I've never heard anyone say that so beautifully," she said, feeling a contradictive sense of joyful sorrow.

"It's because I mean it and feel it. You haunt me '*like a beautiful jewel, hung in ghastly night*'."

Chapter 70

Penny's Magic Carpet

He walked over to the bed, removing the duvet and putting it on the floor.

"Sam? What are doing, sweetheart?" she asked.

"Where I'm going to take you, we'll have no need of that," he replied.

Standing in front of her, he untied the cord of her bathrobe and watched as it parted and then he slipped it off her shoulders to fall freely to the floor. His hands touched her warm and wanting body, sending waves of ecstasy like electrical impulses through her veins.

"What are these for?" he asked, kissing each side of her face, feeling the moisture of her tears on his lips.

"It's because the man I adore is going to make love to me for the first time," she replied, quietly and breathlessly, as she lay on the bed, resting her head on a pillow.

Sam then took her on the magic carpet of passion and desire she had so patiently longed for.

Penny briefly peered through the window from a gap in the curtains, her beautiful, naked form silhouetted by the early light of day. Like a cat her body then crept back into bed and purred as she melded herself around him.

"You've got a mystified look," she said.

"Well," he replied, giving her a loving peck on the tip of her nose, "I was wondering when I was going to wake up and realise that I've been making love to one of those bloody teddy bears instead of you," he replied.

"I'm your teddy bear, Sam, only me," she replied, laughing, running her fingers over the scars on his torso, exploring, caressing.

"I don't remember having scars down there," he told her.

"I don't remember you telling me that last night," she responded, and with a mischievous grin, crooked her foot over his and pulled herself on top of him.

He rolled her over onto her back, pushing her head into the pillow with the force of his lips on hers, and then pulled away, leaving her mouth poised for more.

"Oh, I'm not complaining," he said, hearing her giggle – a saucy giggle.

She then tugged at the duvet and pushed it back on to the floor; she didn't want it impeding her as Sam's magic carpet took her on another journey of passion.

Chapter 71

Sweet Sorrow

"Have you packed everything I promised Canda, sweetheart?" she asked, as they prepared to take Sam to the airport.

He could tell that behind her façade, she was miserable at the thought of him going away after the fabulous two days they had spent together. The previous night she had taken him to the theatre, but this time to stand backstage, high up in the eaves, with Max to get a bird's eye view of her playing Katherine – and she performed even better than the first time he'd seen her. With no first-night nerves or dragons to slay, she only had love on her mind, and the man she was head over heels in love with was watching her.

"Word is," Max had whispered, out of ear shot, as Sam watched her seamlessly, effortlessly become Katherine once more, "she's going to grab a load of theatre awards for this – and me too with a bit of luck."

"That will give your CV a bit of a boost," Sam had whispered back, and Max nodded with a look of glee on his face.

Sam knew Penny's career no longer needed a boost, her star was in ascendancy, and that Angie had every intention her friend should cash in on her well-deserved popularity. One stipulation Penny insisted on, though, was that her relationship with Toby had been like two ships that passed in the night, but this time Sam came first, second and third in order of priorities, and not even Angie was brave enough to argue with her over that decision, especially now she was Sam's girlfriend, as she liked to call herself.

"You won't forget to phone me as soon as you get there, will you?" Penny asked as Sam checked in.

He wrapped his arms around her, feeling her soft, perfumed skin against his face as they kissed and held each other.

She felt almost breathless, and had a physical pain in her heart. She knew he had booked his flight long before they had become a couple, but that didn't make it any easier for her. And Sam knew he had a lot of thinking to do, and he had to do it alone away from the beautiful distraction of Penny.

"'*Parting is such sweet sorrow*'," he told her, his voice betraying his own sadness at leaving.

Her response to the words he had recited was a sorrowful groan.

"'*Good night, good night! Parting is such sweet sorrow. That I shall say good night till it be morrow. . .*'" she added, reciting from *Romeo and Juliet*. Her words tailed off into a forlorn whine.

He kissed her lips, an embrace that attracted the attention of fellow travellers, many of whom had recognised her and were eagerly taking pictures of them on their phones. He then watched as she walked away.

Chapter 72

Turn Around

"Is there anything else I can do for you, Mr Farmer?" asked Martin, the flight attendant, placing a glass of single malt onto the table to the side of his seat.

"There is one thing you can do for me," Sam replied, scanning the email open on his laptop. "You can ask the pilot if he would be so kind as to turn the plane around."

"Oh dear, have you left something important behind?" Martin asked, in his quietly spoken Canadian accent.

"Yes . . . you could say that. I've left something *very* important behind," he sighed, resigned to the fact that he was heading in the wrong direction to where he really wanted to be. His finger hovered over the 'Send' button. *"May the wind fill your sails,"* he murmured, as 'Your email has been sent' appeared on the screen.

Clearing customs at Toronto Airport, he hurriedly made his way to the Arrivals exit, to be met by Oak and his son Jake, knowing the die had been cast and all he wanted to do was get back home to Penny.

"Hi, fella!" boomed Oak, shaking Sam's hand and grinning in disbelief at what his brother in-law was determined to do.

"OK, Sam," said Jake, showing him some paperwork he held in his hand. "You're booked on a flight out which is due to leave in less than an hour, so we'd better say goodbye!" Jake sounded slightly amused that his uncle was prepared to cross the Atlantic twice in less than twenty hours for love of a woman who wasn't much older than he was.

Opening his travel bag, he handed Oak a package Penny had given him for Canda.

"I think these are items for her to auction off to raise money for her drama group," he said, also handing him his birthday card. He laughed. "I don't believe I'm doing this! I should be sitting on your veranda with you, drinking beer and getting drunk!"

"Well, if you balls it up let me know, and I'll put some on ice," Oak guffawed, as he wrapped his arms around Sam for a good luck hug, banging his back with such impact it expelled the air from his lungs!

Sam turned to walk away, the return ticket in his hand, hoping that whatever the future held for him, it wouldn't be the last time he saw Oak. The past that had haunted them for so many years had been put aside, and a bond had formed between them. Sam smiled and realised that like Oak, Canada was in his heart, and somehow knew he would return.

Standing on her half-landing, her body trembling with expectation, Penny watched her front door open, her mind racing and her heart pounding. Not bothering to use the last two steps, she jumped into his arms like a flightless bird.

"Hello, babe! Surprised to see me?"

"No, actually," she replied, holding him with all her might, not wanting him to leave her again. "Call it intuition, but I woke up this morning somehow knowing I'd see you today."

He didn't wonder why that was. He knew she felt and sensed things others didn't, and was too tired to give it much thought. All he cared about there and then was that his mammoth journey was now at an end and he was back where he wanted to be.

"Come on, I'll make you cup of tea, and then you must go to bed, you look exhausted," she said, taking his hand.

He put his hand on her shoulder, gently turning her around to face him, and then kissed her. He inched her away from him, and looked into her eyes.

"Marry me?" he asked, earnestly, softly, never imagining he would hear himself say those words to another woman again.

She stood there, her eyes sparkling at him as she stroked the sides of his unshaven face. But then suddenly her look of joy turned to panic, and her breathing became laboured. Breathlessly she tried to utter his name, "S-Sa, Sam, I-I ca . . . *I can't*!" she cried, but then she became distracted by the sound of a bell ringing and ringing, again and again. From the kitchen, she ran to the front door, forgetting to check who it was through her spy viewer, and opened it to be greeted by the last person on earth she wanted to see.

"Hello, pet," said Toby, barging his way into her hallway.

"Toby! What the hell are you doing here? Go away!" Her remonstrating stopped suddenly as he put his hand around her throat, forcing her backwards into the stair banisters, her spine crashing into the turned wood. The cries of pain and fear were muted by Toby's hand.

"You're making a fucking fool of me and yourself! Have you seen the pictures of you kissing that old man at the airport?" he bellowed, releasing his grip on her.

"You bastard!" she screamed, just managing to slap him hard across the face as she spat out the words. She retched and coughed as she rubbed her throat.

Just then a hand appeared and grabbed hold of Toby's hair, pulling at his scalp until he was forced to back away from her. Sam spun him around and put his hand around Toby's neck, manoeuvring him backwards into the full-length wall mirror; the sound of shattering glass was lost in the tempest of anger.

He said nothing, just looked at Toby, watching his bulging eyes and gasping mouth as he desperately tried to suck in air.

"*No, Sam*! Let him go, please!" Penny yelled, not wanting him to vent his full wrath on Toby.

"I won't have him treat you like that," Sam growled, his face full of hatred.

"Please! I beg you! I love you!" Her voice was now was breaking with shock.

Sam released his grip on Toby's throat, and he dropped to his knees, coughing and choking.

"Go Toby!" she yelled, pointing at the front door. "Get out of my life!"

Toby didn't say another word, just staggered into the street. He heard the door slam shut behind him.

Penny turned to see Sam sitting on the stairs, resting his head in his hands and trying to comprehend why his world, within minutes, had crashed around him.

"I'm sorry, Sam, I really am," she said, kissing him on the side of his face.

She then picked up her coat and bag, and briefly turned to look at him before walking out of the house, and away from him.

Chapter 73

Full Circle

She ran down the road, her mind desperately trying to make sense of the situation she was now in. She wondered why. Why had things gone so badly wrong? With anguish consuming her, she found herself walking briskly, crossing at junctions, and turning into streets. Although she looked at the street names, she seemed unaware of where she was or where she was going; it was as if her legs were taking her on a journey and her mind had not told them the destination.

Entering Regent Street and then Haymarket, she continued down the Mall and then finally to a place that made her realise she had come full circle: Trafalgar Square.

Menacing shadows began to appear from between the buildings as the sun set lower in the afternoon sky, creating a No Man's Land between light and darkness. Instinctively she made her way to the same steps, like a pilgrimage to where it all began for them, remembering how she had crashed in on Sam's life on that fateful day. She recalled how she had been having a row with Toby that day, and then she remembered how Sam hadn't been overly irate with her, considering she had just tripped over the bag containing Annie's ashes, sending it flying into the air. He'd treated her in such a way that she'd naturally responded to the calmness he showed her, and had felt instantly at ease in his company.

Without thinking, Penny stood up and looked behind her, believing she'd heard someone call her name. Her eyes searched frantically at all the faces about her, hoping above hope it was

Sam. Making her way up the steps, she saw an advertising sign outside the National Gallery. Her skin became cold and clammy, and she felt goose bumps rise on her arms as she recalled a riddle in her mind that had been buried in her subconscious. It had obsessed her from the first time they had met, and it was the *answer* to all her whys. Why she trusted a complete stranger. And why her road to loving him had been laid with obstacles. But the final why, that of why everything had unexpectedly gone so wrong for them eluded her. *I should be in his arms making love, celebrating our engagement, now I may have lost him forever*, she thought, and the realisation of those thoughts and her fear empowered her to tell him the truth as to *why they had met*; but first she had to find him.

Tears streaming from her eyes, she reached into her bag for her phone with trembling hands and called his number. '*The person you are calling is unavailable, please try again later*' came the digitalised reply. Then she phoned her home, but knew he wouldn't be there. He had no reason to be. Her last hope was her aunties.

"Come on! Come on!" she cried, in frustration, calm cast aside. "June, it's Penny, is Sam there?" she asked, quickly, without even a 'hello', hoping that although she couldn't say yes to Sam, June would say yes to her.

"Yes, dear," June replied, calmly.

"Oh thank God. Whatever you do, don't let him leave!" Penny ordered, her voice frantic.

"Where are you, dear?" June asked.

"Trafalgar Square. I'll get a taxi," she said, her heart pounding in her chest as both relief and anxiety set in.

She sat in the taxi, thinking that he may have left by the time she arrived, and that she may never see him again.

"No, it can't end like this, it can't. I'll be dammed if I'm going to lose him now," she said, speaking out loud to herself, endeavouring to keep her negative thoughts at bay.

The taxi had hardly pulled to a stop before she was out of the cab, not waiting for her change, and running up the street.

Briefly restraining herself from rushing in, she entered with composure, as if she was walking onto a stage – only to be greeted by a sight that made her blood run cold and her heart sink: Sam was slumped over to one side on the settee, his head resting awkwardly on the arm.

"June!" she cried, trying to put a cushion under his head. "How long has he been like this?"

"About an hour, dear. We tried to move him, but he's too heavy," replied June, watching her as she comforted him.

"There's something wrong! He almost looks unconscious." Her face was riddled with fear and sadness.

"It was me, I did it," came a voice from behind her.

Penny turned to see May walking towards her, her face pale with fright, her hands shaking with unrelenting nerves.

"What do you mean, you did it? You did *what*?" she asked.

"I'm . . . I'm s-sorry," replied May, her speech fragmented with the distress she felt. "He . . . he told us he was going back to Devon and that most likely we wouldn't see him again because . . . because it didn't work out between you. I-I thought if we could keep him here, you might have a chance to talk to him–"

"So, what did you bloody do?" Penny demanded, loosening his belt.

"I gave him some of my sleeping pills," May replied.

"What?" Penny cried, in disbelief. "You stupid *fool*. He might be my Romeo but you didn't have to act it out! You could have bloody killed him! If you'd have just left him alone, he would most likely have just fallen asleep anyway, he's hardly slept for three days!" Penny stood up to try and move him, tugging at his jacket. "How many of those sodding pills did you give him?" she asked, now breathless from her efforts to help him.

"Three, dear. I take one, so I thought three would do the trick."

"Do the trick, for Christ's sake! He's not an elephant!" retorted Penny, helplessly gazing at him, wondering what to do next. "June, go and get Betty *now*! She's a retired nurse and I want her to have a look at him. May, you help me get his jacket off," she ordered, as June scurried away next door.

"I'm so sorry, dear. I only wanted to help you both," said May, her voice shaking.

Penny looked at her aunt and saw her distress; she knew she hadn't purposely intended to harm him, but he'd be pissed with her when he woke up.

"Let me see sleeping beauty, then," Betty said, gently moving Penny out of the way. She lifted Sam's arm to take his pulse. "How many pills did you say, May?"

"Three," she replied, putting the bottle into Betty's hand.

"Oh, these things," she said. "He'll be OK." She looked up with a reassuring smile. "He'll have a bit of a head on him, and he'll be thirsty as hell, but I don't think any harm has been done. Despite his age, he looks pretty fit."

"Oh yes, he's fit alright," Penny remarked, and then noticed Betty and her aunties staring at her with child-like curiosity on their faces. "Oh shut up you three, you're as bad as each other," she snapped, scowling at them. She knelt down and held his hand, lovingly caressing it. "Come on, sweetheart, let's get you upstairs."

Chapter 74

Scared

Sitting on the edge of the bed, watching over Sam, Penny phoned Angie, informing her about Toby and requesting that she contact Max and ask him to use the new understudy for that night's performance.

"I'm not walking out on you anymore," she then whispered, lying down next to him.

A while later, June entered the bedroom with a mug of coffee and a sandwich for her. Standing at the end of the bed, June gazed at him as he slept, oblivious that the woman he loved was only inches from him.

"Poor man, he must rue the day he met us," June said, as her niece caressed his fingers with hers, fuelled by the knowledge that their loving each other wasn't just fate, but somehow devised.

"June, I've got to tell him something, something he'll find hard to believe. I couldn't take it in at first, but it answers everything about why we love each other."

June, as always, was tempted to enquire what it was, but this time she knew Sam had to know first.

Swinging his legs out of the bed, Sam looked around the room at the familiar, but unexpected, surroundings. He stood up and stretched, moving his head from side to side, trying to liven up his drowsy body.

"Christ, my head's banging," he muttered to himself, massaging his scalp with his fingers as he looked through the window. He opened it, filling his lungs with the freshness of a new day. He turned to see Penny enter the bedroom, holding two mugs of coffee.

"Get back into bed, Sam," she said kindly, placing his drink on the bedside cabinet. She stood there, wanting to give him the impression of being relaxed, as if the events of the day before hadn't happened, but he knew better, he could hear the tell-tale sound of clicking from her fingernails. In the past, he had not bothered to stop her, but this time it irritated him.

"There's no need for that," he told her, with a forced smile.

She could see his eyes were ringed with redness, even after all the extended sleep he had been dosed up for.

"I'm sorry . . . for all this," she said, and then stepped nearer to him, hoping for a fleeting kiss on the lips, hoping he would be curious as to why she did that, considering she ran out on him.

"Don't do that," he said, frowning at her. "I've got a mouth like a boat's bilge. I'm going for a wash." He started to head for the door.

"You can't go like that! You've got nothing on. You'll scare the old ladies."

"That's the general idea," he replied, not bothering to look at her.

At least he didn't get dressed and walk out straight away, she thought.

"That's better," he said, climbing back into bed, noticing she had fluffed up his duvet and pillows. Penny was sat by the window in an old armchair. "So, what did the buggers do to me then? Hit me over the head with a frying pan? Because that's what it feels like." He reached for his coffee.

"May put sleeping pills in your tea."

"Christ! They never stop, do they?" he replied, carefully moving his mug away from his lips, tentatively sniffing at it.

"It scared the life out of me when I found out what she'd done," she said, watching Sam lift up the duvet.

"So, who did all this? The old ladies?" he enquired, indicating his nakedness.

"God, no! They didn't deserve such pleasure," Penny replied, risking a small grin. "I did."

"Well, I'm fortunate that May is a better actress than she in an assassin," he replied tersely.

"They . . . they wanted to give us time to talk and to try to . . . straighten things out between us."

"So, do you think we have anything to talk about? I seem to remember you said no," he replied coldly.

"I didn't say no. I said . . . I said . . . I can't. Meaning, I was unable to say yes. I didn't say no, Sam. I really didn't."

He realised she was digging her heels in, and if he had misinterpreted the situation, she intended him to realise the fact.

"OK . . ." he replied, slowly, needing to understand. "Tell me this. You didn't say yes, so what did you mean when you said, 'I can't'? That sounds a lot like a no to me."

She turned her gaze away from him to look out of the window. The morning sun warmed her face, refreshing her. Sam watched as she ran her hand up and down one side of her back, twisting and turning.

"Come over here," he said, sounding insistent. The look on his face was one of concern. "Turn around." He then unzipped her dress down to her waist, and moved his hands across her shoulders, lowering it down.

"I put this polka dot dress on for you, Sam."

She felt him release her bra, and then ever so gently run his hand over her ribs and spine. He didn't speak a word, but she could hear him, his controlled panting fired by rage, and she felt the heat of his angry breath on her skin.

He stared at the left side of her back, smothered in a fiery sunset of bruises.

"The bastard," he growled, realising his love for her hadn't waned, despite what had happened.

She turned to look at him, letting him do what he loved to do: gaze into her hazel eyes. She reached for his hand and held it, buoyed by the fact he made no attempt to withdraw it.

"When you flew to Canada, God, did I miss you," she whispered. "I used to miss you before . . . before I realised I loved you, but this time, like you, I felt the true meaning of *weary with toil.* I cried, I sulked, and cried some more. I behaved like a bloody love-struck school girl.

"I did the play that evening, and I can't say it was one of my best performances. But in the middle of the night, I got up for a pee and, as usual, you were on my mind; but I felt less depressed, like you weren't as far away as I thought.

"When I woke up in the morning, I felt strangely happier than when I went to sleep – when I eventually fell to sleep that is – and I sensed I'd see you sooner than I expected. You'd said you'd phone me when you arrived, but you didn't, and that's when I knew you'd be back. And then I realised why, and I was so elated at the thought of seeing you again so soon, and I was filled with joy at the idea that you might ask me to marry you, to be your wife, and I'd rehearsed saying yes, time and time again. I knew you wouldn't bother to get on one knee, or give a speech on how much you loved me, because I knew already. No, you would just simply say, 'Marry me'."

"That predictable, am I?"

"Don't say that, that's not what I meant. The one thing I know about you, Sam, is that you don't do grey, do you? You're Mr

Black and White: girlfriend and boyfriend; husband and wife." She felt her heart skip a beat on hearing herself say 'wife'. "What is it you said not long ago? No 'what ifs'?

"You're the man I'm in love with, and a man I hope still loves me, and when you did arrive back and you asked me to marry you, you made me feel so happy, you really did. I stroked your face and kissed you, wanting to savour those precious moments for the rest of my life."

"And then it went pear-shaped for us, didn't it?" he told her, still wanting to know the reason why she had said she couldn't marry him.; not wouldn't, but couldn't.

"The truth is, Sam . . . I panicked. To me it was the most important day of my whole life, and I ballsed it up. Stage fright? Call it what you want." She was clearly chastising herself far more harshly than he thought she would. "How bloody hard would it have been to say one sodding word . . . *yes*?" she asked. "When I realised I couldn't say it, I froze. My head was saying, 'You stupid cow, say yes', but I couldn't, I was scared. I was so scared I would say *no* like I said *no* once before, when I was intending to say yes, remember? And . . . I did."

She sighed, and then put his hand to her face, holding it there to comfort her. She looked out of the opened window again, to gaze at the clouds floating by, effortlessly and free, like her heart had been twenty-four hours before; now it was heavy with trepidation.

She left Sam on his own to think about what she had told him, and she wondered if it would have any sway on the deep feelings of hurt and rejection he felt.

Chapter 75

The Final Curtain

He could hear her fumbling at the door and he opened it for her, seeing that she was holding two more mugs of coffee.

"Oh, you're dressed," she said, handing him one, concerned that he may be getting ready to leave before she'd had a chance to tell him everything.

"Don't worry, I won't run off." His tone was reassuring, but there was a sting of pain there too.

He sat back on the bed, placing the pillows against the headboard behind him. He gestured with his eyes.

"No, Sam, not just yet" she replied, standing at the end of the bed, nervously clicking her fingernails again. "Before I go any further with what I must tell you, I need to know if you still love and forgive me . . . well, love me anyway, that would be a start." Her plea reached out to him, hoping his answer would make her heart float free like the clouds.

He looked at her, a deep, searching stare. Then she saw something that made it disappear, like a conjurer clasping a coin in his hand, only to open his palm to reveal that it had vanished: his smile. But not just any smile. *His* smile. The smile that spoke louder that any words he could ever say.

He stood up and walked towards her, and her pulse pounded with every step he took. He put his hands around her waist and gently pulled her against him, feeling her warm body soft against his.

"Maybe you know me less than you thought," he told her. "Do you really think I could stop loving you, just because you panicked yesterday? You knew at the time you'd hurt me; and I really thought you'd ended this. But the question is – do we draw a line through it?"

She didn't want to reply to his question; she hoped he already knew the answer.

They stood there for what seemed an eternity, not saying anything, just gazing at each other. Then he placed his lips on hers.

"Come on, let's go home," he said quietly.

"Sam. I . . . I have to tell you the rest and what happened after I ran off."

Sam frowned and wondered why she wanted to continue; he just wanted to go.

"It doesn't matter, sweetheart, it really doesn't, honestly," he said.

"Oh it does, Sam. Believe me it matters! It answers all the questions about why we are together, and why we love each other. Please, sit down. Please?" she asked, her voice quietly insistent.

She sat next to him on the bed, as close as she could get. He always told her he would be there for her when she needed him, but she knew that once he heard what she was about to say, they would need each other.

"You once said I wouldn't like the angry Sam, and you were right. I thought you were going to kill Toby, and I was frightened about what you might do – not to me, as I know you wouldn't hurt me – but I didn't care about Toby, it was you I cared about. I could see the malice in your eyes when you held him, but when you looked at me, all I could see was a confused and bewildered man. That look will haunt me for the rest of my life."

Sam thought back to the moment he put his hand around

Toby's throat and how satisfying it felt. And had he known the bruises he'd caused to her back, he would have squeezed just that little bit tighter and held him longer.

"So, I did something you were unable to do . . . I ran away. I didn't plan to, Sam, and it was strange that I felt compelled to, but not because of what had taken place . . . it was like I had to go somewhere. All I could do was cry and think of you and why I had reacted the way I did.

"After I left, I walked for bloody ages, and believe it or not, I didn't have a clue where I was heading. I just kept walking until I found myself back to where it all started for us: Trafalgar Square, and the steps of the National Gallery." She took a deep breath and reached for Sam's hand, hoping she'd still be able to hold it when she'd finished speaking. "I need you to listen carefully to this part, OK?" she began.

"So, I walked over to where we met and sat down on the same step, recalling how I was shouting at Toby on my phone, and you were sitting there minding your own business. Then, like you said, 'I crashed into your life'."

He smiled at her. He would never forget that day. That moment, that low point in his life when it took another direction to the one he had in mind – and he'd never looked back.

"I sat in the late afternoon sun, hearing and seeing people come and go around me. And then I thought I heard someone call my name. I hoped it was you, so I stood up and looked around, and as I frantically looked for you, I walked up the steps towards the gallery."

She looked once more out of the window.

"You know when you have a word on the tip on your tongue, and try as hard as you may, you can't remember it?" she asked. "I remember having that sensation soon after we first met, and again yesterday, that same sensation returned to me when I arrived at the steps.

And Don't Forget the Roses

"As I walked up towards the gallery, I glanced at one of those huge poster boards advertising what was going on inside, and noticed they were having a major exhibition on Monet. I remembered you telling me how Annie adored Monet," she said, squeezing his hand.

"You don't have to put yourself though this," he told her, seeing intensity in her eyes he had never seen before – not even when she became Katherine on stage.

"Sorry, but you've got to know," she replied, her voice breaking with emotion. There was no hiding the truth now.

"As soon as Annie entered my mind, I got goose bumps and became cold and shivery, and I started to recall the word which had been on the tip of my tongue again, well, actually it was four words. My mind was telling me something, saying something to me. It was only then I realised what it was: *faire confiance en lui . . . faire confiance en lui.* You know what that translates to, don't you, Sam? Your French is far better than mine. It's *have confidence in him*; but we don't say it that way, do we? We would say *trust him,* instead, wouldn't we?"

"*Annie* spoke to me in French, Sam, telling me to . . . to trust you. That's why I always thought I knew you, despite not knowing you. Annie planted those words in my subconscious to give our friendship a head start.

"She wasn't going to hand over her keys to your heart without being sure I was the right woman for you. I think she's been testing me, Sam. Could I live in your world as well as you live in mine? And I believe now that it was Annie who made me lie to you at the airport, and how I felt like shit for doing it – and I like to think I've passed that one – but yesterday was all my own work."

Sam pulled his hand away from hers and placed it on the side of her face, letting out a long sigh. He shook his head.

"Annie was always a hands-on type of person. She'd never leave anything to chance, and that sounds so typical of her," he said.

"How can you be sure I'm telling the truth? How can you know that that is the answer to why we're together?" she asked.

But he didn't have to doubt it; he knew it was true.

"Because she spoke to you in French, that's why I believe you. You . . . met her once, when you were a teenager."

"What? Why? How?"

"Archie's parents were great patrons of the Arts, and Annie knew them from her time at the Academy. On one of her trips to London they met up, and were invited to a cocktail party hosted by Archie's father . . . who introduced her to your aunties . . . and a certain young lady – you."

He paused. The only sound in the room was their breathing. Penny's was deep and rhythmic as she concentrated on every word he spoke. His was faster, now that he was doing the talking.

"Annie planned to take Estelle, but she had tonsillitis, and Maggie wasn't interested, so Ruth went with her. The reason I know all this is because Canda told me. She recalled how jealous she felt when her mother told her she'd met the Shakespeare sisters, and how her Auntie Annie thought their niece, Penny, was so enchanting as she practised her French on her."

Penny gasped as she struggled to come to terms with how everything had come full circle. Not only had she met Annie, but Ruth too . . . the woman in her dream, the woman in the sailing boat with the pink sails.

"I don't remember her. I'm so sorry. I wish I could remember her. I wish I could remember *them*," she whispered.

"Don't be. She remembered you. The words Annie spoke to you – *faire confiance en lui'* – are from her marriage vows to me: '*To know you is to trust you. To trust you is to love you. To love you is forever*'."

"Oh God, Sam! What beautiful words. But it's true what she said – to trust you *is* to love you forever." His face was alive with emotion as she continued. "I know Annie wants you to be happy after the love and support you gave her, especially in her final years, and keeping your promise to her. I wondered why she thought *I* could do that, and it was a mystery to me, but she knew me. She also knew I was lonely – not because Toby had stood me up, but because I've always been lonely. I suppose it stems from when I was a child, without Megan, and always being on my own. Even after we met, I was still lonely, but only when I wasn't with you. Annie knows how much I love you and she's allowing us to live our lives together."

She instinctively leant towards him as he wrapped his arms around her, holding her tight. Her face was moist with tears, and soon Sam's mingled with hers. Closing her eyes for an instant, she then fulfilled a life-long promise to herself as she recited words of love for Sam:

"'*Of all my loves this is the first and last, that in the autumn of my years has grown,*

A secret fern, a violet in the grass, a final leaf where all the rest are gone.

Would that I could give all and more, my life, my world, my thoughts, my arms, my breath, my future,

My love eternal, endless, infinite, yet brief, as all loves are and hopes, though they endure'."

She paused, knowing that what she was about to say was the essence of her love for him:

"'*You are my sun and stars, my night, my day, my seasons, summer, winter, my sweet spring,*

My autumn song, the church in which I pray, my land and ocean, all that the earth can bring

Of glory and of sustenance, all that might be divine, my Alpha and my Omega, and all that was ever mine . . .'

"I always told myself that I would only recite that to my one true love," she said, taking his hand to kiss.

"Thank you. I am the luckiest man," he replied.

"One last thing, Sam . . . I love you with all my being, and I sure as hell know you love me. Ask me to marry you again, please? Please. I won't mess up again, I promise. I'm spent. I can't do any more." She held her breath, waiting, watching his every expression as he gently stroked her face with the back of his hand.

He could see she was worn out, she didn't have to tell him, so with a loving smile, he pulled her to him and gazed into her beautiful hazel eyes. He then took a breath and held it . . . a breath that would change their lives forever.

"So, where do you want to go on honeymoon?" he asked, with the smile she had come to love.

Absorbing those words into her whole heart and soul, she smiled right back and said, "Niagara Falls, *and don't forget the roses. . .*"

Epilogue

Unable to wear her engagement ring on stage, but vowing to Sam that she would never be separated from it, Penny unclasped the gold chain from around her neck. She slipped off the ring of white gold with its solitaire rose-pink diamond, and held it up to the light between her fingers. She gazed at it with adoring eyes.

"They say diamonds are a girl's best friend, and that ring's certainly yours, isn't it, my dear," Mavis commented.

Penny stared at her, shaking her head in disagreement, and said, "No, Sam is my best friend. This beautiful work of art is just his token of his love for me."

She returned it to her finger with the knowledge that it could have been so different had it not been for Toby failing to keep his promise to her, and Sam faithfully keeping his to Annie.

Dreams of her future with him filled her mind; but for Sam the nightmare of the past would soon come back to confront him, putting his life and those of the ones he loves in jeopardy . . .

To be continued. . .

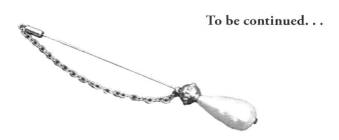

Book Two

The Long Reach Back
P. J. Paterson

"'Yes, I did," Sam answered with a shrug of his shoulders. "You see, I had no choice. Your friends, the Fabers, they showed me an incriminating photograph taken of Kazemi in a restaurant, and with him the Barber who, as we all know, is a depraved assassin, and Sidney, my brother, the drug dealer. I soon realised that it would only be a matter of time before the Fabers would use that picture as part of their condemning evidence to destroy Kazemi . . . a revenge killing if you will."

Sam lingered to savour a sizable mouthful of his single malt before he carried on with his reasoning.

"That night at the theatre, I handed him an envelope, and inside was a copy of the photograph with my name written on the back, nothing more. I wasn't going to make it that easy for him to remember who I was. I needed to force his hand and, on my terms, to come after me, not those I love and care for, like you two or Penny and my daughters. Because he would, you know. He'd get someone to pick you off one by one, and all because of the person who links all of you to that picture . . . *me*.'"

Faced with a seemingly impossible dilemma, Sam must make a choice: to ignore a decades-long commitment to honour and loyalty, or reopen the Pandora's box of past horror to protect those he loves . . .

About the Author

Patrick Jeremy Paterson was born in Marylebone, London, in 1955 and spent his formative years in a small fishing village on the breathtaking River Fowey in Cornwall. It was no wonder that with the saltiness of the sea air his constant companion, he joined the merchant navy. From cook to deckhand, quartermaster and first mate, these years were some of his happiest . . . and darkest . . . and provided the inspiration for many of the fictional characters in his books.

On leaving the sea, he and his wife spent the next thirty years building a successful window repair company, until Patrick retired to pursue his love of writing.

Connect with the Author

www.facebook.com/Anddontforgettheroses
anddontforgettheroses@yahoo.com
www.facebook.com/patrickj.paterson
https://twitter.com/patrickpaterso7
https://www.patersonbooks.com